THE O'ROARKE AFFAIR

TRACY GRANT

The O'Roarke Affair

Ebook ISBN: 9781641972840

KDP POD ISBN: 9798325666094

IS POD ISBN: 9781641972888

NYLA Publishing

121 W 27th St., Suite 1201, New York, NY 10001

http://www.nyliterary.com

...Keep thy friend
    Under thy own life's key
    —Shakespeare, *All's Well That Ends Well*, Act I, scene i

DRAMATIS PERSONAE

*Indicates Real Historical Figures

The Rannoch Family & Household

Malcolm Rannoch, MP and former British intelligence agent
Mélanie Suzanne Rannoch, his wife, playwright and former
French intelligence agent
Colin Rannoch, their son
Jessica Rannoch, their daughter
Berowne, their cat

Laura O'Roarke, Colin and Jessica's former governess
Raoul O'Roarke, her husband, Mélanie's former spymaster, and
Malcolm's father
Lady Emily Fitzwalter, Laura's daughter from her first marriage
Clara O'Roarke, Laura and Raoul's daughter

Lady Arabella Rannoch, Malcolm's mother
Alistair Rannoch, her husband, Malcolm's putative father

Miles Addison, agent, Malcolm's valet
Blanca Mendoza Addison, agent, his wife, Mélanie's companion
Pedro Addison, their son

Valentin, footman

Alexander (Sandy) Trenor, Malcolm's secretary
Elizabeth (Bet) Simcox Trenor, his wife

Helen, Lady Marchmain, Sandy's mother
Lord Marchmain, her husband, Sandy's father

<u>The Mallinson Family</u>

Julien (Arthur) Mallinson, Earl Carfax, former agent for hire
Katelina (Kitty) Velasquez Mallinson, Countess Carfax, his wife,
former British and Spanish intelligence agent
Leo Ashford, her son
Timothy Ashford, her son
Guenevere (Genny) Ashford, Kitty and Julien's daughter

Ralph Allam, claimant to the Warkworth title, their friend
Amanda (Mandy) Allam, his wife

Hubert Mallinson, spymaster, Julien's uncle
Amelia Mallinson, his wife

David Mallinson, MP, their son
Simon Tanner, playwright, his lover (see also At the Tavistock)

<u>The Davenport Family & Household</u>

Lady Cordelia Davenport, classicist

Colonel Harry Davenport, her husband, classicist, and former British intelligence agent
Livia Davenport, their daughter
Drusilla Davenport, their daughter

Archibald (Archie) Davenport, Harry's uncle, MP, and former French intelligence agent
Lady Frances Davenport, his wife, Malcolm's aunt
Chloe Dacre-Hammond, Frances's daughter from her first marriage
Francesca Davenport, Frances and Archie's daughter
Philip Davenport, Frances and Archie's son

Judith Roth, Frances's daughter from her first marriage
Jeremy Roth, Bow Street runner, her husband
Serena Derwent, Judith's daughter from her first marriage
Samuel Roth, Jeremy's son from his first marriage
Dorian Roth, Jeremy's son from his first marriage
Harriet Roth, Jeremy's sister

Cressida Caldwell Beardsley, Jeremy's first wife's sister
William Beardsley, MP, Cressida's husband
Vincent Caldwell, Cressida's son

Aline (Allie) Blackwell, Frances's daughter from her first marriage
Geoffrey (Geoff) Blackwell, doctor, Aline's husband

<u>The Bamford Family</u>

Anthony (Tony) Southcott, Duke of Bamford
Henrietta (Hetty) Southcott, Duchess of Bamford, his wife

Viscount St. Ives, their son
Sylvie, Viscountess St. Ives, his wife

Lady Frederica Rawdon, the Bamfords' eldest daughter
Percy Rawdon, her husband

Helena, the Bamfords' second daughter

Rosalind, Condessa Azevado, the Bamfords' youngest daughter
Gaspar, Conde Azevado, Portuguese diplomat, her husband

Filbert, the Duke of Bamford's valet

<u>The Beverston Family</u>

Humphrey Smythe, Viscount Beverston
Benedict (Ben) Smythe, his son
Nerezza Smythe, Ben's wife

<u>At the Tavistock</u>

Simon Tanner, playwright and part owner of the theatre (see also Mallinson Family)
Manon Caret Harleton, actress
Jennifer Mansfield Smytheton, actress
Sir Horance Smytheton, her husband

<u>At the King's Theatre, Haymarket</u>

Tristram, Lord Gresham, composer and agent
Danielle Darnault, opera singer and agent
Pierre Ducroix, journalist, her husband
Ilia, their daughter

<u>Prebble & Company</u>

Hugo Prebble, manager and part owner

Hypatia, Viscountess Rothermere, his cousin and co-owner
Viscount Rothermere, her husband
Ronald Camden, Rothermere's friend

The Bonaparte Family

*Napoleon Bonaparte, first consul and later emperor of France
*Josephine Bonaparte, his wife
*Hortense de Beauharnais, Josephine's daughter from her first marriage
*Caroline Murat, Napoleon's sister

*Colonel Rapp, aide-de-camp

In the French Government

*Prince Talleyrand, foreign minister
*Dorothée de Talleyrand-Périgord, his nephew's wife
*Count Karl Clam-Martinitz, her lover
*Wilhelmine of Sagan, Dorothée's sister

*Joseph Fouché, minister of police
Georges Curier, his agent
Reynald St. Pierre, official in the ministry of police

Diplomats

*Lord Castlereagh, British foreign secretary
*Lord Stewart, his half-brother, ambassador to Vienna
*Sir Charles Stuart, British minister plenipotentiary in Portugal
Billy Fitzsimmons, British diplomat
Lord Thirleton, British diplomat
Lionel Buckfield, Thirleton's brother-in-law

*Prince Metternich, Austrian foreign minister

Prince Franz Stroheim, Austrian diplomat
Gaultier Barton, French soldier, married to Stroheim's cousin
Régine Barton, Gaultier's second wife
Roland Barton, Gaultier's son from his first marriage,
Mylène Barton, Gaultier and Régine's daughter

*Dorothea, Countess Lieven, wife of Russian ambassador to
Britain, Metternich's mistress

The Varon Family

Henriette Varon, former seamstress to Josephine Bonaparte
Lisette Varon, agent, her elder daughter
Minette Varon, her younger daughter

The Montagu Family

Christopher (Kit) Montagu
Sofia Vincenzo Montagu, his wife
Enrico Vincenzo, her brother

Violetta Barese, their friend

The Laclos/Caruthers Family

Bertrand Laclos
Rupert, Viscount Caruthers, his lover
Gabrielle, Viscountess Caruthers, Rupert's wife
Stephen, Rupert and Gabrielle's son

Others

Désirée Clarineau, French agent
Antonio Diaz, Spanish agent
Charlotte Leblanc, former French agent
Louis St. Georges, French soldier
*Lord Sidmouth, home secretary
*Sir Nathaniel Conant, chief magistrate of Bow Street
Sophie

PROLOGUE

February 1799
Harrow, England

Malcolm Rannoch eased the book from the shelf. He could go to the counter and buy it immediately. One thing he didn't lack for was pocket money. But instead he opened the heavy cover and flipped through the pages, taking in the feel of the paper and the smell of the leather binding, running his finger over lines of text. Some of his schoolfellows liked to get lost in the forest. He liked to get lost in books. Abernathy's Shop in Harrow village was even more of a refuge than the library at Harrow. No one was likely to interrupt him here.

"I've always found Ludlow's response to the Restoration fascinating," a voice said from the end of the aisle. "But then perhaps that's because I've been through the collapse of a cause myself. More than once."

Shock held Malcolm immobile for a moment. He would know that voice anywhere. It was one of the last voices he'd expected to hear just now. But then Raoul O'Roarke had a way of turning up at unexpected moments.

Malcolm turned and saw Raoul leaning against the bookshelf down the aisle. His face was in shadow, as it often was, but the way he stood, shoulder dug into the shelf, one hand braced casually yet at an angle where he could push away at a moment's notice, was unmistakable.

"I wasn't expecting you." Malcolm bounded to Raoul's side, the book held carefully in both arms. "Mama said you'd had to go away."

"Yes. I'm sorry I missed Speech Day."

"It's all right." He couldn't say anything else. Though he'd been surprised how much he'd noticed Raoul's absence. "Mama came this year." Arabella Rannoch was an erratic presence at school events. And Alistair Rannoch almost never put in an appearance. Raoul was the one Malcolm had learnt to count on. "It was Ireland, wasn't it?"

"What do you know about Ireland?"

"I read the papers. And I listen." When he'd been home from Harrow, he'd seen his mother's white face as she scanned the papers in the days after the United Irish Uprising. And he'd heard the servants' whispers. Lady Arabella's friend was on the run. Sometimes they used a different word from "friend."

Malcolm took another step forwards. The dusty light slanting between the books shifted, and he saw a scar he didn't remember next to Raoul's left eye. Raoul had always been lean, but he looked thinner than Malcolm remembered. His cheeks were hollow and there were shadows round his gray eyes. "Were you hurt?"

Raoul shifted his weight from one foot to the other. "I wasn't well for a bit. I'm all right now, that's what matters."

That was one of those things grown-ups said that sounded sensible but left all sorts of questions unanswered. Raoul said those things less than most grown-ups. But even he wasn't immune. "Is it safe for you to be here?"

"It's a bit of a risk for me to be anywhere these days. But it's worth it."

"Did you come to see Mama?"

"I came to see you." Raoul stretched out a hand and touched Malcolm's shoulder. "I think we could risk a visit to the Ink & Quill."

It was a pub not far from Abernathy's. Too shabby to be frequented by most parents visiting and taking their children out, and not dashing enough for the older boys who went out to get a drink. Malcolm and Raoul would sit there for hours, Malcolm with a lemonade, Raoul with a pint of stout.

Despite all the questions that lingered in the air, Malcolm grinned. They made their way to the front of the shop. Malcolm paid for his book and got a smile from Mr. Abernathy, who knew him well. He also knew Raoul and he nodded at him without surprise.

Clouds had thickened in the sky while Malcolm was in the shop, and the wind had come up. He felt a raindrop hit the back of his neck. He tucked his book inside his jacket. Raoul threw a fold of his greatcoat over Malcolm's shoulders as they hurried down the street and rounded the corner towards the Ink & Quill. Harrow was a sleepy village and in the late afternoon the streets were quiet. Malcolm could see the glow of the lamps through the thick glass of the windows in the Ink & Quill.

They passed an alley, closing the distance to the pub. Suddenly, Raoul jerked away. Malcolm spun round. A man in a bottle-green coat had Raoul pinned against the wall of a building in the alley. Raoul slid down and kicked, sending the man thudding over backwards in the mud. Raoul pushed himself to his feet. The man caught his ankle. A knife flashed. Raoul lunged for the man's arm as the man tried to bring the knife down.

Malcolm hurled his book. The man with the knife staggered back as it hit his arm. Raoul dealt him a blow to the jaw, grabbed the knife and the book, and seized Malcolm's arm.

They ran over rain-spattered paving and didn't speak until

they were seated in the Ink & Quill, a glass of lemonade and pint of stout before them.

"I'm sorry," Raoul said. "But that was quick thinking. Thank you."

Malcolm reached for his glass but didn't quite trust himself to pick it up. His fingers were shaking. "I wasn't sure what else to do."

"Use the weapon nearest to hand. I always told you words had power. Though this wasn't quite what I was thinking of."

Malcolm took a drink of lemonade, holding tight to the glass. "Will they come after you again?"

"Not in the pub. That man wasn't an expert. I've faced far worse."

Malcolm nodded. The lemonade glass was cold in his hands, but that wasn't why he felt chilled. And it wasn't even because of the danger, though he'd never been in the midst of a fight.

He couldn't remember a time he hadn't known Raoul. And by the time he was three, he'd understood enough of Raoul's life that every time he said goodbye to him, he wondered if he'd ever see him again.

CHAPTER 1

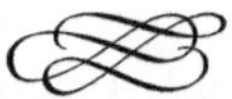

May 1821
London Dock

Kitty Mallinson had to admit she was enjoying herself. The taste of sour beer lingered on her lips. The air was smoky from battered oil lamps and guttering candles in tarnished sconces. The pungent scents of ale and stout and frying oil warred with saltwater and tar. She could feel her hair slipping from its pins with delightful abandon. The laces on her gown were loose enough that her sleeves slid off her shoulders.

A man in need of a shave and bath jostled up against her and slid an arm round her waist. She swatted him away and righted her beer before it could spill. She could take care of herself. Not that she really needed to with so many friends dispersed about the tavern. It was a bit absurd to have brought six of them to a simple meeting with a contact. But after an afternoon spent calling on Lady Debenham, whose husband's support Kitty's husband needed for his abolition bill, even a pale shadow of the adventure of her old life was welcome.

Another man sidled up beside her next to the bar. "Found you."

Kitty grinned. "I was beginning to think you weren't coming."

"Here now," said the man she'd swatted away. "Wouldn't talk to me, but you'll talk to him?"

"He's an old friend," Kitty said. Which was true.

The other man grunted and slinked off. Kitty turned, leaning against one of the posts of the bar, and regarded the man she had come to the London Dock to meet.

He grinned back. "I thought you'd have changed more."

She tilted her head back. The post felt splintery against her scalp. "I'm not sure whether to be flattered or affronted."

He braced one hand on the bar. "Believe me, it's a compliment. I thought you'd have turned into a great lady."

She laughed, and felt a lock of hair slither free of its pins. "I couldn't if I tried. Though I did dress for the occasion." Sometimes choosing tattered lace and faded sarcenet took as much time as dressing for a ducal soirée. More, perhaps. There was less of a formula.

"You always knew how to." His gaze moved over her face. Antonio Diaz had been a member of the guerrillero band in the Spanish mountains where she had lived with her cousin in the early days of the Peninsular War. A dancing partner by the campfire, a comrade in foraging and on the occasional mission. A mild flirt but never anything more serious, and always a friend first. "You look happy," he said.

"I am. I seem to have stumbled into it." She felt the smile that broke across her face as she said it. She'd never expected to marry for a second time. She certainly hadn't expected to become a countess. But perhaps more than anything, she hadn't expected to find love. Or rather, she'd found Julien before Edward died, but she wouldn't have admitted to the possibility of love. She would have scoffed at the word. "You could have simply called on us at Carfax House," she added. "It's a ridiculous pile, but we've made it quite comfortable. My husband would have been glad to meet you." In fact, her husband was in a corner of the tavern, probably slouching with lazy abandon while watching with an all-too-anxious gaze.

"How much does he know?" Antonio asked.

"A great deal. Probably even more than I realize."

Antonio laughed. "It sounds like he might almost deserve you."

"Oh, I'd say we deserve each other. For better or worse."

Antonio's smile deepened. "I'd have liked to meet him. But I didn't have time to come to Mayfair. I'm on my way to the Argentine. As you may appreciate."

Kitty had spent several years in the Argentine with her first husband and was close to a number of people in the current Revolutionary government. She had also begun her affair with her current husband there, though when he'd left she'd thought she might never see him again. "Spain wasn't exciting enough for you?"

"It was a good time for me to get out of Spain. There's a chance to make a new country in the Argentine. And less need to worry the French or the Austrians will interfere."

The barkeep pushed two pints across the bar to customers. "They could use your talents there," Kitty said. She felt a familiar twinge at the thought of the adventure in the Argentine. Her life wasn't there anymore, but it felt like a job left undone. "I'm glad I got to see you."

"So am I, but that's not the only reason I made such an effort to see you." Antonio's gaze went serious. "I have a message to deliver." He shifted, turning away from the bar, so his words were less likely to carry. "About one of our old friends."

Ale foamed and fizzed as the barkeep pulled a pint. "Who?" Kitty asked.

"I hear you still see Raoul O'Roarke."

Kitty curled her fingers round her glass of beer. It shouldn't be surprising. Raoul had a way of being in the midst of everything. But dread bit her in the throat. "We see him a great deal. He's part of our circle." Part of their family, really.

Antonio's eyes narrowed. "He has enemies. Powerful enemies."

"When hasn't he?"

"True. But I have a reliable report someone's out to kill him."

~

JULIEN MALLINSON LEANT BACK in his chair and surveyed the taproom. "Quite like old times. Is it too much to hope for a brawl?"

"Don't be difficult, Julien." Mélanie Rannoch took a drink of Irish stout and let the black lace mantilla she was wearing in place of a shawl slither down over her shoulders.

Malcolm Rannoch watched his wife with appreciation. Mélanie could be at home in any setting and she knew just how to blend in. She sat with easy abandon, chin cupped in one hand. Her walnut brown hair tumbled loose over her shoulders. Her sea-green eyes were lit with adventure. He'd never grow tired of seeing Mélanie in the midst of a mission.

Malcolm grinned at his wife. "I could sympathize. But then I was in the Commons today and Julien was in the Lords. Nothing like cooling one's heels in Parliament to bring on the need for activity."

Julien cast a glance round the taproom over the rim of his tankard. "In the old days Kitty ran off into danger on her own. Now she says she has so much backup she'll scare off her contact. I told her not to wound us. We'd never let a contact be scared off. We're all former agents."

Dice rattled against wood as someone tossed them at the next table over. They were sitting at a table in the shadows of a corner of the dockside tavern. Harry and Cordelia Davenport were at the other end of the taproom, half-hidden by the throng of sailors, dockworkers, tradesmen, women looking for custom. And, no doubt, more than a few pickpockets. Julien's wife Kitty was by the bar, waiting for the contact whose message had brought them all

8

here. Malcolm could see Kitty's tawny hair in the crowd round the bar. Then the crowd shifted a bit and he saw more clearly. "She seems to have found her contact."

"He looks reasonable," Julien said in a lazy tone at odds with the tension in his gaze. "I still want to know why he didn't want to come to see us at Carfax House."

"You know from fieldwork there could be dozens of reasons for that," Mélanie pointed out.

"Fair enough," Julien said, gaze still fixed on his wife.

The man Kitty was talking to looked to be in his late thirties or early forties, dark hair, patched cloth coat, casually tied neckcloth. "He looks unexceptionable," Malcolm said. Though even as he said it, he caught a flash of surprise in Kitty's gaze as the man leant forward to say something. Perhaps—

"Cheat!" A man at the table next to theirs pushed his chair back and tossed the contents of his tankard at the man across from him.

"Did not!" The victim of the splashed ale sprang to his feet and surged across the table at the other man, sending their dice game scattering to the floor. The two men staggered into the next table over. A woman sitting there screamed and kicked the man who'd tossed the ale. A man beside her dealt the man who had upended the table a blow to the jaw.

Mélanie sprang to her feet as the crowd surged towards them. "I think you got your wish, Julien."

A man crashed into Malcolm, swore, turned, and swung a fist. Malcolm ducked and collided with another man.

"Bloody idiot!" Hard metal crashed on Malcolm's head.

Mélanie tossed the contents of her own tankard in Malcolm's attacker's face. Her fingers closed round Malcolm's own. Julien was halfway to the bar, dodging through the melee, making for Kitty. A man skidded on the ale-soaked floorboards in front of him and collapsed on the floor. Julien stepped over him, but the man grabbed Julien's ankle, pulling him down. A dart whistled across the room and caught Julien in the arm.

Malcolm and Mélanie pushed and dodged through the crowd to their friend. They slid between two men in the midst of a fist-fight and reached Julien to find someone else pulling him up.

Malcolm put out a hand and found himself looking at a familiar face. "Raoul. I was wondering when you were going to show up."

Raoul grinned with the same reckless delight with which he'd always faced danger. "Glad to be back. All right, Julien?"

Julien pushed himself to his knees. "The only damage is to my ego. Where's Kitty?"

"Here." Kitty pushed between two sailors and dropped down beside them. "All right, darling?"

"I have a bruise to my ego and probably to my elbow."

"I can kiss both like I do for the children." Kitty pressed a kiss to her husband's left elbow. "You'll have to tell me where your ego is. Raoul. When did you get here?"

"I took a boat up the Thames. I assume you all have your reasons for being here?"

"Antonio Diaz. He had a warning about you." Kitty cast a glance round the tavern. A few were still scuffling, though the brawl had died down. "I don't see him. He may have run. He's on his way to the Argentine."

"What sort of warning?" Malcolm asked.

A tankard sailed across the room, spattering its contents over all of them. Kitty dashed drops of ale out of her hair. "He says someone's trying to have Raoul killed."

Raoul scarcely paused in hauling Julien to his feet. "Hardly surprising. Happens almost every day."

A familiar chill settled over Malcolm. "If—"

A crash rumbled through the tavern, shaking the timbers of the walls.

Of one accord they all stumbled through the crowd and raced to the far door.

Harry and Cordelia had got out the door before them. "There." Harry gestured down the quay. Flames shot up the sails of a ship in the distance. "I think the crash was an explosion."

They ran down the dock through crowds running towards the fire, running away from it, stopping to stare at the flames. A makeshift bucket brigade had already formed to toss water on the burning ship. Gusts of wind slammed against them and fanned the flames. Malcolm stripped off his coat and flung it over a barrel.

A scream cut the air. A woman was on the deck of the ship, flames licking the folds of her dress. Julien, who was nearest to where the woman stood, grabbed the coat he'd just removed, raced onto the next ship over, dodging barrels and coils of rope, and sprang onto the deck. He seized a rope and swung onto the flaming ship.

CHAPTER 2

$\mathcal{J}$ulien thudded onto the ship deck and threw his coat round the woman standing there. He pressed the folds of the coat against her to extinguish the flames, keeping hold of the rope in his teeth. Smoke stung his eyes and scraped his throat. He straightened up and looked into her soot-smeared face. Though he didn't need to see her blue eyes and retroussé nose to recognize her. "Sylvie," he said, meeting Sylvie St. Ives's gaze. "I'm used to seeing you just about everywhere, but I confess this is a surprise." He tossed his singed coat on the deck and caught her round the waist. "Forget this is me and hold on as tight as you can."

Sylvie's arms closed round him with a grip similar to his two-year-old when she was frightened. Julien kicked off from the deck, Sylvie clasped against him.

Kitty and Mélanie were on the deck of the other ship when he swung back to it. They steadied Sylvie as he set her down. If either was surprised to see her, they hid it well. Julien released the rope, hands raw, breath hard. He bent over for a moment, hands on his knees.

Kitty put a hand on his back. "I'm all right," he said.

Mélanie had thrown a coat—Malcolm's—round Sylvie. "Cordy's gone to find a place we can shelter."

As she spoke, Cordelia came running down the dock, blonde hair flying loose from its pins. She froze for a moment when she recognized Sylvie, but merely said, "We can go into the warehouse. This way."

The bucket brigade were still hard at work. Julien spotted Malcolm, Raoul, and Harry amid their number. He started to move towards them, but Kitty gripped his arm. "We need you here. Also, I'm not sure you can stand much longer."

Julien started to protest, then, as often happened, decided his wife was right, and accepted the support of her arm.

Cordelia led the way to a small sitting room in the warehouse on the quay. The wood and brick had the sour, pungent smell of wine. Likely the room was used by gentlemen who came to sample the contents of the barrels stored in the warehouse. A dock official provided a bottle of brandy and cast an anxious glance at them. "We'll manage," Mélanie said. "I'm sure you're needed elsewhere."

Mélanie had a way of at once charming and commanding. The official nodded, then hurried off to help the fire brigade.

Mélanie pressed Sylvie into a straight-backed chair. Cordelia put a glass of brandy in Sylvie's hand.

Sylvie took a swallow, gasped, and choked. "Is he off the ship?"

"Who?" Julien's fingers froze round the glass of brandy Kitty had put in his hand.

"The duke." Sylvie coughed again.

"The Duke of Bamford?" Sylvie's father-in-law was one of Britain's most powerful diplomats.

Sylvie nodded, shoulders shaking.

Mélanie's gaze shot to Julien and then Kitty. "I'll go." She looked at Sylvie. "Malcolm and Raoul and Harry are fighting the fire. If the duke's still on the ship, we'll make sure he's safe." She tossed her mantilla round her shoulders, looked from Julien to Kitty again, smiled at Cordelia, and slipped from the room.

Julien gripped his glass. One had to learn to trust fellow agents, and few could be counted on better than Mélanie. In his state he wouldn't do much good searching for the Duke of Bamford. On the other hand, for a number of reasons, he was probably the best person to interrogate Sylvie. "You came here with the duke?" he asked.

"I followed him," Sylvie said.

"Why?"

"He was meeting someone. I wanted to know whom."

Julien took a drink of brandy. It was a decent vintage. He wondered which barrel the dock official had taken it from. "Is the duke in the habit of holding secret meetings?"

The light from the single lamp in the room bounced off Sylvie's eyes. "My father-in-law is an interesting man."

"So I suspected." Julien glanced down and saw blood on his brandy glass.

"Your hands are bleeding," Kitty pushed him into a chair. "We can talk while I bandage them." She started tearing strips from her petticoat. "What happened when you got to the ship?" she asked Sylvie.

"I hid. Behind some barrels. I could see the shadow of someone in the cabin—the duke or whomever he was meeting. But the wind was loud and I couldn't hear anything. Until there was a crash that sounded like an explosion. I saw the sails go up in flames. I think I heard someone running and a splash, but by then I was running myself. Sparks blew onto my gown and the burning sails were between me and the quay. It was too far to jump." Sylvie folded her arms. "I know you probably aren't inclined to believe me. You're probably thinking I'm telling all sorts of lies. And I can't think why you should trust me. I suppose I could have set off the explosion. But I'd hardly have been on the ship at the time if I had done."

"You might have, if you'd got the timing wrong," Julien said. "Or had trouble with the fuse. Tricky things, explosives. Even to someone with my experience. Or yours."

Sylvie turned her head to look at him. "Maybe. But I didn't."

Kitty splashed brandy on Julien's raw hands. Julien controlled a wince. "If you were following your father-in-law, the question is whom are you working for?" he asked.

Sylvie pulled the folds of Malcolm's coat closer round her shoulders. "Haven't you worked that out?"

Julien held his fingers rigid as Kitty wrapped his hand with the strips from her petticoat. "I'm desolated to disappoint you."

Sylvie took a drink of brandy. Strands of fair hair hung about her face. Not so different from the way she normally wore it, save that usually the disorder was the result of careful work by her maid. "Castlereagh was interested in Bamford's actions."

"The foreign secretary was investigating a senior diplomat?" Cordelia asked.

"It wouldn't be the first time." Kitty looked up from bandaging Julien. "But what did Castlereagh suspect Bamford of?"

Sylvie set her brandy glass down on the gateleg table beside her chair. "He questioned Bamford's loyalties."

"So he had you spying on Bamford," Julien said.

"Gathering information." Sylvie gathered up the loose strands of her hair and tucked them into their pins. "He wanted to know whom Bamford was communicating with."

"So whom was the duke meeting tonight?" Julien asked.

"I told you. I didn't have a chance to find out."

Julien took another drink of brandy. Kitty had his left hand bandaged and his fingers curled stiffly round the glass. "If Castlereagh had you spying on the duke, you can't tell me you didn't go through his papers."

"The duke got a message while he was dressing for a dinner with Mama Duchess. He changed his plans and said he'd meet her at the dinner. By the time I got into his dressing room, all I could find were a few burnt fragments in the grate, with the name of the ship. I went to the ship instead of wasting time looking for more." Sylvie hugged her arms over her chest. "I liked the duke, you know. He supported St. Ives when St. Ives wanted to marry me. He rescued me more than once from people who looked askance at émigrés. He was a charming grandfather. Better than I am a mother." She reached for her glass, took another drink of brandy, and grimaced. "God, I can't believe he's gone."

Cordelia leant forwards and put a hand on Sylvie's arm. "We don't know that he is. Only the sails were on fire and people got there quickly. Malcolm's there, and Raoul and Harry, and Mélanie went to warn them. Whatever you think of all of them, you must admit they're capable. If the duke is there and alive, they'll save him."

Sylvie frowned. "Yes, I have to admit that. Probably at more risk to themselves than I would take." She looked at Julien. "I haven't thanked you, have I?"

Julien considered the woman he'd known since they were both teenagers. Who had helped him escape arrest and execution, been his confidante and lover, and also stabbed him in the back—metaphorically and, on at least one occasion, literally. "No thanks are needed. Or expected. I needed you to get answers."

"And have you got them?"

"Not conclusive ones."

Sylvie took another drink of brandy. "You'd have saved me anyway. At least now. It's this troublesome conscience you've grown."

Julien flexed his right hand, now bandaged as well. "I haven't grown anything I didn't always have."

Sylvie regarded him for a moment. "For what it's worth, it's appreciated."

CHAPTER 3

A damp strip of her petticoat wrapped over her mouth, Mélanie Rannoch hurried down the quay, through the wind and black smoke, along the volunteer bucket brigade slinging water down the line towards the ship. The fire was smoldering. The sails were gone and the cabin was a blackened shell, but the rest of the ship had survived.

She spotted Raoul first. He was coatless, shirt damp with splashed water or sweat or both, face smeared with soot. He saw her and stepped out of the line with a quick look at the man in front of him.

"Sylvie St. Ives was the woman on the deck," Mélanie said. "Julien rescued her. She says the Duke of Bamford was on the ship. She was following him."

A dozen questions shot through Raoul's eyes. His gaze went shuttered for a moment. But he'd never been one to waste time on unnecessary questions in the midst of a mission. "Malcolm's up ahead," he said, voice hoarse from the smoke.

He hesitated a moment, but the quay was crowded with firefighters, buckets, coils of rope. He held out a hand and she put her own in it. Sensible in the crowd.

They picked their way forwards to Malcolm. Her husband was as damp and disheveled as Raoul. Like Raoul, he didn't ask unnecessary questions. And given what they knew about Sylvie, her news was not as surprising as one might have thought. Oddly, Raoul had seemed more shaken than Malcolm. "There's the dock manager." Malcolm jerked his head to the left.

Sometimes it helped to be a duke's grandson. Coatless, his damp cravat stripped off and held over his mouth to ward against smoke, Malcolm still knew how to project the position he had been born to, much as he usually disdained it. So did Raoul, who might be a revolutionary but had been born an aristocrat. Mélanie had had to learn it. But though she might not have been born a lady, she'd been born an actress. Even in tattered black lace and spangled sarcenet, she knew how to convey the authority of a woman who wouldn't dream of being denied.

After a few minutes and a brief conversation with the dock manager, the three of them were able to step onto the charred ship. Smoke hung thick in the air. The sails were blackened tatters. The explosion appeared to have gone off on one side of the deck. The boards were smoke-stained, one burnt away, some still smoldering. But there was a path to the cabin where the boards were untouched and solid beneath their feet. Malcolm nudged the cabin door with his boot toe rather than touch the handle, probably still hot to the touch. He kicked the door open for Mélanie and Raoul, then followed them into the cabin.

They stepped into soot and darkness. Flames had torn through, blackening the walls, leaving only charred remnants of what might have been a table and chairs. Mélanie choked and pressed her dampened strip of petticoat closer to her face as her eyes grew accustomed to the dark. She could make out a shape on the floor. She felt Malcolm and Raoul focus on it as well.

Damp cravat over his mouth, Malcom moved across the floor, holding the lantern the dock manager had given him, skirting a decanter and a cracked glass that had survived the fire. Mélanie and Raoul walked beside him in the dim light of the lantern and the moonlight seeping through the shattered windows. The horror of what they were probably about to see was clear. She could feel it in the air among them. But they all had to see it for themselves.

As they drew near, the shape slowly resolved into outlines that might be recognized as a human form. Splayed legs, twisted arms. Mélanie stared down at the blackened figure on the floor. The body was charred beyond recognition. Malcolm handed the lantern to her and knelt down. When he picked up the corpse's charred hand, the ring on it was plain from the musicale they had attended last March. A lion rampant with a rose in its mouth. Honoring the Plantagenets and Tudors. It belonged to the Duke of Bamford.

Malcolm set the duke's hand down and looked up to meet his father's haunted gaze. Raoul had gone still. "Poor Tony."

Mélanie cast a quick glance at her former spymaster. "Tony?"

Raoul knelt down and touched his fingers to the duke's blackened head. "Anthony Southcott, Viscount St. Ives, and then Duke of Bamford. I knew him. Rather better than I let on to anyone."

With Raoul, secrets were not surprising. But the Duke of Bamford, a Tory politician and diplomat, was hardly a likely friend of a spy embroiled in the French Revolution and the United Irish Uprising who had worked for the Bonapartists during the Peninsular War and Waterloo. And in all the years she had worked for Raoul and all the years since, Mélanie had never heard him mention such a connection to the duke.

Mélanie met Malcolm's gaze and knew they were thinking the same thing. It was Malcom who said it. "Was he—?"

"Not a French spy. Unless he had even more secrets than I knew of." Raoul's gaze fixed on the hollow shell that had been Bamford's face. "We both found our acquaintance useful. And we tried not to presume upon it. That's why I was originally going to let Kitty go alone to the Bamford musicale to talk to Bamford about Spain. It was only when things got complicated with the Ralph Ackerley business that I decided to go as well. And in the end, I didn't speak to Tony much that night."

Malcolm picked up a fragment of metal with a curved handle from the floor. "It looks as though an oil lamp tipped over near him. That would explain why the body is so badly burnt."

Raoul nodded and gently lifted the duke's body and turned it on its side. The back of his coat was less burnt. It had a jagged hole.

Mélanie sucked in her breath.

Raoul grimaced. "However the fire started, someone had already employed a pistol to make sure Tony Bamford was dead."

Mélanie lifted the lantern. All three of them cast quick looks round the cabin. Nothing stirred in the shadows.

Raoul pushed himself to his feet. "Which still doesn't explain how the fire started. Let's have a look."

CHAPTER 4

1791

rue de Richelieu, Paris

Raoul glanced up at the windows glittering with candlelight. Strains of Haydn drifted into the street. "Why are we going to this party?"

Arabella tucked her gloved hand tighter round his arm. "Why do we ever go to parties? To gather information."

Raoul studied the crowd spilling up and down the steps. He could catch traces of talk and laughter carried on the breeze. Not specific words, but the accents were unmistakable. "It's mostly a party of English people. You could talk to them at home."

Arabella twisted her neck, green eyes glinting as only they could, golden ringlets tumbling over her shoulder. She was wearing a red velvet choker. The style was meant to mimic a head cut off by the guillotine. "Tongues will be freer in Paris."

"While the country's being remade and perhaps coming apart at the seams, it's a playground for your set."

Arabella lifted her frothy white muslin skirt as they climbed the front steps, flanked by torches. "For a certain type of English aristo, anywhere is a playground."

"Just English aristos?"

"Fair enough. Though there's a certain insularity about the English."

Raoul paused on the top step. "What are you after, Bella?"

Arabella grinned and tossed her ringlets back from her face. "Information. Half the people at the party are in the Elsinore League. They may treat everywhere as a playground, but they're playing dangerous games. Lord Lovell should have a list of contacts on him. I want to get them."

"Anything I can do to help?"

She slanted a smile up at him. "You're very obliging, Raoul. Have I mentioned that?"

"On occasion." And she had recruited him to her cause when he stumbled across her stealing papers during a ball. Part of her quest against the Elsinore League, a mysterious group of powerful men dedicated to their own advancement rather than any political philosophy. Arabella had gone so far as to marry one of their number as part of her efforts to bring them down.

A liveried footman admitted Arabella and him to the entrance hall. Marble tiled, liberally touched with gilt. The curving staircase was crowded with guests in ruffly gowns and dark coats. Laughter and the clink of champagne glasses drifted down from the salon. The air smelt of wax tapers and expensive scent, snuff and port and brandy. The same sounds and smells as at any aristocratic party. But the laughter was a bit freer, the gentlemen's cravats were tied more carelessly, the ladies' gowns slipped lower on their shoulders. There was a reason Paris was a chosen playground. The same aristos who deplored the Revolution were quick enough to enjoy some of the freedoms it had brought.

"Lady Arabella." A slight young man with sleek fair hair stopped them just inside the salon.

"Lord St. Ives." Arabella extended a gloved hand. "I didn't realize you were in Paris."

"I just arrived. Popped over after a duty visit to my parents in Richmond."

"You always know where to find the best parties, Tony. Do you know Raoul O'Roarke?" Arabella turned to Raoul.

"Only by reputation." St. Ives extended his hand. "I've read some of your articles."

Raoul shook St. Ives's hand. "You have dangerous reading taste, St. Ives."

"I like to know what all sides are saying. But it strikes me you're as likely to get yourself in trouble with your own side as with the Royalists."

"So I'm always telling him," Arabella said with a mock sigh that held a far from playful edge.

"If either of you thinks there are only two sides, you don't grasp the situation in France," Raoul said. "Or in any conflict, come to that."

"Do you think we should be alarmed?" St. Ives asked.

"I think change is inevitable. What sort of change is a matter of question."

St. Ives stopped a passing footman and procured three glasses of champagne. "A more pressing matter now France's king and queen are essentially imprisoned in the Tuileries." He jerked his head towards the dais where the musicians were playing. Haydn had given way to *Ça ira*.

Arabella accepted a glass of champagne from St. Ives. "I can't but feel for them. Marie Antoinette is much cleverer than most acknowledge. But there's no escaping that the king and queen—and more importantly their councillors—managed things abominably." She clinked her champagne glass to Raoul's and St. Ives's. Candlelight sparked on the crystal and bubbles.

Raoul knew enough of fashion to know that her white muslin gown, sashed in scarlet like her choker, was meant to be in the style of the dresses worn by maids and tradeswomen. But he'd never seen a maid or tradeswoman in a gown with such a full skirt, so many ruffles, so much lace. One couldn't but think of Marie-Antoinette playing shepherdess at le Petit Trianon.

Raoul took a drink of champagne. He'd met the now imprisoned queen. He liked her. "England is a very different place from France."

"St. Ives is the Duke of Bamford's heir," Arabella said.

"Oh, Bella," St. Ives said. "Now O'Roarke will see me as the enemy."

"On the contrary," Raoul countered. "And like you, I'm interested in the perspective of those with any number of opinions."

"I hope to see more of France," St. Ives said. "I've been offered a diplomatic post. It seems an important time to be involved."

Raoul took a drink of champagne. Their hosts (whose names he'd forgot) had excellent taste. "There I'd agree with you."

"I hope I can make something of it. A bit challenging with the family." St. Ives looked at Arabella. "How are your boys? They must be quite little men by now."

"So they are. Walking and talking." Arabella's voice was light.

Raoul stood by quietly, face schooled to betray nothing at all. He should be used to it by now. Perhaps one day he'd master the skill.

"My oldest will be at Eton in a couple of years," St. Ives said. "Hard to believe how quickly the time passes." He looked at Raoul. "Do you have children?"

"No." A simple word. Easily enough said. And one of the lies he found it most difficult to tell.

"Well. Plenty of time for that. Certainly comes with its challenges."

"Will your family go with you on your diplomatic posting?" Raoul asked.

"I'm not sure. My wife likes the idea of diplomatic life, but she may wish to remain in London. She says it's for the children, though I suspect it's more to do with London society. She has more power there than I do through any posting. And in truth I think some separation can be of help in a marriage."

"I certainly find so," Arabella said. "Assuming anything can help."

St. Ives gave a light laugh, though a flash in his gaze said he was well aware of the state of Arabella and Alistair Rannoch's marriage. They hardly tried to hide it.

St. Ives moved on a few minutes later, claimed by an acquaintance. Raoul slanted a look at Arabella. "He's not a League member," she said. "At least, not so far as I can make out. But he's worth watching. The charm is effective cover for something far more interesting."

"I thought so." Raoul took another drink of champagne. "Any idea what?"

"No." Arabella touched her glass to his. "That's what makes him so intriguing. Definitely worth an investigation."

"Just what sort of investigation did you have in mind?"

She tilted her head back and laughed. "There's more than one way to investigate, darling. I assume as a spy you know that."

"It had occurred to me. Are you thinking St. Ives could be an ally or an opponent?"

Arabella's gaze shot across the room to where Lord St. Ives stood surrounded by a knot of revelers. "I'm not sure. He's a cipher. And you know how ciphers intrigue me."

CHAPTER 5

May 1821
London Dock

Malcolm followed Mélanie and Raoul into the warehouse sitting room. Sylvie St. Ives was sitting in a straight-backed chair, tendrils of blonde hair escaping round her face, a crumpled brown coat (his own, he realized) clutched over her singed blue gown. A far cry from the polished image the Viscountess St. Ives usually presented.

Malcolm had known Sylvie St. Ives since they were both children. Past events had left him with few reasons to sympathize with her and even fewer to trust her. But it was impossible not to feel compassion at delivering such news. Especially as her gaze held a fear she rarely displayed. He moved into the room, aware of Julien, Kitty, and Cordy looking closely at him, and stopped before Sylvie's chair. "I'm sorry."

A flinch showed in her gaze. "You're sure?"

"His body was badly burnt, but I recognized his signet ring."

"So did I," Raoul said. "I knew your father-in-law rather better than perhaps you realize, Lady St. Ives. I'm sorry."

Sylvie gave a quick nod.

Kitty was staring at Raoul. "You knew Bamford? I mean, I know you'd met him, but—"

"I knew him better than he or I acknowledged when we spoke with him at the duchess's musicale," Raoul said. "Going back to Paris in the '90s."

"Why does everything seem to go back to Paris in the '90s?" Julien muttered.

"I first met the duke at a party with your mother," Raoul said to Malcolm. "When he was still Lord St. Ives. I saw him often through the years. At times it was a profitable alliance."

"You needn't dance round it," Sylvie said. "I know my father-in-law was a spy." She glanced round the group. "It can't be such a surprise. He wasn't the first diplomat to be one."

"The line is often fluid," Raoul agreed. "The duke worked in France."

"Was he—" Cordelia bit the words back.

"He wasn't a double agent, to my knowledge," Raoul said. "It can help to have a contact on the other side. There are often things to negotiate."

"Whom was the duke working with now?" Malcolm asked Sylvie.

Sylvie picked up the glass of brandy from the table beside her and held it with care. "He with dealing with the Austrians over the situation in Naples. And he was also working on the situation in Spain and Portugal. You know all that. If I had more information I wouldn't have been following him tonight."

"Whom was the duke working with when you worked with him?" Julien asked Raoul.

Raoul returned Julien's gaze. "The duke had a varied career."

"Haven't we all?"

"Was he a League member?" Mélanie asked.

"No, I don't believe so. Though I first met him at a League party with Arabella."

"He wasn't," Sylvie said. She had worked with the Elsinore League herself, so she likely knew, though whether or not she'd tell them the truth was open to debate. "Not that you'll believe me."

"We'll question you," Julien said. "It's not quite the same thing."

"I'm afraid there's more," Raoul said. "The duke appears to have been shot in the back before the fire."

Sylvie's eyes widened. "Did the same person who shot him set off the explosion?"

"I'm not sure," Raoul said. "You didn't hear a pistol shot?"

She shook her head. "The wind was howling. And I got there after the duke. I saw the shadow of someone in the cabin. I thought it was the duke, but perhaps it was the person who shot him. I was hiding among barrels on the deck. On the opposite side from where the explosion went off. I heard the explosion, then running feet and a splash."

"I would think whoever set off the explosion would have given themselves more time to get away," Raoul said.

"So the explosion was set earlier?" Sylvie asked. "That means—"

She broke off as the door opened, and went still at the sight of the man standing there.

Hubert Mallinson pushed the door to behind him and regarded the group in the sitting room. Besides being Julien's uncle, he was also his former spymaster. And Kitty's and Sylvie's. And Malcolm's own. Hubert was in evening dress, a greatcoat thrown on hastily over his dark coat and cream-colored breeches.

"This was quick even for you," Julien said.

Hubert took a step into the room. "Is it true the duke's dead?"

Sylvie stared at him for a long moment, then turned her gaze away.

"Raoul, Mélanie, and I saw the body," Malcolm said. "It had the duke's signet ring. It had also been shot in the back."

"Damnation." Hubert gripped his hands behind his back. "And the explosion?"

"Are you accusing us of it?" Julien asked.

Hubert regarded his nephew. "I don't believe I've accused anyone of anything."

"You've been quick enough to accuse us of any sort of violence in the past."

"Connecting you with violence has often been a not unreasonable assumption, Julien."

"Often committed on your order, Uncle. And judging by recent events it could have been guns *you* were shipping that exploded."

"There was gunpowder on the ship," Raoul said. "Packed in a wine barrel, as best we could tell. We found some of the iron that had bound the barrel. But there was also a trail and a candle set to burn down and set it off. Malcolm, Mélanie, and I found the candle holder."

Hubert's brows snapped together. "You're sure?"

Raoul gave a short nod.

"It isn't only Radicals who explode things," Julien said.

"I never said it was. Oh good." Hubert looked up as the door opened again. "We need you, Roth."

Jeremy Roth paused for a moment to take in the company, then moved into the room. "You said it was urgent." He addressed Hubert, though he was far closer to everyone else in the room, except Sylvie.

"It's nothing to do with Judith," Hubert said.

"Yes, I know." Roth had recently married Malcolm's cousin Judith. "I was with her when I got your message. We were dining with friends."

"As was I. We need you." Somehow Hubert's clipped words had the odd ring of a plea.

Roth regarded Hubert. "I don't work for you."

"You're a Bow Street runner and Bow Street report to the home office, which means you work for the British government,"

Hubert said. "I still have a connection to that government. And you're one of the family now."

"Which family?" Roth asked.

"Ours," Hubert said.

"Oh my god," Julien said. "Are there no depths you won't sink to, Uncle?"

It was much what Malcolm would have liked to say, though he probably wouldn't have put it into words.

Roth was looking at Hubert. "Interesting."

"We share an interest in this." Hubert gestured round the room. "All of us."

Roth regarded him, hands jammed in his greatcoat pockets. "I don't know what *this* is."

"A ship exploded and caught fire."

"I've heard. I talked to Harry Davenport, who's still working with the firefighters. He's fine, just tired." Roth glanced at Cordelia as he said it, and caught her smile of thanks, then looked back at Hubert. "It's not Bow Street's jurisdiction."

Hubert pushed his spectacles up on his nose. "The Duke of Bamford was on the ship. The explosion was caused deliberately. And the duke was shot in the back. Now do you understand the importance?"

"A death is always important and worth investigating. But technically it's not Bow Street's case."

"Never mind about that. I'll talk to Sidmouth. It's a sensitive issue. We need Bow Street involved."

"Sidmouth may not agree that that means involving me," Roth said.

"Then Sidmouth's a fool. This is going to take all our resources."

"And I'm a resource?" Roth asked.

"You have the keenest mind at Bow Street."

"Not everyone would think that an asset."

Hubert took a step towards Roth and stared up at him. Roth

was a good four inches taller than Hubert, but Hubert, as Malcolm knew well, had a way of controlling the room and all those in it. "I'm not everyone."

Roth folded his arms. "What do we know about why the duke was on the ship? It wasn't a yacht, from what I could tell."

All eyes in the room moved to Sylvie. "I don't know," she said.

"You didn't come with him?" Roth asked.

"No, I followed him." Sylvie looked from Malcolm to Hubert to Julien. "I know what you're thinking."

"What?" Julien asked.

"I was there. I have no morals and no scruples and I've killed before. Does Mr. Roth know that? Well, it scarcely matters at this point, and if he didn't, I'm sure one of you would have enlightened him."

"You didn't necessarily have a motive to kill the duke," Julien said. "Though you would have known how to set the explosives. I remember showing you."

"Surely I'd have managed to leave sooner in that case. If there's one thing I am it's careful of my own self-preservation."

"You have me there," Julien said.

"What was the duke doing on the ship?" Hubert asked.

"You think I'd tell you?" Sylvie said.

"If you want to learn who killed your father-in-law."

"Surely the answer to that has to do with who killed him. Surely it does for you as well."

"I think you mean what I'd want to do with the information might depend on that," Hubert said.

Sylvie folded her arms over her chest. "I'll give you this, Hubert. You're honest. If you were the one who'd been found shot in the back, I can quite see everyone suspecting me."

"Oh, if Hubert were found shot in the back, we could suspect everyone in this room," Julien said. "Well, almost everyone."

"What were you doing here, Sylvie?" Hubert asked.

"Following the duke."

"Why?"

"Because I was curious about what he was doing."

"And what was he doing?"

"If I knew that, I might know who killed him. I never got a chance to find out." She took a drink of brandy. "If you're so interested in him, you must have an idea."

"He was a senior British diplomat. And a duke. Anything that happens to him is of interest."

"I somehow doubt you're going to take as much interest in St. Ives." She frowned. "Who I suppose is the Duke of Bamford now. What an odd thought."

Hubert's gaze shifted to the others. "What were you all doing here?"

Silence gripped the group. Normally they kept things from Hubert on general principles. But in this case, not telling him risked his thinking them more connected to the explosion and Bamford's death.

"I was meeting a contact," Kitty said. "From Spain."

Hubert tugged at his spectacles. "Bamford had connections to Spain."

"My contact moved in quite different circles."

"Why were you meeting him?"

"He had a warning for me."

"Could it have meant—"

"No." Kitty hesitated a moment. "He gave me a warning that someone was trying to have Raoul killed."

Hubert frowned and rubbed his spectacles. "People are always trying to kill O'Roarke."

"Quite," Raoul said.

"This was a specific threat," Kitty said. "An—my contact thought it important."

Hubert cast a glance at Raoul. "You knew Bamford. Better than either of you let on. Could there be a connection?"

"I don't see how. Bamford and I were working for opposite

sides."

Hubert's gaze snapped round the others in the room. "Could any of your friends be behind this?"

"I know you think Radicals are behind every bit of unrest, Uncle Hubert," Julien said, "but, honestly, doesn't Bamford strike you as an unlikely target?"

"People have been known to pick unexpected targets."

"You think Radicals are behind this?"

Hubert tugged at his earpiece. "No, actually. But I think they're likely to be accused of it. I want to be able to deflect the attacks."

"You surprise me."

"Thank you."

Julien folded his arms. "Of course it's always possible this is one of your agent provocateur attacks."

"Why would I pick this target?"

"Because you wanted to get rid of Bamford?"

Hubert regarded his nephew. "Julien, did you just accuse me of murder?"

"Seems an appropriate question in our family."

"I didn't want to get rid of Bamford."

"So you say."

"You're always telling me not to waste time suspecting your friends. I advise you to do the same."

The door creaked open. Harry stepped in, coatless, brown hair plastered to his sweat-dampened face. He took in the company with a quick glance, gave a smile of reassurance to Cordelia, and said, "The last of the embers are out. The ship apparently belongs to Prebble & Company. They import wine from the Continent."

"That fits with the wreckage we saw," Malcolm said.

Julien looked at Sylvie. "Do you know of any connection Bamford had with a wine importing business?"

Sylvie shook her head. "But I can't claim to have been privy to his business activities."

"You appear to have made yourself privy to a number of his activities."

"Any business investments he had weren't of interest to me. I imagine he did make some investments, but I never heard of anything to do with a wine importer. And whatever he was doing tonight didn't appear to be a business meeting. It was very secretive. Perhaps—"

She broke off as the door opened again, this time to admit another of Malcolm's former employers. Britain's foreign secretary.

CHAPTER 6

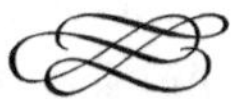

ord Castlereagh hesitated on the threshold. Like Hubert, he was dressed for an evening engagement, though his greatcoat appeared less haphazardly pulled on. Nothing Castlereagh did was haphazard.

"Well, well," Julien said. "Quite a reunion."

Castlereagh looked at Sylvie. "Is it true?"

"Malcolm found him," Sylvie said. "He recognized Bamford's ring."

"He was caught in the blast?" Castlereagh asked.

"And he'd been shot in the back," Malcolm said.

Castlereagh went still. "Take me to see him."

"Certainly, if you wish."

"I do. No need for the others to come."

Satisfying as it would be to refuse Castlereagh, it would probably make things worse. And Malcolm needed to know what the foreign secretary knew. Malcolm exchanged a quick look with Mélanie and led Castlereagh back to the quay. Another exchange with the dock manager, whose gaze widened at the sight of the foreign secretary, and they were cleared to step back on the ship.

The acrid smoke was even stronger than before. The boards of the deck were slick with water the firefighters had dumped on them to douse stray embers. Malcolm pushed open the door of the cabin and lifted the lantern the customs official had given him as they stepped into the charred air.

Castlereagh stared down at the Duke of Bamford's body, gaze on the signet ring in the lantern light. "I don't think I really believed it until now. We need to talk, Malcolm."

Without speaking, Malcolm led the way back onto the deck and then down the quay where they could breathe more easily. The wind cut against them, but at least cleared the air. He could hear voices and the strains of an Irish fiddle from the tavern they had been in. It felt a lifetime ago.

He drew a breath of the briny air and looked at the man he had served for eight years. "Quite like Vienna." Only then, the victim had been Malcolm's fellow agent and half-sister, and Malcolm himself had been a suspect.

"What else do you know?" Castlereagh asked.

Malcolm jerked his head towards the warehouse. "Those are my allies in the sitting room. Do you think I have secrets from them?"

Castlereagh's gaze was hard and steady as polished gems. "Everyone has secrets. Isn't that what you'd say?"

"Not in the midst of an investigation. We're a team."

"What were you and Mélanie and the Carfaxes and Davenports and O'Roarke doing here tonight?" Castlereagh demanded.

"Nothing to do with the Duke of Bamford."

"That's all you're going to say?"

"As I often say to Hubert, I don't work for you anymore. What about you?"

Castlereagh took a step back. "What about me?"

"What do you know about this?"

"Why—"

"You had Sylvie following Bamford."

Castlereagh grimaced and turned away. "Bamford was one of Britain's abler diplomats. You know that."

"He was quite brilliant. And he was also an agent?" He kept it a question, because he wasn't going to reveal Raoul's information. Or even Sylvie's.

Castlereagh's eyes glittered ice blue in the shadows. "The line between diplomat and agent is often blurry. As you know. But Bamford always had connections with the French."

"Are you saying he was a double?" Malcolm kept his voice easy. Mélanie and Raoul had pardons. He didn't have to worry as he once would have. Which didn't mean he didn't worry. Which didn't mean Castlereagh wasn't a threat.

Castlereagh coughed. "I had wondered about that in the past, though he managed to convince me otherwise. But lately I'd heard rumors he was communicating with people who were dangerous."

"You think he was spying now?"

"Possibly. Alliances had shifted. He had a mistress in France for many years. She was French. Is French."

"It happens." Malcolm kept his voice even. "People form entanglements with people on the opposing side. It can lead to conflicts. It doesn't have to lead to betrayal."

"You can't deny the risks."

"Of course not. But at this point surely those risks are in the past."

"Don't pretend to be so naive, Malcolm." Castlereagh flexed his gloved fingers. "O'Roarke goes back and forth to Spain—"

"Raoul O'Roarke is my father."

Castlereagh cast a glance at him. "I wish you wouldn't—"

"What? You don't like me to say it so plainly?"

"I understand family feeling, Malcolm. But he had a history before you can remember."

"He was quite young when I was born. I've known him for over half his life at this point."

"You have a good mind, Malcolm, but you've always had illusions. You certainly have them when it comes to O'Roarke."

"I don't claim to be free of illusions. But I'd say I see Raoul O'Roarke quite clearly."

"In your mind, he's some sort of hero. I've seen the way you look at him."

"Admiration doesn't mean illusions."

"Not everyone has your ideals, Malcolm."

"Oh, I quite recognize that. Raoul would be the first to say he's far more ruthless than I am. But the ideals I have I learnt from him."

Castlereagh's eyes narrowed. "You have a keen understanding. But you're too inclined to let your emotions cloud things."

"If you mean I can't justify everything in the name of the mission—or the supposed name of my country—you're quite right."

A gust of wind ruffled the clouds. The moonlight shifted over Castlereagh's face. "O'Roarke's magnetic. And you grew up with him."

"And he's my father."

"As you say. All of which makes me fear you're in for a hard awakening."

"You and I have often disagreed on what is to be feared, sir."

Castlereagh gave a curt nod. "The Duchess of Bamford is dining with the Marchmains. I was there myself until I received the message about the explosion that brought me here. So was Hubert. My wife is still there. I want you and Mélanie to go to the Marchmains' and tell the duchess before she learns of her husband's death from others."

"Surely it would be easier for you to return."

"I wouldn't be able to note her reaction as you would. I wouldn't know the questions to ask."

"So now you trust my judgment?"

"I trust you as an investigator. I trust Mélanie. You showed me what you could do in Vienna. And you know the Marchmains."

"We know the Marchmains because their son, whom they have disowned, is my secretary and lives with us, along with their daughter-in-law, who is the reason they disowned him."

Castlereagh's brows drew together. He was not fond of scandal. "Alexander Trenor's situation is unfortunate. But the Marchmains are too well bred to let it stop them from receiving you and Mélanie. In fact, I suspect they'll be eager for news of their son. It will make your calling on them less surprising."

"Sir—"

"We're in the midst of an investigation, Malcolm. And a possible international crisis. I've never known you to stand on niceties in the midst of either."

No, it was far more likely to be Castlereagh who stood on niceties. To the point of standing by when Malcolm had been arrested for murder. A murder Castlereagh may at the time have believed he'd committed. None of which Malcolm could reasonably bring up now.

"Mel and I are scarcely in a state to call on anyone in Mayfair." Malcolm glanced down at his damp shirt and breeches. "We'll need to go to Berkeley Square first."

"So you'll do it?"

"Was that ever really in question, sir?"

CHAPTER 7

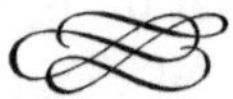

December 1798
Off the coast of France

ater lapped against the boat. Mist hugged the shoreline, but a faint outline shone through the gray curtain. Raoul leant his elbows on the rail and watched the shore come into focus. The country that had shaped him. That had been the site of his first spectacular failure. And was now his refuge from his latest failure.

The boards creaked. Without looking round, he said, "You'll soon be rid of me."

"Not precisely the way I've imagined it in the past," Alistair Rannoch said. "But yes."

Raoul risked a glance over his shoulder. "I won't pretend to know why you've helped me. And I certainly understand that you didn't want to do it. But for what it's worth, I am grateful."

The wintry light caught Alistair's wry grimace. "I thought you were done for."

"So did I." For months after the failed United Irish Uprising,

Raoul had been sure it was only a matter of time before he was discovered and arrested. Until Arabella found him and said she had a way to get him out of the country. And took him to, of all people, her husband. The man they had both betrayed for over a decade.

Alistair closed his hands on the rail. With much the grip he might use to strangle an opponent. "You lead a charmed life, O'Roarke. You always have."

"Forgive me for saying it hasn't often felt that way. But I have escaped far more danger than anyone has a right to expect to do."

Alistair's fingers whitened on the rail. "Arabella's a hard woman to say no to. And I don't mean that the way it may sound."

"I'd never have thought you did."

Lamplight shifted in the cabin behind them, where Horace Smytheton, whom Alistair had inveigled into helping, had settled with a volume of Shakespeare and a bottle of port. Alistair cast a glance over his shoulder. "For all our sakes, no one should hear of this. I hope we can at least agree on that."

"I may be no stranger to betrayal, but common sense, not to mention common courtesy, dictates I not betray those who have helped me."

The boat slid towards shore. Scraggly trees. A makeshift dock. A hut of some sort beyond. A cloaked figured emerged from the mist. Raoul didn't recognize him. But Alistair appeared to, or at least to be expecting someone. He gave a grunt of acknowledgement.

The boat thudded against the dock. Smytheton came out of the cabin to wish Raoul well, in tones that sounded genuine. As were Raoul's when he thanked him.

The cloaked figure came forwards. Raoul swung onto the dock. Alistair followed. The hood of the figure's cloak hood fell back to reveal a fine-boned face.

"Monsieur O'Roarke. We're glad to see you in France."

"Thank you. Mademoiselle—?" He let the question dangle.

"You can call me Chat Gris. Anything more specific is risky, as I'm sure you'll appreciate." Her voice was level and determined. But she couldn't be much over twenty. In fact, Raoul suspected she was younger.

"What agent wouldn't appreciate aliases? Mademoiselle Chat Gris. It appears I am in your hands."

She nodded and looked at Alistair. "I can take it from here."

"I'm relieved to hear it. I assumed my responsibilities ended at the shores of France. I think both O'Roarke and I would prefer it that way."

Raoul turned to him. "I'm sure you want to hear the least possible from me. But thank you."

Alistair met his gaze. His own glittered in the moonlight. "I'm probably going to regret in the future that you're alive, O'Roarke. But for everyone's sake, I hope you have the goodness to not botch the efforts that have been put into saving you. I really don't want to answer to Arabella if you come to grief. You have a catlike ability to escape, but even you must be running out of your nine lives."

Alistair swung back onto the boat. A shadowy alliance that still did not make sense ended as quickly as it had begun.

Mademoiselle Chat Gris led the way across the sand and through the trees. Branches creaked. Another figure came towards them. Raoul tensed for combat, but Chat Gris put up a hand in greeting. "I told you I could handle it."

"I have no doubt of it. But you'll permit me concerns." A man's voice speaking impeccable French. But Raoul would swear the speaker was originally English. And something about those accents was familiar. He studied the figure in the moonlight seeping through the branches. Not overly tall. Regular features, an air of easy assurance, a flexible mouth, and eyes that gleamed with wry humor. "Lord St. Ives?"

"My god. You really do have supernatural abilities." The new arrival's eyes glinted at him in the dark.

"I find it useful to remember faces. And voices. If I'm right, we met at a party in the rue de Richelieu."

"We did. With Lady Arabella. We were all more carefree then."

"Don't be an idiot, Tony," Chat Gris said. "This isn't safe."

"No, it isn't, but O'Roarke has no reason to turn me in. The risk was mine in agreeing to help. And I'd do it again."

"I can't think why," Raoul said. "But I'm grateful."

"I don't like it," Chat Gris said.

St. Ives touched her arm. "You've picked a strange time to be worried about me. But don't think I'm not grateful."

"It's not that I don't worry about you the rest of the time. We just happen to be on opposite sides and our countries are at war. You can't expect me to forget that."

"I never said I did." St. Ives gripped her hand and pressed a quick kiss to her fingers. "Alliances have a way of shifting, O'Roarke, as I'm sure you understand better than most. My friend and I can get you to safety. Or what passes for safety. Assuming you can trust us."

"I don't trust lightly. But in my current circumstances, it is difficult for me to do anything else."

St. Ives jerked his head towards the shadows. "We have a carriage waiting."

The carriage was a well-sprung chaise. Nothing ostentatious on the door, but the mahogany paneling gleamed, the glass didn't let in a draft, and a charcoal brazier burnt on the floor.

"You're probably wondering why I'm here," St. Ives said, when they were settled on the tufted brocade seats. "But politely declining to ask."

"I confess it occurred to me. I didn't take you for a Radical."

"I'm not." St. Ives gripped the strap as they rounded a curve. "Nor am I an adherent of the United Irishmen, though I am not without sympathy for your cause. But let's say a complicated set of alliances pulled me into this. I can't promise we'll be allies in the future. But I can promise you can trust me in this."

"He means it," Chat Gris said. "He's honorable to a degree that isn't good for his safety."

St. Ives shot a look at her. "I can look after myself. I fully accept the limits of any alliance."

"Hmph."

"I imagine O'Roarke does too," St. Ives said. "Or he wouldn't be trusting himself to us."

"I don't have much choice but to trust," Raoul said. "At times one must take one's allies where one finds them."

"Tony and I wouldn't work together if it weren't for that," Chat Gris said.

"Tony?" Raoul asked.

"My given name," St. Ives said. "Anthony Sebastian Richard Aloysius. Scarcely anyone else uses it. Even in the nursery I was St. Ives."

"And your son will be," Chat Gris said. "Silly."

"A silliness our lives are built on. And that my two traveling companions would like to tear down."

"Oh, we'd settle for just expanding the suffrage," Raoul said. "At least, I would. I can't speak for Mademoiselle Chat Gris."

"That would be a start," she said. The hood of her cloak had fallen back again. Her eyes were a shade between green and brown, her hair a golden brown that would serve her well in a variety of disguises. "And no, I never claimed to be entirely in tune with the government I serve. Any more than you are with yours," she added to St. Ives.

"Touché," St. Ives said.

Raoul settled back in his corner of the carriage. "Whom are we going to see?"

Chat Gris's eyes glinted. "How do you know we're going to see anyone?"

"You could have simply left me on the French coast. Or at the most, delivered a purse and a horse. I could fend for myself. Both of your skills and time being put to such use suggests there's someone specific you want me to talk to. Or who wants to talk to me."

Chat Gris shot a look at St. Ives. "You're right. He's sharp as a knife blade."

St. Ives smiled at her, then looked back at Raoul. "You're correct, O'Roarke. But at this point, I don't think you'll object."

"At this point I'd have little reason to do so. I have no claims on my time." When until recently it had seemed there wasn't enough time in the day to accomplish what he needed to do. And then that he had no time before time itself ran out and he faced arrest and execution.

Chat Gris regarded him. "Do you need a doctor? We heard you'd been wounded."

"I was. A maddeningly long time ago. I'm healing." And unlike his friend Edward Fitzgerald, who had died of wounds that should have been minor, Raoul hadn't had his wounds fester.

The carriage came to a stop. They seemed to be in an inn yard, judging by the clatter of carriage wheels and horses' hooves, the creak that sounded like an inn sign, the quick glimpse that he got of mullioned windows and a gabled roof. They drove round to what seemed to be the back of the inn and pulled up. St. Ives and Chat Gris led the way through a side door and down a low-ceilinged, slate-flagged passage. Chat Gris opened the door.

"Here he is," she said to whoever was beyond. "Safely arrived and in one piece. It all went so smoothly it was almost dull."

"Thank you, my dear," said a voice from the shadows. "I knew I could count on you. And your friend, whose presence I won't officially acknowledge. You'll find a nice bottle of Bordeaux waiting for you in the adjoining room."

St. Ives gave a smile that glinted in the shadows. He and Chat Gris stepped to the side to allow Raoul to enter the room, then pulled the door to behind him.

A man sat at the far side of a table in the inn parlor that lay beyond the door. The room was lit only by a branch of candles on the table, and the man was in shadow, but the set of his shoulders, the outline of his wig, and the walking stick leaning against the table told Raoul all he needed to know. "I wasn't expecting you. Though perhaps I should have done."

"Yes, you should," said Prince Talleyrand.

CHAPTER 8

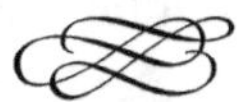

May 1821
London

The Marchmains' house in Upper Grosvenor Street blazed with candlelight. Mélanie smoothed her velvet cloak. She'd discarded her mantilla and sarcenet overdress, and hastily wrapped a pink-spotted black gauze overdress over her pomegranate silk slip when they returned to Berkeley Square. But her hair was still loose, caught back with pearl pins she'd jammed in in those few minutes in Berkeley Square, while also trying to fend off questions from the children. She'd go out in Mayfair attired as she was, but with their friends, not to the home of a Tory family with whom they were at odds.

The footman looked askance at their unexpected arrival in the midst of a party, but recognized Malcolm's card. He conducted them across the high-ceilinged, marble-tiled hall into a sitting room hung with ice blue watered silk. A short time later, Lord Marchmain came into the room. His neckcloth and fair hair were immaculate, but his angular face was consumed not with anger but concern. "Alexander—"

"Sandy's fine," Malcolm said. "So is his wife."

Marchmain let out a breath of relief and flushed in the same instant. "Then—"

"This isn't about Sandy and Bet," Malcolm said. "We understand the Duchess of Bamford is among your guests."

"She is. She and my wife are old friends. The duke was supposed to be here as well, but he was detained."

"That's why we're here," Malcolm said. "There's been an accident. We need to speak with the duchess in private."

Marchmain went still, but nodded and did not ask more questions before he left to fetch the duchess.

Mélanie exchanged a quick look with Malcolm. "I confess I'm still debating the best strategy."

"I confess I'm doing the same," Malcolm said. "Though at the very least we've confirmed part of Sylvie's story. Whatever took Bamford to the docks was apparently not a long-standing engagement."

"Unless he always meant to slip out of dinner."

"Speaking as a spouse who's done the same?" Malcolm asked.

"Possibly."

He gave the quick, sweet smile that was his usual answer when they confronted their past. Then his face went serious. The same feeling settled within her. Because whatever the state of the Bamfords' marriage, they were about to tell a wife that her husband was dead.

A few minutes later, Marchmain returned with the Duchess of Bamford and Lady Marchmain, who hovered protectively beside her friend. Lady Marchmain's presence complicated things, but given that the duchess would certainly need a friend, it was difficult to object.

Lady Marchmain regarded Mélanie and Malcolm with a gaze as cool as her diamonds, but the duchess smiled at them. She was gowned in pearl gray silk, her gray-blonde hair twisted into an elaborate knot, as elegant as she had been when they had last seen her at her musicale a few weeks before.

"Mr. and Mrs. Rannoch. I understand you have some unfortunate news to deliver." Her voice was level but held the strain of fine silk pulled to the breaking point.

"I'm afraid so, Duchess," Malcolm said. He told her, as quickly and gently as possible. Not an easy combination, but Malcolm was good at it. He'd had an unfortunate amount of practice.

It was Lady Marchmain who gasped and went pale. The duchess stayed very still, white-gloved fingers curled inwards. "To think I was annoyed when I got his note saying he wouldn't be able to come to dinner. Another tedious diplomatic negotiation interfering, I thought. The things one doesn't realize."

"Hetty." Lady Marchmain's voice was hoarse. "Bamford is—"

"Yes, I know." The duchess put out a hand and gripped her friend's fingers. "My husband is dead. Though it doesn't quite seem real yet. I imagine it will be a long time before it does. I knew he did dangerous things. I tried not to ask too many questions." Her fingers tightened on Lady Marchmain's hand. "Is Sylvie all right?"

"She was shaken," Mélanie said, "but she's not hurt beyond some scratches."

"Lady St. Ives was at the London docks?" Lady Marchmain said. Malcolm had said as much, but she seemed not quite to have grasped it.

"It's not as surprising as it seems," the duchess said. "Our family have varied interests. With certain common themes. There's a great deal I'm not supposed to be aware of. And generally I stay out of their way. But really, one can't ignore everything. And pretending to be blind can grow exhausting."

"Do you know why the duke didn't join you at dinner?" Malcolm asked. "Forgive the questions, but it may be important."

The duchess released Lady Marchmain's hand and folded her own hands in her lap. "I understand. He said some business had come up. With Bamford that wasn't unusual. When Castlereagh and Hubert Mallinson both left, I should have guessed something. But I assumed they'd been called away for the same reason Tony hadn't made it to the dinner. Some treaty to be discussed. Some diplomatic contretemps to smooth over. Some foreign dignitary to pull out of an embarrassing situation. Or someone's troublesome mistress to pay off. And those were only the ones he more or less told me about. At times it was something more dangerous." Her gaze went from Malcolm to Mélanie. "I'm sure I don't need to tell you that my husband was a—what's the word you use? Agent? It has a more weighted ring than spy."

"We've learnt he was," Malcolm said. "But only recently. I knew of your husband's diplomatic work in Spain. I wasn't aware of his other activities."

"By the time you knew him in the Peninsula, his work was more confined to diplomacy. But he hadn't given up his other activities entirely."

"Can you think of why he'd have gone to the London Dock tonight?" Mélanie asked.

"I imagine to meet with someone who had recently arrived in England. Or was about to depart. My husband had eclectic contacts. But if you're going to ask me whom—" She shook her head. "We didn't have that kind of marriage. His secretary would be more likely to know. Or his valet. Or possibly his mistress, though I can't tell you who that is at the moment."

"Hetty—" Lady Marchmain put a hand on her friend's arm.

The duchess met Lady Marchmain's gaze. "It's the devil of a mess, Nell. But there's nothing to do but move forwards. Has anyone told St. Ives?"

"Lord and Lady Carfax took Lady St. Ives home," Malcolm said.

"Sylvie might break it to him better than I would. Still, I should go home. You're welcome to come with me. I imagine there are a number of people in our household you'll wish to speak to."

"I can come with you, Hetty," Lady Marchmain said.

"No, Nell. You have guests to see to. And I need to see to this myself. It's hardly the first difficult situation I've faced in the course of my marriage to Tony. And I doubt it will be the—" She drew a sharp breath. "No, I suppose it is the last, in that sense. All the more reason for me to get on with it."

Lord Marchmain went to order the carriage. Lady Marchmain returned to her guests, at the duchess's insistence. The duchess said her friend could do her a great favor by not letting talk get about until morning. But in truth, Mélanie suspected the duchess might wish to speak without the Marchmains present.

The duchess let out a small sigh when both the Marchmains had left the room. "Nell's a dear friend, but there are times when a concerned friend is the last thing one wants."

"Can I get you anything before we leave?" Malcolm asked. "A glass of wine?"

"Thank you. I believe Marchmain keeps a decent sherry in those decanters." The duchess drew her shawl about her shoulders. "I still can't make sense of it. If I ever fancied myself in love with him, it ended long ago. I don't know that he ever fancied himself in love with me. We spent months apart. The better part of a year, at times. We went days scarcely speaking, even when we were in the same house. But he was the father of my children. We forged a life together, even if that life took us on separate paths. He was always a part of my life. I didn't realize how much until I learnt he was gone."

"I'm sorry," Mélanie said. Her impulse was to put her arm round the other woman, but they were hardly on terms that would make such a gesture appropriate. Especially with a woman of the duchess's station.

"Tony wouldn't thank me for being sentimental." The duchess shook her head. "I knew he ran risks, but I never thought—especially now."

"He hadn't mentioned what he was working on?" Mélanie asked.

"We didn't have those types of conversations. Some diplomatic wives share their husbands' careers. I know you did when Mr. Rannoch was posted abroad." The duchess cast a quick smile at Malcolm as he put a glass of sherry in her hand. "But beyond Tony's occasional inquiry into the guest list for a party, we did not. Not surprising, perhaps, given the nature of his activities."

"You always knew he was an agent?" Malcolm asked.

"I may not be an agent myself, but I am reasonably astute, Mr. Rannoch. I had an idea of the sort of missions he went on. They created secrecy, naturally. Which isn't the best thing in a marriage. Though in our case, I'd say we were already apart. I never really wanted to know his secrets. That might have meant needing to reveal mine, and I can't imagine anything more appalling. I married to obtain my freedom, not to lose it." She took a sip of sherry. "I thought he'd give it up when he came into the title. His work outside of diplomatic channels. But he didn't. And I could see he didn't want to."

"So you weren't entirely unattuned to his thoughts and feelings," Mélanie said.

"Not entirely." The duchess looked into the pale gold depths of her glass. "I was glad he had something of his own. It left me free to pursue my own life. Where our lives touched, we could assist each other. Mostly we didn't get in each other's way. There are worse partnerships."

Malcolm moved to a chair beside Mélanie. "Had he seemed concerned about anything lately?"

"Not particularly. If anything, he had that air of suppressed excitement he seemed to get when there was a mission afoot. I half expected him to tell me he was going abroad again. A bit too schoolboyish at his age, I sometimes thought, but then I can certainly understand the impulse to chase after one's youth. One doesn't risk one's life dyeing one's hair or ordering a new gown, though."

"Did you think he was risking his life?" Mélanie asked.

"No, or I'd have—well, I don't know what I'd have done. Tony never interfered with me. I'd have been reneging on the bargain if I'd tried to interfere with him." The duchess took another sip of sherry. "If you want to know more about whatever he was involved in, it's possible his mistress knew more."

"Would you happen to know the lady's name?" Malcolm asked.

"Tony and I respected each other's freedom, but we weren't quite so modern we shared names. However, I did hear mention of a former opera dancer named Maria. I imagine with your skills you can find her."

A door clicked open in the hall and footfalls sounded on marble. "The carriage." The duchess swallowed the last of her sherry. "It seems I can't delay facing my family any longer."

CHAPTER 9

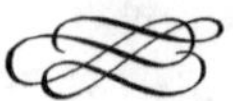

December 1798
France

Prince Talleyrand regarded Raoul across the inn parlor St. Ives and Mademoiselle Chat Gris had conducted him to. "Sit down, O'Roarke. And perhaps you'd be good enough to pour us both some calvados." The prince gestured to a decanter on the table. "My foot is a bit troublesome."

Raoul poured two glasses of calvados and handed one to the prince.

Talleyrand inclined his head in thanks. "You look well. I'd heard—"

"Yes, I was wounded." Raoul dropped into a chair at the opposite end of the table. "I had time to recover before I got out of Ireland. I still move a bit slowly, but I'll mend." Physically, at least. He was never going to be the man he'd been before the Uprising.

"Arabella was worried."

"I'm still rather stunned by the lengths Arabella went to." Raoul took a sip of calvados. Velvet on the tongue. Talleyrand must have brought it with him. It would be a rare inn cellar that boasted something so supple. "I don't suppose you know how she got Alistair to help? Or that you'll tell me if you do."

Talleyrand's blue eyes glinted in the candlelight. "You're right, I probably wouldn't tell you. But if I did know, I wouldn't try to get you to tell me what you knew of the matter."

"Which is precisely nothing."

Talleyrand smiled. "So you say."

Raoul settled back in his chair. "I'm flattered you took an interest in me, sir."

"Don't underestimate yourself, O'Roarke. A great many people are interested in you."

"I don't have a great deal to offer just now." His fingers bit into his glass. He tossed down another sip of calvados. Quickly enough it burnt down his throat. Sometimes it took a jolt like that to remind him he was alive.

"You've been dealt a setback." Talleyrand's voice was cool as the chilled champagne he served at his parties but not without sympathy. "A serious one, I grant. But if either of us had given up at our first setback or even our second, we wouldn't have outlasted the Revolution."

Raoul's fingers tightened on the stem of his glass. "Talking of setbacks."

"We may not entirely agree on what we want to make of the world. But surely we both understand that most progress is achieved by chipping away."

"You're talking to a veteran of two failed revolutions."

"I wouldn't call France a failure, would you? That's talking like Hubert Mallinson."

Raoul took another drink of calvados. "Fair enough."

"It may not be the France you wanted, but a great deal has changed. I'd think you'd want to preserve that change."

"Very much."

Talleyrand reached for his own glass. "Things have a way of shifting. Not so very long ago I was in the United States working at a bank. At times, I wasn't sure I'd ever see my homeland again. Now I'm France's foreign minister. You may not be exiled forever."

"The thought of years of exile is not comforting." He bit back more.

Talleyrand's gaze stayed steady on his face. "I know something about what it is to be a parent to a child one can't claim openly. There are ways to keep the bonds, even with distance."

Raoul turned his glass in his hand. It was more than six months since he'd seen Malcolm. April, a quick trip before all hell broke loose in Ireland. He'd missed Speech Day, for the first time since Malcolm had started at Harrow. He had no intention of allowing his separation from his son to drag on much longer. He'd find a way back into England. It wouldn't be the first time he'd skirted authorities.

Talleyrand's gaze continued steady on his face. "Running risks is part of who you are. Though I hope you've learnt to stop short of recklessness. Meanwhile, there's plenty for you to do in France. Your friend Josephine's husband is going to be even more powerful when he returns from Egypt."

"Am I supposed to be pleased about that?"

"I'm not such a fool as to expect anything of the sort from you. It's not precisely the republic you envisioned, but Bonaparte may be what France needs to stave off a return of the Bourbons. And to give it some stability."

"Or at least to give you a stable position."

Talleyrand lifted his glass with leisurely grace and took a sip. "There's a great deal to be said for stability. I can hardly serve France without stability in my own position. Neither of us wants France to go backwards, the way men like Hubert Mallinson would like to see it do. A great deal came out of the last decade, for all the messiness. You can take pride in the role you played. And you can play a role in the next ten years."

It was what Raoul had told himself, time and time again. It was what he had counseled younger agents, tired and frustrated by the slow pace of change or disillusioned by the turns the Revolution had taken. But just now, fresh off the ruin in Ireland, he could scarcely make the case in his own mind, let alone to anyone else. "Are you asking me to work for you?"

"I have no illusions that you would. Or that I could trust you if you did. But we've been allies at times in the past. We could be so again."

That, at least, sparked curiosity. "What are you asking me to do?"

Talleyrand shifted in his chair and took a drink of calvados. "To begin with, I'd be inestimably grateful if you could keep Josephine from doing worse damage to her marriage before Bonaparte returns. For both their sakes and the sake of France. He doesn't need the distraction."

Raoul choked back a laugh. "I'll admit I'm at a point where I could use almost any distraction. But chaperon is an unlikely role for me."

"I was thinking of friend. I imagine you and Josephine could both use a friend."

"That, I won't argue with." When they'd been imprisoned in Les Carmes, expecting to go to the guillotine any day, he and Josephine de Beauharnais had said things to each other they would probably never say to another person. Some bonds were stronger than any love affair.

Talleyrand shifted in his chair. The candlelight bounced off his pristine cravat. "Julien St. Juste was there the last time I saw her. He's a danger."

Julien's mocking, inscrutable face shot into Raoul's memory. "That depends on which side he's on. Like you, he has a way of shifting. But I'm quite sure he won't turn on Josephine. In fact, she's safer with him about."

"An interesting way of putting it. And possibly true. But he's a threat to her relationship with Bonaparte."

"Josephine may not be any more faithful to Bonaparte than he is to her. But I don't think she and Julien have been lovers for some time. Partly because I think St. Juste understands the risk of harming her marriage."

"You always were an idealist, O'Roarke. And now you're being an idealist about Julien St. Juste, of all people."

"Possibly." Raoul took another drink of calvados. "And St. Ives?" he asked. "Talking of risky alliances. That surprised me. Is he one of yours?"

"St. Ives is very much his own person. And loyal to his country. We have an alliance that is mutually profitable at times. Much like the alliance you and I could have, if for different reasons."

Raoul set his glass down with precision. "You've also been known to ally yourself with Hubert Mallinson."

"It serves France's interests to ally myself with various people at various times."

"Or your interests."

"Or both," Talleyrand said in an easy voice.

"And you also have an alliance with Mademoiselle Chat Gris?"

Talleyrand smiled. "She's a very able agent."

"She was at pains to keep her name hidden."

"She has her reasons."

Raoul shifted in his chair. Easier to talk about others than about himself. "She and St. Ives are fond of each other."

"Yes. That's useful, actually. Poor St. Ives."

"Poor?"

"He's hampered by being the heir to a dukedom. He has the soul of an agent. Much like you. But unlike you, he's weighed down by family responsibilities."

Raoul's fingers tightened on his glass. "There's something to be said for family responsibilities."

Talleyrand's gaze narrowed. "Your wife is still in Ireland?"

"And will be remaining there. It would have been easier for her if I'd managed to get myself killed, but my exile will at least make her life pleasanter. My marriage was effectively over before the uprising."

"I've never been tempted by marriage," Talleyrand said. "One of the advantages, perhaps, of being compelled into the priesthood. And I can't say I'm inclined to try it now I'm not a member of the clergy. But I think you had other expectations."

Raoul took a drink of calvados. "Foolish expectations. A response to the last time my cause didn't go as I anticipated. And to my relationship with Bella. I thought I could put down roots. I should never have put Margaret in that situation. Staying out of her way is the best I can do to make it up to her. I suppose that's one consolation for my present circumstances."

"And now? Are you looking for a refuge?"

"I know better than to think I can find it in my personal life."

"Then I advise you to consider work. However disillusioned you are, there's satisfaction in putting your mind to use. And I know you can't be so disillusioned that you've lost your ideals."

Raoul twisted the stem of his glass between his fingers. "You talk about ideals very freely."

"Just because I'm not driven by them doesn't mean I don't appreciate them. Or that they are entirely alien to me."

"Even I might admit that. Though it may be testament to your charm."

Talleyrand flung his head back and laughed. "Paris is an exciting place. And you've always been happy there."

"As well as profoundly sad at times."

"Josephine will be glad to see you. Like Arabella, she's been worried. She said she hadn't heard from you in a long time."

"I wanted to keep her out of it." Especially given the French involvement in the Uprising.

Talleyrand reached for his glass and frowned into it. "It would have been a mess, you know. If French support had succeeded in helping your friends in Ireland. We'd have got bogged down."

"Yes, I'm inclined to agree. That wasn't the route I wanted. I also didn't want an Ireland governed by the French. Though I'd have taken it over the current situation. It doesn't mean we couldn't have succeeded on our own."

"There's always a 'perhaps' to make one question. Folly to dwell too much on it. And even if you're going to tilt at windmills, you have to pick and choose your battles. That's Bonaparte's weakness. Thinking he can overreach. If we can't manage him, it could be a problem."

"We?" Raoul had respect for Napoleon Bonaparte, as well as concerns about where his ambitions would take him.

"One place we could be allies. You have Josephine's ear. And she has Bonaparte's. Or should, if they can keep the marriage together. Which again is why I need your help."

"My dear Talleyrand. Did you just ask me to save a marriage for the sake of politics?"

Talleyrand lifted his glass. "Can you think of a better reason? Pour us some more calvados, O'Roarke. And let's talk."

CHAPTER 10

May 1821
London

"$\mathcal{H}$e can't be gone." Lord St. Ives stared round the crowd in the salon at Bamford House. "He was just—"

Sylvie put a hand on her husband's shoulder. "He lived a more dangerous life than you realized."

St. Ives put his hand over her own. "You mean someone killed him. Deliberately."

"It looks that way," Malcolm said. They had reached Bamford House to find Sylvie had just broken the news to St. Ives. They were all in a high-ceilinged salon hung with gold silk worked with the Bamford arms—Sylvie and St. Ives, Malcolm and Mélanie, Kitty and Julien, and the duchess. "Whatever was behind the explosion, the duke was shot before the fire started," Malcolm added.

Disbelief clouded St. Ives's gaze. He was taller and more heavily built than his father had been, and though he had his father's blue eyes, they lacked the keen irony Malcolm remembered in the duke. "But who—"

"We don't know yet," Malcolm said. "We know very little. Did your father mention any enemies?"

St. Ives ran a hand over his sandy hair, which always looked rumpled at the best of times. "He was a diplomat. He decided things in council chambers."

"He was also a spy," Sylvie said.

St. Ives swung his head round to stare at his wife.

"You can't have been blind to it," Sylvie said.

"But he never—"

"Told us? Of course not. What spy tells their family? Well, the Rannochs are an exception. And the Mallinsons." She looked from Malcolm and Mélanie to Julien and Kitty. "And the Davenports. But rare exceptions. The hints were all there. The mysterious missions he went on to negotiate in secret. When he was gone for weeks at a time without anyone knowing where?"

"They were missions," St. Ives insisted.

"They were indeed. Spy missions." Sylvie glanced at her mother-in-law. "Mama Duchess knew."

"I had my suspicions." The duchess had been sitting by quietly, hands tightly clasped in her lap.

"Why the devil didn't you say anything?" St. Ives demanded of his mother.

"It was hardly the sort of thing one shares, my dear. "

St. Ives stared at his mother for a moment, then turned to his wife. "Why on earth were you with Father tonight?"

"I wasn't precisely with him," Sylvie said. "I followed him."

St. Ives's gaze shot over his wife's face as though she were a stranger. Which perhaps in many ways she was. "Why?"

Sylvie folded her arms over the stained bodice of the blue gown she was still wearing. "I wanted to know what he was doing."

"But—"

The door burst open. Rosalind Azevado, the Bamfords' youngest daughter, raced into the salon. "Is it true? Was Papa killed?"

"I'm very much afraid so, Rosy." The duchess got to her feet and went to her daughter's side.

Rosalind stared at her mother for a moment. Tall and slender, with smooth pale gold hair, she looked much as her mother might have when she'd married the future Duke of Bamford. At the duchess's musicale last March, Malcom had caught a glimpse of Rosalind's nerves of steel and the lengths to which she was willing to go in political intrigue. She squeezed her mother's hands, but then her gaze shot round the company. "He was at the docks?"

"He was on a ship," Malcolm said.

"What on earth was he doing there?" Rosalind looked at her mother. "I thought you were dining with the Marchmains."

"We were. Your father never arrived."

"Was he on one of his missions?" Rosalind asked Sylvie.

"I'm not sure. I was trying to find out. I thought you might know."

St. Ives took a step towards his sister. "You knew Father was an agent?"

Rosalind glanced over her shoulder at her brother. "Of course. I've known for years. But I never thought—"

"None of us did," Sylvie said.

"How on earth did you know?" St. Ives demanded of Rosalind.

"It was obvious. Well, if one knew what to look for."

"And you went through his papers," Sylvie said.

"*What?*" St. Ives looked from his wife to his sister.

"That's a despicable lie," Rosalind said.

"Don't be modest, Rosy," Sylvie said. "You're quite amazing for someone untrained."

"What is going on here?" St. Ives demanded.

Julien, who had been sitting quietly on a settee beside Kitty, got to his feet and went to St. Ives's side. Julien had been gone from Britain so long, Malcolm forgot that he had known both Sylvie and St. Ives since babyhood. Before Malcolm was even born.

Julien put a hand on St. Ives's arm. "Sometimes the people we're closest to can surprise us the most."

Sylvie turned to her husband. "We live with secrets. You must know it."

"Not those sorts of secrets."

"Difficult to parse the types, St. Ives." Sylvie stared at her husband for a moment. "Oh, lord, I suppose I'm going to have to get used to calling you Bamford."

"You have what you wanted now. You'll be Duchess of Bamford."

"You think that's what I wanted?"

"Isn't it why you married me?"

"I married you because I didn't have many options in life. In many ways. Ask Julien."

"I wish you wouldn't," Julien said. "But it's true, as far as I know."

St. Ives drew in and released his breath. "Honest, at least. We haven't had an honest conversation in a long time. If ever."

Sylvie crossed to his side and put a hand on his arm. They stood together before the Carrara marble mantel, carved with the Bamford arms. The new duke and duchess. "There'll be a lot to do. I'll own I'm not a very good wife. But I can help with that."

St. Ives stared at her fingers on his black superfine sleeve. "I'm not ready for this."

"No one ever is," Malcolm said.

"It's a shock," the duchess said. "I haven't begun to come to terms with it myself. But in time we will all manage. We have no choice. St. Ives, your father said much the same when he came into the title. About not being ready for it. And he managed very ably."

"But I'm not Father," St. Ives said.

"No. You'll make your own sort of Duke of Bamford. Which is what your father would want." The duchess turned to Malcolm. "Mr. Rannoch, I imagine you would like to speak to those who spoke with Tony most recently. I hadn't seen him since last night. I suggest you begin with his valet. A valet knows a man far better than his wife."

～

"I'M SORRY, MR. RANNOCH." Filbert, the Duke of Bamford's valet, dashed a hand across his eyes. "It's come as a shock."

"Very understandable. Please sit down. May I pour you a brandy?"

"I wouldn't—yes. Very good of you, sir."

Malcolm poured the brandy from the decanter on the chest of drawers in the duke's bedchamber. A room filled with oak and dark green upholstery. A writing desk stood in one corner. A brocade dressing gown lay across the bed. There was no sign of the duchess's presence.

Filbert took the brandy with a shaky hand and downed a swallow. "His Grace would share a drink with me on occasion."

"You'd been with him a long time?" Malcolm asked. Filbert looked to be about the duke's age. A tall man with gray-streaked dark hair and an air of quiet self-sufficiency.

"Since he came down from Oxford."

Malcolm poured himself a brandy. It would put them on an equal footing, which seemed both appropriate and helpful. "My own valet has been with me since university. He knows me as few do. In some ways, better even than some of my closest friends." And Addison was also an able agent. He and his equally adept wife Blanca were away with their young son on one of their visits to Addison's family. Their absence would be keenly felt in the investigation.

"My father was an underbutler at Chevenings. I was working

as a footman when I started dressing Lord St. Ives, as he was then."

Chevenings was the Bamfords' principal country estate. "So you'd known him since you were boys."

"Oh yes. We'd played games of tag with the village boys. Gone fishing together on occasion. It's different at that age."

"So it is. Pity we lose that freedom to be friends."

"One has to grow up, sir."

"But into what?" Malcolm took a drink of brandy. "You went with Bamford on his diplomatic postings?"

"Most of them. Sometimes his Grace would travel alone. If it was a short mission. Or one where a particular amount of secrecy was required."

"We're aware of the duke's activities."

Filbert met his gaze. "I thought you would be. I can't say he confided in me, but I couldn't be unaware. One learns discretion. But one has to be aware enough to know when to apply it. If you take my meaning."

"Precisely. When did you last see the duke?"

"This evening." Loss clouded Filbert's gaze. "I laid out his things and helped him dress. He and the duchess were to dine with Lord and Lady Marchmain."

"So I understand. Did you know the duke's plans had changed?"

Filbert took another drink of brandy, then set his glass down with care on the table beside his chair. "A message was delivered while he was tying his cravat."

"From whom?"

"I don't know. Thomas, one of the footmen, brought it in. The duke was already planning to meet the duchess at the Marchmains' due to a late meeting with Lord Liverpool. By the time he returned home to dress, the duchess had already left. When he received the note, he wrote out a note himself and asked Thomas to take it to the Marchmains'. Then he told me he'd be out late and not to wait up."

"Did he seem alarmed?"

"The duke wasn't the sort to show alarm. He seemed"—Filbert frowned—"not excited, precisely, but keyed up, one might say. As though he was going into a situation where he'd need his wits about him, if that makes sense."

"It does indeed. You're a keen observer, Mr. Filbert."

"I learnt from the duke."

"Did he order a carriage?"

"No. I assumed he wasn't going far. Or that he wanted his business to be secret."

"Did he say anything else that might be significant?"

Filbert reached for his glass and took another sip. "He thanked me."

"For what?"

"I wasn't sure. I thought it was simply for making sure Thomas followed instructions and got the message to the duchess at the Marchmains', but it seemed to have a bit more weight. Or perhaps I'm reading into it now."

Malcolm took a sip of brandy. "You must have had a sense of what the duke was working on."

Filbert shifted in his chair. "He was involved in discussions about the British response to the situation in Naples. To the Austrians' response to the situation, I should perhaps say. I don't think that will come as a surprise to you."

"No. But diplomats are generally involved in more than one situation. Was there anything else? Anything perhaps more secret?"

Filbert hesitated. Weighing the consequences of disclosure, as a diplomat would. "He'd been writing to the Continent."

"To whom?"

"I don't know. I only know because he sent the letters through channels he used for communicating abroad."

"Had he had any particular visitors lately?"

"He often meets with people at his club. And I don't see all his visitors. But there was one I was surprised by. Not by the visitor, but by the raised voices. I passed by his study. I couldn't make out the words, but they were plainly quarreling."

"Who was it?"

Filbert hesitated a moment. "I wouldn't have known him, save that he was here for the duchess's musicale. It was the composer. Lord Gresham."

CHAPTER 11

1811
Lisbon

Raoul paused just beyond the door to the grand salon in the house in Lisbon occupied by the minister plenipotentiary, Sir Charles Stuart, head of the British delegation in Portugal. Which Raoul tended to think of as the British embassy, though technically the term was incorrect. He had been there before as a guest, but tonight he was in the guise of a footman, hired on for the night. His powdered wig had his hair plastered to his scalp with sweat, but afforded wonderful anonymity.

He held his tray of champagne glasses out to two ladies in mantillas.

"I'll have one of those as well." A gloved hand shot out towards the champagne glasses. A pair of quizzical blue eyes looked into Raoul's own. "I suppose I should have known I'd see you here."

"So much for my disguise," Raoul returned in Portuguese.

"No, it's good." Tony Bamford made a show of investigating a possible chip in his champagne glass. "Especially the putty round the nose." He frowned. "I just got to Lisbon today, but shouldn't Malcolm Rannoch be here tonight?"

"He is. He's in the library, where he's spent most entertainments his entire life. I haven't got within twenty feet of him. Though it wouldn't be the first time he'd seen me in disguise." A regrettable fact of life since Malcolm had become an agent, and like so much else, he couldn't afford to dwell on it.

"Your audacity never ceases to amaze me. Still, I'm sure you could come up with a story if he recognized you. " Tony took a drink of champagne. "While I can't precisely wish you good luck with whatever you're doing, I can say I'll do my best to stay out of your way. Unless your business in Lisbon tangles with mine. Have a care. The next time we meet, I hope we can share a drink."

Tony moved off. Raoul made his way towards the door to the passage. A few minutes later, another footman slid up beside him.

"Got them," Mélanie said. "It took a bit longer than I expected. Stuart is quite untidy with his personal possessions. Rather like me."

"Good. A few more minutes and we can leave."

She turned, her back to the salon, and regarded him from beneath the wig that half covered her forehead. "I was afraid that fair-haired man was talking to you too long."

"Which one? Oh, the English duke? No, just complaining about a chip in his champagne glass. We can—"

"What are you doing standing about?" A senior footman stopped beside them with the disdain of regular employees for those hired on for the night. "Make yourself useful and take these to the kitchen." He thrust a tray of dirty glasses at Mélanie.

Mélanie nodded and hurried towards the door to the backstairs without so much as a backwards glance.

Raoul adjusted his position slightly with his tray of glasses. Nothing to do now but wait until they could make their escape. Waiting was often nine-tenths of what one did on a spy mission.

And nine-tenths of the challenge was often not doing something stupid because one was bored.

A man with an abstracted expression hurried past him towards the door to the passage. Sir Charles Stuart. Lots of reasons the host might be looking preoccupied at diplomatic soirée. And the fact that he was headed to the passage where the stairs were didn't necessarily mean he was going up to his bedchamber. Even if he did, Mélanie said it was a mess. He'd have to actually look for the papers to realize they were missing. Still—

Raoul cast a glance round and spotted Mélanie across the room with a fresh tray of champagne glasses. Too obvious to leave now.

Stuart came back into the room. Not hurrying, but with an intent expression. He touched another gentleman on the shoulder, and then several of them moved into an adjoining room. A colloquy of those concerned about something. Raoul was about to make his way to Mélanie when a senior footman pushed a bottle of champagne into his hand and instructed him to refill glasses. Good, that gave him an excuse to make his way round the room to Mélanie. But he wasn't more than halfway there when Tony materialized beside him.

"Stuart's valet thinks he saw a footman outside Stuart's bedchamber." Tony held his glass out to be refilled with a perfectly calibrated air of slightly inebriated nonchalance. "He's checking if anything has disappeared."

"Interesting." Raoul poured, letting the champagne fizz just to the rim.

"They're going to keep any of the footmen hired on from leaving." Tony took an appreciative sip of champagne. "So the only way to leave will be not to be a footman."

"Point taken. You're a gentleman, Tony."

Tony lifted his champagne glass in a silent salute. "I believe I've owed you this since Christmas Eve in 1800."

Raoul caught Mélanie's eye and lifted his hand in a coded gesture they'd agreed to. All it took was the briefest eye contact to establish that she knew.

A minute later, his champagne bottle emptied into guests' glasses on his way, he was in an antechamber they had scouted earlier. He tugged off his wig and stripped off his brocade footman's coat and breeches to reveal a plain dark coat and skintight pantaloons beneath. He was halfway done when Mélanie slipped into the room. "What gave it away?" she asked, pulling off her own wig.

"Stuart's valet glimpsed you."

"Damnation." She tugged off her coat and then her waistcoat and started on her cravat. "I hate it when I'm stupid."

"This sort of thing happens." Raoul retrieved the dark shoes and satin slippers they'd hidden beneath the settee in the room. "It's why we make plans."

"How did you know?" Mélanie pulled her shirt over her head and let down the champagne silk slip she'd been wearing underneath, rolled about her waist.

"Footmen are well placed to overhear." Raoul tugged a handkerchief from his pocket and wiped his sweat-dampened forehead. Better for Mélanie not to know about Tony, for his sake and her own.

Mélanie had her breeches and stockings off and was tying the satin ribbons on her slippers round her ankles. Raoul handed her the black lace mantilla and comb they'd hidden with the shoes. She pulled a few curls loose from her pinned hair, stuck the comb at the back and draped the mantilla over her shoulders. "This should do. Didn't we hide gloves?"

"Here." Raoul handed her a pair of long ivory gloves. He already had his own on. "Where are the papers?"

"In my bodice. I may not be wearing a corset, but the darts hold anything in place."

They bundled the footmen's clothes under the settee, where at least it would take a bit to find them. Raoul held out his arm. Mélanie curled her now gloved fingers round it and they stepped into the passage. Guests were still coming up the stairs from the hall below, and others were making their way down. Easy enough to blend in. But as they neared the stairhead, Raoul caught sight of a familiar figure in the hall below. Just a flash of tousled dark hair, and shoulders held at a contained angle. Malcolm.

Raoul pulled Mélanie to the side.

"What?" she asked.

"Someone who might recognize me. Just a minute. Pretend we're flirting."

"You never flirt." She smiled up at him, head tilted, the mantilla cascading down her back.

"Anything for the mission." Raoul had his back to the stairs. No harm really if Malcolm caught a glimpse of Mélanie. He was unlikely ever to see her again.

"Who are we hiding from?" she asked with a bewitching smile.

"Someone I knew in England. A long time ago." He returned the smile, with the air of a middle-aged man besotted by a pretty young girl. A man feeling far more than he'd admit, even to himself, more in many ways then he'd ever felt before, yet aware that she'd soon be beyond him. Which wasn't so far from the truth.

"You knew this person well?" Mélanie asked. Her blue-green eyes glinted into his own, wide and brilliant.

"At one time, yes."

She leant forwards as though to whisper in his ear and peered over his shoulder. "Twenties, dark hair, tall, lean face—what I can see of it—coat a bit rumpled, as though he's been sitting?"

"Yes."

"He just went into the salon."

"Good." The word caught slightly in his throat. He turned and offered her his arm again.

They made their way down the stairs, without haste, across the hall, and out the main door. Mélanie flashed a dazzling smile at the footmen as they passed.

Another mission successfully completed. With barely enough drama to render it interesting. Unless one considered coming within a few yards of the son who was now his enemy.

CHAPTER 12

May 1821
London

"Somehow I don't know that Sylvie's going to enjoy being Duchess of Bamford as much as she always thought she would," Julien said. "A duchess has less freedom of movement than a viscount's wife."

"I manage as a countess," Kitty said.

"Very true." Julien kissed her hand.

They were in the Berkeley Square library. By the time Malcolm and Mélanie and Julien and Kitty returned from Bamford House, the others had all been gathered there, drinking coffee that Laura, Raoul's wife, had made. Including Judith, Jeremy Roth's new bride and Malcolm's cousin, who had come to Berkeley Square and had been waiting with Laura. Laura, to Mélanie's endless gratitude, could handle household details Mélanie had no time for. And though her gaze asked a dozen questions, she'd waited for the explanations with a patience Mélanie would never have been able to muster. While at the same time Mélanie was quite sure Laura regretted not being part of the evening's adventure herself. Mélanie also suspected Laura had exerted all her influence to keep Judith from asking questions the moment they walked into the room.

"So we have another investigation." Cordelia blew on the steam from her cup. "Are you officially involved, Jeremy?"

Roth took a drink of coffee. "I don't think I can avoid it. Hubert will use his influence with Sidmouth."

"I'm glad," Raoul said.

Jeremy flashed a grin at him. "Possibly the first time I've heard you claim to be grateful for Hubert's influence on the home secretary."

"There'll have to be an official investigation. Safer with you involved. And we need your skills. I want to know what happened to Bamford."

Julien settled back on the sofa, coffee cup cradled between his hands. "Now we're all here, and Sylvie and Hubert aren't present, someone has to say it. Did anyone here have anything to do with any of the events at the London Dock tonight?"

"Much what I was thinking," Harry said. "And for the record, no."

"No on my end as well," Raoul said. "I haven't met with Tony secretly for years. And I'd never have chosen a ship owned by a wine company I have no connection to."

"I got us to the docks," Kitty said. "But after I spoke with Antonio, the rest took me as much by surprise as anyone."

"Ditto." Malcolm turned to Mélanie, who was curled beside him in one of the capacious Queen Anne chairs.

"Are you asking, darling?" She looked into her husband's gray eyes, inches away from her own.

"I'd never presume."

"No, then. I had no notion about Bamford."

"Davenport and O'Roarke and I had a look round the ship after the rest of you left," Roth said. "It seems quite clear the explosives were packed in a barrel in on the deck, as you first supposed. With a trail of gunpowder to ignite the explosives. And I think the pistol shot to the duke may have come from the quay. We found a fragment of a window with a bullet hole in it."

"So he wasn't shot by whomever he was meeting with?" Mélanie said.

"Not if we're right," Jeremy said. "The splash Lady St. Ives heard was presumably whomever the duke was meeting with running away."

"After the gunshot?" Kitty asked. "Sylvie didn't hear it, so I've been wondering if it came earlier."

"Precisely," Roth said. "In which case, Bamford may have been lying there dead for a while before the second person came onto the ship and found him. Probably just before the explosives went off."

"But why jump into the water?" Cordelia asked. "Why not escape on the quay?"

"Perhaps because they weren't sure if the murderer was still there," Harry said. "Which leaves the question of where the person who escaped ended up. There was no sign of anyone in the water. We searched."

Roth leant towards Raoul, coffee cup cradled between his hands. "You must have sources you can ask about Bamford. I'm not asking you to take me with you. I'd only get in the way. I'm not asking you to come close to revealing everything you learn. But if you want to discover what happened to him—"

Raoul nodded. His gaze was matter-of-fact, yet Mélanie could glimpse ghosts at the back of it.

Roth looked at Malcolm. "Can you come with me to talk to Prebble & Company tomorrow?"

"Of course."

"Thank you." Roth turned to Julien. "You're clearly the best one to discover whatever Lady St. Ives was up to that she hasn't told us."

"Discovering anything about Sylvie is always a challenge," Julien said. "But I'll do my best."

Cordy set down her tea. "I know Frederica. The eldest Bamford daughter. Or I did when we made our debuts, and we moved in the same circles for a time."

Harry frowned. "Can't say I remember her. Not that I would. I didn't know most of your friends."

"No, love. Frederica was the sort who bored you to tears. I never had much in common with her myself. We rather lost touch when I was abroad. And unlike Pippa Blayney, I confess it's not a lost connection I regret a great deal."

Judith wrinkled her nose. "Frederica always struck me as stuffy when I used to play with Rosalind. But then she was years older. That is, she seemed years older to me at that point—"

"No offense taken. Ten years stretch long at that age." Cordelia took a sip of coffee. "Frederica married Percy Rawdon. I've known him since we were children." She set her cup down with care. "He's a cousin of the Chases."

Harry touched her hand.

"There's no reason for you to involve yourself if you'd rather not," Malcolm said. Frank as they all were, he still avoided mention of Cordelia's former lover George Chase, who had nearly destroyed her marriage to Harry.

"Don't be silly," Cordelia said. "All that horrid mess with George has to be worth something. I'm delighted if I can put it to use."

"I can try to track down Bamford's mistress," Mélanie said. "I'm guessing Cressida Caldwell can help me locate an opera dancer named Maria with a ducal lover. Cressida may be William Beardsley's wife now, but she still has connections among the cyprian set. But we also should talk to Tristram Gresham. From what we learnt at the Duchess of Bamford's musicale, it's entirely possible he and the duke quarreled over his affair with Rosalind. But given that the affair itself was cover for Rosalind's intrigues, and given Gresham's involvement in politics, it's also possible it was more."

"I can talk to Gresham," Kitty said. "I rather ended up in the midst of his intrigue with Rosalind at the musicale." She leant forwards to add more milk to her coffee and looked at Raoul over the milk jug. "Now that Hubert and Sylvie aren't present, what I don't understand is why on earth you didn't simply tell me that Bamford was your friend last March when we wanted to talk to him about Spain?"

"Because Tony's and my friendship was always complicated," Raoul said. "At first it was just you talking to him at the musicale to get support for our friends in Spain. That made sense. Then I thought it might not be bad to have me there. But only with you there as well, so it would be clear I wasn't trading on the past. Tony and I were always careful not to trade on information we had about each other. It was the secret of making our friendship work." He cast a quick glance at Laura, who presumably hadn't known about his friendship with Bamford either.

"Did you just admit to having a friend on the opposite side, O'Roarke?" Julien said.

"Unavoidable. Didn't you?"

"Oh, I was on so many sides I couldn't have avoided it. Assuming I'd admitted to having friends at all."

"Not admitting to it doesn't mean you didn't." Raoul flashed a grin at him, then turned back to Kitty. "Then, before we could talk to Bamford at the musicale, we were caught up in Lady Rosalind's issues. We needed to resolve those to avoid international repercussions. And because she was Tony's daughter, but it wouldn't have added anything for me to go into that with you in the midst of everything. Tony's and my friendship was too mired in secrets on both sides to discuss it. Even with those we were closest to."

Kitty nodded. "I can see that."

Malcolm had been staring at his father throughout the

exchange with Julien and Kitty. "Bamford knew you were working for the French."

"Yes."

"You knew," Malcolm said. "You knew all along that Bamford knew about you. Three and a half years ago. When I learnt about Mélanie. When I came to see you at Mivart's. I asked you who knew about her. And you knew that whole time that one of Britain's senior diplomats knew you were a French agent."

Raoul met his gaze. "You didn't ask me who knew *I* was a French agent."

"I wasn't particularly worried about you at the time."

"Quite."

"But anyone who knew about you could have known about Mélanie."

"I didn't know about Bamford," Mélanie said. "I never even met him until after I married you, darling. Well, I did see him once before, on a mission at Charles Stuart's. But we didn't actually speak."

Malcolm's gaze swung to her. "You were on a mission at Charles Stuart's?"

"Yes, I wasn't in Lisbon often before I married you, but I was occasionally. I was disguised as a footman." She looked at Raoul, the memories coming back. "I saw you talking to Bamford that night. But you told me he was just complaining about a chipped champagne glass."

"It seemed safer for you not to know more," Raoul said.

"So Bamford saw you?" Malcolm asked.

Mélanie squeezed her husband's hand. Malcolm was still inclined to fuss, even though she and Raoul had royal pardons. Though he had agreed they needed to share the truth with Jeremy and Judith recently. Which, given this investigation, was a good thing. "It's all right, darling. I doubt anyone who met me later as Suzanne Saint-Vallier would have recognized me. You were there that night. Though I only saw you briefly."

"You never—"

"Mentioned it? I knew you'd worry and I didn't want to—"

"Make me feel foolish? It's all right, sweetheart." Malcolm grinned and kissed her hand. "If I couldn't handle feeling foolish, I couldn't handle my life." He turned back to Raoul with a hard stare. "Bamford knew about you. All the time I was worrying about the threat of Hubert's learning the truth about you, you knew the risks you were running."

"Tony wasn't a risk."

"For god's sake, Raoul, if you're going to tell me he was a friend—"

"He was. As I just said to Kitty. I'm not fool enough to have thought that was a guarantee. But if he revealed I was a French agent, I could have revealed information about him."

"You really think he believed you'd use it?"

"Probably not. But then I didn't think he'd reveal the truth about me. We both knew the world is complicated and we had a check on the other if we need it. Needed it." Raoul set his cup down and stared at his hands for a moment. "Now Tony's gone, I suppose that at least isn't an issue. But I damn well want to know what happened to him."

CHAPTER 13

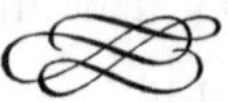

"Raoul." Malcolm caught his father's arm before he could leave the library. Harry and Cordy, Kitty and Julien, and Judith and Roth had gone home, and Mélanie and Laura had gone up to look in on the children.

Raoul set down the coffee tray he was taking to the kitchen and raised his brows.

"With everything tonight, we haven't talked about Kitty's news," Malcolm said.

"With good reason. A man was murdered tonight and the damage could have been even worse. Kitty's friend's report is the sort of threat I've been getting my whole life."

"Don't I know it." Scenes shot through Malcolm's memory. Going back to Harrow, when he was eleven. And words overheard and fears lived with long before that.

Raoul crossed the room and picked up a coffee cup he'd missed. "Most of the threats come to nothing. Remember all the fuss when we were at Lake Como?"

"I remember the League wanted Julien to kill you. The fact that Julien wasn't inclined to do so doesn't change the fact that they wanted to."

"They wanted an excuse to reach out to Julien because they knew he was the rightful Earl Carfax and they could use him against Hubert." Raoul set the coffee cup on the tray. "Also, they thought he could lead them to the dauphin. I was a convenient excuse."

"A bit more than that. Alistair wanted you gone. For various reasons."

"And except for a couple of token attempts, they didn't try much, even when Alistair was attempting to return and take control of the League. Alistair's left the country and has more important things to worry about now." Raoul moved back to Malcolm and clapped a hand on his shoulder. "I don't mean to overstate my role, but I work in dangerous circumstances. People get angry and make threats. This isn't anything I haven't dealt with in the past."

"You've also been attacked in the past."

"Without success. Not counting actual combat, which is rather different."

Malcolm scoured his father's face. Raoul's gray eyes were unusually open, as they were more of late. And yet they were still expertly fortified defenses. "You think this is to do with your work in Spain?"

"I assume so. The warning came from someone in Spain. And working with the Spanish Liberals is the most dangerous thing I'm doing now." Raoul's hand tightened on Malcolm's shoulder. "I appreciate the concern. I'll put out some inquiries to see if anyone has heard anything. I'll be extra vigilant. But I'm not going to earth."

"I wasn't going to suggest you do so."

"What, then?"

Malcolm drew in and released his breath. Because he wasn't sure what to say. Or what he felt. Or, no, he knew what he felt. A choking combination of fear and pleading that tangled in his throat. *Stop. You can't outrun this forever.* The words couldn't be said. The fear was there. And always would be. Unless it turned to grief. "You run risks. Always."

"So do you, for that matter. So does Mélanie. So do Julien and Kitty. It's part of our life. But the nature of the risks has shifted a bit."

"The nature. Not necessarily the degree."

Raoul's grip on his arm tightened. "I love you, Malcolm. I love your concern. We have enough to focus on right now. A friend is dead."

"Leaving children and grandchildren."

"Tony wouldn't thank us for going sentimental. I owe it to him to get to the bottom of this."

"You don't have many friends." Malcolm hesitated, because there was still a lot about Raoul he didn't know. "That is, I don't think you used to."

"Agents can't afford to have friends, in some ways. Or at least, we know the limits of friendship."

"Castlereagh's suspicious of Bamford."

"I'm not surprised," Raoul said. "He's suspicious of me."

"Oh, yes. He brought that up tonight too. He thinks I can't see through you. He's probably right. But I don't think you're trying to deceive me. At least, not in the way Castlereagh claims."

Raoul grinned. "Don't underrate yourself, Malcolm. But no, I'm not."

"Castlereagh said Bamford had a French mistress."

"Yes. For many years. But neither of them was supplying the other with information. At least, not unless they outwitted each other."

"I had more in common with the duke than I realized."

A host of emotions shot through Raoul's gaze, carefully veiled. "Falling in love with an enemy agent isn't as rare as you might think."

"So he was in love with her?"

"Oh yes. And I'd say she was in love with him, though I don't know that she'd admit it."

"Where is she now?"

"I'm not sure. I don't think they'd been in contact for some time. They had a falling out after Waterloo."

"Was she angry at him?"

"I'm not sure." Raoul picked up the coffee tray. "It's one of many questions I need to explore tomorrow. Meanwhile, would you mind opening the door? I'm a rather better spymaster than a butler."

~

JEREMY ROTH LOOKED DOWN at his wife. It was hardly the first time they'd walked home together from Berkeley Square, but it was the first in the midst of an investigation. "I'm sorry."

"So am I." Judith tucked her gloved hand through the crook of his arm. "It's difficult to take in. I can't claim to have known Bamford well, but I'd known him for so long. I keep remembering how he'd stop to admire Rosalind's and my sketches. He showed far more interest than my own father ever did. Which isn't saying a lot. But Bamford genuinely seemed to care."

The hood of her cloak slipped back and the lamplight caught the diamond pins in her golden blonde hair. They'd been dining with friends of hers when Hubert summoned him to the docks. Lord and Lady Pelham. A pleasant couple. Pelham had an interest in biology and had asked some quite keen questions about investigating physical evidence. Lady Pelham had been intrigued as well. She was a watercolorist and deplored strictures against women taking life classes. On the whole, it had been a less challenging dinner than Jeremy had feared. Which wasn't to say it had been easy. Nothing about moving into Judith's world was easy. And being married to Judith was worth all of it.

"I'm also sorry our evening was disrupted," Roth said.

"Oh, that's all right. Pelham and Eliza understood. I mean, it was an agreeable dinner, but this is bound to happen with your work. I'm glad I was there when you got the summons. I must say, so many of our friends were at the docks, they might have sold tickets. I'm surprised Mama and Archie weren't there as well. And I begin to think I should have insisted I come with you."

"Judith." Roth hesitated as they reached her mother's house in South Audley Street where they were staying.

Unlike the Rannochs, Lady Fanny hadn't quite got to the point of answering her own door in the evening. Will, the second footman, admitted them. Judith told him to lock up and go to bed when he had taken their things.

Alone in the hall, Roth tightened his grip on his wife's hands and drew her into the library. Malcolm and Mélanie did this. Talked things over in their library. At least, he assumed they did it alone. They often did it with their friends, as they had tonight. He went to pour two glasses of whisky, and then realized he was doing precisely what Malcolm would probably do. He still felt like an interloper in this house, despite the warm welcome of Judith's mother and stepfather. He put one of the glasses into Judith's hand and took a sip from his own. He had a feeling he was going to need it. "This is a case. It happens to involve people we know, which makes it challenging. But I've been called in in a professional capacity."

"Well, of course. It's your job." Judith dark brows drew together. "Are you saying that means I shouldn't be involved? Malcolm and Mélanie and a number of our friends and family are. I don't see why I'm different."

"Malcolm and Mélanie were tangled in it."

"Well, now I am too. You ask Malcolm and Mélanie for help with investigations."

"I'm not married to either of them."

"No, thank goodness." Judith took a drink of whisky. "If I was still your mistress, would I be allowed to help you?"

"Judith. Malcolm and Mélanie are agents—"

"See, this is what I hate. At one point, they weren't agents. Cordy isn't an agent. She's just learnt how to be one from being married to Harry. Mama isn't either, and now she does all sorts of things, even though she wasn't there tonight. I know I don't have their skills. I'm not proposing to rush into the middle of where I shouldn't be. But I'm tired of being kept out of things everyone else in my family—and most of our friends—are involved in, because I'm not an agent."

"Understood." Roth leant against the sofa, glass cradled in his hand. "But this isn't about your family. It's about my work."

"You're my husband. You're part of my family."

As Hubert Mallinson had said. But then Hubert would say just about anything to score a point. "I have to try to keep a distance between my work and my personal relationships."

"Other wives help their husbands in their careers. Diplomats, politicians, soldiers."

Roth put a hand on the sofa back. He was still afraid of leaving a mark on the cream watered silk whenever he touched it. "Being a Bow Street runner is rather different."

"I'm not asking you to share secrets with me." Judith gave one of her bewitching smiles.

"You must realize it would be difficult not to do so."

"Not secrets that were inappropriate."

"It's a fine line to draw."

Judith set her glass down and moved across the room to him. "You turn to Malcolm and Mélanie for help in your investigations because they can ask questions you can't. Especially in Mayfair."

"Yes. They know everyone. And anyone they don't know Cordelia does. Or your mother."

"Precisely." Judith twined her arms round his neck. "But, except for Raoul, whose connection to the Duke of Bamford is a bit mysterious, none of them knows the Bamford family that well. I grew up taking drawing lessons with the duke's youngest daughter. Who we now know from her mother's musicale is involved in all sorts of international intrigue. Cordelia's going to talk to Frederica Rawdon, but I know Rosy much better. Tell me you don't want to know what Rosalind Azevado has to say. And then tell me who's a better person to get her to talk than your wife?"

Roth looked down into her blue eyes, which he doubted anyone could say no to. He certainly couldn't. "You know perfectly well I can't say anything of the sort."

"Precisely." Judith kissed him. "I'm so glad you weren't unreasonable, Jeremy. This is going to work out splendidly."

CHAPTER 14

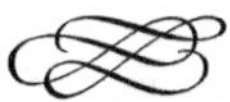

itty pressed her fingers to her temples. "Sorry. But it hits me sometimes."

"What?" Julien asked.

She pushed her fingers into her hair. She was hunched on her dressing table bench, wrapped in an emerald silk dressing gown, feet bare, hair tumbling over her shoulders. "The feeling that I should be there. Trying to make a difference."

"In Spain?"

"Or the Argentine. Talking to Antonio today. The future's being decided and I'm here safe in London."

"But you're helping make a difference in Spain."

"With conversations in diplomatic salons."

"Sometimes conversations in diplomatic salons decide the fate of nations. In fact, all too often they do."

"I know. To a degree. But when it comes to risk—"

"You think you need risk to show commitment?"

"No. Not precisely." She tented her fingers together. "But I know I have it so much easier than so many others."

Julien perched on the bench beside her. "Are you saying you want to go to Spain? Or the Argentine? We could. I could look after the children while you ran risks. Not saying I wouldn't be concerned, but we could make it work."

"My darling. You'd be following me on missions."

"Only if you didn't tell me about them."

Kitty shook her head. "No. Our life is here. The people we love are here. We both have work here. And while I'm not going to hide, I'm also not going to rush into danger as a parent." She cast a glance at the door to the nursery where their three children slept. The children had been home tonight, looked after by Ralph and Mandy Allam, who had been the cause of their adventures at the Bamford musicale. Ralph was close to proving his claim to the Warkworth earldom thanks to the events of the night, but what-ever happened, he and Mandy had become part of the family. "I wouldn't want to. It doesn't change the twinges."

"I rather envy those twinges."

"You'd rush into danger for a cause. You upended your whole life for a cause."

"And to get back at my father. But, yes. And I don't regret it. Though it would be harder to upend the life we have now. I didn't value the life I had before."

Kitty smiled. The smile that made his heart turn over. God, when had he started using that phrase? "Well, no, nor did I, before the children. Even then it was practical. I wanted to be there for them. I didn't envision what we have." She hesitated. "I feel selfish sometimes. Because we have so much."

He reached for her hand. "Oh, don't think I don't. That is, I would if I admitted to things like selfishness. I don't admit to such scruples at all. They aren't part of my makeup."

Kitty twined her fingers round his own. "You're a fraud, my love."

"You're confusing me with O'Roarke."

"Not in the least. I'm very fond of Raoul, but I know very well whom I'm married to. Though I do think you've learnt far more from Raoul than you or he tend to admit. Perhaps more than either of you recognizes."

"O'Roarke's gone after a cause his entire life. He may have tilted at windmills, but they were windmills that needed to be taken down. That were—are—doing active damage."

"And to use the metaphor, the windmills you took on? They are certainly doing unconscionable damage."

"I struck a blow. And then I ran to save my skin. Which I don't regret. I had no desire to be hanged for treason to salve my father's excuse for a conscience. And I worked for Uncle Hubert to protect myself and for anyone else who'd pay me enough, because I had colossal contempt for all of them."

"Which rather proves my point. You have to care a lot to be as angry as that."

"But I can't claim to have been fighting for anything."

"I think Malcolm would say the same about working for Hubert and Castlereagh and Wellington."

"And he'll never forgive himself for it. But he tried to help round the edges. I stood on the sidelines and laughed. I wasn't trying to create a better world any more than Puck is trying to unite true lovers."

"Puck does manage to unite true lovers in the end."

"After some massive bungling. And I think he'd have been just as amused if he hadn't."

"Perhaps." Kitty folded his hand between her own. "It depends how it's played. I tend to think he's a romantic underneath."

"You aren't going to make that mistake, are you, KitKat? Romanticizing everything?"

"It would take a lot to romanticize you, Julien. And since when have I romanticized anything? But you've often said I see you more clearly than most."

"Possibly. But one could make a good case you're deluded or you wouldn't put up with me."

"Believe me, Julien, I have no illusions. And I also recognize what you're trying to do in Parliament."

"It's little enough, probably, but it saves me from feeling completely useless." He watched her for a moment. "You could go to Spain if you want. I could stay here with the children. It works for O'Roarke and Laura."

"No." The word came out quickly and with force. "I don't blame Raoul, but that isn't what I want. I think the children would be fine, but I'd miss them." She shook her head, her amber hair falling over her shoulder. "It's a conundrum. Mostly I suppose I'm lucky we make it work as well as we do." She smiled. "Insanely, absurdly lucky."

"Oh, when it comes to luck"— he took her hands and kissed each in turn—"I marvel at my good fortune every day. None of which changes what we started with. Your feeling sidelined."

"Not sidelined. And I don't think there really is an answer. Except to keep doing what I can do. Balancing it all as best as possible. Constantly feeling I'm failing on one front or another. And your putting up with me when I complain about it."

"I wouldn't call it putting up."

"Darling. Putting up with each other is what marriage means."

Julien laughed and gathered her into his arms. "It means a great deal more."

"I'M SORRY," Laura said, tucking the covers over Clara, who, at almost two, still slept in a cradle in their room. "There's scarcely been time to focus on it, but you've lost a friend." A man she hadn't even known was his friend, but then, after three years together and two years of marriage, there was still a great deal she didn't know about her husband.

Raoul looked up from unbuttoning his waistcoat. "I remember Tony congratulating me on our marriage. With a touch of envy.

He made a practical marriage himself, but he was always much more of a romantic than I was."

"Sweetheart. You're an impossible romantic."

Raoul tossed the waistcoat aside. "I'm a hardened spymaster."

"The two aren't mutually exclusive."

"Perhaps. Tony never found that sort of happiness."

"Did he come close?"

"I think he thought he had, at one time. It was a long time ago." Raoul hesitated, but didn't say more.

Laura knew better than to press her husband. Raoul's brows knotted as he undid the buttons on his shirt cuffs, but not about Bamford, she thought. "What is it?" she asked.

"Malcolm's worried. About Kitty's report."

Laura brushed her fingers against their daughter's red-blonde hair. "I'm not surprised. I'm worried too."

Raoul shot a look at her.

Laura took a step towards her husband. The man she was still surprised she shared a life with. Three years ago, they had both seemed destined to be alone. Neither of them had been willing to let their guard down enough to be anything else. "I know you run risks. I accept them. You can't blame me for being concerned when one of those risks is verbalized."

"I'd never blame you for anything. But it's the sort of noise I've always had to live with."

"And that anyone who loves you has to live with. I understand that. I understood it when I fell in love with you. To the extent I could think logically at all."

He closed the distance between them and touched her cheek with one long-fingered hand.

"I'm sure Malcolm understands it," Laura said.

"Malcolm has an admirable instinct to take care of everyone. I seem to be included in that."

"Of course. You're his father."

Raoul cast a quick glance down at his youngest child. "It still surprises me. Not that I'm his father, obviously. That he sees me as his father. More than that, that he's concerned. It wasn't so very long ago that he could barely speak to me."

"Long enough ago that you and I were barely acquaintances. But then you lived a complicated life before we knew each other at all. I often feel I've come into the play late." She said it lightly. But the past echoed.

"Often the most interesting part of the story. Though I hope not too near the curtain."

She twined her fingers round his own. "You know I don't like to fuss."

"Perish the thought."

"So I won't say anything tiresome about being careful. I know you do what you need to do. But do your anxious wife a favor and be on your guard."

Raoul kissed her fingertips and then touched a hand to Clara's hair. "I know what I have to lose, sweetheart. It's enough to make anyone wary."

Laura smiled. But her heart tightened. Because she knew he meant it. And she also knew he'd never stop running risks.

Mélanie tugged loose the ties on her gauze overdress. "Not what I envisioned when we went out tonight."

"No." Malcolm leant against the closed door of the nursery. He'd gone to look in at the children when he came up, a few minutes after her. She'd heard Colin wake up and ask questions. He never seemed to sleep well when they were on a mission.

Mélanie tossed the overdress on her dressing table bench. "I remember Bamford in Vienna. He was kind, though I scarcely exchanged more than a few words with him."

Malcolm's brows drew together. "Of course. Somehow I didn't realize you talked to him there."

"You had enough on your mind, dearest. It seems half the people we later knew in Paris and London were in Vienna."

Malcolm's arms tensed against the door behind him. "He wasn't—"

"I had no notion he had anything to do with intelligence. Certainly not that he was connected to Raoul." Mélanie's fingers froze as she tugged one of the pearl pins from her hair. "You do believe me, don't you, darling? There'd be no reason for me not to tell you now."

Malcolm gave a twisted smile. "There could be a hundred reasons, Mel, as we both know. Raoul knows a lot about Bamford that he's not telling us."

"That's different. They were colleagues. I don't really understand how." Mélanie folded her arms over her chest. She'd been Raoul's agent for six years. And his lover for three of them. She'd never had any illusions that she knew all his secrets. But it still shook her to realize the depths of the things she didn't know. Although, given that she hadn't known he was the father of the man she'd married as part of a mission, why should anything surprise her?

"Nor do I." Malcolm frowned as he moved into the room and tugged off his coat. "None of us talks lightly about a source. I understand why he's not volunteering details. There's no need for him to tell us more until we see how the investigation unravels. We all know we have secrets from each other."

"We just haven't faced it in a while." Mélanie tugged the pin free. Two strands of her hair snapped.

Malcolm tossed his coat onto the frayed green velvet chair he resisted her every attempt to re-cover. "Quite."

"This isn't the first investigation where we've had to confront the past. We've got through it before."

"We have. But this time—"

Mélanie studied her husband's eyes. They looked more deep-set than usual. "Kitty's warning was concerning."

"Yes. I pointed that out to Raoul just now. He didn't want to talk about it. But that's not surprising."

"No, he wouldn't. He's always faced risks." She could see the reckless glitter in Raoul's eyes. She'd often thought he fed off the risk.

Memories shot through Malcolm's gaze. "Growing up, whenever we said goodbye, I'd wonder if I'd ever see him again."

"So did I once I knew him. Though that was partly because I wasn't sure I'd survive myself." In the midst of the Peninsular War, her family dead, staying alive had seemed a low priority beside the need to fight. "It's not quite as extreme now. For any of us."

"Not quite."

Mélanie moved to her husband's side. "You can't change who he is, darling."

"I don't want to. But the risks won't go away for his denying them."

Mélanie reached for Malcolm's hand. "He's very good at taking care of himself."

He squeezed her fingers but looked down at her with a keen gaze. "Tell me you're not worried."

"All right, I'm worried. I've always worried about him. Although, I suppose—I can't really imagine the world without him."

"Nor can I. It doesn't mean it isn't possible."

Mélanie leant her head against her husband's shoulder. "It's difficult to see what a warning from Spain had to do with a shipping explosion in London and the murder of an English duke."

"Bamford was connected to Spain. Though I admit we have no reason to see a connection between his murder and the threat to Raoul. And Raoul says they hadn't spoken much recently. Raoul and Kitty wanted Bamford's support in Spain." Malcolm shook his head.

"What?"

"The Bamford musicale. Raoul going along with all of us, part of the mission, talking to Bamford but not saying a word about their connection. I suppose I shouldn't be surprised at this point at how adept he is at deception."

"You can't blame him, darling. We'd both have done the same with a contact."

Malcolm released her hand to wrap his arm round her. "I don't blame him. I just know I haven't a hope in hell of keeping up with him."

CHAPTER 15

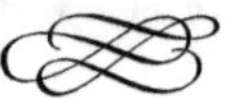

July 1790
Lake Como

Raoul knelt down in the sand to let Malcolm clamber off his shoulders, and watched as he ran to splash his feet in the lake.

"He's going to get sand everywhere." Arabella's voice caught on the breeze.

"Isn't that the point of summer on a lake?" Raoul said.

"I thought it was drinking wine and eating strawberries and tomatoes."

"Not when one's two years old."

"A point, perhaps." She came to stand beside him with a swish of muslin skirts. "I can't remember being two years old."

"Nor can I. Well, no." Raoul dropped down in the sand and kicked off his shoes, one eye on Malcolm. "I have the vaguest memories of Ireland that I know are from then."

"Your memory is remarkable. It always has been." Arabella leant forwards. Her hyacinth scent washed over him, shooting through the smells of lake water and summer air. "I prefer to forget things. Much more comfortable overall."

"Splash!" Malcolm tossed a pebble into the water and toddled further. Raoul ran after him and tossed another pebble. Malcolm giggled in delight as the pebble skipped over the water.

Arabella gave a mock sigh from the beach. "You'd swear you'd been doing this for years."

Raoul grinned at her over his shoulder. "Maybe it's just that I never grew up."

"That's one explanation."

"Mummy!" Malcolm turned and waved.

Arabella waved back. "Splendid."

Raoul sent another stone skittering across the water, gaze on Malcolm. Malcolm clapped and jumped as the stone pinged over the water, sending up ripples. "It's amazing," Raoul said.

"What?" Arabella asked.

"Watching the world through his eyes. It's like discovering it anew. The simplest things seem fascinating."

"That's a charming way of explaining a life that's restricted."

Raoul shot a look at her. "Is that what you think parenting is?"

Arabella folded her arms and arced a brow. "Can you honestly tell me you think it isn't?"

Raoul turned back and caught Malcolm's hand as he took another step into the water over the slippery stones. "I'd say it's opening a door. One stops doing some things and starts doing others. Things that one would never have thought of doing without a child in one's life."

Arabella moved to the water's edge. "I still say it's a charming way of making the mundane sound interesting."

Raoul scooped up a pebble and handed it to Malcolm. "There's nothing mundane about learning to navigate the world. It's perhaps one of the most remarkable journeys of discovery any of us goes on."

"I'm delighted you find it so interesting. I'll have more to say to him when he's older. For instance, when he can talk."

"He's talking quite well now."

Arabella watched as Malcolm threw another stone. "It's probably just as well."

"What is?"

"That we couldn't have more together than this." She gestured round, encompassing not so much the lake and the villa above as the golden fragility of the summer. "I have a feeling you might have quite changed your life if you could have been a father full time."

The light slanted across the sand, blinding for a moment. "Would that be so bad?"

"Would it be bad?" Through the glittering light he could feel Arabella's gaze cutting into him. "Does it take so little to forget all your ambitions?"

"Perhaps to reconsider them."

"And everything you want to accomplish?"

"Perhaps to reframe it."

She shook her head, strands of dark gold hair and the blue ribbons on her hat stirring about her face. "Is this something like the world being well lost for love? What about the loss to the world?"

"I wouldn't say the world has felt the impact of my work particularly."

"Don't underrate yourself. Or what you can achieve. Would you really not want to be part of what's happening in France?"

Raoul bent over Malcolm and helped guide his hand as he threw another pebble. "I don't think it's one or the other."

"You'd be torn. If you were with Malcolm all the time."

Malcolm's head jerked up as he heard his mother say his name. He cast a quick glance at Arabella. When she didn't meet his gaze, he focused on the pebble in his hand.

"What about you?" Raoul asked.

"I'm not there all the time," Arabella said. "I don't mind leaving things to nurses and governesses. They're much better at it than I am. But I don't think you could do the same. In some ways I'm much more suited to parenthood than you are."

"Because you can walk away?"

Arabella waved at their son as Malcolm turned again. "Given the lives we lead, yes. You can't be forever fussing in the nursery and spooning out pudding and jam and wiping runny noses and change the world at the same time. Fortunately I was raised in a world that doesn't expect parents to be in the nursery."

Raoul put a steadying hand on Malcolm's shoulder. "Bella. Did you just say aristocrats make better revolutionaries?"

Arabella blew a kiss at Malcolm. "Possibly. If we have the right priorities."

"Need I remind you my own mother was an aristocrat?"

"I didn't say we were all the same. Surely you'd be the first to claim one can't look at any group as a lump. You'd also be worried, I think, if you had loved ones who could be in harm's way."

"Do you worry?"

"There's more than one reason Malcolm's usually in Scotland. And Edgar too."

This was the time to graciously cede the argument. Which usually worked best with Bella. But his throat tightened with the impulse not to do so. Somehow, they had ventured onto ground it was vitally important to defend. "There are risks in absence too. Or perhaps I'm just too arrogant to think someone else can do my job for me."

"Which job?"

"Both—all—of them if it comes to that. But I was thinking of being a parent. Assuming that applies to me."

Arabella's mouth curved with mocking irony. "You've rather made it your job. And no one appears to be fighting you for it."

He bit back a dozen retorts. "I don't see it as a job." He put a steadying hand on Malcolm's shoulder as Malcolm studied a white-veined gray stone. "More a privilege."

Arabella sighed. He could see her mocking smile thought he didn't turn round. "People who don't try domesticity tend to romanticize it."

"Since when have you tried it?" Raoul asked.

"I never had the least desire to."

Raoul guided Malcolm's hand as he skipped another pebble. "That, I'm well aware of."

Arabella went silent for the length of a heartbeat. "It wouldn't have worked. And the scandal is the least of it. We'd have driven each other mad. Or at least I'd have driven you mad."

Raoul looked at her over his shoulder for all part of his instinct was to ignore her words. Her gaze caught and held his own. Defiant, as Arabella always was, and at the same time apologetic. "We'll never know," he said.

Malcolm looked round, as though aware of the tension between the two adults who were his parents, though he couldn't call them that. Though he didn't know that, Raoul reminded himself. "Excellent shot, old chap," Raoul said. "Let's try another." He reached for another handful of pebbles.

On the shore, Arabella laughed. "I'll leave you to it."

May 1821
London

Archie Davenport poured Raoul a cup of coffee in the garden of the house he shared with his wife, Malcolm's aunt Frances, and their three children. And, at present, with Fanny's daughter Judith and Jeremy Roth and their children, as well as Roth's sister. "Jeremy left before breakfast, but Judith had quite a bit to say, and Cordelia was just here. I understand we missed a lot of excitement last night. Pity. Though firefighting is not among Frances's bountiful talents, and with my leg I don't know that I'd have been of much help."

Raoul took a drink of coffee and smiled at the man who had been his fellow agent and friend before he had even acknowledged that he had friends. "You're always a help, Archie."

Archie smiled, but then his face turned serious. "I'm sorry about Tony Bamford. I liked him. And I know you did."

"Yes." Raoul looked across the rain-spattered garden. It had rained in the night after their adventure at the docks, though the sky was now clearing. "Hardly the first time I've lost a friend. But I confess it's hit hard."

"Cordelia said you received a threat last night as well."

"That was an associate of Kitty's, reporting some gossip from Spain. Unconnected to the business with Bamford."

"Are you sure?" Archie moved to a wrought-metal chair beside Raoul, leaning on his walking stick. "Coincidences happen, but they're also worth investigating. Quite a coincidence that Bamford was killed on the same night you got a warning someone was making an attempt on your life. With you only a few yards away."

Raoul leant back in his own chair, arms folded, and breathed in the aroma of the coffee. Which was superb, like everything offered in the Davenport household. "All right. I'll confess it's occurred to me." He set the cup on the table between them. "But Tony and I had barely spoken in years."

Archie picked up his coffee. "We both know the past has a way of intruding on the present."

A dozen moments shot through Raoul's memory. Secrets traded, confidences whispered, compromises that had seemed necessary at the time. He reached for his coffee and blew on the steam. "Castlereagh warned Malcolm about Tony last night. And about me."

Archie's brows tightened, though he did not appear surprised. "How much does Castlereagh know?"

"Not much, I think. He doesn't seem to realize how entangled Tony and I were. Though he had Sylvie St. Ives investigating Tony. You heard she was there last night?"

"And that Julien rescued her from the fire."

"She talked surprisingly frankly, for Sylvie. Which probably means there's a great deal more she's holding back."

"Castlereagh thought Tony was a threat now?"

"Seemingly. Though Castlereagh tends to see threats in any

shadows." Raoul took a drink of coffee. Strong and bitter, like the kind they had shared in France. "When did you last talk to Tony?"

"At Covent Garden a few nights ago. But we only exchanged pleasantries. Talk about the children and grandchildren. I didn't have any notion he was working on anything. You talked to him more at the duchess's musicale."

"With Kitty there. I wanted to make it clear I wouldn't use our past in an effort to get his support in Spain." That had always been part of his relationship with Tony, the thing that had allowed them to stay friends on opposite sides. They reached out to each other, they worked together when it was helpful. But neither traded on what they knew about the other.

Archie took a drink of coffee. "What else about the past could Castlereagh know? Or Hubert? Or anyone?"

That was the question that had haunted Raoul ever since he looked down and saw Tony's signet ring on the dead body on the ship. "I'm not sure." He looked at Archie for a moment. Sometimes one had to step into parts of the past one had thought one could leave safely locked away. "Do you know where she is?"

"No. I assumed if anyone did, it would be you."

"She didn't turn to me for help after Waterloo."

"I thought she and Bamford had ended things."

"So did I. In theory. But I'm not sure that's the sort of relationship that can fully end. I rather wonder if Tony was looking for her. And where that search might have led him. I don't know what he was doing at the docks last night. But he was on a ship from a wine importing company that traded with the Continent. He could have been gathering information from someone from the Continent."

"Someone who killed him?"

"It seems the pistol shot came from outside the ship. And the explosives may have been set by someone else entirely. Perhaps someone learnt of the meeting and used the opportunity to kill

Tony. For reasons that might be wholly unconnected with the meeting or the explosion."

"Or someone really didn't want Bamford to find her."

"Yes, that did occur to me."

Archie hesitated a moment. "Or she didn't want to be found. How far would she go?"

"Not this far." Raoul shifted in his chair. The intricate iron-work pressed into his back. "At least, I don't think so. A lot's changed since Waterloo."

"Of course, it could be someone trying to cover up the past. Which might mean the same person is after you."

Raoul took a slow sip of coffee. "It might." It was the first time he'd admitted it, outside the dim recesses of his mind.

Archie's gaze fastened on a white-painted wooden carriage by the steps to the house, filled with a red-haired doll, a stuffed cat, and a wooden dog. "It's a different game from what it was when we were working with Tony a decade or two ago. And not just because we're older. A lot has changed since Waterloo as you say. For good, in some cases. We both have more to lose."

Like Raoul, Archie had married in his fifties, in Archie's case for the first time. He had two-year-old twins, slightly older than Clara, and an eleven-year-old stepdaughter. "Don't I know it," Raoul said. For a moment he saw Clara in her cradle last night, and Emily and Colin and Jessica at breakfast this morning. "There's no reason for you to be pulled into this."

"I wasn't thinking of that," Archie said. "I can look after myself and my family. We all know we can never really leave the game. But you haven't left it at all."

"Malcolm and Laura said something of the same last night. I promised them both I'd be careful. Which I will."

Archie nodded. He wasn't the sort for warnings. "Perhaps that's why it hits hard. Tony was part of the game too. He under-stood the risks. But he always seemed invulnerable."

A gust of wind blew through the garden, ruffling the trees and scattering raindrops on the carriage and toys. "So he did," Raoul said.

CHAPTER 17

1795

Hyde Park, London

Archie Davenport dropped down beside Raoul on a bench beside the placid waters of the Serpentine. "Sorry I've been out of touch for a bit. My brother and his wife died. A carriage accident."

"I heard." Raoul folded his copy of the *Morning Chronicle* and turned to Archie. Davenport had been passing information on the Elsinore League to him for some months. And occasionally information on Ireland as well. "My condolences."

"My brother and I hadn't been close for a long time. Not since he was born and joined the nursery, if it comes to that. His wife was a diamond of the first water, without much beneath the surface that I could ever tell. But they left a son. I've become his guardian."

"He's fortunate to have you. How old is he?"

"Nine."

Not much older than Malcolm. Odd that Archie could now

openly be more of a parent than Raoul could. "A challenging age, as I recall from my own childhood."

"Yes." Davenport's gaze fixed on a family of ducks making a leisurely journey down the water. "I never aspired to be a parent. My own parents didn't put much effort into it, and I had no desire to follow their example. But Harry—that's my nephew—deserves more than he's had thus far in life."

"If you're saying you want to stop—"

"No. Not in the least. If anything, having Harry in my life makes me more aware of the world I'd like him to have when he grows up. And he hardly relishes my hovering over him. In fact, he seems happiest when I give him time with his books. Our most agreeable moments have been when I sit with him and read while he's reading. He's fascinated by history. Classical history, in particular. I share the occasional bit, but he knows more than I do, and his Greek and Latin are already better. I think he'll be happier if I give him space. He doesn't seem to have a great many friends at Eton, but he also wasn't reluctant to go back."

"Speech Day," Raoul said.

"Speech Day?"

"It's a good day to be there. Especially with boys who have a lot to talk about. They appreciate the attention."

Archie nodded. "That's what you plan to do with Malcolm Rannoch?"

"When I can. I don't think his parents will always put in an appearance. It's little enough. But it seems to make a difference."

Archie watched him for a moment. "Until Harry came to live with me, I don't think I appreciated the challenges you face."

"Malcolm's never been a challenge."

"I don't mean Malcolm. It's clear what you get from your relationship with him. I meant the challenges of keeping that relationship going."

"One could say I have it easy. I don't have to do a great deal." Raoul hesitated. "It's hard sometimes, getting them to talk at this age. But as you noted, the company matters. I think those moments mean more than we realize."

Archie nodded, then sat back on the bench and looked sideways at Raoul. "You must have had reasons for wanting to talk now."

"It's always important to catch up. But I also wanted to share some news of my own before you hear it elsewhere." Raoul hesitated, because it still seemed so odd to put it into words. "I'm going to be married."

"My dear fellow." Surprise flared in Archie's blue eyes, but his voice was warm. "Congratulations."

"Thank you. It happened quickly." Still difficult to credit that Margaret had accepted him or that they were going to attempt to build a life. "It won't change things. That is—it's changed a great deal in terms of my relationship to Arabella, but it won't change our work."

Archie, who was well known for his string of beautiful mistresses, inclined his head. "I understand."

"Do you? I'm not sure I do." Indeed, it was difficult to see quite how his life was going to work, save that he knew it was vital to make a change.

"I may not have felt the inclination to marry, but I can't imagine your not taking marriage seriously."

"No." Raoul watched as two of the lagging ducklings scurried to catch up with their family. "I wouldn't attempt it otherwise. But I won't—I'll stay close to Malcolm."

"There," Archie said, "I certainly can't imagine you doing otherwise."

CHAPTER 18

May 1821
London

Hugo Prebble, current manager of Prebble & Company, received Malcolm and Roth in an office heavy with gilt and brass and mahogany. He was a man in his early forties, with dark hair that curled over his forehead despite being closely cropped, and well-tailored clothes that conformed to fashion while being more sober than the styles affected by those tooling curricles on Rotten Row.

"Thank you for seeing us," Malcolm said, shaking hands.

"Thank you for calling. I've been trying to gather any intelligence I can about the wreckage of our ship." Prebble waved them to chairs covered in bottle-green leather opposite his desk.

"Do you know of anyone who might have had cause to attack your company?" Roth asked.

"No one. Importing wine is not generally a controversial activity. Our competitors, such as they are, are quite friendly with us. My family have been in the business for three generations."

"A man was found dead on the ship," Malcolm said. "And identified as the Duke of Bamford."

"I heard. It is tragic. And very concerning."

"Do you have any idea what Bamford might have been doing on your company's ship?" Roth asked.

Prebble sat forwards in his chair, hands locked on the ink blotter. "His Grace of Bamford would have moved in very different circles from me."

"He wasn't an investor in your company?" Malcolm said.

"No. Mostly our connections to Mayfair involve delivering wines to be served at parties. But occasionally Rothermere hosts gentlemen at the docks to try some of our wines in advance."

"At the docks?" Roth said.

"It's done," Malcolm said. He'd been invited to taste wines at the docks himself on a few occasions, though he had never done so. "Viscount Rothermere?" he asked. "Is he an investor in the company?"

"In a manner of speaking." Prebble adjusted the chased silver penknife on the ink blotter. "He married my cousin Hypatia. Our grandfather founded the company and left it to his two sons. My father was his younger son. Hypatia is the only child of my uncle, my grandfather's eldest son."

It was a not uncommon arrangement. Hypatia Prebble would have been an heiress. The Rothermere family, Malcolm vaguely recalled (he needed Cordy for more) had had pockets to let.

"So Rothermere married into the business," Roth said.

"He prefers to leave the business to me. And I confess I prefer it as well." Prebble's expression, studiedly neutral, nevertheless spoke volumes about his opinion of his cousin-in-law. "Rothermere wasn't born or bred to it. But he does like to entertain friends and let them sample our wines. And that helps us secure clients. It's beneficial for all of us."

"Was the Duke of Bamford one of Rothermere's friends?" Malcolm asked.

"Not to my knowledge. And Rothermere does—enjoy— mentioning the names of his friends. I suspect I'd have heard if he was entertaining a duke. And even if he had been entertaining the duke, he wouldn't have taken guests onto the ship itself. Not in usual circumstances."

"The circumstances last night were evidently unusual," Malcolm said. "We'll want to talk to Rothermere to see if he can shed light on this."

"I expected as much. And I am ahead of you in wishing to do the same. I had hoped to have him here today to meet with you. But I haven't been able to reach him."

"He's out of town?" Roth asked.

Prebble drew in and released his breath. "I called on Rother- mere and Hypatia this morning. I trust you will keep this in confi- dence when I say that Hypatia reported that Rothermere did not return home last night and has not sent word."

Malcolm sat forwards in his chair. "Does Lady Rothermere have any idea where he might be?"

"No. He went out last night to a dinner at White's. She heard nothing that would suggest he planned to go to the docks."

"And I assume he is not in the habit of staying away overnight?" Roth said.

"No. Hypatia is most concerned. I take it the search of the ship—"

"Only the duke's body was discovered," Roth said. "The fire was not so extensive I would expect another body could go unnoticed. The only other person we know to have been on the ship at the time was rescued." Which didn't account for the splash Sylvie reported hearing.

Prebble nodded. "That will relieve Hypatia."

"We'll want to speak to her," Malcolm said.

Prebble inclined his head. "I expected as much. And in truth, I'd be grateful, because if she has anything to share, we should discover it. And it may reassure her, at the very least. I can take you to call."

~

"Hugo." Hypatia Rothermere came forwards to greet her cousin as the footman ushered him, Malcolm, and Roth into her drawing room. She was a tall woman with dark hair swept elegantly back from her fine-boned face. Her hair was immaculately dressed, her gown without a crease, her pearl necklace and earrings perfectly aligned, but her eyes were shadowed with strain. "Mr. Rannoch. Mr. Roth. I'm happy to receive you, but couldn't Hugo have told you what you need to know?"

"Better they hear it directly from you, Patsy," Prebble said.

Her brows drew together. Malcolm suspected the nickname, probably from childhood, was not one she cared for. But she lifted her chin above her frilled collar. "Of course. I want to do everything I can to help. And to ensure Rothermere is safe."

"We understand you aren't sure of your husband's whereabouts, Lady Rothermere," Malcolm said.

Her fingers stilled on the gathered fabric of her sleeves. "He went to dine at his club last night. I went to the opera and then on to Lady Southby's. It was only this morning, when Hugo sent word of the fire, that I realized Rothermere was not at home. And when I spoke to his valet, I learnt he had not returned." She folded her hands in her lap. "I know what you are no doubt thinking, but it was not customary for my husband to remain out all night. I sent word to Ronald Camden, who had been one of the party at White's. He reported that my husband had gone to Mannerling's with him after they left White's, and then left about midnight. Mr. Camden said they shared a hackney, and he believed my husband was headed home after the hackney dropped Mr. Camden at his lodgings."

"You had no reason to believe your husband meant to go to the London Dock last night?" Roth asked.

"None. And from the timing Mr. Camden gave, it doesn't seem he did. Unless it was after midnight—which would have been long after the fire."

"Are you and your husband acquainted with the Duke of Bamford?" Malcolm asked.

Hypatia Rothermere pleated a fold of her gown between her fingers. Malcolm saw the conflict in her eyes. It would be tempting to claim the Bamfords as friends, but she could not bring herself to do so. "We were once at a party at the Trenchards' where the Bamfords were present, but we were never introduced. I can't imagine Rothermere inviting the duke onto one of his ships. Indeed, I can't imagine Rothermere going onto one of the ships himself. As Hugo will have told you, Rothermere stayed away from that side of the business. He did occasionally entertain friends at the docks, but I have no hint he did so last night. Or that he would have included the Duke of Bamford."

"And yet the duke was on a Prebble & Company ship."

"As you say. I have no explanation for you. I would very much like an explanation myself." Hypatia Rothermere drew in and released her breath. "I do not mean to sound hysterical, Mr. Rannoch. Mr. Roth. I am not given to hysterics, as Hugo could tell you. But I should very much appreciate it if you could find my husband."

"WHAT DO YOU MAKE OF IT?" Malcolm asked as he and Roth descended the steps of the Rothermere house in Brook Street. Hugo Prebble had remained behind with his cousin.

"She's a formidable woman. But I don't have the sense that she's lying. Not obviously, at any rate."

"Nor do I," Malcolm said as they turned down Brook Street. The pavement was still damp from last night's rain, but patches of sunlight now shone through the clouds. "There may be something she or Prebble or both of them are holding back. But I think they genuinely don't know where Rothermere is. Otherwise, it would be easy to invent a journey out of town that would at least cover for his absence temporarily."

"Do you know Rothermere?" Roth asked.

"I've met him once or twice. He sits with the Tories."

"So you don't belong to the same clubs, and it sounds as though you didn't go to the same schools."

"In a nutshell. His wife brought him a tidy fortune, and I suspect she surpasses him in understanding."

"Bamford could have been meeting someone who came the Continent on the ship. It sounds as though he could have had a number of reasons to do so. But it's a damnable coincidence if Rothermere's disappearance is unconnected."

"So it is."

Roth cast a sideways glance at Malcolm. "Any chance Rothermere was actually an agent?"

"I have no reason to think he was. But there's always a chance."

Roth frowned, gaze fixed down the street on the leafy trees in the Grosvenor Square garden. "Rothermere could have disappeared because he was involved in what happened on the ship. He could have had reasons unconnected with Bamford to have been behind the explosion. But that doesn't explain who shot Bamford."

"Unless someone went on the ship to set the explosion, stumbled across Bamford, and shot him to keep him quiet. But we still have the question of what Bamford was doing on the ship."

"And the person would have had to leave the ship to shoot Bamford, if I'm right about the pistol shot coming from the quay."

"I think you are. But it's possible the killer set the explosives, left, and then shot Bamford. Or realized Bamford was in the cabin and decided the quay was the best place to get a shot. Doesn't account for the splash though."

"No," Roth said. "I have a patrol seeing if anyone heard the pistol shot. That would give us a timeline at least. But there's a lot unaccounted for."

"So there is."

CHAPTER 19

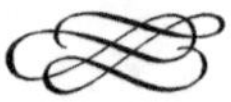

January 1799
Paris

Josephine held out her hand. "I'm glad to see you. I know that sounds selfish when you're only here because things went so wrong for you."

"On the contrary." Raoul took her hand and squeezed it. "Seeing you again is one of the best compensations for my current situation."

She smiled, though her eyes stayed serious. "I was afraid—it sounded very desperate."

"It was." Raoul bent over her hand and pressed a light kiss to it. "I owe my life to a number of people."

"Arabella Rannoch," Josephine said.

"And allies she found." Including, amazingly, her husband. Not to mention Horace Smytheton, and Talleyrand and Chat Gris and Lord St. Ives, whose role in the whole he still didn't understand at all.

Josephine settled against the back of the chaise-longue, where she sat curled sideways, the white folds of her gown falling round her. "And now you'll be in Paris. It's an odd place these days. Less dangerous than during the Revolution. Or so it seems. But I can't help but feel there are knives out on all sides."

Raoul drew a chair up next to the chaise-longue and sat beside her. "You're in a prominent position."

She shrugged, sending her flowered silk shawl slithering down her shoulders. "It's not as agreeable as it sounds. People watch me all the time. Even when I'm not in public, his family watch me. They didn't want him to marry me. I thought it might be better as we settled in, but the more important he gets, the worse it seems to grow." She spread her ringed fingers over the pink and violet of the shawl. "Especially when time goes on without my giving him a child."

Raoul leant forwards and touched her arm. "I don't think anyone ever *gives* anyone else a child."

"You know what I mean."

"Sadly, I do. Some people desperately want children and have difficulty having them. And other times children arrive when the parents were trying to achieve just the opposite."

Josephine put her hand up and squeezed his fingers. "When did you last see him?"

"In the spring. I managed to get to Harrow, where he's at school. I was afraid it would be the last time I'd ever see him. Which I suppose it still could be."

"Don't be silly. You're far too clever not to get back to England. Probably long before it's safe. You always manage."

"I always have managed. It's not quite the same thing." Though he was already planning how to slip into Britain in the next few weeks.

Josephine leant towards him and rested her head against his shoulder. "I thought Les Carmes was the worst. And in a way it always will be. But I had no idea how complicated the world that came after would be."

"Nor did I. Fortunately, we never know."

Josephine straightened up and pulled her shawl round her. "He loves Hortense and Eugène. That was one of the first things I loved about him. And I do. Love him. As I never thought I could or would. It sneaked up on me."

"Love has a way of doing that."

She frowned. "It should make it better. But it makes it worse, in a way. I have so much more to lose now."

"You're his wife."

Josephine lifted her head, her gaze locked on his own. "We both know how little that can count for."

"Given my own marriage, I have little grounds to argue that. But I have seen the way he looks at you."

She shrugged, gaze sliding away. "The way he used to look at me. I don't know what it will be like when he comes back from Egypt."

"He isn't the only one to determine that. He's going to play a position, without doubt. A powerful one. You'll need to decide the position you want to play with him."

Her gaze swung back to his face. "Did Talleyrand put you up to this?"

Raoul smiled. "How did you know?"

"He's one of the obvious people to have helped you. And I mentioned to him that I hoped he would."

"Ah." Raoul smiled. "He didn't say that part."

Josephine rested her elbow on the curved back of the chaise-longue. "He wants you to spy on me."

"He knows better than to ask. He wants your marriage to succeed. Because he wants Bonaparte happy and stable."

"And you?"

"I want you to be happy."

"I am. When I'm not anxious about the future."

Raoul settled back in his chair. "Did you know Lord St. Ives when he was in Paris?"

Her gaze lit with recognition. "Oh, yes. He's charming. Probably the most charming Englishman I've ever met. That's not an insult."

"None taken."

"You're Irish. But St. Ives was very amusing. I actually thought I saw him in Paris a few months ago."

"Where?"

"In the Bois de Boulogne. I was passing in my carriage and moved on before I could be sure. I told myself I must have been mistaken. Though I'm sure there are Englishmen who find a way to slip over. Perhaps he has a mistress here."

"Perhaps." Raoul was quite sure St. Ives did have a mistress in France. And also quite sure that Mademoiselle Chat Gris was not the sole cause of St. Ives's visits to an enemy country.

"If so, I'd be curious to meet her," Josephine said. "It would take a very interesting woman to make a man risk going to a country his own country was at war with."

"So it would," Raoul said.

CHAPTER 20

May 1821
London

"Malcolm. Julien." Hubert regarded them across the ramparts of his desk in the house where he now lived with his wife and youngest daughter. Far simpler than the desk he'd used to preside over in Carfax House, but somehow as much of a fortress. "Aren't you supposed to be out investigating?"

"We are." Julien dropped into one of the ladder-back chairs in front of the desk.

Hubert frowned. "I told you everything I knew last night. I want to know who killed Bamford. I have no reason to keep anything back."

"There's always a reason to keep things back." Malcolm dropped into the other chair. "Castlereagh wants us to investigate too."

"Us?" Julien shot a look at him.

"Me, at least." Malcolm turned his gaze back to Hubert. "Castlereagh's the one who had Sylvie following Bamford."

"Yes, I thought he might have been." Hubert tugged off his

spectacles. "Castlereagh and Bamford never got on that well," he added, polishing his spectacles. "Bamford's a Tory, but more of a Canningite." Castlereagh and the more moderate Canning were longtime rivals, and had once even fought a duel.

"I know," Malcolm said. "Like Canning, Bamford supports the revolutions in South America."

"And O'Roarke and Kitty hoped Bamford would sympathize with the rebels in Spain," Hubert said. "No, you needn't say more. It's plain enough. In any case, I think Castlereagh has always half suspected Bamford is after his job, though frankly I think Bamford would rather retire from public life than find himself in the cabinet and be required to answer to so many people."

"What are you suggesting?" Julien asked.

"I don't believe I suggested anything. I stated facts."

Julien sat back in his chair. "Castlereagh and Bamford were at odds. Castlereagh feared for his job. That could be called motive."

"Oh, well. If you're going to claim anyone with political tensions has a motive for murder, then we all do."

"But in this case, the object of the tensions ended up dead," Malcolm said.

"A point," Hubert conceded.

Julien folded his arms over his chest. "Speaking of which, you had your own tensions with Bamford."

Hubert raised a brow. "Are you suggesting I have a motive?"

"What do you think?"

"Since when you do you care what I think, Julien?"

"I'm always curious. I just don't always agree."

"Fair enough." Hubert clasped his hands on the tooled-leather blotter. "Bamford and I crossed swords. He was occasionally frustrating. He had a tendency to sympathize too much with those better regarded as opponents. But overall I found him a reasonable ally. If I had a motive to kill him, I'd have a motive to kill half my colleagues."

"Who says you haven't?" Julien asked.

"My life would be easier if I had done," Hubert said.

"Castlereagh questioned Bamford's loyalty," Malcolm said.

"He had a French mistress." Hubert tucked one page under another in the stack of papers on his desk. "You should understand that."

"Malcolm doesn't have mistresses," Julien said.

Hubert adjusted his spectacles. "Bamford was willing to take certain risks. Foolish, but understandable to a degree. I don't think he was a double."

"*Think?*" Julien said.

"Can one ever be sure?"

"That's meant to be funny, right?" Julien said.

"I didn't see any reason to get rid of Bamford. But by all means, waste time investigating me. If you learn he was a traitor, I'd be very interested to know."

"Do you think he revealed things to his mistress?" Malcolm asked.

"Doesn't everyone?"

"You know what I mean. Bamford was competent."

Hubert aligned the corners of the stack of paper. "Why don't you ask O'Roarke?"

Malcolm held his former spymaster's gaze. "I have. I'm also asking you."

"Interesting."

"Always good to examine all sides of a question. You and Raoul both taught me that."

"Really?" Hubert shifted a half-empty cup of coffee to the edge of the ink blotter. "I thought I tended to suggest thinking too much was a problem."

"You have a way of putting things in multiple ways," Julien said. "And meaning about five other things you aren't saying."

"Glad to know you pay attention, Julien."

"Sometimes."

Hubert took a sip of coffee and grimaced, perhaps at the taste. "Bamford was competent. More than competent, actually. I also think he was besotted. Which can lead to all sorts of errors. As I would think you'd both appreciate."

"I was going to say I haven't been besotted in my life," Julien said. "But I don't think you'd believe me."

"I've seen you with Kitty."

"Yes, it all depends on one's definition of besotted."

"What if Castlereagh really believed Bamford was a threat?" Malcolm said. "Castlereagh was ready to see me convicted of a crime in Vienna. Granted, one I think he actually believed I'd committed. But if he did think Bamford was a traitor—or even a threat—"

"It's possible," Hubert said. "More than possible. Especially given Castlereagh's attitude lately. He sees enemies everywhere."

"Unlike you?" Julien kicked his foot against the chair leg.

"There's a difference between rational analysis and paranoia."

"A difference that may be in the eye of the beholder."

Hubert clinked his cup back in its saucer. "That's of course up to you to say. The main thing is that you learn who killed Bamford. And why. Before this becomes more of a crisis."

"So now we have the usual question after we leave Uncle Hubert," Julien said as he and Malcolm walked down Bolton Street. "Do you believe him?"

"I think he suspects Bamford of working with the French. As Castlereagh apparently does. And I tend to think Raoul's right and they're wrong. Though it's always possible Raoul's wrong."

"He isn't often."

Malcolm put up a hand to anchor his hat against a gust of wind. "Or that he's lying to us."

Julien shot a look at him. "He doesn't do that often these days."

"Still. It's always a possibility."

"With all of us. And our spouses."

"Just what I was saying to Mel last night."

"Keeps things interesting. Let's go in here. I could do with a drink." Julien tilted his head towards the Rose & Crown pub sign at the corner.

The pub was dark and discreet, with mellowed wood and polished brass. Quite different from last night's dockside tavern. They said nothing more until they were settled at the back with pints of porter.

"If Hubert were behind this, I think he'd be steering us away from it," Malcolm said.

"Probably." Julien took a long drink of porter. "He'd know he couldn't keep us out of it. But hard to see him dragging Roth into it if he didn't have to."

"And Castlereagh must have had real suspicions to have engaged Sylvie."

Julien stared into his glass. "I suppose we'd gone too long without tangling with Sylvie."

"Unfortunately."

Julien shot a look at him through the cloudy light filtered by the thick glass of the windows. "You're never going to forget, are you?"

Memories washed over Malcolm. A shocking revelation about someone he'd known since childhood. Quickly swamped by the revelation that Hubert knew about Mélanie, and the need to flee the country. But not forgot. "She killed a man."

Julien sat back on the bench and folded his arms. "I've killed any number of men. And some women."

"Sylvie did it to protect herself."

"Well, so did I. On occasion."

"I don't mean self-defense. She did it to cover up her past. I don't think you ever did so."

The lamplight bounced over Julien's eyes. "Would it change your opinion of me if I said yes?"

Malcolm claimed not to trust his instincts about people anymore. How could he when his wife, his father, and many of his closest friends had deceived him? And yet so much came down to instinct in relationships. "Julien—"

"I didn't, as it happens." Julien folded his arms. "However lethal my actions, they were in the service of a mission. Use your judgment on whether that makes it better or worse. And I'll confess Sylvie's actions bother me. Though I may be drawing false parallels in an effort to excuse my own actions. Which many would call worse than Sylvie's. The fact that you put up with me at all is remarkable."

"Don't talk rot, Julien."

"I'm serious."

Malcolm dragged his glass closer. "You're my friend."

"So you excuse anything your friends do?"

"You know what I meant."

Julien met his gaze. Perhaps it was a trick of the lamplight that made his own more open. "I do. I'm grateful beyond measure for your forbearance. I don't know that it excuses my actions. I certainly don't know that it should. By any standards, my actions were appalling. There's little sense in dwelling on them, but I am aware of just how appalling they were. It seems important to say as much, at times. Which doesn't mean I'm not aware of Sylvie's actions. Or that I don't struggle with them. While at the same time feeling I have no right to cast aspersions."

Malcolm tossed down a drink of porter. "There's no sense in dwelling. Raoul taught me that."

Julien reached for his glass. "You don't have anything to dwell on, Rannoch. And Raoul doesn't follow his own advice."

"Oh, he does. He gets on with his life. While not forgetting what he's responsible for. And yes, I do. Have things to dwell on. Some of them—"

"Involving my wife?" Julien asked.

"Among other things."

Julien gave a faint smile. "Kitty can take care of herself. She certainly could by the time she met you. I'm older than Sylvie. I was an earl's son, not the daughter of an émigré, when we were first caught in Uncle Hubert's games. I should have been able to protect her. Or so I tell myself."

"I understand."

Julien shot a look at him. "Do you?"

"I can't forget what she did to Ben Coventry. I can't look at Sue Kettering or their son and not think about it. I find it difficult to look Sylvie in the eye. But I do understand. I may not be able to forgive her, but I recognize that she was a victim at the start. As were you."

"I got myself into it. With actions for which I'm not sorry." Julien hesitated for a moment, the way he once had before he'd opened up and revealed the truth of his past. "At the start we were in it together. She helped me get out of Britain when my father wanted me prosecuted for treason. And Uncle Hubert used that to make us both his creatures. For many years she was one of the few people I was connected to who knew the truth of who I was. Well, other than Uncle Hubert, but Uncle Hubert hardly ranks as a confidant. Not that Sylvie was a very good choice of confidante. I told her things I never should have done. Talking of unforgivable."

There was a time when Malcolm would cheerfully have planted Julien a facer for revealing Mélanie's past. A lot had changed. "Hubert would have learnt about Mélanie somehow, at some point."

"Talking of being charitable."

"Difficult now to quarrel with how things played out. Including your emerging from the shadows."

Julien turned his glass on the table in a shaft of light filtered by the mullioned panes of the windows. Dark amber lights shot through the rich brown of the porter. "Funny how we see people.

I'd have said I was free of illusions when it came to Sylvie, but I saw her as more like me than she is. I can't forgive Uncle Hubert either, by the way. But I probably give him more latitude than I should."

Malcolm took a drink of porter. "God knows I do. He manages to make me believe he's feeling something genuine. And just as I realize I'm being manipulated, I find myself questioning if it's manipulation at all."

"An excellent way of putting it." Julien tossed down a drink of porter. "Which brings us back to the original question. What do we think Uncle Hubert is doing?"

"A question I've never been able to answer about Hubert. But in this case I think we're better off trusting him than Castlereagh."

"Agreed. God help us."

Malcolm sat back on the bench. "And Sylvie? Do you trust her account of last night?"

"I don't trust a word Sylvie says. But if she'd been behind Bamford's death, I think she's clever enough not to have been anywhere near the ship when it happened. On the other hand, if Castlereagh's told her more, I don't count on her sharing it with us."

"If she'll talk to anyone, she'll talk to you."

"Regrettably, yes. I was resigned to having to talk to Sylvie from the moment I recognized her on the deck of the burning ship. Which was before I swung across and rescued her, by the way." Julien reached for his glass. "There's one other person whose story we haven't discussed."

"Raoul."

Julien raised a brow. "He is our best source on Bamford."

Malcolm stretched his legs out under the table. "I'm hardly an expert at reading Raoul. In fact, I've been rather disastrous at it in the past. But I believe most of what he says about Bamford."

"And?" Julien asked.

Malcolm ran his fingers along his glass. "I don't think he's telling us all of it. I probably wouldn't, if a case involved someone from my past as an agent. There are likely to be too many secrets that touch too many people."

"Quite." Julien took another drink of porter. "Which means it's up to us to work out what those secrets are."

CHAPTER 21

24 December 1800
Paris

Raoul turned up the collar of his greatcoat. The wind sliced between the tall, smoke-stained buildings, driving the light rain. Brightly colored handbills flapped on the walls beside him, a blur of crude images and bold words advertising *Instruction in Swordsmanship; A painless cure for the pox; La Belle Marguerite: The Loveliest Dancer in Paris*. A raw stench rose from a mound of garbage at the street corner. The pile of refuse seemed to shift as he turned the corner into the Place du Carrousel. The wind, perhaps. Or a rat burrowing deeper.

Christmas Eve. Or 3 Nivôse, Year IX by the French Revolutionary calendar. Malcolm had been about to leave for Dunmykel, his family's country house in Scotland, when he last wrote from Harrow. Dunmykel, with both Arabella and Alistair present, could be a challenging place, though at least at Christmas Arabella's sister Fanny would be there as well with her children, and the Duke of Strathdon, Malcolm's grandfather. Strathdon would probably retire to the library and wander in and out at inopportune moments, often with a comment that showed he'd been paying far more attention than one credited. Fanny, who professed to loathe the sentimentality of the holidays, had a suspiciously soft gaze at this time of year.

Not that Raoul had seen it often. He avoided holiday celebrations unless a mission called for them. During the few years he'd attempted to make his marriage work, the season had only served to emphasize his wife's religion and his own lack of it. Margaret lived on surfaces, but she honestly believed a number of things that went against the core of his own beliefs.

He cast a quick glance at the gates to the Tuileries, where Josephine now lived with her husband, France's first consul. Josephine was there now, unless she'd already left for the opèra, where Raoul himself was bound. Raoul jammed his hands into the pockets of his greatcoat, turned another corner into the rue Saint-Nicaise, and nearly collided with another greatcoated man.

"My apologies." Raoul stepped back and put a steadying hand on the other man's arm before they both tumbled to the cold pavement. Then, in the lamplight, he saw the familiar features beneath the curly hat brim. "St. Ives. I didn't know you were in Paris. But perhaps that's the general idea?"

The gleam of St. Ives's blue eyes and the bones of his face were unmistakable. But he wore a worn olive-drab greatcoat and a low-crowned salt-stained hat, not precisely a disguise, but not the garb of a future duke either. Not that one would expect to find a future English duke in Paris these days, with the countries at war. "Let us say I'm here on private business."

That St. Ives was an agent had been apparent when he helped Raoul reach safety in France. Not a French agent, according to Talleyrand. One always had to take what Talleyrand said with a grain of salt, but Raoul would hazard a guess that St. Ives was a British agent who had a convenient alliance with Talleyrand. Far be it from Raoul to interfere, especially given the service St. Ives had rendered him. "I won't keep you. I hope you have somewhere warm to go on a cold night. If you see Mademoiselle Chat Gris, give her my regards."

St. Ives smiled. Down the rue Saint-Nicaise, at the corner of the rue Malte, candlelight and voices raised in cheer spilt from the windows of the Café d'Apollon. A horse and cart, drawn up at an odd angle, half-blocked the street, Raoul realized. A young girl held the horse's reins, but the driver seemed to have run off somewhere. Perhaps to the café for something to ward off the chill. He'd been damned clumsy in parking the cart.

As Raoul and St. Ives watched, a carriage clattered by, turned down the rue Saint-Nicaise, then swerved to avoid the cart. Of one accord, Raoul and St. Ives sprang back from the spray of mud. Raoul caught the flash of a crest with laurel leaves and an eagle in the lamplight. The first consul's carriage. Not surprising. Like Raoul himself, Napoleon Bonaparte was no doubt on his way to the Théâtre de la République et des Arts for the French premiere of Haydn's *Creation*.

"The first consul is in a hurry," St. Ives said.

"He often is. In a number of ways."

"You're probably on your way to the theatre yourself," St. Ives said.

"Yes, as it happens."

St. Ives grinned. "No point in not admitting I am as well, as we'll walk in the same direction."

Raoul had no desire to interfere with St. Ives's business. To a degree. If St. Ives was working with Royalists—which was likely— and information fell into Raoul's lap, he wasn't going to ignore it. Presumably St. Ives knew that and could take care of himself. They were veterans of the same game.

Two grenadiers cantered by in the carriage's wake. Raoul and St. Ives waited for the mud to settle back onto the cobblestones and then started down the pavement again. The narrow side street was crowded with those entering or leaving the Café d'Apollon. A couple hurried down the pavement ahead of them, his beaver hat brushing her bonnet, his arm wrapped about the velvet of her cloak. Across the street, a man in a fusilier's uniform shouted to his companion, who was lagging behind. A girl with a basket of toothpicks or matches crossed the street at the next corner. Raoul heard the rumble of another carriage behind them. He and St. Ives stepped to the side again. Then light and sound exploded all round them.

The impact knocked them into a brick wall. Shards of glass, chunks of masonry, and fragments of tile rained from the sky. Smoke and screams filled the air. Raoul pushed himself up on one elbow. St. Ives, who had scrambled to his knees, held out a hand and pulled Raoul up. A man stumbled past them, half-carrying a bleeding woman, a gash in his own head. Another man—wiry, dark-haired, younger than Raoul and St. Ives—had been thrown at their feet, pinned by a fallen beam. Raoul grabbed one end of the beam and St. Ives the other. They shifted the beam to the side and Raoul lifted the man into his arms. Only to look into his vacant eyes and realize he was dead.

The cart that had blocked the street was gone, blown to bits, along with the horse and the girl who had been holding the reins. A spray of blood dripped from the wall of the building. Raoul looked back towards the Place du Carrousel. A carriage was drawn up at the gates of the Tuileries, the windows blown in. A dark-haired man in uniform had sprung from the carriage and run to the coachman, who was slumped on the box. A woman's screams came from inside the carriage. Raoul ran towards the carriage, then went still, halfway across the Place du Carrousel, the implications thud-ding through him. But he couldn't ask St. Ives to hold back, and in truth he might need the help. He stumbled to the carriage, St. Ives beside him, and wrenched open the door.

A woman slumped in one corner in a dead faint, chestnut hair slipping from its pins, a brilliantly patterned shawl twisted round her filmy white gown. A fair-haired girl was screaming, clutching her wrist, which spurted blood. A dark-haired girl, heavily pregnant, was fumbling in her reticule. "Hortense! Get hold of yourself." She pulled a vinaigrette from her reticule.

"Revive Josephine," Raoul said to the dark-haired girl—Bonaparte's sister Caroline, who was married to Marshal Murat. Raoul tugged out his handkerchief and reached for Hortense de Beauharnais's bleeding wrist.

Her screams stopped. She stared down at her spangled skirt, splotched with crimson. For a moment, he thought she too was going to faint. Then she looked up at him, eyes widening with the shock of recognition. "What are you doing here?"

"I was nearby. The merest chance." Raoul smiled at the girl he'd known since she was a child, much the age Malcolm was now, and bound the handkerchief round Hortense's wrist, pulling the fabric tight to staunch the flow of blood.

"Thank you." Hortense gave a trembling smile.

"Madame Bonaparte? Can you hear me?" St. Ives had leapt into the carriage and was bent over Josephine along with Caroline Murat.

Raoul reached across the carriage and gripped Josephine's wrist. "Rose."

It was her name from the old days, before Bonaparte began to call her Josephine. As Raoul spoke, the man in uniform leant in through the open carriage door. Colonel Rapp, Bonaparte's aide-de-camp. "A cart in the street was set with explosives."

"Bonaparte?" Josephine's eyes fluttered open. Her face was like bleached linen.

"We think he was ahead of it."

"You *think*—"

"We saw your husband's carriage swerve into the next street just before the explosion," Raoul said.

Josephine let out a ragged breath. "Thank God."

Colonel Rapp turned his gaze to Raoul, brows drawn. "Monsieur—? Oh, forgive me, Monsieur O'Roarke. I didn't realize you were here."

"Monsieur O'Roarke was in the street," Hortense said. "Along with this gentleman—" Her gaze flickered to St. Ives.

"My name is Fourmier," St. Ives said, in perfectly accented French. "Monsieur O'Roarke and I have been acquainted since university. We had just run into each other when the explosion occurred. We heard the screams, so we ran to the carriage."

"We are indebted to you." Josephine spared him a brief smile. "Hortense—?"

"I'm all right, Maman." Hortense's voice was weak but steady. "Some of the flying glass must have struck me. The bleeding has stopped, and Raoul bandaged the cut. It was shock more than anything. Are there many injured, Colonel Rapp?"

"I fear there are many dead, mam'selle," Colonel Rapp said, his face grave. "Particularly in the café."

"Can't we—"

"There is little we can do, mam'selle. Help is on the way."

"I thought the Jacobin plotters had been caught," Caroline Murat said. "My brother said the police had them in custody."

"Perhaps this wasn't Jacobins," Raoul said.

Colonel Rapp cast a sharp look at him. Bonaparte and Raoul were on friendly terms, but Raoul's views were known to be far more Republican than France's current government. On the other hand, Colonel Rapp too must realize it could have been Royalists behind the plot. Such as those St. Ives was almost certainly in Paris to meet with.

St. Ives was quietly helping Caroline Murat gather up the contents of her reticule, which had slipped on the floor and come unclasped. But Raoul saw Rapp cast a sidelong look at the other man.

"We must continue to the opèra," Josephine said.

"*Mon dieu*—" Caroline Murat looked up from tucking a comb into her reticule.

"But Maman—" Hortense said.

"I need to be sure Bonaparte is unhurt."

"You've received too great a shock, madame," Colonel Rapp said.

Josephine waved his protests aside with a flick of her gloved wrist. Sweet as she was, she could turn to imperious in an instant and she knew her own mind. "We can take you and Monsieur Fourmier with us," she said to Raoul. "It's the least we can do in thanks."

Raoul squeezed her hand. "You're kind. But we should see what we can do to help in the street. I'll see you at the opèra." He touched Hortense's arm, nodded to Caroline Murat, and swung down from the carriage. St. Ives followed.

"My thanks to you both," Colonel Rapp said as he closed the carriage door. His tone was easy.

But his look implied he and Raoul would speak later.

CHAPTER 22

May 1821
London

Mélanie had a shrewd notion of the best way to find Maria, the former opera dancer who had been the Duke of Bamford's mistress. She called at an elegant house in Jermyn Street with a shiny red door. Once this house had been the site of some of the most notorious parties in Mayfair. Now Cressida Caldwell, who had hosted those parties, shared it with her new husband, William Beardsley, a fellow Radical MP of Malcolm's. But Mélanie was quite sure Cressida, more than anyone of their acquaintance, could help find Maria.

To her surprise, when Tim, Cressida's footman, admitted her, Cressida herself came hurrying down the stairs. "Mélanie, thank goodness. I saw you from the windows. You're just the person we need."

Cressida's dark hair was caught back with a gold clip and she wore a loose ivory gown with a scarlet and gold shawl wrapped hastily round her shoulders, but as usual she looked impossibly elegant. She seized Mélanie's hands. "Come upstairs. There's someone you should speak with."

A young woman sat in the same yellow and red sitting room where Mélanie had first met Cressida the previous February. She had chestnut hair, elegantly cropped but haphazardly pinned, and clutched a handkerchief in both hands.

"This is my friend Maria Parker," Cressida said. "Mrs. Rannoch, Maria. Whom I was just saying we should seek out."

Maria Parker lifted her tear-smudged blue gaze to Mélanie. "Mrs. Rannoch."

"Miss Parker," Mélanie said. "Am I correct that you were acquainted with the Duke of Bamford?"

Miss Parker drew a choked breath and turned her head away.

"Maria came to see me because she'd just learnt her lover had been killed," Cressida said. "And I believe you are here because you are investigating the duke's murder?"

Trust Cressy to grasp the fundamentals quickly. "We are indeed," Mélanie said. "My condolences, Miss Parker."

Miss Parker's eyes widened. "Thank you. I hadn't—"

"A loss is no less a loss because it occurs outside the legal bonds of family," Mélanie said. "Sometimes it is all the more so."

Miss Parker's eyes widened in surprise and then in reappraisal.

Cressida splashed more brandy into the tea Maria Parker was drinking and then poured a cup for Mélanie.

Maria Parker took a quick drink. "I only heard because my maid reported a rumor when she went to the baker's this morning. I called on Cressida to see if she knew more." She dabbed her eyes. "I can't quite believe it. He seemed so alive. So vital."

"When did you last see the duke?" Mélanie, now seated in one of Cressida's elegant and surprisingly comfortable chairs, took a sip of the fragrant spiced tea.

"Three nights ago. We went to the opera and to supper at the Piazza. He was quite charming, as he always was, though he seemed a bit distracted. As though he had some serious business running through his mind the whole time he was pouring champagne and dispensing clever double entendres. But then he was often like that."

"Did he mention anything particular he was concerned about?" Mélanie asked.

"No. That is—" Maria took a careful sip of tea. "He said there'd been some unpleasantness earlier at White's. A group of Radicals had confronted him. I mean—" She looked from Cressida to Mélanie.

"You mean people like our husbands," Cressida said.

"Yes. No. I'm sure they weren't like Mr. Beardsley or Mr. Rannoch. He called them young hotheads."

"Did the duke say what the confrontation was about?" Mélanie asked.

"Politics, I assume. He said he had to admit they had a point. He didn't seem to want to talk more, and it was surprising he said that much. Though he was always kind and charming, His Grace and I existed on the surface." Maria set her cup down. "Cressida said you were likely looking into the duke's death and you'd be able to tell us more. Though I couldn't credit it when she said we should call on you." Her gaze ran over Mélanie's lilac-striped sarcenet gown and violet Juliet spencer. "I'm even more surprised you'd call here, Mrs. Rannoch. Though Cressy's certainly shown that the world is more open than most of us would have thought."

"Mrs. Rannoch is no ordinary Mayfair lady," Cressida said.

"You're a Mayfair lady yourself now, Cressy," Miss Parker pointed out.

"Perish the thought." Cressida shifted her arm, as though deliberately letting her shawl slither lower on her shoulders.

Maria curled her hands round her cup. "I was surprised when you first called on me after you married Mr. Beardsley."

"Marrying William didn't change who I am. I wouldn't want to change who I am. I made that clear to William before we married. Amazingly, he wanted to marry me anyway."

"Of course he did. He's besotted. One in a long line of men who've been besotted with you." Maria Parker surveyed her friend with rueful acknowledgement. "I was rather surprised Bamford didn't choose you the night we met."

"Well, I was already entwined with his son," Cressida said. "I suspect that was why the duke showed up in my salon that night. Though St. Ives looked horrified. I still remember him spattering champagne all over my skirt and saying, 'Good god, it's the pater.'"

"Bamford admitted it was curiosity about his son's latest entanglement that drove him there," Maria said. "Later. He said he wasn't as attentive a father as he should be, but he'd decided he should pay some attention to what his heir was up to. I asked him if he was always curious about his son's mistresses, and he said, 'No, but he hasn't had a great many.'"

"I think that's true," Cressida said. "St. Ives admitted as much. He was—is—unfashionably obsessed with his own wife."

"Very true," Mélanie said, remembering the scene in Bamford House the previous night.

"Bamford said any unexpected break in the pattern made him wary," Maria said. "And then he laughed and said that made him sound stodgy. But he wasn't really, not at all." She took a sip of tea and regarded Cressida over the rim of the red-flowered cup. "He also said his son had excellent taste."

Cressida smiled. "The duke was very polite that night, I remember. And to his credit, he was just as polite to me when he met me at his wife's musicale. He seemed more comfortable with the situation than St. Ives, though even St. Ives was kind."

"The duke had a way of—" Maria hesitated. "I suppose I'd say, seeing the person. Which is quite odd. And rare."

"You liked him," Mélanie said.

"Yes." Maria smiled in memory, then pressed her crumpled

handkerchief to her eyes. "More than a number of gentlemen with whom I've been entangled in any way. Though I can't say I ever felt I knew him. Some men like to pour their hearts out—"

"St. Ives notably being one," Cressida said. "I think he needed a shoulder to cry on more than a mistress."

"Bamford certainly didn't need a shoulder to cry on. He was a pleasant conversationalist but he was disarmingly rather more likely to ask about me than to talk about himself."

"Was he a—" Cressida broke off, coloring.

"Cressy, are you embarrassed?" Maria asked.

"Me?" Cressida reached for her teacup. "Of course not."

"Yes, you are. You were going to ask if Bamford was a good lover."

"It's a reasonable question. Though I'm not sure it's relevant to the investigation. And yes, perhaps the fact that I hesitated shows I've changed more than I'd like to admit. Though I don't think Mélanie will be shocked."

"Not in the least," Mélanie said. "And while I have no wish to pry, I will say any information about the Duke of Bamford could be relevant."

"That makes sense." Maria spread her hands over her lap. "And this could be relevant. Though perhaps not in the way you think. I can't comment on what sort of a lover the Duke of Bamford was. The most he ever did was kiss my hand."

Cressida clunked her teacup down, spattering tea in the saucer. "And to think I thought nothing an English aristocrat could do would shock me. Was he not—"

"Oh, he wasn't incapable. That is—we never got anything like far enough for me to find out, but he never indicated that he had any difficulty performing. He was very clear about it the first night he took me to dinner and then escorted me home. He said he appreciated my company and thought it could be a useful relationship for both of us. I laughed and said I always found relationships useful. He said he had no doubt that I enchanted any number of gentlemen, but in his case he would find the appearance of having a mistress useful, but he had no desire to ask more of me. He asked if I'd consider assisting him."

Cressida frowned. "Did he prefer men?"

"That was my first thought. He certainly wouldn't be the first gentleman to want a mistress in name only for that reason. But every so often I'd catch him looking at me. Not in any sort of—well, 'improper way' sounds funny—but you know the way a man can look at you, and even if he's being very respectful and has no designs and may be desperately in love with another woman, you can tell he's appreciating you in a certain way."

"I know," Cressida said. "The way I can appreciate an attractive man, even though I have no desire to be in anyone's bed but William's. Or ours, as he'd say. I suppose it's possible Bamford fancied men *and* women, but that doesn't account for why he didn't want to bed you."

"The obvious explanation being that he was in love with—felt committed to—someone else," Mélanie said.

"Such an obvious explanation. I tend not to think of it with men of his sort." Cressida frowned. "It's certainly possible. But why on earth would he have needed a pretend mistress?"

"Presumably to put people off the scent of his actual love, be it man or woman," Mélanie said. "And since he had no problem being thought to have a mistress, if the actual lover is a woman, it must have been on her account. A married woman, perhaps. With a less than compliant husband." She looked at Maria. "Did he ever allude to anyone?"

"No." Maria spread her handkerchief in her lap and looked down at the embroidered roses on it. "Not in so many words. But I'd catch a look in his eye. When he was handing me in or out of a carriage, or once when we were dancing. As though he was thinking of someone else. Holding her hand, sweeping her into a waltz. A lost love, I thought. But it could have been someone in the present. He was the sort who lived his life with a lot of illusions." She reached for her tea and cradled the cup in her hand. "To be honest, I always thought at some point I'd see through the illusions. That was part of what made him so intriguing. But I never did." She dashed a tear from her eye with an impatient hand. "And now it's too late."

CHAPTER 23

24 December 1800
Paris

As the carriage moved off with Josephine, Hortense, and Caroline Murat, Raoul and St. Ives ran back to the rue Saint-Nicaise and up the street to the damaged café. The once gleaming front windows had shattered. Cloaks had already been thrown over dead bodies. They helped shift fallen beams, surrendered their greatcoats to two girls who were shivering with shock, improvised a sling for a young lieutenant's broken wrist. A crowd of rescuers began to gather. When a trio of police arrived on the scene, Raoul cast a sidelong look at St. Ives. His papers were no doubt expertly forged, but would be forgeries all the same. And in the wake of an assassination attempt on the first consul, the police were bound to be asking questions. St. Ives gave a quick nod. Of one accord, they turned and started up the street.

They paused in the light of a streetlamp in the rue St. Honoré. St. Ives gripped the lamppost, as though struggling for self-command. Raoul drew a deep breath of the night air, filled with the acrid tang of smoke. Bile rose up in his throat.

"That girl holding the horse couldn't have been more than fourteen or fifteen," St. Ives said in a rough voice. "And the horse. Whoever set the explosives had to have known—"

"Quite," Raoul said.

St. Ives's gaze shot to Raoul. "I didn't realize how well you knew Madame Bonaparte."

"We were in Les Carmes together during the Terror. When she was Rose de Beauharnais."

"You must have both—"

"Come close to the guillotine? Oh, yes. But we were fortunate. More fortunate than those caught in the rue Saint-Nicaise today." Raoul pulled his watch from his pocket. "We can make it to the opèra." He still had time to meet his contact. And St. Ives presumably had time to keep his own appointment.

St. Ives nodded and brushed the crumbled plaster from his coat. Raoul glanced down at his own coat and did the same. Fortunately, the mud and blood spatters didn't show much against the black cassimere, and his lost greatcoat had taken the brunt of the damage.

They walked in silence along the rue de la Loi. Which had once been the rue de Richelieu, where they had met at that party with Arabella in what seemed another world. They reached the glittering elegance of the Théâtre de la République et des Arts. In the ornate, high-ceilinged lobby, St. Ives turned to Raoul. "We both have people to meet. Better for both of us and our contacts if we do it separately."

Raoul nodded.

St. Ives inclined his head and then touched Raoul's arm. "And —thank you."

The oratorio was underway by the time Raoul entered the house. A dark-haired young woman in a diaphanous white gown was singing in a honey-toned voice that carried throughout the theatre, for all its delicacy. Danielle Darnault, who had burst onto the scene, already had Paris at her feet. From his vantage point in the pit, Raoul could see Bonaparte in his box, Josephine now beside him, Hortense and Caroline just behind. Bonaparte leant back in his chair with an iron calm. Josephine was pale but composed. Hortense clutched her bandaged wrist. Caroline had her opera glasses turned to the other boxes.

News of the assassination attempt had already spread. He could hear the whispers over Haydn's music, heads bent close together and then turning to the side as the news spread. The talk rose to a murmur at the first interval. Raoul made his way to the lobby for his appointed rendezvous. But as he moved to the stairs, a hand fell on his shoulder. Colonel Rapp. "Your friend Fourmier. How well do you know him?"

"We've been acquaintances for some years."

"A bit coincidental, his arrival on the scene."

"He was on his way to the theatre. As was I. As were a number in Paris."

"So you say. But we need to make inquiries of everyone. We've taken him in for questioning."

Easy enough to deny any further knowledge of his friend, the supposed Fourmier, and leave him to his devices. St. Ives would probably understand. It was one thing to support a colleague on a mission. It was another to support someone on a competing mission. "We met at the University of Paris, as he said. But his parents were émigrés later."

"So he's a Royalist."

"His parents were. He supported the Revolution. We were friends, after all."

"Was he a Jacobin?"

"I'd say the word fits him less well than it does me," Raoul said truthfully.

"Damn it, O'Roarke. You know as well as I do it was almost certainly Jacobins or Royalists behind this. Bonaparte's convinced it was Jacobins. Fouché isn't so sure. Of course, he assured Bonaparte he'd dealt with the Jacobins, so he has a vested interest in this not being a Jacobin plot. In any case, Fourmier could have ties to either."

"I told you. He's less of a Jacobin than I am."

Rapp met his gaze squarely. "I don't think you were behind this, O'Roarke. I'm quite sure you wouldn't put Madame Bonaparte and Hortense at risk. I don't think it likely you'd attack Bonaparte. But I do think you may know people who were involved."

"It's possible I do. But I don't *know* they were involved, if that's the case. And if people I know were involved, I don't think Fourmier was one of them."

"So you say."

"Let me talk to him." Raoul held Rapp's gaze. "Believe me, I'm not unaware of the risks."

Rapp gave a curt nod and led the way to a small anteroom across the passage. A single brace of candles burnt on a polished table. A man about Raoul's age, with close-cut dark hair, garbed in a civilian coat of dark blue, stood just behind the table, regarding St. Ives over the light of the candles. Curier, one of the senior agents of Fouché, the minister of police. Raoul didn't know him well, and found it best to steer well clear.

Curier looked over his shoulder at the opening of the door.

"I've brought O'Roarke," Rapp said. "It seemed best."

Curier gave a curt nod.

"I'm still trying to determine what this is about," St. Ives said, blending polite concern with mild affront.

"There was an attempt to assassinate the first consul this evening," Curier said. "He narrowly escaped. As did his wife and stepdaughter and sister. I've had reports that you were at the scene of the incident. Along with O'Roarke."

St. Ives allowed his shoulders to relax. "O'Roarke and I had just run into each other—literally—and we were in the rue Saint-Nicaise on our way to the opèra when the explosion occurred. We didn't realize what had happened at first. We heard a lady screaming and went to the carriage. O'Roarke is acquainted with Madame Bonaparte, as you must know, but in the confusion it was some minutes before I realized the occupants were Madame Bonaparte and her party."

Curier inclined his head, though his face gave nothing away. "Your name?"

"Fourmier."

"And you and O'Roarke met—"

"At university."

"I've told Rapp your parents were émigrés," Raoul said, filling the gap before he could be seeming to interrupt St. Ives. Rapp and Curier would probably suspect he was feeding the information, but they couldn't prove anything. "But that your own sympathies were much closer to mine." That gave St. Ives something to work with that could also explain any seeming ties to England.

"Just so," St. Ives said. "I haven't seen my parents in some time."

"They're in England?" Rapp asked.

"Yes, actually. I spent some time there in the '90s, but haven't been back for years." Which neatly explained any trace of an accent that bled through. "It doesn't make for much family unity."

Curier nodded. "Your papers?"

"Certainly." St. Ives drew the documents from his pocket. He should have the funds to pay for good ones. But even good ones weren't foolproof, as Raoul knew to his cost.

The papers crackled. Curier unfolded them with the seeming slowness of an executioner mounting the scaffold. He glanced through them, held them to the light of the brace of candles. His face remained impassive. "Very cleverly done," he said at last. "But not authentic, unless my eyes deceive me." He drew a pistol from inside his coat and leveled it at St. Ives.

"Georges." The door had opened without sound. A slender figure in silver net stood there, golden brown hair swept up with a diamond comb. It took Raoul a moment to recognize Mademoi-selle Chat Gris. She pushed the door to behind her and looked from Curier to Rapp to Raoul to St. Ives. "Oh, dear, I was afraid of this."

"Désirée?" Curier spoke without turning round, the pistol still leveled on St. Ives. "You know this man?"

"He's here to give me a report. He's one of my best sources. Couldn't you have set them straight, Raoul?"

"I didn't want to interfere with your mission," Raoul said without a blink.

Rapp's gaze shot from Raoul to Chat Gris to St. Ives. "You all know each other?"

"You might call us colleagues." Mademoiselle Chat Gris walked forwards, into the circle of light cast by the brace of candles. The diamonds in her hair and at her ears and throat sparkled like shards of cut glass. "Really, Tony, you might have told them the truth from the first."

St. Ives smiled into her hazel eyes. "Like O'Roarke, I wasn't sure how much I was supposed to reveal to whom."

"He was at the scene of the assassination attempt," Curier said, the pistol still leveled at St. Ives. "He entered Madame Bonaparte's carriage."

"Yes, he was likely to be there, it's a common route to the theatre, and once there, he was bound to offer his help. He's nothing if not chivalrous."

"He was with O'Roarke. Who didn't tell us any of this."

"As I said. I didn't know how much Désirée would want me to reveal." Raoul smiled with familiarity at the woman whose name he had just learnt.

Curier spared her a brief glance, the pistol still on St. Ives. "This is no time to take chances."

"I'll answer for any risk to Talleyrand and Fouché," Désirée said. "And anyone else concerned. Colonel Rapp, do make him see sense."

"O'Roarke wouldn't allow any risk to Madame Bonaparte and Mademoiselle Hortense," Rapp said. "I'm sure of that."

Curier swung his gaze back to Rapp, then looked at Désirée again.

"Surely you have others to question," Désirée said. "It would be dreadful if the true culprits escaped because of your misplaced zeal."

Curier hesitated a moment longer, then moved to the door, still holding the pistol. "I leave him in your hands."

"Thank you, Georges. I know just what to do with him."

Rapp met Raoul's gaze for a moment, then gave a curt nod. "I'll leave you all to it. O'Roarke, Madame Bonaparte would like to see you before you leave."

CHAPTER 24

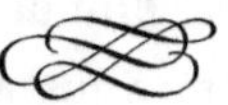

May 1821
London

The sound of French washed over Raoul as he stepped into the coffeehouse in Piccadilly. For a moment he was back in Paris. Not the Royalist city he'd last visited a few months ago that made his throat clog with tears he'd never let himself shed. The city two decades earlier, still vibrant, still echoing with the hope of change. The city where he'd first met Charlotte Leblanc. Who had become an ally and perhaps more, and then more recently perhaps an enemy. But who might have the information he needed.

Charlotte looked up from her table at the back of the coffee-house. The same table at which he'd found her two years before. She was not a creature of habit, but like most agents, she grasped hold of some routine. She was wearing gray rather than blue, but her blonde hair was coiled in the same low knot.

She raised a brow as he approached the table. "This is a surprise."

Raoul dropped into the chair across from her. "Unpleasant?"

"I'm not sure."

"Fair enough." He signaled to a waiter for coffee.

Charlotte stirred her own cup. "I thought we were enemies now."

"Don't we both know how elastic that term is? And we've never been the sort for hard feelings."

"About any number of things." Charlotte took a sip of coffee. "I hear you got divorced not long after I last saw you. Only to shackle yourself again."

"I was fortunate. To have the opportunity to marry. And so much depends on the person."

"That sounds distinctly cloying." She added more milk to her coffee. "And you have a child."

"Two. Laura already had a child who now does the honor of considering me her father."

"Charming." Charlotte's smile always had had a sardonic curl.

"It's the most important thing in my life." The words came out easily, without planning, without artifice.

"But it hasn't made you give up the game."

"No. Though I'm hardly the only agent I know with a family."

"You used to say you were unsuited to family life."

"So I did. I thought I'd make a mull of it. I'm still afraid I will. But the risk is worth it."

"You used to not resort to such platitudes." She took a drink of coffee. "Why did you want to see me?"

"You must have heard."

"That the Duke of Bamford was killed?"

"You always had good sources."

"And you thought I'd be a good source of information on the death of an English duke?"

"On two counts, actually. As an enemy and an ally."

Charlotte closed the book she'd been writing in and settled her elbow on the tabletop. A lace frill escaped the gray sleeve of her spencer and fell over her fingers. "You intrigue me."

"Was Bamford connected to the Elsinore League?"

"I thought Bamford was your friend."

"He was. He's not the first friend I've had questions about."

"Do you think I'd tell you if he had been a member of the League?"

"That depends on a number of things. Your current relationship to the League. The status of the various factions. Bamford's and your own relationship to them."

She turned her saucer on the table. "Cogently put." She took a drink of coffee. "Bamford was never connected to the League. To my knowledge. In fact, many in the League see him as an enemy."

"An enemy they'd like to get rid of?"

"Not that I've heard directly. At least, I haven't heard recent threats. Now you can decide if you think I'm telling the truth about any of this."

"Even if it's only a fraction of the truth, it's interesting. Even if it's all lies, it's interesting."

"I'll be intrigued to hear how you sort it out." She stirred her coffee. "You said you had questions for me as an ally and an enemy. I assume the Elsinore League question was the enemy. What do you want from me as an ally? Assuming I ever was one."

"Désirée Clairineau."

Charlotte's fingers stilled on her cup. "That's a name I haven't heard in a long time."

"What do you know about her?"

"She makes me look tame. Quite out of my league, I freely admit. One of the more dangerous agents I've ever had anything to do with. I can't but admire her. While being rather relieved to move in different circles."

Charlotte didn't lightly admit fearing anyone. Of course, she might have been doing it at least in part to put him off the scent. "Bamford was involved with her."

"Yes, I know. She had a number of lovers and used them freely in her work. But Bamford may have been her most spectacular conquest."

"Where is she now?"

"No one seems to know. I haven't heard she was arrested. Which argues she managed to escape the White Terror. Or that the Ultra Royalists were particularly effective in getting rid of her."

"Bamford was willing to risk a lot for her."

"He wouldn't be the first or last man to do so. More fool they."

"He told me they had a falling out after Waterloo. I never got the details."

"Yes, I heard they'd fallen out quite spectacularly. But I didn't get the details either. It's more surprising whatever was between them lasted as long as it did."

A waiter set down Raoul's coffee. Charlotte ordered another for herself. "It's amazing how love makes fools of us," she said. "I hear even Julien St. Juste is acting the faithful husband."

Raoul took a drink of coffee. The rich Parisian taste brought a host of memories. "I wouldn't say he's acting."

"But then you're besotted yourself. That's the thing about love. It makes us build illusions. About others. About ourselves." Charlotte picked up her fresh cup of coffee and blew on the steam. "Bamford did that with Désirée, I think." She watched the vapor dispel. "Built a fairy tale round what they meant to each other. When all the while Désirée was bent on winning the game. He thought she was the love of his life, and she may have been his greatest enemy of all."

Raoul's fingers tightened on his cup. "What are you suggesting?"

"Someone killed Bamford. Someone, apparently, with skill at arranging convenient accidents. Someone ruthless. Someone who found Bamford inconvenient. Désirée more than fits the first two. And depending on what Bamford knew about her, she might well fit the third."

"Interesting. You think she's in England?"

"I had no reason to think so until now. But she certainly wouldn't be the first French agent to go to earth here. She has to have found refuge somewhere, assuming she's still alive. Somehow, I doubt she's in France. And something about this has her scent all over it." Charlotte took a drink of coffee. "Save that Désirée Clairineau would never leave even a trace of her scent. She's far too skilled."

CHAPTER 25

24 December 1800
Paris

The door swung shut behind Curier and Colonel Rapp. St. Ives held himself perfectly still, staring at Désirée. "I don't—"

"Not so fast." In two strides Désirée was across the room and had a knifepoint pressed to his throat.

St. Ives studied her over the polished steel. "You wanted the honor of killing me yourself?"

"Did you have anything to do with the explosion in the rue Saint-Nicaise?"

"You overestimate my reach."

"Your government have a long arm. There'd be much rejoicing in Whitehall if Bonaparte died. Don't deny it."

"I wasn't going to. But—"

"You have Royalists in your pay. I've seen the papers."

"Don't I know it." His grimace spoke volumes about where she might have seen those papers.

Désirée Clairineau looked at Raoul over her shoulder, the

157

knife still on St. Ives. "What do you know about what Tony's doing in Paris?"

"We met on the street tonight, just before the explosion. That part of our story was the truth."

"So you must have the same questions I do."

"I confess they have crossed my mind."

"Why did he say he was going to the opèra?"

"He didn't."

"But it has to have been to meet a contact. A Royalist contact."

"That was my assumption," Raoul agreed.

"Am I permitted to get a word in?" St. Ives inquired.

Désirée's fingers tightened on the knife. "You haven't answered my question."

St. Ives met her gaze. Raoul was quite sure the last time they'd been this close there'd been no knives involved and also considerably less clothing. "I'd scarcely admit it if I had had anything to do with the explosion," he said. "But as it happens, I truly didn't know of it or have anything to do with the planning. On my word of honor. Though I don't imagine honor's a word you take very seriously."

"But you do." Désirée's gaze scoured his face. "You said you didn't know of it or have anything to do with the planning. You didn't deny involvement outright."

"You were always damned acute with words."

"And?" Her knuckles were white round the knife hilt.

"I was supposed to deliver a payment to a contact at the opèra tonight. I was told it was for information. But I can't claim with certainty there's no connection to the explosion."

"In fact, you suspect there's a connection."

St. Ives drew in and released his breath. "It's possible."

"An impressive admission."

"Or a clever feint," St. Ives said. "You'll have to decide."

Désirée glanced over her shoulder at Raoul. "What do you think?"

Raoul saw again the sick horror in St. Ives's gaze in those moments by the lamppost after they helped the victims. Horror at the plot he might have unwittingly been involved in? Or horror that a plot he had known about and assisted had taken innocents? *That girl holding the horse couldn't have been more than fourteen or fifteen. And the horse. Whoever set the explosives had to have known—*

"I'm inclined to believe him," Raoul said. "Though of course one can never be sure."

"No. One can't. One has to make a choice." Désirée relaxed her hand, though she still held the knife a hair's breadth from St. Ives's jugular. "I confess I wasn't looking forward to killing you."

St. Ives didn't move from his position inches away from her. "What makes you so sure it was Royalists behind the plot?"

"Call it an instinct. Though I expect they'll try to blame Jacobins. They usually do."

He studied the hard eyes a knife's length from his own. "You still consider yourself a Jacobin?"

"I'm a Republican. Like Monsieur O'Roarke."

"Under your first consul, France seems to be a republic in name only."

"He's the best guarantee we have against a return of the monarchy that your government are doing their best to bring about."

"I don't agree with everything my government do. I've told you as much."

"And yet you work for them."

"I'm an Englishman. I have a job to do. A job I do rather well."

"I always said we were much alike." She took a step back, the knife at her side, still between him and the door. She cast a quick look at Raoul. "Lord St. Ives and I have met more than once since we last saw you. Though our mission to help you was a rare occasion on which we were allies." She looked back at St. Ives. "I meant it when I wrote that you were a formidable opponent after our last encounter. I trust you didn't suffer too badly with your superiors over my deception."

"They were remarkably understanding of my lapse into idiocy."

"You saw what you expected to see."

"Which I pride myself on never doing." Without a change in inflection, he added, "Three people on the list you took met their deaths."

"They were traitors. How are you in the habit of rewarding treason in civilized England?"

"They loved France."

"And I imagine Guy Fawkes would have said he loved England." She folded the knife blade into its enameled hilt. "Their deaths are on my head, Tony, not yours."

"You can't possibly expect me to be fool enough to believe that."

"You'll have to decide for yourself what to believe." She tucked the knife into the Grecian drapery of her bodice. "Your government appear to have paid for a plot that took innocent lives tonight. Though I won't pretend mine haven't done the same. Who was the contact you were meeting at the opèra?"

"I don't know his name. He was supposed to be by the stairs in the lobby at the first interval, and to have a pink carnation in his buttonhole."

"Which is no doubt conveniently abandoned now. You wouldn't tell me his name if you knew it. Nor would I, in your circumstances. Nor would Monsieur O'Roarke."

"No," St. Ives agreed. "But we'd also all take care to conceal our identities from someone we were meeting in such circumstances."

"And you, Monsieur O'Roarke?" Désirée turned to Raoul. "What were you doing at the opèra tonight?"

She was theoretically his ally. She reported to Talleyrand, who was also theoretically an ally, at least in some things. And possibly to Fouché. Who wasn't an ally at all. "I expect you won't believe it was merely to hear Haydn's music and Danielle Darnault, though both interest me. But as I'm sure you've surmised, I was meeting a contact of my own. Whom I completely missed, given the events of the evening."

"On business for Madame Bonaparte?"

"On personal business." In fact, he'd been chasing down information about the Elsinore League for Arabella.

"I don't think you do anything for personal reasons, Monsieur O'Roarke. We haven't met since Tony and I brought you to Talleyrand, but I've heard rather a lot about you. You're close to Madame Bonaparte. Bonaparte appreciates your talents. As does Talleyrand. And they both know you wish France were still more of a republic."

"None of that is secret."

"No. But a great deal of what you do is. Even Fouché says you gather better intelligence than almost anyone."

"A compliment indeed."

She smiled unexpectedly. "I don't count Fouché an ally either. He'll undoubtedly investigate tonight's attack. I'm less certain what he'll do with the information. I'd be interested in hearing what you discovered yourself."

"You would? Or Talleyrand would?"

"Do the two need to be in conflict?" She watched him a moment. "I think you'll find it hard not to investigate, Monsieur O'Roarke. And I think we all agree we don't want to see the wrong people pay the price for tonight's events. And you and I at least agree that we don't want Jacobins blamed. There could be far wider implications than simply for those wrongly arrested."

"Agreed."

Désirée glanced at St. Ives. "Tony could help. Not with names. I wouldn't ask that. But at least with making sure the wrong people don't pay the price. I think he wants that."

"What makes you so sure?" St. Ives asked.

"Your morals are rather better than mine."

St. Ives folded his arms. "I do admit we have common points of interest."

"Well, then."

"What are you suggesting?" St. Ives asked.

"You and Monsieur O'Roarke learn who was behind tonight's attack. I'm not fool enough to think you'll share it all with me. But do consider what I can do with proof that it's Royalists to blame rather than Jacobins."

"I can't speak for St. Ives," Raoul said, "but you're quite right that I'd have a hard time not investigating."

"It was a damned mess," St. Ives said. "I don't like to feel responsible for messes."

"Good." Désirée drew a sealed paper from a pocket in her skirt. "This will get you out of Paris. It's not a forgery, it should stand up to hard scrutiny. But don't delay. The city will already be swarming with agents after tonight's attack. You don't want to answer any more questions than you can help."

St. Ives stared at her.

She crossed to his side and pressed the paper into his hand. "For God's sake, Tony. Don't start acting like an idiot now."

He took the paper, but kept his gaze on her face. "Why?"

"Because I believe in settling my debts." She gripped his fingers for a moment, then released him and stepped back. "Whatever you may think, I'm not entirely without honor."

CHAPTER 26

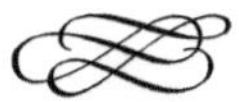

May 1821
London

"*L*ady Carfax." Tristram Gresham leapt off the stage and came forwards to take Kitty's hands as she walked into the King's Theatre, Haymarket.

"Surely we're on a first name basis after the Bamford musicale," Kitty said. Rosalind, the Bamfords' youngest daughter, had attempted to provoke jealousy from Gresham, her former lover, at the musicale. Or so it had seemed. In fact, Rosalind and her husband had been trying to steal papers from Gresham, who in turn had taken them from Countess Lieven, the Russian ambassador's wife. Gresham was as able an agent as he was a composer and roué.

"One never likes to presume." Gresham kissed each of Kitty's York tan—gloved hands in turn. "I don't normally allow guests at rehearsals, but I'm delighted to see you here."

"And I'd be thrilled to watch." Kitty cast a glance at the stage, where several performers and stagehands and a thin man at a piano were looking round with interest. "But as it happens, I need to talk to you."

His brows drew together, though he did not release her hands. "It's not the best time for talking, as I'm sure you'll appreciate from Mélanie Rannoch's comments on the rehearsal process."

"Yes. But I fear it can't wait. The Duke of Bamford was killed last night."

"Good god. Was he—"

"A ship at the docks that he was on exploded. And he'd been shot."

"My god." Gresham looked genuinely horrified. But then she had cause to know what a good actor he was.

"The talk is all over London," Kitty said.

"I slept at the theatre last night. And there wasn't time for chitchat when the cast and stagehands got here." He cast a glance at the group on the stage. "Half an hour, everyone." He looked back at Kitty. "Come into the green room."

"I'm happy to talk," Gresham said, when they were amid the green room's faded tapestry sofas, only slightly less worn than those at the Tavistock, where Mélanie's plays were performed. "But I don't know how much I can tell you. My connection with the Bamford family was not with the duke, as you know. The last time I saw him was at the duchess's musicale. He was polite when I left, but I sensed a distinct chill. Not surprising, given that he knew about Rosalind and me."

"Quite." Kitty smoothed her amber lustring skirt and set her reticule on the settee beside her. "Which makes it all the more remarkable that you were overheard with the duke the day before yesterday."

Gresham went still. "I should have known."

"Yes, you should."

He flicked a speck of lint from his sleeve. "The duke was concerned about Rosalind. Understandable in a father."

"Yes, it is. And I don't believe it for a moment."

"Yes, I thought you wouldn't. But it was worth a try." Gresham moved to a set of decanters beside the tea table, poured himself a brandy, poured one for her. "Bamford's and my politics didn't agree. But we both had interests abroad."

Kitty accepted the brandy he was holding out, despite the early hour. Drinking with Gresham was a good way to get him to talk. "You'll have to do better than that, Tristram. This is a murder investigation."

Gresham took a drink of brandy. "If you must know, Bamford wanted information."

"About?"

"My most recent visit to Paris." Tristram dropped into a chair across from her. "He was trying to find someone."

"An agent?"

"I'm not sure. A woman. He seemed concerned."

"What was the woman's name?"

"He said she used a number of names, but most often went by Désirée Clairineau."

"And you hadn't heard of her?"

"No. But as I told Bamford, his contacts in Paris were probably better than mine."

"His valet heard you arguing."

Gresham frowned over his brandy. "I didn't think we were so noisy. But yes. I wouldn't say we fought, but Bamford was reluctant to believe I couldn't help. I was rather annoyed, save that he seemed so genuinely concerned I couldn't but have sympathy." Gresham sat back his chair. "There are reasons I make it a point never to fall in love."

"You think this woman was a lover?"

"Given his level of concern, I strongly suspect she was, or at least had been."

"And you really hadn't heard of her?"

"If so, why would I have kept it from Bamford?"

"Any number of reasons. Including that she asked you to. Bamford wasn't your political ally. Or mine."

"All good points." Gresham twisted the stem of his glass between his fingers. "But as it happens, I really did have no knowledge of her. Whether or not you believe that is, of course, entirely up to you."

The green room door clicked open. Danielle Darnault came into the room, garbed in a cherry red pelisse and bonnet. "I just got here, and they said Kitty had called and you were in the green room. I assume it's about Bamford."

"You know?" Gresham asked.

"The news about Bamford is all over town." Danielle pushed the door to. "Did you really not know until Kitty arrived, Tristram?"

"As I told Kitty, I slept at the theatre. You probably know more about Bamford than I do."

"Most of what I know is from our performance at the duchess's musicale."

"You never met him in France?" Kitty asked.

Danielle shook her head. "But for most of my career in Paris, the British couldn't travel to the Continent."

"We've learnt that Bamford was on the Continent more than one would think. He was a British agent."

Danielle perched on the arm of Tristram's chair. "Interesting."

"You didn't know?" Kitty asked.

"There are a lot of agents on both sides. Even granted the shocking leaks in intelligence, we certainly don't all know each other's names."

"But you know a number of agents," Kitty said.

Danielle smoothed the black braid on the cuff of her pelisse. "That's undeniable."

"And you haven't heard any talk that could relate to Bamford's death?"

"Kitty. I know you don't want to leave the game. But I'm now an opera singer and a mother and a newspaper publisher's wife. That's quite enough to keep me busy."

"She won't believe you," Gresham said.

Danielle tilted her head to the side. Her dark ringlets and the cherry ribbons on her bonnet fell against her cheek. "No. But then that's the challenge of an investigation. Finding which shadows really have secrets hiding in them."

"RAOUL." Jennifer Mansfield leant forwards to accept his kiss on her cheek as he stepped into the green room at the Tavistock Theatre. "This must be about Bamford."

"You've heard?"

"It was the talk of rehearsal. Simon had a hard time getting us all to pay attention."

"We were there. On the docks last night."

Her eyes widened. "I hadn't heard that."

"I'd just arrived in London. Malcolm and Mélanie and the Carfaxes and Davenports were in a tavern nearby. We got there just after the explosion. Along with a number of others."

Jennifer moved to the tea table. "Everyone was asking what a duke was doing on a ship at the London Dock. The theories ranged from a tryst to fleeing the country due to debts. I have to say, knowing what I do about Bamford, I was less surprised than many."

"You knew him?"

Jennifer poured a cup of tea and handed it to him. "Of course. He was a breath of fresh air at all those parties in the 90s flooded with English aristos. And no, he was never more to me than an agreeable flirtation."

"Did you know—"

"That he was an agent?" Jennifer refilled her own cup and

moved to the faded tapestry sofa. "Of course. And remarkably skilled. Though he was only just beginning in those days."

"And later?"

She took a sip of tea. "Later, I'd left the game."

Jennifer had been a brilliant agent, but she'd left Paris and come to England with Horace Smytheton, who was now her husband. Who had once helped Raoul flee Ireland along with Alistair Rannoch. "Was Bamford connected to the British who were working with the Royalists in the 90s? Alistair Rannoch and Dewhurst and—"

"My own Horace."

"Yes. I got to know Bamford later, but I was never sure about his connections to the others."

"Not that I know of." Jennifer leant back on the sofa. Her red hair stood out against the faded print for *The Rivals* that hung on the wall behind her. "And I believe I would have known." She'd been in the thick of it herself, working with the Royalists but actually a double agent for the Revolutionary government.

Raoul took a drink of tea. "Does the name Désirée Clairineau mean anything to you?"

Jennifer's hand stilled on her teacup for a moment. "I never met her. I was out of France before she became active. But I quite admire what I've heard about her."

"She met me on the coast when Horace and Alistair brought me to France in '98. And took me to Talleyrand. Along with Bamford, back when he was still St. Ives. They were lovers off and on for years."

Jennifer took a thoughtful sip of tea. "I hadn't heard that. Bamford grows more interesting. He wasn't—"

"He wasn't a French agent. Unless I am very much deceived. Which is entirely possible. Bamford found it useful to work across lines on occasion. As does Talleyrand. As do I, from time to time."

Jennifer set down her teacup, as though debating what to say next. But before she could speak, the door opened to admit her fellow actress, Manon Caret. "I don't mean to interrupt, but Simon said Raoul was here. I assume this is about Bamford, and I thought you might want to talk to me as well."

"It is, and I do," Raoul said. Manon, like Jennifer, was not only an actress; she had been an agent, though in Manon's case, a decade or so later, as part of Raoul's network under the Bonapartist government. "Did you ever meet him in France?"

"No. Though from some of the rumors I've heard, it sounds now as though he was there more during the war than I realized."

"What about Désirée Clairineau?"

Manon froze in the midst of pouring herself tea. "She was connected to Bamford?"

"They were lovers off and on. While working against each other and occasionally collaborating."

"Well, that's interesting. It's a wonder he survived as long as he did."

"Was she so dangerous?" Jennifer asked.

Manon took a drink of tea. "She wasn't the sort to go sentimental about a lover."

"She told me as much herself," Raoul said. "Do you know where she is?"

Manon shook her head, her loosely dressed blonde hair stirring about her face. "She'd already disappeared from sight before I escaped Paris." She perched on the arm of the sofa and regarded him. "It sounds as though you knew her better than I did."

Raoul turned the handle of his cup and looked into the swirling tea. "At one time, perhaps. But I can't claim to have understood her. I'm not sure anyone did."

"Even Bamford?" Jennifer asked.

"Bamford least of all."

CHAPTER 27

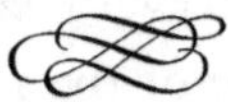

1801
Harrow

"Thank you." St. Ives—or Tony, as Raoul now thought of him—looked up from the book he was leafing through as Raoul approached down the aisle in Abernathy's Shop. "I know it's not easy to get into Britain."

Raoul paused a few steps away. "Not easy for you to get to France either. And I can use it for other purposes."

"The reason we're meeting in Harrow?"

"Fortunately, it's a quiet village. I've found it useful in the past."

Tony gave a faint smile. "Have you seen him yet?"

"Later this afternoon." And hopefully it would go more smoothly than his visit with Malcolm in the bookshop a year ago. But assassins rarely chose the same spot twice.

"And Lady Arabella?"

"I'm not sure. It can be difficult to find time, given the complications of her own life." Raoul scanned Tony's face. He was smiling easily and his cravat and coat were as immaculate as usual, but tension showed in the lines of his arm braced against the bookshelf. "I assume this is important."

Tony's gaze was dark, but held the glint of an agent with information. "Reynald St. Pierre. Younger son of Vicomte de St. Pierre."

"An émigré family. They came to London during the Terror." Raoul remembered meeting the vicomte and vicomtesse at a reception with Bella.

"Reynald returned to France when Talleyrand got the laws against émigrés loosened, though his parents and brother and sisters stayed in England. Reynald now has a minor position in the ministry of police. I don't know that you'd have come across him."

"I can't claim to be well acquainted with all those in the ministry of police."

"Not surprising." Tony tucked the book back into the shelf. Seventeenth century poets. "He's been reporting to the British for years."

Raoul held Tony's gaze, his own steady as still water. Tony was a skilled agent. And he looked after his sources. "And yet you're sharing his name."

St. Ives turned, leaning against the bookshelf, gaze on the shelf opposite. "He was working with Saint-Régent and Limoëlan and Carbon on the rue Saint-Nicaise plot."

That was not entirely a surprise. Raoul's own inquiries had led him to suspect there was someone else involved in the explosion and the plot to kill Bonaparte, still unknown to the authorities, along with those who had been arrested or fled. But he hadn't come close to learning a name. "You said you'd help, but not disclose names. What's changed?"

Tony tugged his shirt cuff smooth beneath the dark blue superfine of his sleeve. "St. Pierre is a loose cannon. He's reckless. But not out of belief. He wants the family's estates restored. His brother married an heiress and seems happy in Britain. His sisters have settled there. His parents seem content. But I think Reynald would sell himself to anyone for power. "

"So you want me to get rid of him for you?"

St. Ives adjusted a cuff button. "I want him removed from the field of play."

"You could simply cut him loose."

"He has connections in Britain. Highly placed connections. His brother married a Cavendish. Through his sisters he's connected to a half dozen other powerful families, and his mother's British. If I cut him loose, he'll object, and they'll get someone else to work with him. Which will be worse, because the new person won't be able to keep an eye on him."

Raoul dug his shoulder into the shelf and folded his arms. "You realize I may be able to get actual information from him."

Tony grimaced. "I don't trust him not to sell us out, in any case. At least this way I can keep an eye on him and limit what he knows."

"You aren't worried I'll try to turn him, now I know?"

"Actually," Tony said, "that's exactly what I want you to do."

Raoul was used to Tony's flexibility, but that startled even him. He was quite sure Tony, for all his willingness to work across the Channel, hadn't changed sides. So—

"I can't cut him loose, as I explained," Tony said. "If he were taken into custody by Fouché's people, he'd be out of our way, but there would be questions, and some might want to effect a rescue. If you turn him, he stays right where he is. But I can build up evidence to use against him, if I need it. You can keep an eye on him and make sure there are no more extravagant plots. And between the two of us, we can make sure he doesn't get his hands on anything too important."

"And if any actual information slips through? He can't be a complete idiot."

"We both know that's part of the risk. But we both might find it useful to have someone to feed information to. And if he blunders into something like the rue Saint-Nicaise plot again, one or both of us will learn and can stop him. Whatever my own government's role in the plot, I don't want to see it happen again. There's a fair amount you and I agree on."

"So you want me to recruit a double agent who will be giving me false information."

"Which you will know is false going in. I also want to see how easily Reynald St. Pierre can be bought. My sense is it's very easily, and that's what makes him such a liability."

"Meaning I'll have to worry about him becoming a triple."

"Quite. That will ensure you never trust him with anything important."

Raoul crossed his legs at the ankle. "It's an intriguing premise. What if he refuses?"

"Then that will tell us a great deal about him. And we can move on to another plan. One way or another, he can't be allowed to go on as he is. And yes, I have thought about what would happen if he simply met with an accident. But there'd be questions."

"And that isn't your style."

"No."

"Does Désirée know?" Raoul asked.

"Not yet. I haven't seen her. And I wanted to see what you said first. But I'd like to tell her myself."

"Talking of reasons to go across the Channel."

"You're too polite to tell me I'm a fool."

"There's a great deal of sanity in seeing across lines."

"Désirée would likely call that weakness and warn me she'd exploit it." Tony looked down at the volume of Lovelace that he'd been scanning. "I was beyond fortunate in the life I was born to. I'm a churl to be dissatisfied. I've found ways to be a rebel round the edges, but mostly I've done what's expected of me. With Désirée, though, it's as if all that's been cut away with a knife and

I've found my way to reality." He ran his finger down the gilded book spine. "Don't you dare tell her I said that."

"That's between the two of you."

"Désirée warns me quite openly that she'll take advantage of me. And god knows I wouldn't want her to change. Then she wouldn't be the woman I—well, she wouldn't be herself." Tony pushed himself away from the shelf. "Let me know what you decide about St. Pierre. I've left an address where you can reach me tucked in the book. At *To Lucasta*. It seemed apt. Think about it and let me know. And meanwhile, enjoy your time with your son."

❧

1801
Paris

DÉSIRÉE LOOKED from Tony to Raoul. "You're telling me an employee of the ministry of police was a British agent and now he's reporting to both of you, and I'm supposed to think this solves anything?"

"Well, it's better than his just reporting to Tony," Raoul said. "At least from my perspective."

"And he was involved in the rue Saint-Nicaise affair."

"It looks that way," St. Ives said.

Désirée regarded her lover. "But you want us to leave him in place."

"You can arrest him if you like. But I don't think he has more information to share. You'll provoke retaliation from his friends in Britain. He'll make up whatever story he thinks will best serve him with Fouché, implicating whomever he most thinks Fouché wants implicated."

"And it will make your life complicated."

"That too. I wouldn't expect that argument to weigh with you."

She folded her arms. "That depends."

"I have no illusions some information won't get through to O'Roarke. You'll have that. Meanwhile I'll be able to build a case against him. You won't give Fouché a victory. And O'Roarke and I can use St. Pierre to get information about Fouché. Which would benefit all of us."

Désirée crossed the inn parlor where they were meeting to Tony's side, smiled up at him, and put her hands on his chest. "You're a good diplomat, Tony. You know how to make a case. Even an improbable one." She glanced sideways at Raoul. "You seem to think this is a good idea."

"I think it's a workable way to deal with St. Pierre. Even an intriguing one."

She looked between them. "You could have simply kept this from me and done as you pleased."

"So we could," Raoul agreed.

"But I told you I'd report back," Tony said.

"Honorable to a fault."

"And you'd have worked it out anyway."

"Probably." She reached up and kissed him lightly. "I may be a fool, but I see your point. Best we're all fools together."

CHAPTER 28

May 1821
London

"I can't believe it." Rosalind dragged her handkerchief across her eyes and looked at Judith across a sitting room in Bamford House where they had once sketched and gossiped together. "I know you must think me the worst daughter imaginable after everything Gaspar and I were doing at the musicale—"

"Don't be silly, Rosy." Judith put an arm round her friend. "In my family, how could I not understand that intrigues can strain loyalties?"

Rosalind choked. "The truth is I did rather take Papa for granted. He was always there, sometimes interfering where I didn't want him to be. But it never occurred to me he could be *gone.*"

"I'm so sorry. I remember how it was when my father died," Judith said. Well, not her father in biology, but the man she had grown up calling father. "I can't say we were close, but I certainly felt his absence. How can one not? And I always thought Bamford was quite splendid."

"He didn't fuss." Rosalind spread her handkerchief in her lap. "It was easier to get my way with him than with Mama most of the time. And sometimes he'd ask questions that showed he was paying a surprising amount of attention. It was a bit disconcerting, actually. But also sweet." She fixed her gaze on Judith. "Your husband is looking into this, isn't he?"

"He's been asked to, yes."

"And the Rannochs. Which I suppose means you too. Is that why you're here?"

"No! I wanted to see you, Rosy. And I'm not really an investigator." Not that she wouldn't like to be, but she had to admit she still had a great deal to learn. And while she was genuinely concerned for Rosalind, there was no reason she couldn't put her skills to the test. As she had told Jeremy last night.

"Stuff. I'm quite sure you can learn to be one. Look at what I've learnt to do. Don't apologize for yourself, Judith. I want all of you working on this. I want to know what happened to Papa."

"You hadn't heard anything that might relate to why someone would have wanted to kill him?"

"Just because Gaspar and I were involved in our own intrigues doesn't mean we knew about Papa's."

"No, that's a fair point. But anything at all about what may have threatened him—"

Rosalind went still for a moment. "There was one thing. Funny. I should have said something sooner. But I've been thinking he must have been killed because of some vast international conspiracy. And this certainly wasn't that. Whatever it was."

"Anything could be a clue to what happened." That was what Jeremy would say.

"It was three days ago. I was dressed early for a family dinner and I went to the library to get a book to while away the time.

That's when I heard them arguing in Papa's study. I couldn't make out the words, but the voices were raised. I did hear Papa say 'You can't ask that,' but I couldn't make out more."

"Could you make out whom he was quarreling with?"

"Oh, yes." Rosalind gripped the handkerchief in her lap. "It was Percy. Frederica's husband."

Judith sat back. Rosalind's eldest sister Frederica was almost ten years Judith's senior, and they'd never been friends. But she knew whom to go to. She needed to talk to Cordelia.

CHAPTER 29

1801
London

$\mathcal{A}$rabella stirred and stretched, dislodging the covers. The morning light filtering through the muslin subcurtains caught her hair, picking out strands of gold. "You didn't tell me what you'd been doing."

Raoul pushed himself up on one elbow. "We didn't have much time for talking last night."

She reached for a shawl dangling haphazardly from the headboard and tossed it over her shoulders. "First things first. I hear you've seen St. Ives."

"Ah." Raoul's meeting with Tony at Harrow had been six weeks ago, but it should have gone unnoticed. "How?"

"Sources."

Given Bella's focus, that was interesting. "I didn't think he was part of the League."

"I don't think he is. But he's a British agent."

"Oh, yes." Raoul pushed himself up against the headboard. "I've known that for some time."

"Does he know about you?"

"Most definitely. But we have a mutual agreement."

Arabella turned her head, brows drawn together. "Is he a double?"

"No."

"So why is he dealing with you?"

Raoul drew his knees up under the covers and linked his arms round them. Bella apparently didn't know Tony had met him in France and taken him to Talleyrand. Which was interesting, "He has his reasons."

Arabella's eyes narrowed. "You don't trust me."

"I thought it was taken for granted we didn't trust each other with everything."

"We're allies."

"In some things. When it comes to this, I'm a French agent and you're English."

She tossed her hair over her shoulder. "I'm not an English agent. Nothing I do is in the service of the British crown."

"Still."

"My mother was French."

"England's your country, whatever you may think of it. I'm not going to put you in the position of committing treason."

She smiled, one of those smiles that lit a room like a blaze of candlelight. "I think I've already done that. I helped a fugitive escape the crown. And I have no regrets."

He reached out and touched her face. "A palpable hit. Still. We can't entirely claim to be on the same side in this. It isn't your fight. And can you really say you tell me everything?"

"About what?"

"Precisely. We're allies in some things. Not in everything. That's true of most allies."

Her gaze skimmed over his face. "But we're—"

He dropped his hand to the coverlet and sat back against the headboard again. "Past time to stop romanticizing what we are, Bella, don't you think?"

Arabella reached for the half-full glass of wine on the night table. "If your reluctance to share information is about Désirée Clairineau, I know about her."

That was interesting. "What do you know about her?"

"She's a French agent. And linked to Tony St. Ives. Who is rather foolish about her. More fool he. I suspect he drew you into something about her. Am I right?"

"You're a witch, Bella. And no comment."

Arabella took a meditative sip of wine. "St. Ives has always intrigued me. I thought at first he might be connected to the League. But I'm quite sure he isn't. He seems to go his own way."

"Not everyone involved in intrigue in Britain is part of the League, Bella."

She swirled the wine in her glass. "I know that."

"But it consumes you."

"The rights of man consume you. In various countries."

"Fair enough."

He watched her for a moment. Her gaze was focused on her wineglass, as though it held hidden secrets. Secrets were always the best way to get Bella's attention.

"You haven't told me how he is," Raoul said softly.

Arabella turned her head towards him. For a moment, he wasn't sure she knew who he meant. "I last saw him at Christmas. He spent most of the holidays buried in books, but he seemed happy enough. Hard to believe how tall he's getting."

"I know. I saw him the day after I met with St. Ives."

"More recently than I did."

"I try not to be gone more than two months."

She shrugged her shoulders, the shawl slithering to her elbows. "You have more of a knack for it than I do."

"What?"

"Parenting."

He laughed, tasting the bitter bite. "I'd hardly say it's a knack. I like seeing him."

"That's what I mean. Oh, not that I don't like it. But I don't feel the need. At least, not as often as you. I get caught up in other things. I don't realize how much time has gone by. And I think he's happier without me."

"I doubt that's true."

Arabella took a drink of wine. "He looks at me as though he wants something I can't give him. If he saw more of me, he'd only find me even more wanting."

"Bella—" He put out a hand, then dropped it to the covers. "How's the little one?"

"Chattering away. She has quite a will of her own. She has most people wrapped round her finger. Even Alistair, surprisingly. Malcolm's quite good with her. Edgar's adjusting. On the whole, the nursery and schoolroom seem to run better when I don't intrude too much. Then I can focus on enjoying the time I do have with them." She glanced at him. "Somehow I think that shocks you."

"By no means. I'm certainly an absent parent. If I can be called one."

"In a lot of ways, you're more of one than I am." She took another drink of wine and passed the glass to him. "I hoped Malcom would make friends at Harrow. But he still seems on his own much of the time."

"Not necessarily a bad thing." He took a sip of wine. "I was much the same myself. Which may not be a recommendation. He's close to David Mallinson. Who seems far more sensitive than his father."

"Yes, David's an outlier in the Mallinson family, from what I can tell. I suspect he'll have a hard time dealing with Hubert's expectations. Whereas Malcolm—"

The unspoken words hung in the air.

"Would it have been easier with Alistair if I'd stayed away?" The words caught in his throat.

"No." Arabella turned to him, face unexpectedly soft. "Alistair knew before Malcolm was born. He was never going to see Malcolm as his. You give Malcolm someone who cares about him. There's nothing to regret in that." She folded her arms over her bare chest. "In truth, Alistair is a challenging father to Edgar. Edgar never quite seems to meet his expectations. It may be easier on Malcolm that they don't have a closer relationship." She frowned. "Alistair doesn't have expectations about Gisèle. That makes it easier."

Raoul studied her in the gathering light. She'd never revealed who Gisèle's father was. Though she didn't flaunt her affairs, she didn't go out of her way to hide them. So whatever entanglement had led to her youngest child's birth was something she had her reasons for keeping secret.

"Fanny's had a hard time disentangling herself from Prinny," Arabella said. "Personally, I can't begin to see the attraction, even if I'm not as much of a revolutionary as you. But I suppose being the Prince of Wales's mistress—one of his mistresses—is another sort of avenue to power. Honestly, my sister could achieve a great deal if she just focused a bit more."

"Fanny's always been clever."

"She told me the last time I saw her that it was harder and harder to find someone who amused her. I must say, I take her point. Present company excepted."

"Thank you."

Arabella leant over and kissed him. "You're an exception to just about everything. Don't worry so much, Raoul."

"Is that what I'm doing?"

"It seems so. Children do better when one doesn't fuss too much. I can't imagine you liked being fussed over."

"No." Though he had liked his mother's presence. He could have done without his father's, but that was because of the man his father had been. "But there's a difference between being fussed over and being present." He said it carefully, because with Bella he had learnt to be wary of pushing.

"I'm better at it in short bursts." Arabella pushed her hair back from her face. "I can dazzle for a few hours or days. Then I need time to recover. Better they see me in the dazzling moments."

"One might suggest they should know their mother in all her facets."

"Perish the thought. I wouldn't wish that on anyone. I drive you mad enough, and you're an adult." She pulled the shawl round her. "The children are perfectly well cared for. Better than I could manage. They'll understand when they're older."

"I think any parent can't help but hope for that. If Malcolm understands and accepts me, I will be very grateful." Of course, Malcolm probably wouldn't know Raoul was his father. Not in so many words, at least. Not unless Bella told him. Raoul couldn't take that action on his own. She had set the terms of Malcolm's childhood very clearly. And given the situation for a married woman, he had to abide by her decision.

"He's quite good at codes," Arabella added. "Almost frighteningly so."

"Yes, for all he loves history and books, he's always had an affinity for maths as well."

"I wouldn't be surprised if he ends up an agent."

"God, I hope not."

Her brows rose. "You don't want him to take after you?"

"Into a life of compromises and twisted loyalties? My god, no. And then there's the not insignificant fact that we'd be on opposite sides."

Arabella's eyes widened, then narrowed. "I'm not used to thinking of it that way. It's a game. There are different sides of the chessboard. More than two—an octagon might be more appropriate than a square."

"So it is. But as mutable as sides and loyalties are, they exist.

And I have no desire to find myself on the opposite side from my son."

The words hung in the air like frost. Or cannon smoke. He almost never called Malcolm his son. At least not out loud.

Arabella inclined her head. "In the future—"

"I'll still be Irish and Spanish and connected to France. He'll still be British. Certain things aren't going to change."

"The war can't go on forever. In my parents' day, they and their friends went back and forth between London and Paris all the time. Don't you want a life of adventure for Malcolm?"

"I want Malcolm to be happy."

"What on earth does that mean?"

"Different things to different people. I hope Malcolm can work it out for himself."

Arabella reached for his hand. "I'm sorry."

"For what?"

"You tried to get away from me and have a normal life."

"Ha. Yes, one of my more misguided moments. I'm not sure how I ever imagined that anything about my life could be normal."

"You're better suited to it than I am, I think."

"If so, I was ruined long ago." He turned her hand over in his own. "I've made mistakes. More than I can count. They aren't your fault."

"No, I have my own mistakes." She gripped his fingers. "Some-times I think I should stay away from you."

"We both tried that. It didn't work."

She looked into his eyes, her own unusually open. "I couldn't have managed it, you know. And I don't mean the scandal and being poor. I wasn't suited to that life."

She meant being a family. In a garret in Paris or on the edge of Lake Como. For anything more than a few weeks.

He lifted her hand and kissed her palm. "I've learnt to take what I can get."

"Try to enjoy the dazzling moments. You get more of them

than most people. You're better off without me the rest of the time."

He tightened his grip on her hand. "Never."

"Don't think I'm not grateful for the rescuing. But you've never been able to control what I do." Her shawl slid down, revealing the curve of her shoulder and the dark gold hair tumbling down her back.

He almost caught her to him and pulled her back into the pillows. Instead, he said, "Do you know Reynald St. Pierre?"

Arabella settled back against the headboard beside him. "What on earth brought him up?"

"Someone mentioned him recently. He's in the French ministry of police, apparently."

"Yes, he went back to Paris. The rest of the family are still in London. The Vicomte de St. Pierre and my mother knew each other. The vicomtesse is English and some sort of very distant cousin of ours. But I never found the family that interesting. And Reynald was quite impossible. He couldn't bear being an exile."

"It's not easy being an exile. But I imagine it's not easy for him now back in Paris, away from his family. Someone thought he might be a British agent."

"Interesting. I was surprised when he went back to Paris. There was an English girl he wanted to marry, but her parents wouldn't give their consent. Not surprising. The St. Pierres fled without anything, and he was a younger son. I suppose at that point he felt he had nothing to stay in England for."

"Who was she?" Raoul asked. "The girl he wanted to marry?"

Arabella flicked an end of her shawl over her shoulders. "Oh lord, I don't remember. It seems centuries ago. And I'm not sure I even knew. It was one of those secondhand bits of gossip. Surely he's not important enough to interest you?"

Raoul stretched out an arm and pulled her against him. "You never know what may prove interesting."

CHAPTER 30

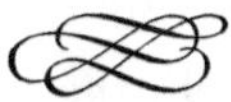

May 1821
London

"Cordy." Frederica Rawdon kissed Cordelia's cheek. She was tall and fair-haired like her mother and younger sisters and, like them, always exquisitely gowned. Today, the day after her father's death, her black bombazine was impeccable and her straw-colored hair elaborately dressed, but her eyes were red-rimmed. Tragedy had a way of stripping away social artifice. And yet Frederica's surface instincts remained. "It's been too long."

"I know." Cordelia squeezed Frederica's hands. "I'm so sorry, Freddie. Your father was always so kind. I was at your parents' musicale not long ago. He was charming that night."

"People always liked Papa." Frederica put a hand to her mouth. "I can't really believe he's gone. I suppose it will settle in. It will have to." She glanced round her sitting room as though it were a foreign country and gestured to the blue and gold striped chairs by the fireplace. "Do sit down. It's kind of you to come. I know it's a bit awkward now to see us."

"Why on earth should it be awkward?"

"I mean with Percy being the cousin of—"

"Oh, stuff." Cordelia seated herself and smoothed the French gray gros-de-Naples of her skirt. "I see Johnny and Violet all the time, and Violet was George's sister. Though I quite understand it might be difficult for *you* to see *me*."

"Don't be silly, darling." Frederica sank into a chair beside Cordelia. "Especially not now. But Colonel Davenport must—"

"Oh, Harry doesn't mind in the least. He's the first to say we have to confront the past and move forwards."

Frederica's fair brows rose. "He sounds remarkable."

"He is. I only wish I'd appreciated it properly sooner."

Frederica scanned her face. "You investigate crimes. With the Rannochs. I heard they were looking into this. Mama said she was pleased. Is that why you're here?"

"Not entirely. I'd have wanted to offer my sympathies. But Harry and I did see the Rannochs last night."

Frederica nodded. "People are bound to ask questions and I'd rather talk to you than others. But I don't think I can tell you anything. Percy and I only just got back from Paris. That's why we weren't at the musicale. We hadn't seen Mama and Papa much since our return. And before we went abroad Papa was abroad himself. He was always away a great deal, and more than ever lately."

"Freddie." Cordelia hesitated. "I don't quite know how to say this. But we've had a report that Percy was heard quarreling with the duke only three nights ago."

Frederica's back straightened. "From whom?"

"I'm afraid I can't say. But I thought you'd rather talk about it to me. Was I wrong?"

"No. But why on earth—"

"You think they did quarrel?"

"I can't be sure. But I think it's possible. We dined at Bamford House three nights ago." Frederica pressed her hands over the dull black fabric of her skirt. "Cordy, your marriage seems happy now, but it can't be a shock to you that couples don't always share everything."

"Certainly not. Harry and I are happy, but we certainly don't share everything."

The door opened on her words. Percy Rawdon stepped into the room, then hesitated on the threshold. "Cordy."

Cordelia met his gaze. He was heavier than she remembered, but his curling dark hair and blue eyes were the same, as was his general air of self-satisfaction. "It's been a long time, Percy. I'm sorry it took tragedy to bring us back together."

"Terrible business. If—"

"Percy." Frederica's voice was sharp. "Did you quarrel with Papa the night we dined at Bamford House?"

"What?"

"Oh, don't deny it. You were overheard."

Percy's gaze snapped to Cordelia. "That's why you're here."

Frederica's gaze swung to her husband. "Better she's here than a Bow Street officer."

Percy stalked across the room, poured himself a brandy, downed half the contents. "It's a family matter. You should appreciate that, Cordy."

"Unfortunately, it stopped being a family matter when the duke was murdered," Cordelia said.

"You can't think this has anything to do with his being murdered. That was obviously the act of some deranged lunatic."

"Whoever was behind it, I don't think they were deranged. There was obviously a great deal of careful planning involved."

"But it wasn't anything to do with us."

"When someone is murdered, everything about them becomes important. You don't know what detail could lead to another detail."

"You're an expert on it now?"

"Not really. But I have learnt a lot from the Rannochs. And Jeremy Roth."

"The upstart runner who married Fanny Dacre-Hammond's daughter?" Percy demanded.

"He is married to Judith. But more important, he's a brilliant investigator."

"Percy," Frederica said. "You're not answering."

Percy slammed his glass down, spattering brandy, refilled it, downed another swallow. "Do you have any idea how expensive it is to live in these circles? Not just the London house, the country one, the shooting box, school fees, the race horses. Frederica's dressmaker alone—"

"Don't put this on me," Frederica said. "I have a perfectly good allowance."

"Not to cover everything for all of us."

"As a matter of fact, I do know," Cordelia said. "My father was horribly in debt. For all the reasons you describe. But more because of gaming."

"Mmm," Frederica said, gaze on her husband.

"All right." Percy picked up his brandy and took a more measured sip. "A fellow has to keep up appearances. The crowd I run with has dipped deep since university."

Frederica was staring at her husband. "You asked Papa for money?"

"Well, who else was I supposed to go to? You know my family haven't a feather to fly with."

"You asked him *again*?"

"Damn it, he's your father. He should want his daughter and grandchildren taken care of."

"Did he refuse?"

"Yes. Well, not precisely. He said he'd pay the boys' school fees and any of your bills I forwarded. But he wouldn't give me another 'carte blanche', as he called it, and he wouldn't pay any more gaming debts. As if he didn't know those are the debts one can't get out of paying. The rest we could put off. As long as needed, really."

"How charming for people you owe money to," Cordelia said.

Percy shot her a look. More surprised than annoyed. It was, she supposed, not the way she should talk to get him to confide more. Regrettably.

"So that's why you quarreled," Frederica said. "Because Papa wouldn't pay your debts." She stared at her husband, horror gathering in her gaze. "And now he's gone—"

"No." Percy clunked down his glass and took a quick step towards her. "It wasn't like that. He did refuse to cover my debts, but that wasn't when we quarreled. I mean, that wasn't the worst quarrel. The one three nights ago. I still had hope that night. I went to talk to him when we arrived for dinner. I was waiting in the library and the door to his study was ajar. So I went in. I mean, I knew that's where he'd go, so it seemed I might as well wait for him there."

"Percy." Frederica regarded her husband like one opening a wall and discovering rot has gone further than they had thought. "You went through Papa's papers."

"No. I mean, the truth is he keeps better liquor in the study. I went in to pour myself a drink. I told myself it was the least he owed me. And damn it, there were papers lying about on his desk. Didn't seem any harm in wandering over and taking a look. Can't believe he left such things just lying about."

"Nor can I," Cordelia said. "The duke was a skilled agent. If you were able to find anything in his desk, I can't believe picked locks weren't involved. I never knew you were so enterprising, Percy."

"Oh, well. One learns a bit, after all. Don't mean to brag, that is—" Percy broke off, perhaps aware of just how much she'd tricked him into saying. He moved back to the drinks table and picked up his brandy. "In any case, that's when I stumbled across Sophie."

"Sophie?" Frederica said.

"Papers about a Sophie. He's been paying money to her for years. Since 1815, at least. Regularly. He has money set aside for her. I mean, hardly a shock the old boy has a mistress—sorry, Freddie."

"Oh, for god's sake, Percy. It's hardly a shock you have a mistress. Next you'll be saying it's a shock I have a lover."

Percy stared at her. Even Cordelia was startled. Not at the words, but at Frederica's uttering them. She was more interesting than Cordy had realized.

"We're rather beyond pretending," Frederica said. "And Cordelia's scarcely in a position to cast aspersions."

Cordelia reached for her tea. "Very true."

Percy stared at his wife a moment longer, as though she'd transformed into another person, then reached for his brandy. "But obviously Bamford was at pains to keep this Sophie a secret. So when he came in at last, it seemed worth a try."

"What did?" Frederica asked.

"Seeing if he was willing to pay up, to keep the secret of this Sophie, of course."

"Of course," Cordelia said. "Why didn't our minds go there at once? And was he?"

Percy frowned into his brandy. "Well, at first he lost his temper. Called me all sorts of foul names. I actually thought he might plant me a facer. That must be when we were overheard. But then he told me not to breathe a word of this. And that we'd work something out."

"So he gave you the money?" Frederica said in a voice stripped of color.

"Not then, but I was quite sure he was going to." Percy took a drink of brandy and smiled at them with confidence. "So you see I'd have had no reason to hurt your father. He was going to help me."

"Quite, Percy." Frederica, who had hardly seemed to have illusions about her husband, regarded him as a particularly loathsome form of insect.

Percy's brows drew together again. "In fact, now he's gone I'm in the deuce of a mess. I don't suppose St. Ives—"

"Oh for god's sake, Percy," Frederica said. "St. Ives has enough to deal with. Don't you dare make things worse."

Percy clunked his glass down. "This is your life too. Your expenses. Your gowns and the house and your pin money."

"My pin money comes from my portion. I'll talk to Mama when she's had a bit of time. I'm sure she'll cover the boys' school fees and give me something for the housekeeping. But your debts are your problem."

"I'm your husband."

"Don't remind me."

Percy reached for his glass. "This Sophie must be important. St. Ives is going to have to deal with her now if she makes trouble. Which she might, if her money stops coming in. St. Ives won't want a scandal as he settles into the dukedom. I wonder—"

Frederica pushed herself to her feet. "Don't. You. Dare."

Percy returned her gaze for long moment. Frederica didn't give way. Percy turned on his heel and stalked out of the room.

Frederica strode to the table, poured two more brandies, and held one out to Cordelia. "I imagine you could do with this. I know I could."

Cordelia accepted the glass. "I'm so sorry."

Frederica took a drink of brandy. "I knew my husband was a beast and a boor. I just didn't know how much of one. What on earth was I thinking when I tied myself to him?"

"What are any of us thinking at eighteen or nineteen or twenty? I certainly wasn't thinking when I married Harry. I'm fortunate in how it turned out."

"I don't trust him." Frederica took a drink of brandy. "I don't trust anything he says."

"I can't say I'm inclined to, but I'm not sure he'd have made the Sophie story up. Had you ever heard of her?"

"Had I ever heard of a mistress of my father's?"

"Well, I knew about a few of my father's. One hears the servants gossiping."

"I've been out of the house for years. Of course, I'm hardly surprised that Papa—and really, why would it be such a secret? I can't imagine Mama would care very much. It would hardly be a scandal if talk got out about him."

"Perhaps he was worried about Sophie. Perhaps she has a reputation to be damaged."

"I suppose that's possible. But if she's married, why was he supporting her?"

"Not every married woman is comfortably situated."

Frederica frowned over the rim of her brandy glass. "Yes, but do you think her husband knows? No, I take that back. After what we just witnessed, I suspect Percy would be all too ready to take money from a lover of mine. Although you'd think in that case Papa and this Sophie would have been less concerned about being discovered. And Papa must have been concerned indeed if he was ready to pay Percy off to protect the secret of his payments to Sophie."

"There could be other reasons for the payments than that she was his mistress."

Frederica returned to her chair, her face thoughtful. "Someone had Papa killed. I know he was shot, so it isn't just that he was caught in a bad situation. I've been assuming it was something to do with politics. Or all the other things he's involved in that are associated with politics, that no one in the family seems to think I know about. Which is silly. You don't have to actually be dabbling in espionage like Rosy and Sylvie to recognize that it's going on under your nose. But I realize now that we don't know that it's that at all. It could be something personal. It could be people we know."

"Given the life your family lead, it could be political *and* be people you know."

"That's true. But not—"

"I've learnt enough to know one can't be sure of anything in an investigation," Cordelia said. "Or anyone. But I'm not sure Percy would have the ability to have organized the explosion."

Frederica choked on her brandy. "An excellent point. Percy would have a difficult time organizing his cravats. Not that it would ever occur to him to try. I'm not sure how comforting it is that my husband's idiocy may be the best argument against his having murdered my father, but I suppose it is something." She took another sip of brandy. "Do you remember how handsome he was in his Horse Guards uniform?"

"Yes, but having known him since childhood, I don't think I appreciated it."

"To think I fancied myself in love over that. And we accuse gentlemen of being caught by a pretty face. I can't claim Mama or Papa pushed me into it. In fact, Papa asked me if I wanted to wait, as I'd only really known Percy for a season. Papa was quite kind." Frederica hunched her shoulders and folded her arms across her chest. "I suppose I didn't know Papa very well. I mean, one doesn't really know one's parents, does one? Knowing them better seems a rather ghastly prospect."

Cordelia took a sip of brandy. It had been her father's favorite drink. "Well, some people know their parents better than others. I hope my children grow up knowing me. Flaws and all."

"That's an odd way of putting it. I wouldn't have said that about my children. But I suppose—" Frederica stared down at the black bombazine of her skirt, as though surprised to find herself wearing it. "I'm beginning to think I didn't appreciate Papa enough. He always seemed so busy, and yet he did take time to talk to us. He'd ask what we were doing, and want to discuss it. And I'd roll my eyes and want to get on with playing dolls or finishing a watercolor or planning a new gown."

"That's being young."

"Still." She shook her head. "It seems different knowing I'll never see him again."

"There are all sorts of things I never said to my father. You'd think it would make me do better with my mother, but I don't know that it has."

Frederica looked at her. "You're being very kind, Cordy. I know you came here to make inquiries."

"Not just for that."

"I don't think I ever properly appreciated you."

Cordelia smiled. "I'm thinking the same."

Frederica returned the smile. "That's something out of this whole wretched business." She smoothed the black lace on her cuff. "I'm sorry, Cordy."

"For what?"

"For not being more of a support—not being any kind of support at all—when you were going through everything you did."

"You have your position to think of."

"Yes, but what was I really worrying about? I'm a duke's daughter. I was comfortably married, as far as position goes, however uncomfortable a husband Percy is. My daughters were babies. Years before I had to worry about bringing them out. I could have afforded to be kind. I rather think Papa would have been kind. And Mama."

"Your mother invited me to one of her soirées. That was kind."

"I remember. I'm afraid I was surprised she'd done so."

"You needn't apologize. You didn't owe me anything."

"All of this does make one think about people differently. Papa's gone, and suddenly there's so much more I want to know about him. I wish I paid more attention sooner." She reached for her glass, took a sip, and stared into it. "I can't say I really knew my father. And yet I'm quite sure he was a far better man than the man I married."

CHAPTER 31

1802
London

Frances Dacre-Hammond put a hand to her mouth to stifle a yawn. "Sorry, it's not you. I didn't get home until after four. Hetty St. Ives's party was surprisingly lively. I must say, she's a very accomplished hostess. Between that and St. Ives's diplomatic skills, they've quite carved out a place for themselves. Not that they needed to as the heirs to ducal coronets." Frances frowned over her chocolate. "In fact, so many dukes and duchesses don't seem to try."

Raoul smiled. "You have a way with words, Fanny."

"One gets used to observing. Hetty and St. Ives seem to have settled into a comfortable arrangement. I don't think it was ever a love match, but whatever they're up to, they're discreet. And believe me, I had my eye out last night. London needs some new scandal." She sat back on the chaise-longue, gold-rimmed cup cradled in her hand. "Talking of observing, you look a bit haggard. How are you, my dear?"

"I don't have your eternal youth, but I'm surviving. I'm not sure I should expect much more."

"Have you seen Bella?"

He reached for his cup and turned it in his hand. "I thought she was in Scotland."

"She's back. Two nights ago. She didn't write to tell you?"

He took a drink of tea. Hot and astringent. He missed tea sometimes on the Continent. "She doesn't apprise me of all her movements."

"Have you seen Malcolm?"

"I came back for Speech Day."

"It's tomorrow, isn't it?"

"Do you want to come with me?"

"I don't want to spoil it."

"As if you could spoil anything for me."

"I wasn't thinking of you, I was thinking of Malcolm. You don't have a lot of time alone."

"I don't know that that matters to Malcolm."

"Of course it does. He may not know the precise nature of his connection to you, but you've always been special to him. I may not be the most discerning parent, but I do understand that."

"You're kind, Fanny. And quite discerning."

"Those times are what they remember. The special times, just the two of you. At least, that's what I tell myself to make up for the times I'm not there." She frowned into the translucent porcelain of her cup. "Though I'm rather coming to the conclusion that I'd prefer to be there more often. I find I laugh more in the nursery than I do at the latest gossip."

"Some of my most sensible conversations are with Malcolm." Raoul set his cup down. "Do you think he's happy at Harrow?"

"He has David Mallinson. Sometimes all it takes is one good friend. And he likes visiting the Mallinson family. Whatever I think of Hubert and Amelia, I have to admit there's more affection in the family than in his own."

Raoul reached for his cup again. He had to do something to cover the tumult of his thoughts. He knew his son was growing up in a world that in many ways was the enemy of everything he was working for. But that was one thing. That Malcolm was finding refuge in the home of an enemy spymaster was something quite different.

Fanny watched him. "Whatever you think of Hubert's politics, at least he and Amelia are an example of a happy marriage." She frowned. "Odd that I'm wanting to give happy examples of the married state. Or rather, odd that I like the idea of the children seeing it as something agreeable. Considering what I've made of it myself. Not that I'd precisely say I'm unhappily married. Dacre-Hammond and I have a comfortable understanding. But it's certainly not what I envisioned as a girl. Of course, whose future is what we envision at that age?"

Raoul took a drink of tea. "Mine certainly isn't."

"Didn't you want to change the world even then?"

"Oh, yes." He returned his cup to its saucer with a click. "And I actually believed I could."

~

December 1806
Calais

THE LIGHTS in the tavern were dim and smoky. The dark paneling had worn to a fine patina that soaked up the glow instead of reflecting it. Raoul poured a glass from the bottle of Bordeaux he'd ordered and took a sip. The meeting was risky. More so for Tony than for him. So it had to be urgent.

The door opened, letting in a blast of cold air that carried to the back reaches of the tavern and bringing the smell of brine and tar. A greatcoated figure made his way through the tavern. Without the urgency that would draw attention. He didn't look directly at Raoul, but he made his way to Raoul's table at the back with unerring instinct. Only when he dropped into a chair across from Raoul did he meet his gaze.

"Thank you for coming," Tony said. "I know it was short notice."

"More challenging for you than for me."

Tony shook out of his greatcoat, scattering raindrops on the floor, and accepted the glass of Bordeaux Raoul was holding out. "I have a cover story ready if I need it. I wanted you to hear this at once. And to hear it from me."

Tony's gaze was dark, steady, but weighted with the grief of one bearing bad news. It was worse than Raoul had feared. Because that look and tone spoke of grave news that was personal, not political. Which could only mean one of two things. "Bella?" he said. Please god it wasn't Malcolm.

Tony's fingers curled round his glass, not quite steady. "I'm sorry."

"How did she do it?" He didn't need to ask if she'd succeeded this time. From Tony's look, he knew.

Tony's knuckles whitened round the glass. "It was an accident with a pistol. At Dunmykel."

The world before him swam to the red of the wine. All these years. All the fearing, intervening, wondering. Pulling her out of the water. Taking the knife from her hand. Talking her through the night. The threat always there at the back of his mind. For a moment, he thought he was going to seize the table and smash it onto the tavern floor. But he didn't. He'd learnt control. "Malcolm—" he said, his voice rough.

"He was at Oxford, apparently, though he's gone to Dunmykel. Edgar was with her when it happened."

"At Dunmykel?"

"In the room, apparently."

"Christ. And Gisèle?"

"She was at Dunmykel. Fanny's gone to Dunmykel. The duke as well."

"Poor Strathdon. No one should have to bury a child." Raoul swallowed a drink of wine, scarcely aware he'd lifted his glass. "I don't suppose Alistair was there?"

"Not at the time, from what I can make out. Though I imagine he's gone there now."

Because that was what family did when there was a tragedy. They gathered together. Even a man like Alistair, who had been as estranged from Bella as it was possible for two people to be and still be married. But Raoul couldn't go anywhere near Dunmykel. The last thing the family needed was tension, the risk of scandal. He was merely a family friend who could write a concerned letter and offer his condolences. To Strathdon, Bella's father. To Fanny, her sister. To Malcolm, her son and his own. He knew how to play that role. It was the role in Bella's life he'd been assigned long ago.

"It could have really been an accident," Tony said.

"I'm sure it wasn't. I stopped her from similar attempts more than once. Others did as well." Raoul reached for his glass. It tilted in his fingers, splashing wine on the table. "She can't—couldn't bear being out of control. I was always afraid one day it would be too much." Memories rose up, choking his senses. The scent of her skin, the feel of her hair through his fingers, the sound of her laugh. The sparkle in her eyes when she turned her head to look at him over her shoulder. "I should have—"

"My dear fellow." Tony's hand closed on his arm. "I don't pretend to have understood Lady Arabella. But I do know one person can't be responsible for another's happiness. And that loss tends to bring guilt and a thousand questions of what one might have done differently. It did as much when my father died, though we were never particularly close."

Raoul drew in his breath with a rough scrape, forcing every-thing back to a place where he could look at it later. Sometime.

When he had world enough and time. "You're a good fellow, Tony. You had no need to risk so much to bring me this."

"It's what friends do. Stand in when their friends need them."

"Is that what we are? Friends?"

"Don't you think the word applies after all this time?"

"Yes. Though I've got out of the habit of admitting I have friends."

"I can't say it's a word I use often either. But somehow I think we know who they are." He scanned Raoul's face. "If you want me to take messages—"

"Yes, I'd like to write to Fanny. And Malcolm. Fanny can deliver that. I should send something to Strathdon as well." At least with Fanny he could be open about what he felt. To a degree.

Tony nodded. "I'm sure it will mean a lot."

"It will be woefully inadequate and they'll be feeling too much to really focus on it. That's how it was for me when my mother died. But it's better than nothing. It saves me from feeling entirely helpless. And hopefully at some point it will mean something to them that someone reached out."

Tony inclined his head. "I can't imagine how it feels. To lose someone one loves that much."

Raoul dragged his glass closer and forced down a sip. "No?"

Tony met his gaze. "I haven't lost her. Or at least, she's still here. I have no illusions as to what the future holds."

Raoul set his glass down. Before he smashed it on the floor. "I think we all have illusions. That's the only thing that makes life bearable."

~

1811
Brooks's, London

"I FORGET," Raoul said, dropping into a leather-covered chair. "How distinctive a London club feels. I think I could close my eyes and know where I was just from the smells of tobacco and port and old leather."

"Clubs have their uses." Archie Davenport folded his copy of the *Morning Chronicle*. "No one's inclined to bother one."

Raoul scanned his friend's face. "What is it?"

Archie set the paper on the table between them. "Harry's joining up."

No wonder Archie looked so concerned. "I thought he was dedicated to classical studies." Raoul had often regretted that Malcolm didn't have a similar interest to consume him.

"He wants to get out of the country. You've been away, you probably haven't heard the gossip. Cordelia's left him. Run off with her old love, George Chase."

Raoul had an image of Harry Davenport on the edge of a ball-room, gaze fixed on his beautiful wife. "I'm sorry. That must have been a wrench."

"But not surprising, you're thinking? I was concerned when they married. Difficult when one person's head over heels and the other isn't."

"I know a bit about that." Raoul settled back into the soft leather. One was scarcely aware of the hard wood beneath. "Or least about the imbalance."

Archie nodded. He'd seen too much with Bella to ask questions. "But it was what Harry wanted. And I hoped with time—she's a brilliant woman and quite courageous. At first, I thought she might be trying to get Harry's attention. And I still wonder—but in any case, it's come to a separation. I've told Harry I'll help with his commission. It's what he wants. He's set on it, in any case." Archie met Raoul's gaze for a moment. "This changes things when it comes to anything to do with the Peninsula."

"Naturally."

Archie's gaze skimmed over his face. "It hasn't necessarily changed for you when it comes to—"

"When it comes to Malcolm?" Raoul shifted in the chair, exerting every effort of will to keep his fingers easy on the arm instead of digging his nails into the leather. "It's different. He's not fighting. He's not in danger most of the time. And you and I began this differently."

"Meaning my commitment wasn't the same as yours?"

"I can't speak for you, but it seems to me you started because you saw injustice and wanted to help. Which is nothing but commendable."

"And you didn't?"

"I started sooner. I suppose I feel—I have more obligation. We all have different loyalties."

"That's rot, O'Roarke. You can't tell me you aren't loyal to Malcolm."

"No. There are different ways of defining it. I've often thought you tumbled into more than you bargained on. And had the grace not to back out."

"I found something of meaning after years of being an idle fribble." Archie eased his bad leg out in front of him. "I'm not walking away. Just telling you I'll have to be careful. Have to balance things."

"Which we all do."

Archie pushed himself to his feet, crossed to a table with decanters, poured two glasses of port, and gave one to Raoul. "You told me once that the most helpful thing I could do was perhaps to sit and listen to him. I've tried to remember that. Tried to remind myself that I can't fix everything, no matter how strong the urge." He dropped back into his chair and took a drink of port. "Can't fix anything, for that matter. But it's damnable. Watching him make decisions. Watching Cordelia make them. Thinking that a nudge to one side or the other might make all the difference."

"Things can still change," Raoul said. "God knows I've seen that in my own life. I thought Bella and I were finished more times than I can count. And for what it's worth, from what I've seen of Lady Cordelia, I don't think she's an Arabella."

"No. Though just as unsatisfied, in many ways." Archie frowned into his glass. "If I thought she'd be happy with Chase, I'd think it was for the best. But I don't think she will be. That could be my delusions again."

"From my experience, you're a good judge of character. And not prey to delusions."

"We're all prey to delusions, at times." Archie took a drink of port. "All I can do is try to make sure the scandal isn't too bad for Cordelia. Harry's ready to give her a divorce. We'll see if Chase goes through with a divorce himself. Either way, it won't be easy for her. Would have been easier in our day, in some ways. People are more inclined to moralize these days. But there are things I can do. As to Harry—" He stared into his glass. "I only hope he's enough of a cynic not to try to be a hero."

"I can't tell you how many times I've thought the same about Malcolm." While at the same time desperately wanting his son to have something to keep him going. Arabella had shown them both what despair could lead to.

Archie nodded. "You've taken the time to come to see me. Can I do anything?"

"I don't need an excuse to see you. But—what do you remember about Vincent St. Pierre?"

Archie grimaced. "Tiresome fellow. Every conversation turned to complaints. It was a distinct relief when he went back to Paris. I'm sorry if you have to deal with him now."

"He was apparently feeding information to the British when he went."

"Interesting." Archie's gaze narrowed. "So that means—"

"Now he's feeding information to me. Has been for the past

decade. Under duress, but I think he likes keeping a hand in anywhere he might curry favor."

"That fits what I remember of him." Archie reached for his port. "Why bring this up now?"

"He's been pushing lately. Wanting to be paid more. I think he's worried about which side will prevail, and where it will leave him. I wouldn't be surprised if he tries to become a triple and report back to the British." In fact, Raoul knew from Tony that St. Pierre had tried to do just that.

"Careful," Archie said. "Those who bend with the wind can be the most likely to blow you over along with themselves."

Raoul reached for his own glass. "Don't I know it."

CHAPTER 32

May 1821
London

Danielle Darnault stepped into the small basement room, careful not to make the boards creak. "I'd forgot how exhilarating a mission can be."

"I'm sorry." The woman sitting on a straight-backed chair at the gateleg table in the room got to her feet. "I didn't want to complicate your life."

"It's complicated enough, in any case. I don't like things simple." Danielle set the hamper she'd brought on the table. It was her second visit today and she doubted it would be her last. "I'd have brought more, but I didn't want to look too obvious."

"You have a cosy nest in Britain."

"And I appreciate it. More than I ever thought I'd appreciate anything approaching domesticity. But that doesn't stop me from being restless. Oh, not with Pierre. Not with Ilia." Danielle noted a doll that was lying on the sofa in the corner. She should bring some toys when she returned. "But there are times I do quite long to go on a mission, even a simple one. Or shock someone just for the rush of freedom."

"I understand the feeling. Though right now I have enough adventure."

"Are you safe here?"

"For the moment. But I need information. I don't have as many connections in London as I do in Paris. Not that I'd do well in Paris at this point." She was silent for a moment. "You're quite tactfully not mentioning all the things people are saying about me."

"It wouldn't really help the situation. And I doubt you'd tell me the truth if you did have things to hide."

"Probably not. A reputation for ruthlessness has got me quite far. I shouldn't sacrifice it now."

Danielle opened the hamper. "A number of people I know are looking for you."

"I have enough sources to understand that."

Danielle took a bottle of wine and a corkscrew from the hamper. "I'm amazed at the friends I've made here. But sometimes older loyalties come first." She uncorked the wine and pulled two glasses from the hamper. "Tell me what you need."

"I wish I could help." Sandy Trenor regarded Mélanie across the marble table in the Berkeley Square library.

"I know the feeling," Laura said.

Mélanie set her bonnet and reticule on the library table and looked between them. She had returned to Berkeley Square to see the children and check if anyone had come back with news, but the rest of the team were all still out gathering information. "I'm not sure what to do next myself. My own contacts in the Duke of Bamford's world are limited. Though I did manage to locate his mistress. Who apparently is his mistress in name only."

"Interesting." Laura raised her brows. "Bamford meant a great deal to Raoul, I think. But I'm certainly feeling that I don't have contacts to help with this. As I said to Raoul last night, it's a story from the first act and I came in late in the third."

Mélanie touched Laura's arm. Laura was a brilliant strategist, but if Mélanie and Malcolm found Raoul an enigma, it must be even more challenging for his wife.

Sandy was frowning at the gnarled branches of the plane trees in the square garden outside the library windows. "I have less knowledge than anyone. But I suppose I can't help but think I should be able to help because you saw the duchess at my parents' house last night."

"How well did you know the duke?" Mélanie asked.

"Not well. That is, the duchess and my mother were childhood friends, but I can't claim to know any of my parents' friends well. There was a firm line between the nursery and the rest of the house in our household. Quite unlike here." He looked towards the garden again, where his wife Bet—who was the reason he was estranged from his parents—had taken the children to play. "The duke was always kind," Sandy added. "Used to ask after my studies. I was afraid he considered me an idle fribble. Which I suppose I was until I met Bet and went to work for Malcolm."

"You're anything but a fribble, Sandy," Mélanie said. "And honestly, you can be a great help by making sure Malcolm doesn't neglect anything he needs to do for Parliament while he's consumed with the investigation. Perhaps—"

She broke off as the door opened and Valentin, their footman, stepped into the room. "The Countess Lieven, Mrs. Rannoch."

The Russian ambassadress stepped into the room. She was exquisitely clad in a bronze-green velvet pelisse and high-crowned bonnet, but her gaze, which could dominate any ballroom, darted round with uncertainty.

"Dorothea." Mélanie quickly assumed the Mayfair hostess

manner she seldom wore these days. Though she already knew this was no ordinary Mayfair call.

Dorothea cast a quick glance round the group in the library.

"Countess Lieven." Laura smiled. "Please forgive me, I need to assist Mrs. Trenor with the children in the garden. And I believe Mr. Trenor has work to do for Mr. Rannoch."

"What? Oh, yes. Definitely." Sandy sketched a bow to the countess and withdrew to Malcolm's study. Laura nodded and went into the hall.

Mélanie smiled at Dorothea and gestured to the fireplace furniture grouping with the Queen Anne chairs and the sofa and settee, where conversation felt more intimate. She had seen the ambassadress navigate any number of situations, from a diplomatic uproar at her dinner table to an interloper at Almack's, where she held court as one of the patronesses. But she had never seen Dorothea look so uncertain as she did now. Or so afraid.

Dorothea moved to the fireplace and then hesitated. "Mrs. O'Roarke was kind. As was Mr. Trenor. Every instinct tells me I shouldn't be here."

"You're welcome to leave. I won't press you. I don't even know enough to try to learn why you came here. But my every instinct tells me you're too capable to have come here without good reason."

"You are far too insightful. As always. Pour me some of that brandy. I'm going to need it."

Mélanie poured two glasses from the decanters on the drinks cart, and put one in Dorothea's hand. Dorothea's fingers felt cold when she brushed against them.

Dorothea took a deep drink and moved to one of the Queen Anne chairs. "I know you can't promise to keep this to yourself. You're too sensible to try to say so, and I hope you have too much appreciation of my own understanding to think that I would believe it, if you tried. So I can only ask you to treat this with the caution you would give to anything delicate. Because I am probably committing treason."

Mélanie's fingers froze on her glass. "Dorothea—"

Dorothea put up a hand. "Don't warn me. I know what I'm doing. It's a delicate business sharing political secrets. And yet it's the currency of our lives." She took a drink of brandy. "You're looking into the Duke of Bamford's murder."

Mélanie no longer attempted to deny their investigations. Especially those like this one, sanctioned, or at least encouraged, by elements in the government. Their role, and that of their friends, was known and even in accepted, in that odd way the British ton accepted eccentricity in their own ranks. "We are. Though, so are Bow Street."

"Meaning Jeremy Roth, who is one of you."

"Jeremy Roth is very much his own person."

"He's now married to Judith—who, from what I've seen, can wrap him round her little finger—and very much part of your family."

"But then our family don't always agree. As you must know." That was perhaps skating on thin ice. Dorothea didn't know Mélanie had been a French agent. At least, Mélanie profoundly hoped she did not.

"And yet you all work together." Dorothea took a drink of brandy, as though fortifying herself. "I'm not asking you to share your discoveries, but I assume you don't yet know who killed Bamford?"

"We aren't anywhere close."

Dorothea nodded. "As I expect you know, Castlereagh wanted Bamford to handle the Naples situation, and Bamford had been asking uncomfortable questions."

"Such as what the Austrians meant to do with those they arrested? Or what they were doing at all?"

"Don't be difficult, Mélanie. Bamford wasn't a Radical, by any means. But he didn't always toe his government's line. And that had happened more, of late."

"What else do you know about him?"

Dorothea shifted in her chair. "You mean that he was an agent? Well, yes. But the line between diplomat and agent is always blurry. You should know that better than most."

"There are degrees."

"Quite."

Dorothea set down her glass and tugged off her gloves. "Metternich quite admires you, you know."

Mélanie set down her own glass. She had seen a great deal of Prince Metternich, Austria's foreign minister, in Vienna, but she hardly considered him an ally. "You shock me. Though he was faultlessly polite, I always thought he considered Malcolm and me a nuisance. Or dangerous. Or both."

"Oh, he thinks you're dangerous. You, in particular. Because you're so capable. He's also expressed that you'd be a powerful ally, if we could get you on our side. Which I've suggested is not likely to happen."

"Define 'side.' As Raoul says, there are multiples of them."

"Yes, Metternich does have a tendency to divide the world up too neatly into sides." Dorothea's cool voice warmed with affection. Not surprising, considering her own long-term relationship with Prince Metternich. "But the world he wants is a world you'd live comfortably in."

"The question is, who else would?"

"I thought you'd say that." Dorothea raised a brow as she reached for her glass. "It sounds charming, and completely ignores reality."

"Whose reality?"

Dorothea took a sip of brandy. As though she had finally come to the point and was steeling herself. "These aren't just my secrets. But they need to be shared. Metternich trusts me, and I trust him.

We've achieved a great deal for our countries through that trust. He is trying to achieve a great deal right now."

"He's trying to shift the balance of power on the Continent."

"Yes, I know I can't convince you of the dangers of the rabble in Naples. Or Spain or Portugal or anywhere else. But Austria's and Russia's relations with Britain are more precarious than at any time since Bonaparte's fall. And Metternich needs Britain's support."

"To walk all over the Continent?" Mélanie asked.

"To protect the order in Europe. I don't ask you to agree with me, I only say as much for the context." Dorothea took another drink of brandy. "The British are hostile to the alliance between Austria and Russia. And Prussia."

"The British don't like the idea that Austria—and Russia and Prussia—can intervene wherever they want."

"No, the British would prefer to do the intervening themselves."

"I won't argue with you there." Mélanie took a sip from her own glass. It was French brandy, laid down by Alistair Rannoch, Malcolm's putative father, in the days before Napoleon Bonaparte had risen to power.

"It's a particularly delicate time." Dorothea said. "Castlereagh prefers not to get too closely involved. I think he regretted sending his half-brother to Laibach. Which any of us could have said was a mistake."

Lord Stewart (not to be confused with Malcolm's former superior, Sir Charles Stuart, whom she quite liked) was hardly suited to a delicate diplomatic situation. Mélanie still had keen memories of the time he had cornered her in a passage at the British embassy in Paris. "Again, I won't argue with you. Though I think any diplomat would have had trouble pulling off representing Britain at Laibach."

"And there I won't argue with you. Still." Dorothea's fingers tightened round her glass. "As I said, Castlereagh had deputized the Duke of Bamford to communicate with Metternich."

"Yes. We knew that."

"But diplomatic channels were proving cumbersome. Metternich thought a more direct approach was needed."

"He asked Bamford to come to Austria?"

"No." Dorothea took another drink of brandy, then folded her hands round her glass. "He sent someone to meet with Bamford."

"In secret?"

"Even Castlereagh didn't know. Metternich hoped they could make progress in quiet talks."

"Who? Whom did he send?"

"Prince Franz Stroheim."

Mélanie remembered Stroheim from the Congress of Vienna. Young, charming, but more than able in the swirl of intrigues. Several of which had cut uncomfortably close to Mélanie herself. Metternich had obviously trusted him then. And he'd be more senior now. "You're saying the prince is on his way to London? Or—"

Dorothea's gaze was as steady and unblinking as the faceted yellow stones of her earrings. "He just arrived in London. He and Bamford had a private meeting arranged. They were to meet—"

"On—"

"Yes. A ship owned by a wine importing company. One of our attachés had a connection. They thought it was less likely to draw attention."

"But Prince Stroheim never got to the meeting? Or he left before the explosion and fire?"

"I don't know." Dorothea's voice sounded as though the braided collar of her pelisse had tightened round her throat. "No one has seen the prince since last night."

Mélanie sat back in her chair. "Does the Austrian embassy know?"

"They didn't know he was here. Metternich had only written to me."

"Dorothea." Mélanie set her glass on the table beside her chair, careful not to jostle the brandy. "Could Prince Stroheim have attacked Bamford?"

"I don't see why. They didn't know each other well."

"But they'd met? They were both in Vienna at the same time."

"Bamford had been abroad on missions a great deal. It seems more likely to me that the killer attacked both of them."

"But Stroheim wasn't found. And neither was Lord Rothermere."

"Lord Rothermere was there?"

"Not that we know of. But it's his company's ship. And he and Stroheim are both missing."

Dorothea's shoulders tensed, pulling at the frogged bodice of her pelisse. "You understand the risks of my sharing this."

"Yes. Why did you?"

"Because I need to learn what happened to Stroheim. I'm going to have to let Metternich know. If it comes out that an Austrian envoy disappeared while on a secret mission to London, a mission known to the wife of the Russian ambassador, and that his disappearance is connected to the death of a senior English diplomat who is also a duke—the only thing worse than that coming out, is its coming out without my having any answers. I may disagree with you and Malcolm on almost every matter of policy, but I trust you to get answers. Which I desperately need."

Mélanie nodded. "Does your husband know?"

"No. It would be risky." Dorothea took a careful sip of brandy. "It was a risk for me to help arrange this. It was a risk for Metternich to send Stroheim. And it was a risk for Bamford to agree."

"It explains his secrecy about his activities that night. Whom else did Stroheim know in London?"

"Diplomats he'd met in Vienna and other places. For that matter, he knew you and Malcolm." Dorothea hesitated.

"No," Mélanie said.

"Not that you'd tell me, if so."

"Probably not. But it happens to be true. I haven't seen Prince Stroheim in years."

Dorothea nodded and reached for her brandy.

"I realize what a great act of trust this is," Mélanie said.

Dorothea, who did not trust anyone lightly—or at all—in Mélanie's experience, smiled. "In the circumstances. I have little choice."

CHAPTER 33

22 January 1815
Schönbrunn

orchlight glinted off the snow. Sleigh bridles jangled. Gold sphinxes sparkled on sleigh axles. The horses that had drawn the sleighs stood by patiently, plumes nodding on their heads. Guests relaxed against the emerald and sapphire velvet upholstery of the sleighs, or walked about on the snow, sipping spiced wine. Talk and laughter filled the air, along with strains of music from the band that had driven out with the party from the Hofburg Palace, but on the edge of the crowd the world felt still. Mélanie looked up at the clear sky, turning to rose gold as the sun began to set. The velvet hood of her cloak fell back from her head, and she could feel tendrils of her hair escaping their pins. She laughed, caught for a few seconds in the crazy beauty of the moment. The lavishly dressed elite of Europe playing in the snow while deciding the future of millions. Insane. Wrong. Yet the brilliance of the moment could not be denied.

Someone pressed a cup into her hands. "You'll need this to keep warm."

She took a sip of the spiced wine, fingers curled round the metal cup, and smiled at Franz Stroheim. He couldn't be more than a year or two older than her own one-and-twenty. But his eyes had the cynicism of one who had been raised in the old world as it teetered on the brink of falling apart. Along with the exuberance of youth on holiday. "I wish my son was here," she said. "He loves the snow."

"Meaning this is an activity for children?"

"Playing in the snow? Sleigh rides? Fancy dress? Skaters on a frozen lake?" She glanced at the skaters in the guise of Venetian gondoliers, steering sleighs dressed to look like gondolas over the polished surface of the lake by the Schönbrunn Palace. Her son Colin would be entranced.

His blue eyes glinted. "So the Congress is really a game for children?"

"Children whose toys are the population of the Continent."

"You're an insightful woman, Mrs. Rannoch. Most would simply be enjoying the game."

"I saw too much in Spain to think of it as a game." Or so much she couldn't think of it as anything else and keep her sanity.

His gaze moved over her face. "I keep thinking you look familiar. Perhaps we met in France?"

She was used to such comments. There were easy ways to deflect them. Though the prickle of fear would never ease completely. "I went to Spain as a baby, during the Terror." That was more or less true, though her parents' theatre troupe had performed on both sides of the border. "Unless you've spent time in Spain, it doesn't seem likely we've met." Even as she said it, an image shot into her mind. The garden at Malmaison. She'd been talking with Hortense Bonaparte and Julien St. Juste. A young man in uniform had come up to the group and bowed to Josephine, who was reclining in a chair a little way off. Seemingly inconsequential. Save that, just as a detail in the first act may suddenly seem key as the plot unfolds in the third, she was now sure that young man had been Franz Stroheim.

Better to come up with some excuse to explain it. Yet almost impossible to do so, given the outlines of her supposed life as Suzanne de Saint-Vallier. "My father came from a large family," she said. "I have a number of cousins who remained in France, whom I have never met. But family resemblance runs strong in our family. In fact, I probably have even more cousins than I'm aware of. My grandfather was known for his liaisons."

"That must be it. " He took a sip from his own wine cup. "Are you enjoying Vienna?"

"It's a beautiful city." She glanced towards the band, playing an Italian song to go with the gondoliers on ice." And magical to be surrounded by so much music."

"But—?" He quirked a brow. "I sense a but."

"Not about Vienna. I think the city would feel quite different if we weren't at the Congress. The pace is exhausting. It's difficult to find time to breathe."

"I was in Paris until recently, but having been back less than a week, I can fully appreciate that. Not much time to be oneself. Particularly hard, I would think, for one quite newly married."

It was a likely enough comment. No reason to think he was digging for information. "Oh, Malcolm and I've been married over two years. We're quite a settled couple."

"Though you've hardly been able to lead a settled life. You married in Spain during the war, didn't you?"

"In Lisbon, actually. But, yes. We've never had what one could call a home. Fortunately, our son is very adaptable." That was true. So much of what she had said was true. Amazing how often the truth served in the midst of a deception. Yet she couldn't rid herself of the sense that he was probing for more.

"I hope you and your husband have more time with him soon. My apologies for the disruption the city of my birth is causing."

"It's hardly Vienna's fault. And how can one not love—" She

gesture to the snow-dusted landscape, the skaters gliding on the ice, the glittering pile of the palace. "Not to mention the coffee. Especially since we came here after visiting my husband's family in Britain. There's much to love there, but I couldn't get a decent cup of coffee for weeks."

Stroheim threw back his head and laughed. "I think you have a talent for finding humor in any situation, Mrs. Rannoch."

"A necessity of diplomatic life, don't you think?"

"Most definitely." He smiled and extended his hand. "May I escort you to a better view of the skaters? And beg for a waltz at the ball tonight?"

His smile was dazzling. And as she put her hand in his own, she suspected he knew just how to use that dazzling smile for his own ends. What good agent didn't?

"Rannoch." It was Franz Stroheim. A favorite of Prince Metternich's, with a keen mind across the negotiating table. He had an easy smile. "I was just talking with your wife. It seems I may have met one of her cousins years ago at Malmaison."

Malcolm had never heard his wife mention a cousin who might have been at Malmaison. Or any cousin at all. Suzanne rarely talked about her family. Understandably. However their relationship had progressed, there were still things they both kept to themselves. Certainly there were places he wouldn't intrude. And he was grateful she did the same. "My wife left France as a baby."

"Yes," Stroheim said in an easy voice. "And with the war, she wouldn't have been able to easily communicate with any family still there. Especially those at the imperial court. Odd how alliances have shifted through the years. That day at Malmaison I wouldn't have thought to find myself negotiating with British diplomats in the future. At least, not in these circumstances. No offense intended."

Malcolm, grinned. "None taken. I wouldn't have expected it either."

"You're a talented delegation," Stroheim said. "Your colleague was impressive on the ice just now."

One of the younger British attachés had performed an elaborate skating routine and traced the initials of the queens and empresses in the ice. "Some of us have hidden talents," Malcolm said. "I only hope he can make up for the behavior of our ambassador." Lord Stewart, Castlereagh's brother, had drawn up his carriage and blocked the path of the sleighs leaving the Hofburg.

"That was indeed an interesting spectacle," Stroheim said. "I've rarely seen Trauttmansdorff so rattled."

Prince Trauttmansdorff, the Austrian court marshal, had had to personally convince Stewart to move his carriage. "I wish I could say that was unusual behavior for Lord Stewart," Malcolm said. "Unfortunately, it wasn't."

"I imagine he'd had too much to drink."

"That is also not unusual. Castlereagh does not suffer fools gladly, but he's very fond of his brother."

"Families ties are complicated." Stroheim cast a sidelong glance at him. "I've watched you in conferences. You don't always agree with Castlereagh, do you?"

Lord and Lady Castlereagh were talking with Tsar Alexander and his current favorite, Princess Gabrielle Auersperg, who still reclined in their sleigh. "Is it that obvious?" Malcolm asked.

"Only to one who feels the same conflict." Stroheim clasped his hands behind his back. "My father is a diplomat. My course was set without my ever considering it. And I enjoy diplomacy. I enjoy the game, if truth be told. But lately"—he drew in and released his breath. It frosted in the cold air. "Metternich wants to turn the clock back."

"And you don't?"

"No, but even more, I don't think it can be done."

"Nor do I."

"So how do you manage?" Stroheim took a step closer. "Manage to stick by your mission working for a man and policies you disagree with?"

"Not very well, judging by your seeing through me."

"No, you're brilliant at it. You take meticulous notes at endless meetings. You argue points that I'm sure aren't your own."

"It's my job. To make others' arguments. But it's a job I do with increasing self-disgust." Malcolm hesitated. He didn't talk about these issues easily. And Stroheim was the representative of another country's delegation. But something about the raw earnestness of Stroheim's question compelled him to speak. That and perhaps changes in his own thinking. It grew harder and harder to swallow his own thoughts in council meetings. "When I started in the diplomatic corps, I was too numb to do anything but go through the motions." He didn't add that he'd still been recovering from an inexpert attempt to slash his own wrists in the wake of his mother's suicide.

Stroheim watched him. "It can be painful when numbness wears off."

"So it can. But it can also remind one of what it is to be alive. I can't just go through the motions anymore." He glanced towards the lake and spotted Suzanne's gilded sugar plum gown and ivory cloak in the crowd. She was talking with Dorothée Talleyrand and Wilhelmine of Sagan. He looked further and found himself staring at a familiar figure, who lounged like a panther even amidst the snow. He hadn't known Raoul O'Roarke was in Vienna, but he was never surprised to see Raoul anywhere.

"What is it?" Stroheim asked.

"A family friend I've known since childhood. I don't know what he'd think of the choices I've made, given the ideas he discussed with me growing up."

Stroheim followed his gaze. "Raoul O'Roarke?"

"Yes. You know him?" Surprising, for Raoul's work was in Spain, but then Malcolm had long since ceased to be surprised at his wealth of connections.

"He knows my father."

Probably going back to Paris in the '80s and '90s when so much had happened, and which so many of today's alliances and conflicts seemed to go back to. Raoul had some surprising friends, including Lord Liverpool, now the prime minister.

"Is he a friend of your father's?" Stroheim asked.

Malcolm managed not to choke on his spiced wine. "No. Of my mother's." Which was true, on the face of it. And didn't nearly begin to get at a complex tangle he couldn't unravel himself. Secrets he wasn't quite sure he had the right to probe, for all they went to the core of his life. Or at least how his life had begun. After all, there were different things that made a parent. He was Colin's father. Nothing would convince him otherwise.

"He's a fascinating man," Stroheim said. "And a tolerant one. I'm sure he understands the choices you've made. He's not the sort to be judgmental."

"No." But they wouldn't make him proud. Malcolm had never particularly thought about making anyone proud. But it suddenly occurred to him that he would quite like Raoul O'Roarke to be proud of him.

CHAPTER 34

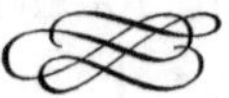

May 1821
London

"Christ," Malcolm said.

He and Raoul had returned to Berkeley Square shortly after Dorothea left, and Mélanie had quickly updated them. She had Dorothea's permission to share the story with the team.

Mélanie leant back on the library settee, where she was sitting beside Malcolm. "I was shocked. But it's the best explanation we have for what Bamford was doing on the ship."

Malcolm scraped a hand over his hair. "If Bamford was meeting secretly with Stroheim, and someone tried to kill both of them, we've gone from murder to international incident."

"I liked Stroheim," Mélanie said.

"You were afraid he knew the truth about you," Raoul said.

Malcolm's gaze shot from Raoul to her. "Stroheim knew the truth about you?"

"I was afraid he suspected. I have no reason to be sure he did."

"You're telling me Stroheim's known who you are since Vienna?" Malcolm persisted.

"We don't know that he ever knew who I was," Mélanie said.

"But you started suspecting it in Vienna."

Mélanie folded her arms. Best to be honest. She should have learnt it was never wise to try to manage Malcolm. "To say I was concerned would be an understatement. But there wasn't a great deal I could do. I told Raoul and we had a plan in place."

Malcolm looked between the two of them again. "What? You running?"

"A story about a by-blow cousin who looked like me."

Recognition lit Malcolm's eyes. "At the sleighing party. Stroheim told me he thought he might have met one of your cousins at Malmaison. I was startled because you'd never talked about cousins. But then there was a lot we'd never talked about."

Mélanie shifted on the settee, curling her feet under her. "I couldn't very well tell you any of it in Vienna, darling."

"And after I knew the truth? Did it occur to you to warn me about Stroheim? Either of you?" His gaze moved to Raoul, who was sitting in one of the Queen Anne chairs.

"Stroheim wasn't in Britain," Raoul said.

"And you were already threatening to have us all run to Italy the moment you heard anything in the least concerning," Mélanie added.

"With good reason," Malcolm said.

"Hubert was good reason," Mélanie said. "Stroheim wasn't. And whatever risk Stroheim may have posed in the past, what matters now is that he's missing in the present."

"We need the others," Raoul said. "Julien in particular. And we need Hubert."

Malcolm frowned. "Are you suggesting—"

"If Bamford was killed because he was meeting with an Austrian representative, and the Austrian representative may have been targeted as well, it's an international incident, as you say."

Malcolm regarded his father. "Raoul, are you saying you want to protect British interests?"

"I've never tried to damage British interests except when the British were trying to interfere with the governments of other countries. And Hubert will have the best idea of who may have been involved in this."

"Unless he was himself," Malcolm said.

"If he was, discussing it may be the best way to gauge his involvement."

"What have we come to?" Malcolm said. "I want to keep secrets from Hubert and you're counseling confiding in him."

"As I've said, a lot shifted at the end of the war."

Malcolm was still frowning.

"Hubert knows about me, darling," Mélanie said. "And about Raoul. Even if Stroheim knew, there's no risk of Hubert's learning anything he doesn't already know."

"It's not that. Just my general wariness when it comes to Hubert."

"We need to learn who killed Bamford," Raoul said. "And to find Stroheim. As soon as possible. I don't want another murder."

"None of us does." Malcolm's gaze settled on Raoul. "You know Stroheim as well."

"And I like him. And he knew Bamford. There's a lot to share. But that should wait until we have everyone here."

CHAPTER 35

22 January 1815
Schönbrunn

"O'Roarke." Malcolm at last managed to make his way to Raoul's side on the edge of the sleighing party. The company were beginning to move into the palace for supper and an opera (a French version of Cinderella, apparently). "I didn't realize you were coming to Vienna."

Raoul smiled, the smile Malcolm remembered from childhood, though it didn't quite seem to light Raoul's eyes the way it once had. "It seems all the world is making its way to Vienna just now. And decisions in Vienna will impact a good portion of the world."

Malcolm tightened his grip on his wine cup. "I'm sorry. I don't imagine you're happy with the outlook for Spain." Though the restored Bourbon King Ferdinand had originally agreed to rule by the Liberal constitution established during the war, he had later abolished it, and seemed set to revive the most repressive measures of the past. Many journalists Malcolm had known during his time in the Peninsula were now imprisoned.

"No. Though I'm not surprised by how things are playing out. Disappointed, but not surprised."

Malcolm took a quick drink of wine. Perhaps he was nearing the dregs. It tasted bitter. "I hope I need not say that my country's opinions are not my own."

"It's a challenge in diplomacy. One's opinions rarely align completely with the official position. I admire you for navigating the challenges."

Malcolm cast a quick look into those keen gray eyes that had meant so much to him. "That's kind of you."

"I didn't say it to be kind."

Memories were thick in the cold air. Memories of a time the world had seemed full of possibilities and Raoul had been the one who would unlock them. Walking by the stream at Dunmykel. Bending over a book together in the library. Sitting across from each other at the Ink & Quill. "I don't imagine this is the future you'd have foreseen for me."

"I never saw any particular future for you, save that I wanted you to be happy."

"I don't know that I'd want Colin to become a diplomat," Malcolm said, and then immediately wondered if drawing any sort of parallel between himself and Colin and Raoul and himself was too much.

Something flickered in Raoul's gaze, but he smiled and said, "Plenty of time for that. He must be quite the young man by now."

"Chattering away. And he can understand us and we can understand him better, which helps."

For a moment, Malcolm saw memories shoot through Raoul's gaze. Raoul took a drink of wine. "It must be exciting to watch one's child master new skills."

"Most people don't put it that way, but yes, it is. He's discovering so much. Unfortunately, the Congress isn't the easiest place to be a family." Funny, that word. He'd never thought to have a family. He wasn't sure he was very good at having one. But he couldn't keep the wonder from his voice.

"The Congress won't last forever. You'll have more freedom then to decide what you want to do. Will you go back to England?"

England. The site of his greatest failure. It had been hard enough to go back for a few weeks, though he'd wanted Mélanie and Colin to see it. And Scotland. He already knew he didn't want Colin to go away to school, but suddenly he wanted to show his son the Ink & Quill. "I'm a diplomat. I'll go where I'm posted. Are you returning to Spain?"

"I don't know." Raoul took a measured sip of wine. "I'm not precisely welcome in certain quarters. And it's not agreeable to see the Bourbons back."

"Things have a way of changing. That's what you always said."

Raoul gave the smile that had comforted Malcolm from boyhood, though it seemed a bit frayed round the edges. "That's what I try to hold on to."

MÉLANIE MOVED THROUGH THE CROWD, laughing, talking, sipping wine, moving on before any conversation became too serious. Typical behavior at a diplomatic reception, even if this one did happen to be outdoors. And all the while, her senses were keyed. Malcolm was talking to Stroheim. And then to Raoul. Which didn't necessarily mean anything. There were a hundred reasons he could talk to both. Stroheim was a diplomatic colleague. Raoul was a family friend. Still—

As the company began to move into the palace, she found herself standing on the edge of the crowd again, without consciously planning to do so. The torchlight caught a blue sparkle in the snow. And a glint of gold. She bent down, careful not to spill her spiced wine, and picked up an oval sapphire pendant set in gold. She'd seen it earlier in the day, half hidden in the folds of her friend Dorothée Talleyrand's cerulean blue cloak. It was a favorite of Doro's, a gift from Prince Talleyrand. But Doro had already gone into the palace. Mélanie turned to follow and heard a familiar voice through the buzz of conversation and lilt of a waltz played by the orchestra. "What is it, *querida?*"

A ridiculous relief washed over her. She took a sip of wine. "Nothing. Or perhaps everything. I realized I met Franz Stroheim years ago. At Malmaison. Or rather, we were both there in the garden at the same time."

Raoul's gaze remained steady in the flickering torchlight. Perhaps only she would have been aware of the shock of alarm that ran through him. "Did he recognize you?"

"He was just aware that he'd seen me in the past. Or thought he'd seen me. I mentioned I have a number of cousins in France. Including some illegitimate ones."

"Clever."

"He may never piece it together. Or he may. He obviously has a keen understanding."

"We'll figure something out if he does."

"What?" She heard her voice sharpen like the wind. "Pull me out?"

"Not unless that's what you want. And I don't think it is."

"Of course not." Mélanie glanced through the torch smoke to where her husband was standing with Adam Czartoryski. "It might be better for Malcolm though."

"You don't mean that."

"No?" She turned her gaze back to her spymaster. "I'm a fake. I'm never going to belong here."

"Do you want to belong?"

"No, of course not." She cast a quick glance from the gilded sleighs drawn up beside the frozen lake to the candlelit palace to the gleaming sapphire that dangled from her fingers. "Sometimes I forget. I sit still for endless minutes while Blanca pins my hair, go to dress fittings, answer cards of invitation, work out seating arrangements. Change my clothes four times a day. It actually starts to seem normal. And then there I am, paying a call or sipping champagne at a reception or standing in the snow drinking spiced wine surrounded by gilded sleighs, and I want to start screaming. I want to smash something or curse or steal something. Anything to prove I'm still alive."

"Do you want to leave?" Raoul asked quietly.

"You don't want me to."

"If you need to for your sanity, of course I do." His voice was level and matter-of-fact, but she felt it like the warmth of a cloak on a cold day.

"What about the mission?"

"If you're this close to breaking, you can't complete the mission."

"So that's what it's about?"

"It's about making sure you can survive."

"So I can go on being an agent."

"So you can be yourself."

She gave a sharp laugh and hugged her arms round herself beneath the velvet of her cloak. A fashionable shade known as Isabella ivory. "I don't know who that is anymore."

"It happens," he said softly. "Undercover. You can't go on if you don't learn to believe the role. If you don't forget it is a role."

"Is that what you did?"

"Sometimes. I've never done this as long as you. What you've managed is remarkable."

"It doesn't feel remarkable." For a moment she was acutely aware of the pins in her hair, the tight lacing of her stays, the scratchy gold net of her overdress. "I'm such a fake I can't believe anyone believes me."

"You make it look effortless."

"I lie awake going over things. Which fork to use, how many

dances to dance, who takes precedence. I'm terrified I'll make a mistake."

"Would that be so bad?"

"*What?*"

Raoul nodded at an Austrian count and countess whose names she couldn't remember, moving past them towards the palace. "Do you think people born to this world never make mistakes?"

"They learn it in the cradle."

"Not all of them. I very much doubt Malcolm would care."

Raoul was usually careful not to talk about Malcolm. So was she. But sometimes she had to. "Malcolm pretends he thinks it's all silly. Maybe he really does. But he doesn't have to think about it. He simply does the right thing. Or if he doesn't, it's a conscious choice."

"Who says if you do it, it wouldn't be?"

"Because it wouldn't be a choice at all. It would be me desperately trying to remember and then forgetting at just the worst moment possible."

"Why does it matter so much?" he asked in a quiet voice.

"Because I don't want to fail."

"At what?"

"At the mission. What else?"

"Most people don't question what they've accepted. They've accepted you."

"Hardly. You should hear the diplomatic wives. Especially the British ones."

"You're accepted as an émigrée aristo. Émigrée aristos have their own challenges to deal with in British society."

"All right, I don't want to disappoint Malcolm. I know that sounds absurd, but I've put him through this. I'm using him appallingly. The least I can do is give him the sort of wife he can be proud of. For as long as things last." She hunched her shoulders beneath her cashmere-lined cloak. "I know that sounds absurd."

"No. It makes a great deal of sense."

Mélanie shook her head. "You're always so sure you understand things. It's very provoking."

"Oh, there are any number of things I don't understand. But I can see a certain shape to the logic of this."

Mélanie glanced at the golden candlelight in the windows of the white palace. "You were born to this world too."

"More or less. It doesn't mean it doesn't drive me to distraction at times."

"You can slip in and out. It's harder being a woman. More constraining."

"Without a doubt. But I very much doubt that a perfect diplomatic wife is what Malcolm wants."

"Malcolm would say he doesn't. But the truth is he doesn't have a clue how much he needs one. To make sure he goes to the right parties and has the right attire and actually talks to people instead of hiding in the library. And if the magic ever faded, if the mask slipped, if he saw the real me, he'd be horrified."

"That I very much doubt."

She stared at him.

"I have known him since he was a boy."

She forgot that sometimes. It was disconcerting. On any number of levels. "Trust me. He may think he's Radical and free-thinking. He may actually be. But that doesn't extend to loving a woman like me. I mean, why on earth would he?"

"My dear girl. The answer to that is blindingly obvious."

"Poor man." She pulled the folds of her cloak close against the chill air. "He could do so much. I mean, he's constrained by the world he's in. But there are things he could do. A lot of them."

"I agree."

"You do?"

"There's more than one way to fight for change."

"Well, I'm not helping him do it."

"No? You just told me you helped him write a speech."

"That's not the sort of help he needs."

"That may not be the sort of help that's valued. Which is a rather different thing."

The line of guests going into the palace had stalled. A crowd clustered by the doors, velvet pelisses and cloaks, caped greatcoats and gold uniform braid shimmering in the torchlight. "The truth is I don't really know who I am anymore. I'll never belong in this world, but I'm not the girl I was when I married him either. You're right, you play the role enough you start to believe it. Perhaps that's why I'm so determined to follow all the ridiculous rules." She shook her head and felt Blanca's careful ringlets stir about her face. "God. I don't want to turn into someone I despise."

"You couldn't."

"What did you do? When you were lost in a role?"

He hesitated. "I suppose I fell back on the mission. But I'm not sure that's always the answer."

"No? The mission is what matters. It's why we're doing this, after all. Why else put—"

"Yourself through it?"

"I was going to say, put Malcolm through it." She looked down at the sapphire pendant. "Doro called me sweet yesterday. Can you believe it? It's the last thing I am."

He gave a faint smile. "I wouldn't say that."

"Don't be silly, Raoul. I'm not a very nice person. What I'm doing now proves it. But then I've always known that." She tightened her fingers round the chain of the pendant. "I can't leave, Raoul. Even if I were in worse shape than I am. I couldn't walk away." She hesitated, drew in her breath, released it. "I can't take Colin away from Malcolm."

"I know." His voice was low and soft.

"I never saw marriage as a tie. I didn't realize parenthood could be."

"Parenthood is a number of things."

"So I have to make this work. I won't let you down."

"*Querida.* There's no way you could let me down."

"Poor Malcolm. His idea of wild is so much tamer than anything I am. And while he's a brilliant agent, I don't think he understands deception on this level. God, I hope he doesn't. I wouldn't ever want him to see that side of me. For his sake as well as mine. I risk destroying him every day."

"There are different types of destruction."

"Just as there are different types of loyalty, as you always say?" She took another drink of wine. It wasn't as warm as it had been. "Don't worry, this isn't the time to indulge in guilt. I need to get through this for the mission. That's what matters."

"*You* matter."

"I'm doing this for the mission. If my scruples were stronger, I wouldn't have done the things that got me here. Sorry to complain."

"My dear girl. We all need someone to complain to."

"Who do you complain to?" The words came out unbidden. It was one of those moments she realized there was so much she didn't know about him, for all they had shared.

"You, on occasion." He turned slightly, his gaze settled on her face, his back not obviously to the crowd, but his expression hidden. "I'll work on a strategy if Stroheim does become a threat. Lay a trail about a Saint-Vallier by-blow who was in Josephine's court. That was a good thought."

"Julien was there. That day Stroheim saw me. We were talking to Hortense."

"That could be helpful."

"Or not. One never knows with Julien."

"He's fond of you."

"There are other words for it."

Raoul gave a faint smile. "Yes, there are. Words Julien wouldn't even use in the private recesses of his mind."

"That's because they apply to things he has no understanding of." Mélanie tossed down a swallow of wine. "He was in Vienna a few weeks ago. I saw him once in a café disguised as a

Cossack, and another time at a ball in the guise of an Austrian lady."

"I caught a glimpse of him tonight. By the lake edge."

Mélanie cast a quick look round the group remaining by the lake. She'd been too busy worrying about Malcolm. The fair-haired lady in the crimson velvet pelisse and the dashing shako was definitely Julien. "Who's he working for now?"

"I'm not sure. I'm not sure Julien is sure. Or rather, he may be playing more than one side against the other."

"He's quite professional about his commitments, though."

"And if he's loyal to anyone, it's Josephine. That extends to Hortense. And to you. I don't think he'll say anything to Stroheim. Even if he has the chance, which isn't likely because Stroheim's unlikely to be able to identify him."

"Unless Julien wanted to make contact. He's quite expert at appearing when he wants to."

"A good point. But I don't see what he'd have to gain from betraying you to Stroheim."

"Difficult to know what Julien ever has to gain, without knowing his goals. Or even who he is."

"No. And I may judge him wrong. But I do think he has limits."

She laughed and nearly spilt her wine. "Maybe. But I'm not sure even you know what they are."

"Oh, I'm not sure I know anything, *querida*." Raoul's gaze stayed steady on her face. "Malcolm may understand more than you realize."

"Raoul. I trust a lot you say. I believe most things you say. But nothing is going to make me believe in fairy tales."

"Pity." He put out a hand as though he was going to touch her cheek, then dropped it to his side. "Occasionally, they come true."

CHAPTER 36

May 1821
London

Hubert Mallinson regarded Mélanie with a surprisingly open gaze. "Do you trust Countess Lieven?"

"In this case, yes," Mélanie said. "Probably more than you trust me."

"Or than you trust me," Hubert said. "And yet, you told me this."

"It was Raoul's idea," Malcolm said.

Hubert transferred his gaze to Raoul. "I'm impressed."

"We needed to know how much you knew."

Hubert gave a faint smile. "Honest, as always."

Malcolm had sent for Hubert, and Raoul had found Julien and Kitty. Laura had made coffee. They were all gathered in the Berkeley Square library where they usually shared information. Save that it was odd to be sharing it with Hubert.

"Did you know?" Julien asked his uncle. "That Franz Stroheim was meeting with Bamford on the ship?"

"Don't you think I'd have told you last night if I had?"

Julien regarded his uncle. "No."

Hubert jammed his hands in his pockets. "Fair enough. I might not have, at that. But I didn't know. According to Countess Lieven, even Castlereagh didn't know. Metternich apparently set this up with Bamford on his own. The perils of civilians taking things in their hands."

"Bamford was hardly a civilian," Raoul said.

Hubert met Raoul's gaze. "No, I suppose not. But worse, he may have been a traitor."

Raoul took a drink of coffee. "He wasn't. Or, if he was, he was betraying Britain with someone other than me. And I didn't know about it, if he was. Not that there isn't a great deal I didn't know about in French intelligence."

"Don't sell yourself short, O'Roarke."

"Well, then."

Hubert took a turn round the hearthrug. "Metternich, who has gone round official British channels more times than I can count, sent Stroheim to meet with Bamford. And I'm very much afraid someone found out and blew up that ship to cause an international incident."

"Who?" Malcolm asked.

Hubert pulled off his spectacles and stared at them for a moment. "The Russians would like to drive a wedge between us and Austria. So would the Prussians, I suspect. And I'm sure there are factions in Austria that would like to do the same." He tugged out a handkerchief and wiped off the spectacles. "Of course, the rebels in Spain and Portugal might like us distracted and at odds with Austria so we aren't tempted to back any moves Metternich makes against them, as he did against the revolutionaries in Naples." He cast a quick glance from Raoul to Kitty. "And conversely, the Spanish Royalists might like us distracted so we're less likely to arm the Argentine rebels. Or it could be English Radicals who don't care for Metternich or Bamford."

"That last is a stretch," Malcolm said.

"Possibly, but not outside the realm of possibility." Hubert jammed his spectacles back over his ears. "The point is really we're spoilt for choice. And whoever's behind it, we need to find Metternich's protégé before Metternich gets wind of this."

"Were Metternich and Bamford close?" Mélanie asked.

"Bamford was a senior diplomat. So they'd dealt with each other scores of times."

Mélanie added more milk to her coffee. "But this was a secret mission to try to win over the British government. Castlereagh doesn't trust Bamford. You've accused Bamford of being too close to the French during the war. You've hinted he might have been a double, though Raoul disagrees. All of which makes him seem an odd choice for a secret mission of this sort. What would have made Metternich think Bamford would be sympathetic?"

Hubert's gaze settled on her. "You think well, Mélanie. It's a good thing you aren't on the opposite side anymore."

"Who says I'm not?" Mélanie said. Words she'd have once not dared speak to Hubert.

"Who says there are only two sides?" Malcolm said.

"I can assure you there are more," Julien said. "And I've worked for most of them. And played them off against each other."

Raoul set down his cup. "I can't speak for Metternich. But Bamford and Stroheim knew each other. I worked with both of them."

Mélanie cast a quick glance at her former spymaster. Raoul had alluded to this but hadn't told her and Malcolm the full story. Or rather, he hadn't told Malcolm the full story. She knew it, or part of it. Because she had been involved.

Hubert stared at Raoul. "Do you mean to say Bamford and Stroheim were both French agents?"

"No, neither was. To my knowledge. As I keep saying. But we worked together to get people they both knew out of France after Waterloo."

Hubert went still for a moment. "That's quite an admission, O'Roarke."

"Yes, it is. But I don't think there's much you can do with it at this point. Especially with Bamford dead. And if we're going to find Stroheim, we need to pool our information."

"Who were the people they rescued?" Hubert asked.

"I'm not going that far."

"No. I didn't think you would. Still, it was worth a try." Hubert picked up his coffee from a satinwood console table and tossed down a swallow. "Did Metternich know?"

"That we all worked together? I sincerely hope not. That Bamford and Stroheim knew each other? Bamford had been friends with Stroheim's father before the war."

"So Metternich might have been trying personal diplomacy," Kitty said. "It's a lot to trust Stroheim with, though. He's quite young."

"He's quite clever," Mélanie said. "I think he'd worked out the truth about me."

Hubert's brows snapped together. "Did he tell anyone?"

"We were afraid he'd tell you," Malcolm said. "Well, Mel and Raoul were. They didn't tell me. And they didn't know you already knew. Well knew eventually."

"O'Roarke had me trying to find out what Stroheim knew about Mélanie," Julien said. "I never could determine for a certainty."

Malcolm shot a look at Julien. "Why—no, never mind. I'm used to everyone knowing things before me. Or I should be."

"You were the one we were trying to keep it from," Julien said. "Well, one of the people, along with Uncle Hubert and others. That was before Raoul knew the truth about me, come to think of it. I was trying to keep that secret too."

"Thank you," Malcolm said. "For trying to help Mélanie."

Hubert set his cup down on the console table again. "Do you think Metternich knows? About Mélanie?"

"We don't even know for a certainty that Stroheim does," Raoul said. "And if Metternich does know and tries to use it as diplomatic pressure, Mélanie has a pardon."

"And we could always go to Italy again," Mélanie said.

"That's the last thing I want," Hubert said. "It took far too much time getting you back last time."

"*You* got us back?" Malcolm said.

"You can't imagine I wasn't working on it. Well, after I—"

"Drove us away in the first place?" Malcolm said.

"All right, perhaps that was a bit of a reach."

"The question now," Laura said, speaking up from the sidelines, where she'd been quietly observing, as she often did, "seems to be what happened to Franz Stroheim. If he went to the meeting and found Bamford dead, he could be the person Sylvie St. Ives heard jump off the ship after the explosion."

Malcolm nodded. "That was my first thought. Which doesn't explain where he is now."

"Whom does he know in London?" Laura asked.

"Any number of diplomats. Including Malcolm and Mélanie." Hubert looked at Raoul. "This friend of his you helped escape. Are they in London?"

"Possibly. And yes, I'll make inquiries. I'm doing you the credit of thinking you won't have me followed."

"You could shake any tail I put on you, O'Roarke. And I have more important uses for my resources. I'm not really interested in Bonapartists at this point."

"What an admission," Julien said.

"Unless they're involved in current disruptions."

"I knew there'd be an 'unless.'"

Hubert looked round the group. "I won't state the obvious by saying we disagree about a lot. But I don't think any of us wants Britain at odds with Austria. Difficult to tell where that might ripple."

"Possibly in some positive directions, if you put it that way,"

Julien said. "But we do want to find Stroheim. And I think we all agree the ripples could also be unfortunate." He frowned at his nails. "Of course, there could be a different explanation for Stroheim's setting up the meeting with Bamford, then disappearing."

"Julien," Kitty said. "Are you suggesting Metternich sent Stroheim to Britain to assassinate Bamford?"

Julien looked up at his wife with a crooked smile. "I'm suggesting it's a possibility we should consider. Not that I necessarily think it likely. But it's intriguing."

"Stroheim's morals and abilities as an assassin aside, the question is why Metternich would want to attack Bamford," Malcolm said. "Metternich wants to get Britain on his side, not to widen the gulf."

"Unless the plan was to blame someone else for the attack," Mélanie said. "That could push Britain and Austria together. But those are extreme lengths to go to."

"Unless Metternich had other reasons to want to get rid of Bamford," Laura said. "Or Stroheim did?" She looked at Raoul.

"Not to my knowledge," Raoul said. "They appreciated each other when we worked together. I can't speak for what may have shifted since."

"We need answers," Hubert said. "Julien, you're the best positioned to see what talk there is among agents working for foreign governments."

"You mean because I've worked for so many of them?"

"I thought that was implied."

Julien looked at his wife. "Help me, KitKat?"

Kitty took his hand. "Of course."

Hubert looked round the group. "I assume I don't need to impress on any of you the gravity of what we're dealing with?"

"No," Malcolm said. "On that, at least, we're all in agreement."

Hubert took his leave soon after, but before the rest of them could depart on new investigations, Valentin showed Cordelia into the library. She stopped short on the threshold, taking in the group.

"We have a lot to catch you up on," Mélanie said. "But you look as though you have news."

"I've been to see Freddie. Frederica Rawdon, Bamford's eldest daughter." Cordelia moved to the settee beside Mélanie. "Judith saw Rosalind this morning, and Rosalind told her she'd overheard Percy Rawdon and Bamford quarreling." Cordelia accepted a cup of coffee from Laura and told them about her visit to Frederica and Percy.

"It's odd how people can surprise one." Cordelia took a sip of coffee. "Often for the worse. But sometimes for the better. Frederica is far more interesting than I ever credited. When we were younger, I suppose I was too wrapped up in my own concerns to pay much attention. A good lesson. We actually talked today, as we never did when we were girls. As perhaps we couldn't have when we were girls. One has a distinct lack of self-knowledge. What a pity she married Percy. And how easily I could have made a similar mistake." She frowned. "I always used to think how dreadful it would be if I'd married George. But the truth is, if it weren't for Harry I could have married someone else who was just as bad. Well, perhaps not as bad. But you know what I mean."

"Sadly, yes," Kitty said. "I married Edward Ashford."

Mélanie turned to Raoul. "Do you know a Sophie who had anything to do with Bamford?"

"No, though that's hardly proof of anything. We did sometimes discuss our personal lives—more perhaps with each other than with others either of us knew, because we knew it was secret. But we hardly shared everything. He'd have had ample time to fall in love with this Sophie after things ended with Désirée. For that matter, he never said his arrangement with Désirée was exclusive. I think he assumed it wasn't, on her side."

"His relationship with Maria Parker seems to have been meant as cover for another relationship," Mélanie said.

"Yes," Raoul said. "If his relationship with Désirée is anything to go by, Bamford was very much a romantic. I had the sense he never got over her. But it's been almost six years. I could see him tumbling into love again. And doing everything he could to protect the woman."

"Sophie can be a French name," Kitty said. "Another spy?"

"That rather seems to be asking for it," Raoul said. "And yet spies know spies. Tony was drawn to excitement outside of his typical life in London. So it's possible. Or simply a French woman he met after Waterloo. With secrets to keep."

"Could Désirée Clairineau be jealous?" Cordelia asked.

"Are you suggesting she had Bamford killed in a fit of jealousy?" Raoul settled back on the sofa beside Laura. "I can't claim to know her well. But though she could be ruthless, she never struck me as the sort to act ruthlessly on personal feelings. Still, a lot's changed since Waterloo. And from the little I grasped from Tony, their relationship ended in a tangle."

"Whoever this Sophie is," Laura said, "if the relationship is so secret he took on a pretend mistress as subterfuge and was ready to pay off his son-in-law's debts to keep the secret, there could be others who'd have been willing to kill him over it. A jealous husband or lover?"

"There's another angle we haven't discussed." Julien stretched his legs out. "Especially if Sophie was another spy. Castlereagh thought Bamford was a risk. It wouldn't be the first time a difficult spy was killed to get rid of the risk."

"You think Castlereagh would have risked killing Stroheim too?" Malcolm said.

"Perhaps he didn't know Bamford was meeting with Stroheim."

"But he'd have had to know Bamford would be on the ship, somehow," Kitty said. "Sylvie claimed she didn't know. Unless—" She broke off and met her husband's gaze, not quite able to say it.

Julien had no such qualms. "Unless Sylvie shot Bamford on Castlereagh's orders and someone else was behind the explosion?

Believe me, I've been wondering that from the moment I took Sylvie off the ship. Although I can't work out why Sylvie would have shot Bamford and then waited about."

"She could have gone on the ship to go through Bamford's pockets after she shot him," Kitty said. "We only have her word for it that she wasn't in the cabin when the explosion went off."

Julien's eyes narrowed. "True."

Malcolm got to his feet. "I promised Roth an update."

Raoul swallowed the last of his coffee. "I need to look for Stroheim's friends."

"And Kitty and I need to make general inquiries about foreign entanglements." Julien reached for his wife's hand.

Mélanie smiled at Cordelia. "A lot's happened. Come check on the children with Laura and me, and we'll catch you up."

CHAPTER 37

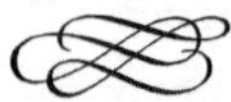

January 1815
Schönbrunn

"Tony." As the fairy tale came to a close onstage, and the crowd moved towards the supper room, Raoul stopped beside the Duke of Bamford. A casual meeting that wasn't casual at all.

"O'Roarke." Tony's greeting was cordial, but his smile seemed a trifle less warm than usual. "I heard you'd come to Vienna."

"Only just. But it seemed impossible to stay away from the Congress completely."

"I found the same myself."

Raoul stepped to the side as two ladies in trailing gowns swept past them. "You got here before I did."

"By a bit." Tony took a drink from the glass of champagne he held. "I've had enough time to see the able work Malcolm Rannoch is doing."

It was perfectly true and a credit to Malcolm, yet something in Tony's tone made Raoul go cold. "He's a skilled diplomat."

"I've got to know him a bit more since I've been here. And the charming Mrs. Rannoch."

The gilded wall was only inches behind Raoul's shoulder. Which was a good thing, as he suddenly did not feel steady on his feet. "Malcolm is fortunate. Suzanne Rannoch strikes me as quite brilliant."

Tony stared at Raoul, as though he were an experiment about to blow up. "If I'm right—my god, you're a cold bastard."

All the snow on the ground outside seemed to have suddenly lodged in Raoul's throat. "Didn't you always know that?"

"Not quite how much. He's your son."

"And circumstances have placed us on opposite sides. You've known that ever since he went to work for Hubert Mallinson. I knew it was inevitable the moment I heard. I was aware of a strong desire to throttle Hubert. But I have to treat Malcolm like an adult. Which means treating him like an opponent."

"This is different." Tony's voice was level, but the horror in it carried a knife cut.

Amazing how something he'd always known was a risk could still bring the slice of dread. "I'm not sure how you mean."

Tony's fingers tightened round the stem of his glass. "I don't know whether to be overwhelmed at your audacity or appalled at your lack of parental feeling. I used to envy the relationship you had with him. So much more than I have with my own children, for all you couldn't openly be a father. Or perhaps that saved you from the trappings of what parenthood means in our world. By the time it occurred to me that more was possible with my children, it seemed too late. I've had my share of guilt for that. But I couldn't contemplate—"

Raoul rested his arm on a marble pillar. To keep it from shaking. "It's often not a matter of contemplating. For all we talk about strategy, it frequently comes down to which moves are possible, given the arrangement of the board at a particular moment."

Cold horror filled Tony's gaze. "I don't think I ever appreciated how ruthless you are."

"Désirée once said much the same to me about your attitude towards her."

"She's probably right. But I think I gave you more credit." Tony glanced away for a moment, gaze fixed on a gilded mirror, as though he were seeing into a different time through the reflected candlelight. "I'd claim to have no illusions about Désirée, but I'm clear-sighted enough to know that would be a delusion. We've both betrayed each other more times than I can count. Désirée's almost certainly betrayed me additional times I don't know about. But at least I've always known we were opponents. Not to know and then find out—I can't imagine that."

Raoul's fingers scraped against the marble. "I find myself difficult to live with. One reason I wouldn't expect anyone else to do so." Raoul had last seen Mélanie with Malcolm as the opera was starting. He didn't risk looking round for her, but it occurred to him that he might have to get her out of Vienna very quickly.

Tony's gaze settled on his face. Within the horror was something else. It might have been compassion. "We both have the power to ruin each other. If I want you to keep your side of the bargain, there are certain secrets I have to hold close. I think this is one of them."

Raoul inclined his head. The candle-warmed air between them was weighted with so much that couldn't be said and so much that they'd never said. "Thank you, Tony."

"I was talking about bargains, not favors."

"Sometimes it takes a friend to understand a bargain. Particularly significant, given what you think of me at this point."

"You surprised me, O'Roarke. You surprised me by what you're capable of. But I never said—"

Tony broke off as a woman in a green velvet gown approached them.

"I should have known I'd find you both here," she said. "Quite a reunion."

How surprising. And how inevitable. "So it is," Raoul said.

Tony stared at her. "What are you doing here?"

"What's anyone doing in Vienna just now? Or rather, what would anyone be doing anywhere else?" Désirée reached for Tony's champagne glass and took a drink. "My name is Baroness Krumlov, by the way." She shifted into flawless Viennese German.

"If you're working for Talleyrand, we're practically allies," Tony said. "And O'Roarke's your opponent."

"We've always known how those things shift." Désirée took another sip of champagne. "Does all of this make the two of you more or less allies?"

"We've always found points of mutual agreement," Raoul said.

She glanced into the supper room. Candlelight flickered off the gilding and bathed the white walls in gold. "It's mad. As though they can will the world back to the 1780s by throwing parties more lavish than anything at Versailles. But one can't deny the glamour." She tossed her beaded lace shawl back from her wrist and considered Raoul. "I don't suppose you're happy about what Tony's doing to Spain."

Tony snatched his glass back. "I'm not doing anything to Spain."

"The government you serve are. At least, they've handed it back to the Bourbons. Just like they did with my country."

Tony took a drink of champagne. "I've never claimed to agree with everything Britain does. Name me one diplomat who agrees with everything their country does."

"And yet you still support them," Désirée said.

"You never claimed to agree with everything Bonaparte did."

"Touché, darling." Désirée tilted her head to the side and smiled at him. Emerald and diamond earrings swung beside her face. "You have to permit me a bit of bitterness. I'm on the losing side, after all. You know I hate to lose."

Tony handed her back the champagne.

She took a drink. "Damn, there's something about this city that brings on nostalgia."

"I won't argue with that," Tony said. "Even Talleyrand doesn't seem immune." He looked at the prince, who was standing beside his nephew's wife, Dorothée, who was serving as his hostess at the Congress. During the opera, Dorothée had been sitting with Count Karl Clam-Martinitz, who was rumored to be her lover, but now she was smiling up at Talleyrand. She reached up to touch the sapphire pendant round her throat, the one Mélanie had been holding by the lake, Raoul realized. Talleyrand returned her smile. The look in his eyes was unlike anything Raoul had seen in the prince's gaze before.

"Oh, I think what Talleyrand's feeling isn't nostalgia at all," Désirée said. "In fact, I'd hazard it's something he may never have felt before." She watched as Dorothée touched Talleyrand's arm and then moved off to rejoin Clam-Martinitz in the supper room. "Interesting to see him caught in the trap after all this time."

"Is that what love is?" Tony asked. "A trap?"

"What would you call it?" she inquired.

"A bit of honesty."

"Oh, Tony. There's nothing as deceptive as love." Désirée's gaze narrowed. "But Talleyrand is an interesting case. We're all capable of change, for good or ill. At least we don't feel these things as hard as the younger generation." She swallowed the last of the champagne and held the glass out to Raoul. "Do you mind?" She held out a hand to Tony. "There's dancing in the next room. Waltz with me, Tony? For old times' sake?"

22 January 1815
Hofburg Palace, Vienna

"WELL, I do believe this is a first, O'Roarke. For all the places we've met, I don't believe we've ever danced together before." Julien moved with lithe grace in Raoul's arms, head tilted at a beguiling angle that made his hairpiece of golden ringlets tumble round his shoulders. His voice was lighter and higher. But the tone of mockery and the glint in his eyes behind his beaded mask were pure Julien St. Juste. Raoul had masqueraded as a woman on occasion, but Julien had turned it into an effortless art.

"The dance floor is an excellent place for private conversation."

"Why do you think I dress as a woman on missions so often?" Julien twirled under Raoul's arm. They were among the crowd in the Hofburg Palace, where the sleighing party had returned to end the night with a public ball. "You don't dance idly with anyone, O'Roarke. What do you want?"

"When did you last see Franz Stroheim?"

Julien's gaze wandered across the ballroom. "Just now. He's dancing with Marie Metternich."

"When did you last interact with him? In any persona?"

"I danced with him a fortnight or so ago. At Julie Zichy's. Or the Duchess of Sagan's. All the events do run together."

"They do indeed. Though they keep coming up with novelties, like a sleighing party. What did you need from him?"

"I needed someone to dance with to escape Lord Stewart's wandering hands. Also, he had notes from Metternich in his shirt cuff. I left with them. And no, I'm not going to share whom I took them for."

Raoul spun Julien to the side, their hands linked overhead. The polished floor made for fast twirls and slippery footing. Much like the Congress itself. "I wouldn't dream of asking."

"Why the interest in Stroheim?" Julien asked, with a flirtatious smile for the benefit of anyone watching them.

"Mélanie talked to him this afternoon at the sleighing party. She remembers seeing him at Malmaison. She thinks he recognized her today. Or at least, knows he saw her, and is trying to piece it together. She says you were there that day as well."

Julien's artfully plucked, delicately penciled brows drew together. "I was at Malmaison a lot. And Mélanie was there a fair amount as well."

"She says you and she were talking to Hortense."

"Also not unusual." As difficult as Julien could be, he also seemed to be genuinely considering. "A lot of the Austrians tended to avoid Malmaison because of Marie-Louise. But I think I remember—he was there with some French officers. Josephine was charmed, as I recall. I don't think we spoke that day. I don't think he spoke to Mélanie. But he visited Malmaison quite a bit, for a time. I think he found other things to interest him there. But I don't recall his seeing Mélanie again. How serious do you think this is?" The dance required Raoul to spin Julien forwards. But Raoul caught the edge of concern under Julien's even voice.

"Depends on if and when he pieces together who she is. If he did, how do you think he'd react?"

"I can't quite take his measure." Julien smiled up at Raoul with the artlessness of a debutante as Raoul spun him back. "He's clever. Not so clever I couldn't steal the papers from him when we danced, but then few would be. With all due modesty. Or not. Also chivalrous. I could gauge that from dancing with him. Though whether that chivalry would extend to this situation—" Julien's gaze drifted across the ballroom. Mélanie was talking with Dorothée Talleyrand and Karl Clam-Martinitz. "Mélanie makes it look effortless," Julien murmured. "And I imagine you and I are the only ones who can see how mad it's driving her."

The strain was there round the corners of her mouth and eyes. But Julien was right. It would be difficult for anyone else to see it. She was that good. "It's a challenging time."

Julien shot a look up at him. "You actually believe the fairy tale, don't you?"

"What fairy tale?"

"That they've fallen in love and can be happy."

"Is that so impossible to believe?"

"Well, I've never been one to believe in love, but I will concede they may well think they're in it. As to happy—that's hard to imagine. But I think you need to believe it. Or you wouldn't be able to live with yourself."

"My dear Julien. Do you imagine I'd have been able to live with myself since the age of twenty without accepting compromise and turning a blind eye to my failures?"

"See, that's the sort of thing you say, O'Roarke. But you don't mean it. Underneath, you're the world's last romantic. You think all sorts of lost causes can have happy endings."

Malcolm had joined Mélanie, Dorothée, and Clam-Martinitz in the last few moments. Uncharacteristically, for him. He was usually conferring with someone at entertainments. As Raoul and Julien watched, he put his hand at Mélanie's waist.

"Do you think she wants to stay with Rannoch?" Julien asked. "When this is over? Assuming any of us knows what 'over' means?"

"I'm quite sure she does."

"Interesting." Julien's gaze narrowed in appraisal. "And damnably uncomfortable. Though I suppose there are worse foundations for a marriage. In fact, I know there are. Not very comfortable for you."

"There's considerable comfort in seeing those one cares about happy." Raoul spun Julien again. Because those words had perhaps been a mistake, and he wanted to hide his expression.

Julien gave an elegant shrug that sent the swirls of gauze that were the sleeves of his gown slithering down on his shoulders. "Always the idealist, O'Roarke. You really should give up the pose of cynical spymaster. I don't know why you try."

"Perhaps because it isn't a pose."

Julien glanced at Malcolm and Mélanie again. Mélanie had slid her own arm round Malcolm. "I have to admit they look rather sickeningly content. Perhaps the most disturbing part is that it's not sickening at all." Julien tilted his head to one side, ringlets falling against his cheek. "I imagine when you say you want those you care about to be happy, that includes Malcolm."

"I've known him since he was a boy." Odd that Julien knew that much, but then it wasn't precisely a secret, and Julien had a way of knowing things. And his own origins remained shrouded in secrecy, though Raoul often suspected they were far closer to British political circles than anyone, very much including Julien, would admit.

"You're a first-class manipulator, O'Roarke. You're also a far better father than most. Including my own, if I mention him. Which I don't care to do." Julien spun again in a swirl of sparkling gauze. "What do you want me to do?"

"Learn what you can about Stroheim. If it looks bad, I may need help laying a false trail."

"My dear O'Roarke. Are you actually trusting me?"

"I've had no choice but to trust you many times, Julien. It usually leaves me with my heart in my throat."

"But so far, we've all survived. The frozen lake at the Schönbrunn this afternoon is a good metaphor for the ground we tread on. Don't worry, I quite want to see Mélanie continue this fascinating fairytale masquerade. If for no other reason than to see how it turns out. I do love a good drama."

"It's good to see you, O'Roarke." Talleyrand moved to stand beside Raoul, leaning on his walking stick.

"Is it? I'd have thought I was an inconvenience."

"Anyone one can speak to with a modicum of frankness is welcome. Rarely have I endured so many days on end of artifice. And given my career, that is saying something indeed."

"Your maneuvering at Vienna has been masterful."

"I've averted some disasters. I can't say I've done much more. But given the climate, that may be something of a feat." The prince shifted his weight from one foot to the other. "Whatever you're working on, I don't want to know about it."

"Believe me, there we are in agreement."

Talleyrand's gaze drifted across the room. Mélanie and Malcolm were still standing with Dorothée and Clam-Martinitz. "The Rannochs look happy. As much as anyone is."

"Yes, I think they are."

"Challenging if he ever learns the truth. Certainly if she leaves."

"I don't think she has any intention of leaving."

"No?" Talleyrand raised his brows. "She'll be in an interesting situation then when things settle down."

"I thought things were settling down."

Talleyrand turned his walking stick. The diamond handle flashed in the candlelight. "Is that what you call the Congress?"

"Britain and France are no longer at war."

"Are you telling me Suzanne Rannoch is content as a diplomatic wife?"

"You'd have to ask her."

"I'm fond of Malcolm."

"I know."

"And I think he means even more to you. So I'll confess your actions have surprised me."

"My dear Talleyrand. You should understand hard choices better than anyone."

Talleyrand watched him for a moment. "I'll give you this, O'Roarke. You're as hard on yourself as you are on anyone else." He smoothed a lace ruffle over his fingers. "Suzanne Rannoch is remarkable. She reminds me a bit of Désirée Clairineau. The obvious parallel would be romantic attachment to an Englishman. But they're also quite brilliant and ruthless. Though I rather think Désirée is more ruthless. Of course, Suzanne has time to grow into it."

"As I recall Désirée, she was quite ruthless at nineteen or so."

"Quite. Are you saying Suzanne isn't?"

"Not in the least. Though perhaps in a somewhat different way. Speaking of Désirée, how is she?" Raoul asked. He assumed Talleyrand knew she'd been at the sleighing party, but he couldn't be certain.

"You'd have to ask her. I never controlled her, and I have less influence on her now than I ever did. I half thought she'd turn to Bamford when Bonaparte fell from power. But she seems to have kept her distance."

"She's proud. And her own person. She'll betray Bamford and make alliances with him, but she won't turn to him for help. I can understand that. I can admire it. I admire Désirée. But I wouldn't care to cross swords with her."

MÉLANIE MOVED ACROSS THE BALLROOM. Her gown was black gauze over champagne satin, instead of the figured gold net over rose silk she'd worn to the sleighing party earlier in the day, with a more trailing skirt for the evening. And she was wearing a crystal-beaded black mask, which was a good thing, because it concealed the dark circles under her eyes. As she moved towards the windows to get some air, she nearly collided with a fair-haired lady in pink gauze.

"I'm so sorry." She stepped back and met a familiar pair of blue eyes framed by a profusion of ringlets.

"Pity we can't dance," Julien said. "I've just had an interesting waltz with O'Roarke, but I'd rather dance with you."

Julien was as comforting as a naked blade beneath the covers, yet for some reason seeing him, after a day of worrying and artifice, made her throat prickle. "Probably just as well. My ability to smile through anything is sorely tried today."

"You? You're in splendid shape." Julien pulled up a trailing fold of her shawl and gave her arm a squeeze in the process. "O'Roarke told me about Stroheim. Don't worry, we'll sort it out."

"It's my problem." She drew the shawl about her shoulders. Black lace. It reminded her of the white lace mantilla she'd worn for her wedding. "My marriage is a farce. Perhaps I'm the fool to think a farce can continue indefinitely."

Julien caught her hand. "I think you're mad to stay in this marriage. I think you're mad to think you can find any sort of happiness as a wife in the British beau monde. But don't ever think you aren't good enough for him. In any way. He's damned lucky to have you. And if he has a grain of sense—which I actually think he does—he knows it."

Mélanie's gaze flickered over Julien's face. Behind the mask and the artful paint and powder, his gaze was unwontedly serious. "Why are you saying this?"

"Because I'd hate to see you make a mistake."

"But you think my marriage is a mistake."

"Perhaps I realize that what I think will make you happy isn't necessarily what actually will."

"That makes no sense, Julien."

"Only if I think I'm always right. Which is one sin I don't believe I've committed. I have little to offer when it comes to using my own life as an example for anyone. But I have learnt that you have to make your own choices. You can't follow anyone else's idea of what's right for you." He squeezed her fingers. "You have ten times the understanding of most of us, *cara*. You can sort out what's right for you. Just don't let it get caught up in what's right for everyone else."

CHAPTER 38

May 1821
London

Jeremy Roth stared at Malcolm. "So this isn't just a murder investigation anymore. It's an assassination. Possibly by a foreign country."

"It's beginning to look that way." Malcolm leant against the mossy balustrade. They were on the terrace off Somerset Place, holding cups of coffee from a Covent Garden coffee stall. Their favorite place to confer in the old days. Roth was now a member of the family, but he still worked out of the Bow Street Public Office, and it seemed to comfort him to stick to aspects of his life prior to marrying into the beau monde. "It's hard to believe the explosion, at least, doesn't have to do with Stroheim and Bamford's meeting on the ship."

Roth blew on his coffee and watched the steam disperse in the chill afternoon air. It was a cool day for May. "So someone wanted to disrupt the meeting. Or to disrupt relations between Britain and Austria, as Hubert suggests. I can investigate, but you'll know suspects and motives better than I do."

"Hubert spelt them out well just now. I'd like to think those in our government would be above interfering like this, but we certainly can't rule them out."

"Can you rule out Hubert?"

Malcolm choked on his coffee. "I've learnt never to rule out Hubert. If he was behind it, I think he'd have played the scene just now much as he did. It's true he doesn't want closer ties between us and Austria. But this seems excessive."

"Unless he had reasons for getting rid of Bamford as well. It sounds as though neither Hubert nor Castlereagh trusted him."

"No." Malcolm curled his fingers round his cup. "There's also the question of what Bamford may have known. I'm not sure even Raoul can answer that."

"I haven't had any luck tracing Rothermere," Roth said. "We haven't been able to locate his friend Camden either, but they left White's early and no one else at Mannerling's remembers seeing Camden or Rothermere last night, so Camden may have been lying to Lady Rothermere. Possibly for reasons that have nothing to do with the explosion. But this raises the question of whether Rothermere could have disappeared because he was involved in the explosion."

"My thought as well. He could have run when he realized what he was involved in. Or his associates could have killed him and his body could be elsewhere."

Roth nodded, gaze on the roiling water of the Thames below the terrace. "My constable found a barkeep who works at the tavern nearest to where the explosion occurred, who heard a loud noise about seven-thirty. Said it sounded like a thunderclap, but there was no rain. It was difficult to hear with the noise in the tavern and the wind knocking things about. But if that was the pistol shot, Bamford was killed almost half an hour before the explosion."

"A risk," Malcolm said. "To shoot in public. Although it would only have taken a few seconds to pull a pistol out and shoot through the window. If the killer caught a moment when the dock was empty—"

"Yes, that was my thought." Roth took a drink of coffee. "There's more. And unfortunately it ties in with Hubert's suggestions about Radicals. I've had reports that Enrico Vincenzo and two other of the Levelers confronted Bamford at White's three nights ago."

Enrico Vincenzo was the brother of their friend Sofia Montagu, recently come from Italy. He—along with Sofia and her husband Kit—was involved with the Levellers, a Radical organization started by their friend Simon Tanner and others at the Tavistock Theatre. Roth was a member himself.

"Bamford's mistress told Mélanie that Bamford said he'd been confronted by some young Radicals that night," Malcolm said. "But not their names. Do you anything about the reasons for the confrontation?"

"No." Roth frowned into his cup and then tossed down another swallow of coffee. "But we've been tracing Bamford's movements before he was killed. The night before last, he called on Kit and Sofia Montagu. Whom Enrico is living with at present. I don't suppose they've said anything to you about Bamford?"

"No." Malcolm's fingers tightened round his cup. "Of course, we haven't asked. We haven't seen them since Bamford was killed."

Roth nodded. "I'd like to dismiss it. But as an investigator, I can't. Difficult to know what anyone might do under certain circumstances, as we both know." He stared down at the green-brown water thudding against the stone. "And that applies to those closest to us."

～

RAOUL FOUND Bertrand Laclos in the library of the house he shared with his lover, Rupert Caruthers, Rupert's wife, Gabrielle, and their young son. An arrangement that was somehow making all of them happy, for all Bertrand had once been convinced the only happiness he could find was in continuing to pretend to be dead.

"O'Roarke." Rupert flung open the library door. "It's good to see you. I imagine you're up to your neck in this Bamford business."

"Something like that."

"It's a pity," Rupert said, genuine compassion in his eyes. "I liked him. He was very decent, for a Tory. Had the good sense not to get on with my father."

Nine-year-old Stephen ran over to Raoul. "Are Colin and Jessica and Emily here? And Clara?"

"Not this time, I'm afraid," Raoul said. "But I'm sure you'll see them soon."

"It sounds like you're here for Bertrand, then. Stephen and I were on our way to the park, in any case." Rupert touched Bertrand Laclos's arm. Even in front of friends, they were discreet. Much as Raoul and Laura had once been.

Bertrand regarded Raoul when Rupert and Stephen had left the room. He was unflappable in any crisis. Most of which had involved people he helped escape France, before and after the Restoration. "Who is it?"

"Gaultier and Régine Barton. They're in London?"

"Is that a statement or a question?"

"Only you knew where they settled."

Bertrand folded his arms. "We agreed that was safest."

"And it was. But Stroheim is in London. Or, at least, in Britain. And he's gone missing."

Bertrand's blue eyes widened.

"He was here to meet with Tony Bamford."

"The Duke of Bamford?" Bertrand said. "So was he—"

"Stroheim was supposed to be on the ship where the explosion occurred. But his body wasn't found. And now he's disappeared. So he either ran, or someone took him. But if he ran for some reason, the Bartons are two people in London—Britain—he might have sought out."

Bertrand gave a contained nod. "How much does Hubert know?"

"What makes you think he knows anything?"

"There's no way he wouldn't investigate the explosion. And these days he goes to you."

"You're quite right on both counts. But I didn't use the Bartons' names. I only said we'd got friends of Stroheim's and Bamford's out of France. Because any connection between Stroheim and Bamford is important. A secret meeting between them over Naples doesn't quite add up. Why Metternich would have approached Bamford secretly, why he'd have sent Stroheim. Unless he knew of the other connections between them. You don't—"

Bertrand's gaze was steady and open. The gaze of a friend. Which he had been. Even before Raoul knew his name. "I had very few dealings with either of them away from you. But I can take you to the Bartons." He hesitated. "They should be fairly safe now. But—"

"Quite," Raoul said. "I'll be careful. Or rather, Malcolm and Mélanie will. I think it might be better to send them."

Bertram's gaze narrowed. "Does Malcolm know about Mélanie's connection to the Bartons?"

"Not yet."

CHAPTER 39

August 1815
Paris

The table at the back of the café was dimly lit, but not private. As usual, it was better to have secret meetings in the view of a lively crowd, who would never suspect three innocuous gentlemen sharing a drink. Raoul arrived first and ordered a bottle of Bordeaux. The waiter had just uncorked it when Tony dropped into a chair beside him. He accepted the glass Raoul poured and took a sip. "A good vintage. There are distinct compensations to being back in Paris."

"I thought your side wanted nothing but to be in Paris."

"Touché." Tony set down his glass and regarded Raoul. "I'm sorry."

"For winning at Waterloo?"

"No, but for what I have no doubt you are going through."

Raoul's fingers tightened round the stem of his glass. "It's not the first time I've lost."

"When I met you at the coast in '98, you were recovering from a loss."

"I'm not precisely sure I'd say I recovered. But I did find new causes. Right now, my main cause seems to be limiting the damage." Raoul took a drink of wine. To prove he could keep his hand steady. "I don't imagine it's been easy for Désirée either."

"You haven't seen her?"

"No. I thought—"

Tony took a careful drink of Bordeaux. "I haven't seen her since Waterloo. Safer, she says. She pointed out she no longer needed to extract information from me. And that she doesn't like losing. Désirée always had a devastatingly acute way of putting things."

He said it lightly. But Raoul could imagine what it cost him. He might have said more, but a wiry young man with tawny hair slipped through the crowd and stopped beside them.

"Stroheim." Bamford held out his hand. "It's good to see you."

Franz Stroheim smiled and shook Bamford's hand. "You as well."

"I didn't realize how well you knew each other," Raoul said.

"We saw each other a fair amount during the war," Tony said. "It was a complicated time."

"And things are so very simple now?" Stroheim raised a brow.

"A palpable hit." Raoul poured a third glass and gave it to Stroheim. "Which brings us to why we're here."

"O'Roarke." Stroheim took a drink of Bordeaux. "Father said you kept the United Irish Uprising alive single-handed, at the end."

"Hardly." Raoul reached for his own glass. "I managed to stay alive, which is more than can be said for a number of my colleagues."

"O'Roarke stands on his principles," Tony said. "A rare thing, these days. A rare thing at any time."

"You're Irish," Stroheim said, looking at Raoul.

"In part. And Spanish. And I went to university in Paris. My alliances have always been more ideological than geographical."

Stroheim's gaze flickered. Half confused. Half intrigued. Mélanie had been impressed by him in Vienna. Impressed and concerned about what he might know.

"Which brings us to why we're here," Tony said.

Stroheim took a drink of wine. "Gaultier Barton. He signed the oath to the Bourbons and then fought for Bonaparte at Waterloo. He's in the Conciergerie."

"And you know him?" Raoul asked.

"He married my cousin Christine. She died two years ago, but Gaultier and I have stayed friends. His second wife contacted me when Gaultier was arrested."

Raoul nodded. He knew Gaultier Barton's wife. But since he knew her as a Bonapartist agent, it wasn't something to share with Stroheim. At least, not yet. Raoul flicked a gaze towards Bamford. "And you, Tony?"

"Louis St. Georges," Tony said. "His mother and mine were childhood friends. I used to see him in Paris in the 80s. During the 90s and after, he fought under Bonaparte. And passed me useful information. Don't comment, O'Roarke."

"No comment made."

"St. Georges also went over to the Bourbons. And also went back to Bonaparte after he escaped Elba. Genuinely. I got no information from him during the Hundred Days, save for a brief note with 'Apologies' scrawled across the bottom." Bamford set down his glass with a clunk. "He's now in the Conciergerie. In the cell next to Gaultier Barton."

"And you both want to get them out," Raoul said.

"Do you disagree?" Stroheim asked.

"By no means. I'd rescue every prisoner of the Bourbon government, if I could."

"Well, then," Stroheim said.

"But I can't. Rescue all of them."

"You have resources we don't," Tony said.

Raoul sat back in his chair. "There are people I could reach out to."

"And you're wondering why help us out of all the people you could help?" Tony asked.

"I didn't suggest that. But it's never easy."

"We can help." Stroheim leant across the table. "I can get paperwork to cross the Austrian border."

"And I can get paperwork to get people into England," Tony said. "We aren't self-centered enough to think you'd only help our friends and not others. If you help Barton and St. Georges, we can help others you want to get out of France."

"That's how it works, isn't it?" Stroheim said. "A favor for a favor? Even across enemy lines."

"Partly," Raoul said. "Favors are currency, in intelligence. I'm sure your father told you that."

"My father said I'd be better off out of the whole—er—sordid business. Only he used sharper words."

"I'm sure he did. It's not anything I'd wish for any son of mine." Though his son was still working ably against him. And had nearly died at Waterloo, until Raoul shot an ally to save him. Perhaps the most chilling moment of his life.

"But you can't expect us to stay on the sidelines," Stroheim said.

"No, I don't suppose we can. One of the many conflicts of being a parent. Wanting to see one's children take on the world, and wanting to keep them wrapped in cotton wool."

Stroheim smiled. "You don't seem one for cotton wool."

"You'd be surprised."

"It's not just currency." Tony's voice was even, but soft. "It might have been for me, once. It's because it's the right thing to do. We may disagree about a number of things. We can agree that the reprisals against Bonapartists have descended into madness."

Raoul met his gaze. "I can contact the Kestrel. He's very helpful."

"Do you know who he is?" Stroheim asked, voice eager.

"There's no need for me to know who he is. And it's safer for him—and for me—if I don't." That still held true, despite the fact that, after recent events, Raoul did indeed know the Kestrel's identity.

"I admire him a great deal," Stroheim said.

"So do I." Raoul looked between Stroheim and Barton. "There are others I'm trying to get out of France. It's my main work these days. So if you can help with passage into England or Austria, it would be most appreciated."

"Of course," Tony said.

"You're not going to ask for guarantees?" Stroheim asked.

"Why? We trust each other. Guarantees can be broken."

"So can trust."

"Yes. But I've learnt it's rather more resilient."

Stroheim met his gaze for a long moment and inclined his head. "Why does he do it? The Kestrel."

"You'd have to ask him," Raoul said. "But I believe it's because he doesn't believe in imprisoning and executing people for their political beliefs. He rescued people imprisoned by the Bonapartist government before it fell."

"What does he want?"

"Again, you'd have to ask him. But I think he wants to keep people safe from injustice. He sees a lot of injustice in the world. As I do."

Stroheim nodded, eyes narrowed and thoughtful.

Tony pushed his chair back. "I'm due at the embassy. You know where to find me, O'Roarke. I can make myself available at a moment's notice."

Stroheim lingered at the table after Tony left. He clearly wanted to talk, though Raoul wasn't sure about what. It would be helpful to learn more, so he refilled their glasses.

Stroheim took a sip. "I have happy memories of France in the days when we were allies with the French. Malmaison, in particular. The empress—the empress dowager—Josephine—was kind to me. I loved the lack of formality."

Raoul reached for his own glass. "Malmaison was always meant to be a home."

"I'm sorry." Stroheim shifted in his chair. "For what she suffered. And for the role my country played in it."

"The divorce is hardly Austria's fault. And Josephine herself wished Napoleon and Marie Louise nothing but happiness."

"She was a remarkable woman."

Raoul looked into his glass, remembering afternoons drinking wine at Malmaison. In the gardens or by a rain-spattered window. "She was indeed. I miss her greatly."

"I remember Queen Hortense as well," Stroheim said. "She seemed more a girl than a queen. She was very kind."

"Her mother's daughter."

"Is she—"

"She's happy to be free of court life, I think. And perhaps to be away from France. It holds a number of memories."

Stroheim nodded. "That was a golden time, in my memory. I'll always cherish it."

The words seemed to be spoken in all sincerity, yet Raoul couldn't shake the sense that Stroheim had an agent's skill at using sincerity to probe for truths. "I hold on to my memories of those days as well," Raoul said.

Stroheim shifted in his chair. "So much has changed in the past months. It's like a kaleidoscope that one shakes and sees different people from the past in different settings." He took a drink of wine. "I hear you saw the Rannochs in Paris recently."

"I did." Raoul kept his voice easy.

"I have pleasant memories of them from Vienna. Though I didn't quite put together then where I knew Suzanne Rannoch from. She's led an interesting life."

Raoul reached for his glass with leisurely care. "She has. She fled France as a child and lost her family in the war in the Peninsula."

"Yes, I know that's the story." Stroheim said it easily, but there was just the slightest emphasis on the word story. "I glimpsed her and Rannoch again in Paris. They look happy. Easier than they were in Vienna."

"I think so. Vienna was hard for everyone."

"Malcolm Rannoch told me you were a family friend."

"I was. I knew him as a child. The war took us in different directions."

"So you don't see them anymore?"

"I do occasionally."

"And Suzanne Rannoch is—"

"Suzanne Rannoch is the wife of an English diplomat."

"Not an easy role in Paris. Whatever one's background."

"She's at least safe. Which is more than can be said for many."

"So they plan to go back to England?"

"I don't know. But their life is with the British delegation."

"Difficult to divide the world up into delegations. Whatever Metternich says, I find it hard to believe the new alliances will be stable. I had a talk with Malcolm Rannoch about that in Vienna. I don't think he agrees with Castlereagh much of the time." Stroheim took a drink of wine. "He said he didn't think you'd be very happy with what he'd made of his life."

"He said that to me in Vienna as well. He could be said to have done rather better than I've done with mine." He was certainly a better father.

Stroheim twisted the stem of his glass between his fingers. "Metternich's my father's friend. But his positions aren't mine. Neither are my father's. It makes for challenges. And now the war's over, the paths seem even more uncertain. I understand this Kestrel fellow. Trying to save those in need. There's a clarity in that. There's a clarity in this mission. I welcome that. But it doesn't help me decide what the devil I'm going to do with myself afterwards."

CHAPTER 40

May 1821
London

The house in Montague Street that Bertrand had directed Mélanie and Malcolm to had worn bricks and peeling red paint on the door, but there were well-tended flowers in the window boxes. A young woman in a print dress opened the door, regarded them with surprise, looked at Malcolm's card, and said Mr. Barton was out but if they would wait in the sitting room, she would let Mrs. Barton know they had called.

The sitting room, which opened off a narrow hall, had faded tapestry furniture tossed with colorful pillows covered in silk and wool that looked to have been cut from lengths of dress fabric. A basket beside the hearth rug held wooden and cloth animals. A stuffed dog and cat were arranged on the settee, as though for a party. Framed children's drawings hung on the wall beside prints of Paris. It was the kind of home Mélanie could imagine having had if she hadn't married a member of the beau monde. Of course, before she'd married Malcolm, it had been difficult to imagine having any sort of home at all.

A few minutes later, the door from the hall opened to admit a dark-haired woman with elegantly boned features and striking dark eyes. She had a little girl of perhaps two in her arms, and a boy of about eight clung to her ruby lustring skirt.

Mélanie smiled into those familiar eyes. Because the last time she had seen this woman was on a mission in the Pyrenees.

Régine Barton met Mélanie's gaze but did not otherwise acknowledge that they had ever met before. "Mr. Rannoch. Mrs. Rannoch. I'm afraid my husband is out. I don't know if I can help you. My son Roland. And my daughter Mylène."

Mylène grinned with the unabashed delight of a toddler. Roland gave them a shy smile.

Régine looked down at her son. "Roland, can you be a very great help? Take Mylène to the kitchen and ask LouLou to send in some cookies and tea? And to give you some cookies yourselves?"

Roland grinned, as much at the responsibility as at the promised treat, Mélanie suspected, and went off, holding his sister's hand.

"He's delightful," Mélanie said when they were all seated. "He's about the age of my own Colin." She smiled at Régine Barton. "But then you probably remember that."

Régine went still.

"It's all right," Mélanie said. "My husband knows my history."

Régine relaxed against the settee back, though Mélanie didn't think she had entirely let her guard down. "I'm glad to hear it. Mine does as well. So we can speak plainly. Or as plainly as agents ever can." She glanced at Malcolm, who was sitting by in alert silence. "How much do you know about me?"

"I'm afraid, as often with my wife, I am ten steps behind. But she did update me on the way here. I know you met Mélanie on a mission in the late days of the Peninsular War, and that you were getting aid and messages to wounded French soldiers trapped behind the British lines and then coordinating their escape. I wish I'd known. I would have helped."

"You'd have got yourself in a great deal of trouble," Mélanie said. "I was trying to protect you."

"Also, you assumed I wouldn't help."

"That, too. And that it would end our marriage."

"Hardly."

"But I didn't know it then."

"Mélanie was very concerned about you," Régine said. "Not so much that you'd learn the truth, as that her actions would impact you."

"Yes, considering she was spying on me, she was always very careful about that." Malcolm shot a look at Mélanie. "Sorry."

"Point taken." Mélanie turned back to Régine. "We have no wish to disrupt your life. Bertrand only told us where you were because the situation was so grave. Franz Stroheim was in London and has disappeared. We need to find him."

Régine's eyes widened. "Where did he disappear from?"

"He was supposed to be on a ship at the London Dock last night," Malcolm said. "Did you know he was in London?"

"No." Régine shook her head. "But though he was very kind to us, he wouldn't necessarily have let us know he was here. Not if it was secret. And, given his work, it likely was."

"Are you saying he's an agent?" Mélanie asked.

"You didn't know?"

"Not conclusively."

"I don't know a lot of details." She drew a breath, then broke off as the maid who had admitted them returned with the promised tea and cookies. When they were alone again, Régine poured tea. "I met Gaultier after I had worked with Mélanie. He wasn't the sort of man I'd have been involved with in the normal run of things. I never saw myself with an aristo. Not even a Republican one who served Bonaparte. I never saw myself married. But in the midst of a war, a lot changes. I needed his help on a mission. His wife had died the year before. With the world changing so rapidly, we were both looking for something to grasp hold of. It was only when he left for Belgium that I realized quite what he'd come to mean to me. Afterwards—" She shrugged. "You know how it was. I can't imagine—" She broke off.

"It was hell," Mélanie said. "It's all right, Malcolm knows that now."

"It was a time when one hangs on to what one has. With the world falling apart and Gaultier in danger, marriage didn't seem so mad. Or perhaps madness seemed the only option. He asked me to marry him so Roland would have someone if he was arrested. We'd scarcely been married a fortnight when he actually was arrested. I was the one who wrote to Franz Stroheim. Whom I had only met once. Gaultier had wanted me to take Roland and leave the country. Instead, I waited, and we all escaped together and came here. Well, you know that." She handed Mélanie a cup of tea. "You helped us."

"I played a very small role." Mélanie accepted the cup and took a sip.

Régine glanced round the sitting room. "It's not the sort of place I ever imagined living. I'd have said this life was far too tame. But somehow"—she shrugged—"things change. The marriage that began out of necessity began to seem real. We had Mylène. A life that might have seemed confined seems unexpectedly rich."

"I can understand that," Mélanie said.

Régine handed the plate of cookies to them. "Though we owe our safety to Franz and I was wholly dependent on him when it came to getting Gaultier out of the Conciergerie, our communication was mostly about practicalities. And Bertrand and Raoul handled many of the details. But Franz had an agent's skills and grasp of the situation. And Gaultier confirmed that Franz was an agent." She looked from Mélanie to Malcolm. "As you haven't told me why he was here, and he hasn't contacted us, I suspect he was here on a mission?"

She made it the slightest question. Mélanie sat quietly. She had to let Malcolm handle this. She'd told him what she could on the drive here. She could feel him taking Régine's measure. It was a matter of instinct as much as anything. Instinct born of experience and keen observation. "He was here to meet with a senior British diplomat," Malcolm said. "Secretly and unofficially. The British diplomat was killed and the ship they were meeting on blew up."

"But Franz wasn't injured? Or killed?" Régine's voice was taut.

"We didn't find another body. So, we think he wasn't on the ship at the time of the explosion, or that he jumped into the water. But for some reason, he disappeared."

Régine squeezed her eyes shut. "Hard to believe I've become so fond of someone who works for Metternich."

"I used to work for Castlereagh," Malcolm said. "Mélanie doesn't hold it against me."

Régine gave a quick smile. Then her gaze went serious. "When someone disappears from the scene of an explosion, there's an obvious assumption."

"You're suggesting Stroheim set off the explosion?"

"No, I'm wondering if you think he did."

"We considered it," Malcolm said. "As you point out, it's an obvious possibility. But we couldn't see a motive. Can you?"

Régine gave the question honest consideration. She'd never been one to shy away from difficult questions. "You'd know more about the present relations between Austria and Britain than I would. But however tense they'd become, it's difficult to imagine. And while it may sound sentimental, it's difficult for me to imagine Franz engaging in that sort of violence."

Malcolm nodded. "Did he ever mention the Duke of Bamford?"

"The English aristo who was also involved in getting Gaultier and Louis St. Georges out of the Conciergerie?"

"Yes, though I didn't know Bamford was involved at the time," Mélanie said.

Régine went still. "Is that the British diplomat who was killed?

I'm sorry. I never met him, but we owe him a debt as well. Franz had a lot of respect for him. That makes it even harder for me to imagine Franz's being involved in the explosion."

"So why would he run?" Malcolm asked.

Régine sat back on the settee. "You're an agent, Mr. Rannoch. You must know there are numerous reasons one might run in a foreign city. Seeing someone from the past comes to mind."

"Who?" Mélanie asked.

"He didn't share his work with me. I can't claim to be in his confidence any more than he could claim to be in mine. But I'm sure he knew any number of people in London. I imagine he met both of you?"

"He did," Mélanie said. "I suspect he suspected I was a French agent. Which gives me reason to be afraid of him, but not him reason to be afraid of me."

"Interesting," Régine said.

"He never said anything to you about it?"

"No, but he'd have had no reason to know I knew you. Raoul kept that from him when you helped us. As I recall, Raoul kept you away from Franz completely."

"He did."

Régine stirred her tea. "Franz has a keen mind. And he's also chivalrous. I don't think he'd have betrayed you. But of course, one can never be sure."

"No," Mélanie said. "One can't. But unless Franz Stroheim was a double agent, I can't see him having the same fears."

"I can't quite imagine his being a double agent. And, given shifting alliances, one would wonder for whom."

"Can you think of anyone in London he'd have run to?" Malcolm asked.

Régine shook her head. "As far as I know, he had colleagues in London, but not anyone he was particularly close to. Wherever he ran, he didn't run to us. Which doesn't entirely surprise me. I don't think he'd have wanted to put us in danger. And while I think he trusts us, trust only goes so far. As I think we all know."

"Indeed," Malcolm said. "It's also possible Stroheim ran because he thought he'd be accused of being behind the explosion. Or feared he was a target of it."

"I wish I knew more," Régine said. "I'm not a sentimental person, as Mélanie could tell you, but I'm quite fond of Franz. All of this leaves me a bit terrified. My only comfort is that he's excellent at taking care of himself."

～

"I'M SORRY," Mélanie said as they descended the steps of the Barton house. "I should have said so earlier."

"Sorry?" Malcolm asked.

She tugged her glove smooth, staring at the black stitching on the lilac cloth. "I wasn't expecting my past to intrude."

"We're both going to run into people we worked with. Useful, in this case. She wouldn't have talked to us so much otherwise. That's why Raoul and Bertrand suggested we talk to them."

Mélanie tightened the ribbons on her bonnet as they turned down Great Russell Street. Clouds scuttered across the sky and patches of sun dappled the pavement. "Raoul told me we were helping Stroheim. Well, he told me he was, and I insisted on helping. But he never mentioned Bamford."

"There's a lot Raoul's kept secret about Bamford," Malcolm said in a level voice.

Mélanie cast a quick glance at him, but this wasn't the time to go into what other secrets Raoul might be keeping. She slid her hand through Malcolm's arm. "I always liked Régine. I think she truly is happy here. I think what she said about her husband and children was genuine. I think she's genuinely fond of Franz Stroheim."

"But?" Malcolm asked.

She smiled at her husband. "How well you know me, darling. It's a bit surprising she hadn't heard about the explosion, though I suppose she might not have seen the papers today. But I think she was holding something back. Perhaps that's just me seeing too much in shadows. Reading in my own actions—"

"No," Malcolm said. "I sensed it too. You think she knows where Stroheim is?"

"I think she knows more than she was telling us."

"Not surprising. Even though she worked with you—and obviously is fond of you—she'd have no reason to trust us, necessarily."

"Depending on why Stroheim disappeared."

Malcolm frowned into the distance. "Quite."

They had passed the British Museum. Mélanie tightened her fingers round Malcolm's arm as they turned down Charlotte Street. "Are you going to see Jeremy?"

"At some point. I'd like to learn precisely whom Rothermere entertained at the docks. Harry and Cordy could help Roth with that. No one's better than Cordy at drawing connections between prominent members of the beau mode. Meanwhile, we need to call on Kit and Sofia—and Enrico—and ask about Bamford's visit to them the night before he died."

"You go alone. Or take Kitty. She knows the most about Bamford's recent political involvement. I'm going to the Tavistock. We need to find out what Simon knows about Enrico and the other Levellers confronting Bamford at White's."

Malcolm looked at her, eyes narrowed in the slanting afternoon light.

"It's easier for me to stop by the theatre and bring it up."

"I don't want this to cross into your work."

"You're an MP, darling. If you talk to him, it crosses into yours."

Malcolm held her gaze. "But—"

"And if he reveals anything to me, I don't have the burden of whether or not I'm obligated to share it."

Malcolm frowned. "You think Simon will reveal—"

"I don't know what he'll reveal."

"And if he does reveal something to you—"

"It will be up to me to decide what to tell you. The same as always." Mélanie looked into her husband's eyes.

Malcolm looked back. "Simon is—"

"Your friend. And mine, too. But I'm not a member of the government."

"If any of the Levellers are involved in this—"

"I'll sort it out."

"Mel—"

"I know it seems absurd to say, 'Trust me, darling.' But I'm afraid that's what you're going to have to do."

CHAPTER 41

August 1815
Paris

The man called the Kestrel, whom Raoul now knew was Bertrand Laclos, presumed dead for five years, leant back, keeping his face in the shadows of the buildings over-hanging the narrow street without obviously seeming to do so. "If you've sent for me, it must be important."

"You flatter me," Raoul said.

"On the contrary. I see how thin you are stretched. Anyone you are trying to help must need help indeed."

"Sadly, these days that applies to nearly everyone who had minimal work for the Bonapartist regime."

"And today?" Bertrand asked.

"Gaultier Barton and Louis St. Georges. They're lodged next to each other in the Conciergerie."

"I know." Bertrand moved further back into the shadows. "I keep a chart of who is lodged where in the Conciergerie. They're high-level prisoners."

"I have contacts in the British and Austrian delegations who will help."

"That will make it somewhat easier."

"They're—"

"No." Bertrand put out an arm. "No names until we know we need them. Safer for everyone. It's enough of a risk at this point that you know mine. It won't be easy, but we've breached the Conciergerie before. It's getting out of the country that will be harder. Might be easier to take them two different directions, across the Channel and over the Austrian frontier."

"My thought as well."

Bertrand nodded. "Suzanne Rannoch was a great help with Paul St. Gilles and Juliette Dubretton and their children. She could help here." He hesitated. He didn't mention asking Malcolm for help, though Malcolm had also assisted with the rescue of the St. Gilles-Dubretton family. The implications were clear. And concerning. "I understand the risk," Bertrand said, a tacit acknowledgement of what he knew or suspected about Mélanie. "I wouldn't blame her if she didn't want to take it."

Raoul nodded. "She's quite fearless when it comes to taking risks. Reckless, even."

"She isn't the only one."

"The people we're saving aren't the only ones with lives to protect."

Bertrand's gaze was dark and steady in the shadows. "I understand."

"You run incalculable risks yourself." It was the closest Raoul had come to asking Bertrand anything personal. But if Bertrand knew this much about Mélanie, Raoul felt the need to learn more about Bertrand.

Bertrand gave a faint smile and shrugged. "You do the same. I think perhaps that to run great risks one has to either feel very secure or have nothing to lose. I think I can guess which applies to you, and I suspect you can guess which applies to me. I'm fortunate to still be standing. I'd like to help others do the same." He shifted his position, not quite so much in the shadows. "I had word from the St. Gilles-Dubretton family. They seem to be settling in well." He smiled. "It's a relief when they can make it work. Thank you, by the way."

"For what?"

"For not trying to force my identity into the open before I revealed it."

"That was for you to do," Raoul said. "Thank you for not blaming me for my own role in your misfortune."

"You were doing your job."

"Not as well as I should have done." Raoul watched him for a moment. "You just said you were fortunate to still be standing. Rather remarkable to call your case fortunate."

"I was nearly killed."

"You had your life destroyed by the father of the person you loved."

"Dewhurst is a monster. But there wasn't a place for Rupert and me. I can't argue with Dewhurst over that."

"And now?" Raoul could see the way Rupert Caruthers's gaze had lit up when he realized Bertrand was still alive.

"Nothing's changed."

"Or everything has."

"There still isn't a place for us."

"Isn't that what you do? Find places for those who seem to have no place to be safe?"

Bertrand gave a faint smile. "There's no country for Rupert and me to run to. Even assuming I could ask him to run. Which I couldn't. Especially not now he has a family."

"At the risk of oversimplification, if former Bonapartist spies can build lives in London, I think you and Caruthers could do the same."

"Rupert doesn't need to hide."

"My dear fellow. Rupert has been hiding his whole life, and particularly since he fell in love with you."

"I don't want him to lose—"

"He's lost something incalculable. But with you he has a chance to recapture it."

Bertrand shifted his shoulders against the wall. "Why so intent on this, O'Roarke? It's—"

"None of my business? You're right."

"It's nothing to do with your work."

"I do occasionally notice things not to do with my work." Raoul met Bertrand's gaze for a moment in the dim light. "I've seen the way you and Caruthers look at each other. One doesn't throw a feeling like that away."

"Is that what you've done?"

"I wouldn't say I've found it. Not where the balance was equal on both sides."

"And if you did? Would you take your own advice?"

"Does any of us take our own advice?"

"Or is it that you don't think you deserve it?"

"Foolish to talk about deserving. But I'm a bit past it, don't you think?"

"Is anyone ever really past it?"

"I'm at an age where I tend to scoff at romance." Raoul put a hand on Bertrand's shoulder. "Different things make different people happy. What we call love doesn't always lead to happiness. But I think you and Caruthers could be happy together. And I don't think either of you will be happy apart."

 through the trees in the Bois de Boulogne. The scent of fresh grass and roses carried on the breeze. Mélanie adjusted her white lace parasol over her shoulder. She caught sight of a familiar figure walking down the avenue of trees. His face was in shadow, but his gait was familiar anywhere. Unless he changed it on a mission.

He tipped his hat. "Mrs. Rannoch. You're looking well. Paris agrees with you."

In any direction, she could see British soldiers without trying. And Austrians and Prussians and Russians. Foreign troops overwhelmed the city. White Royalist cockades were everywhere. At least they no longer fascinated Colin as they had when he first saw them in London a year ago. He seemed to sense that they bothered his mother. "It's an interesting time to be here."

"It is indeed."

She studied his face. She couldn't say Paris agreed with him. His eyes looked deeper set than usual, and his face, always thin, had a gaunt cast. Most disturbing, the vital spark that always lit his eyes had dimmed to an ember.

She turned slightly, angling the parasol so it shielded both of them from the passersby. "Have you had any news of Paul and Juliette?" The last time she'd seen him, he'd been engaged in getting the St. Gilles-Dubretton family out of Paris.

"I saw Bertrand Laclos. They're well. Probably best not to say more. For everyone's sake."

"Meaning you can't trust me."

"I'll always trust you, *querida*. But while this may sound laughable coming from me, you have to contend with enough divided loyalties as it is. There's no sense in straining you further."

"Or risking that I'll say something."

"It's always a risk. Even with the best, which you are. And we aren't colleagues any more. We may care about the same people, but our loyalties don't always align." He watched her for a moment. "You don't owe me anything. You didn't even when you were my agent. But it's even more true now."

Absurd to feel a pang in her throat. "We're friends," she said. "We always will be. On my side, at least."

"And on mine, it goes without saying. Why did you want to see me, *querida?*"

Sometimes for simple reassurance that the part of her that had been Mélanie Lescaut was still alive. That she wouldn't get so used to being Suzanne Rannoch she'd forget who she'd been. But it was more than that. "I saw Franz Stroheim again. At a reception at the British embassy. He was faultlessly polite. Quite kind, actually. He asked after Colin. But I swear I could see the questions in his eyes. Perhaps I'm being fanciful, but I think he's piecing it together." She shifted her grip on the parasol, forcing her fingers not to clench. "I know I'm not your problem anymore—"

"Don't be absurd, *querida.*" The impulse to reach out his hand shot through his eyes. "I'll always be here to help you. Nothing can change that."

"Is that what spycraft is?"

"At the moment, my singular focus is protecting those I care about. And while I may keenly regret the failure of my other enterprises, I can't imagine any work that matters more. I told you before I'd help if Stroheim became an active threat. That still holds."

"More challenging to come up with a by-blow cousin in Josephine's court now we're back in Paris. I spend enough time dodging questions about my fictional Saint-Vallier family as it is. I tried to limit details and make sure everything added up, but impossible not to say things on the spur of the moment. Stroheim caught me off guard in Vienna."

"A cousin, especially one with a different name, who had been connected to Josephine's court, could have fled. Or died. If necessary, we can come up with documentation."

"Of the death of someone who never existed?"

"It wouldn't be the first time. Or we could document someone who left Paris with Hortense. Hortense would help. She's very fond of you."

"I think of her a great deal. I wonder if she's ever able to see her youngest son."

"She has news of him, at least."

Mélanie nodded. Four years ago, she and Julien St. Juste had traveled with Hortense when she went to Switzerland in secret to give birth to her child with her lover the Comte de Flahaut. It had shaken Mélanie more than she'd thought possible to see Hortense send her baby off to be raised without her. And that was before Mélanie had thought to have children of her own.

Raoul hesitated. Mélanie scanned his face. She could still read nuances in his expression. "What?"

"I saw Stroheim myself recently. He mentioned you. For what it's worth, I think he does suspect, but won't do anything. And I have leverage if he does."

"What?"

"I'm helping him get his cousin's husband out of the Conciergerie."

"With Bertrand? No, don't say it, I know you won't want to share details, but of course it's with Bertrand. Can I help?"

Raoul drew in and released his breath. "Bertrand suggested as much."

"And you didn't want to ask me? Honestly, Raoul—"

"I was considering it. But if Stroheim's been saying things to you—"

"You just said you think he suspects but won't do anything. Besides, unless we both assist with the rescue in person, he'd have no need to know I'm involved. I owe Bertrand. And I need to feel I can help." She shifted the parasol against her shoulder. The light shifted over both of them, sunlight shooting through the leaves, dappling the moss green sarcenet and white muslin of her gown. "I never expected to end up where I did."

"I don't know that any of us do. The point is to be as happy with it as possible. Often one ends up somewhere one is happier than anticipated."

"That sounds singularly positive coming from you."

"I'm capable of being positive."

"Are you—"

"I'm better off than most of our friends. If I dwell on my regrets rather more than is comfortable, that's because of the luxury of being able to do so without fearing for my safety. "

"That's why I want to help. Because I'm all too aware of those who aren't as fortunate. I'm not only dancing and dining with the victors, I'm happy doing it. Honestly, if you don't let me help, I'm more likely to get myself into trouble on own, trying to find something to do or dwelling on the unfairness of the world."

He gave a twisted smile. "Put like that—I'll see what Bertrand has in mind. I think he knows, by the way."

"Did he say so?"

"No, but he mentioned you helping, but not Malcolm."

She nodded. "Oddly, I'm not afraid of him. Of all people. I don't think he'd betray anyone. I only hope he can manage to seize happiness himself."

"I tried to tell him as much."

"If you let me help, perhaps I can convince him."

"I'm too much of a pragmatist to refuse help in a crisis. Especially help as able as yours."

She put a hand on his arm. It hadn't seemed wise for so long. But sometimes it was unavoidable. And it seemed less of a risk now. And also more needed. "I'm here. I know you can't trust me with everything, but if you need my help. In this or in any other way. Also if you need to talk. Not about secrets, but as you once said to me, everyone needs to talk. Even if it's just to rail at the world."

"I've done enough of that to you."

"And I'm still here. A lot has changed. Some things never will. I have to hold on to that."

He touched her hand, briefly, lightly. "Thank you. That is a great deal more than I deserve."

CHAPTER 42

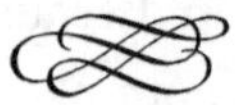

May 1821
London

"Melly." Simon grinned as Mélanie came into the green room at the Tavistock Theatre, where he was part owner and her plays were performed along with his own. Then his face went serious. "I didn't think to see you today. I thought the Bamford business would keep you busy."

Mélanie moved to the worn tapestry settee where her children liked to nap. "It is. That's why I'm here."

Simon's brows tightened. He went to the tea table and poured her a cup from the teapot that was always kept hot when anyone was in the theatre. "I didn't know Bamford well. But he and the duchess attended performances, on occasion. He was polite and made some quite keen remarks on my plays. Including those skewering Tory politicians like him. I was sorry to hear of his death." He handed her a cup of tea. "If you've brought this to me in the midst of an investigation, I assume it's because there's talk that the disturbance is tied to Radicals?"

Mélanie took a sip of tea. It was a drink that could soothe the most difficult conversation. "Because there will be questions, and we'd like to get ahead of the questions. Even Hubert said as much."

Simon grave a dry smile at the mention of his lover's father. With whom he was now on reasonably good terms. "Good of him."

"There's new evidence that makes it look as though the explosion may have been an attempt to create an international incident."

Simon leant against the tea table, legs crossed at the ankle. "And you can't say how."

"It's not that I don't trust you, Simon—"

He waved a long-fingered hand. "Information has to be carefully guarded. Safer for everyone not to share it. Believe me, I understand."

Mélanie tugged loose the ribbons on her bonnet and pulled it off her head. It was choking her. "Members of the Levellers confronted Bamford recently. At White's."

Simon grimaced. "Bamford was dealing with Metternich over the suppression of the uprising in Naples. He was the face of British tacit acceptance of the uprising's being put down. There was a lot of anger among the Levellers over it. Understandably."

Mélanie set her bonnet on the table beside her. The blanket was missing from the settee, she noticed. As were two of the pillows painted to resemble watered silk. Odd. New pieces from productions were always finding their way to the Tavistock green room, but it was rarer for anything to be removed. "Could that have led any of them to attack Bamford?" she asked.

Simon's fingers tightened on the handle of his teacup. "We don't advocate violence."

"I'm not accusing you of being behind it, Simon. You're talking to me. Not David. Not Malcolm."

He tossed down a swallow of tea. "And if I admit something to you?"

"Do you have something to admit?"

Simon clunked his cup down on the tea table. "Enrico Vincenzo is furious at Bamford. Kit was trying to restrain him, but he's obviously furious too. What's happening in Naples cuts close to both of them. I think Kit is extra furious because his father supplied guns to the Austrians."

"And, knowing Lord Thurston, he probably supplied guns to the rebels as well." Mélanie set her cup down. "I remember what it is to be angry and want to lash out."

"But what would you do if you had to confront those feelings now?"

Mélanie tugged the violet ribbons on her bonnet smooth. "I'm not sure."

"Fair enough. Neither am I."

Mélanie reached for her tea and started at a sudden creak. Not unexpected in an old theatre, but it sounded as though it had come from the basement where Simon had his office, where things were generally quiet.

"We're getting some props out of storage," Simon said. "We need a bit more to bring the garden scene to life." He dug his fingers into his thick dark hair. "It was easier at Oxford. We could say more, but it was all more theoretical." He moved to a giltwood chair and dropped into it. "As I've heard the story, three Levellers went to confront Bamford at White's that night, but Enrico was the one ranting at the duke. Later I heard Enrico say he wished he could have planted Bamford a facer the night of the musicale. But it's a long way from that to actually planting someone a facer. Let alone to murder."

"But you're worried."

Simon reached for his teacup and turned it on its saucer. "Tensions are running high. Men like Castlereagh and Metternich have smashed too much. I like to think the tide is running against them. But for the moment they have too much power. To many of my friends it can seem that we keep losing. We think it's those of us who've been fighting longer who can grow cynical. But sometimes it's the young who give up first and try something drastic. Not that I have any reason to think anyone did."

"No."

Simon took a drink of tea. "Thank you."

"For what?"

"For not telling me more and giving me enough rope to get into trouble."

Henriette Varon greeted Raoul with her usual bright smile, though there was concern behind her eyes. She poured coffee in the warm jumble of the sitting room in the lodgings she shared with her two daughters, and listened to his story. As a former seamstress to the Empress Josephine, she was used to stories that touched on the fate of countries.

"I remember Bamford," Henriette said. "I knew him as Lord St. Ives. I met him first in the '90s. Before Josephine married Bonaparte."

"So did I."

"He came to Malmaison during the Peace of Amiens. Josephine liked him."

"He was an easy man to like."

"And I knew he was connected to Désirée Clairineau." Henriette took a drink of coffee. "She undertook missions for Josephine on occasion. She had a terrifying reputation, but she was kind to Josephine. Much like Julien St. Juste."

"Yes," Raoul said. "She was kind to me, as it happens. Do you know who she was? Before she became an agent? I never learnt."

"I'm not sure. Her past wasn't as much a mystery as Julien's, but it wasn't well known. Rumor had it she was the daughter of an aristo family who had mostly fled in the Revolution."

Raoul reached for his coffee. "What about Franz Stroheim? Do you remember his visiting Malmaison?"

"Oh yes. He was quite a regular guest at Malmaison for a time. Hortense had a circle of young people round her. Sort of an informal court of her own. He was very kind."

"I don't suppose you know anything about him and Bamford?"

"The duke wasn't in France by then."

"No, not officially."

"But I do remember Stroheim talking to Désirée Clairineau."

That startled him. More, in retrospect, than it should have done.

"I didn't realize they knew each other."

"She greeted him quite familiarly. No, I don't mean they were lovers. At least, I don't think they were. But I believe she may have been connected to his father."

Raoul clunked his cup in its saucer. "Désirée Clairineau was the mistress of an Austrian noble?"

"Does that surprise you?"

"Not if it was part of a mission. But for it to be so acknowledged that the elder Stroheim knew her real identity and his son knew it as well? That does surprise me. Of course, alliances keep shifting. And it's possible Désirée Clairineau's did as well."

Henriette reached for her cup. "I hope Franz Stroheim is all right. I liked him."

"So did I. He was questioning his diplomatic work and what it meant to argue policies he didn't agree with, in a way that was quite impressive."

"You think he was working for someone else? Besides the Austrians?"

"If so, it seems Metternich didn't know it. Assuming Metternich really sent Stroheim to meet with Bamford, and it's difficult to see why Countess Lieven would have made that up." Raoul set down his coffee cup. "Would Lisette know more? About Stroheim or Désirée Clairineau?"

Henriette's fingers froze on the delicate handle of her cup. "Lisette might. She was quite young when Stroheim was at

Malmaison, but she met him. And Désirée was always kind to both the girls. But I'm afraid Lisette isn't here."

"When will she be back?"

Henriette set her cup down, as though weighing her answer with the weight of the porcelain. "Lisette left today. Early in the morning. Or perhaps during the night. Minette and I awoke to a note telling us she had to go away for a few days and that we mustn't worry."

"Has she done this before?"

"On occasion. She left friends in France. Issues arise. As you know. Often when she disappears, I assume she's doing something for you."

"She has on occasion. Though not this time."

Henriette reached for her coffee and curled her fingers round the cup. "I don't see what Lisette could have to do with the murder of an English duke."

"Nor do I. Save that they are both connected to Désirée Clairineau."

"Désirée Clairineau is in France."

"No one seems to know where she is. Unless Lisette did?"

"Lisette hasn't spoken of her in years." Henriette took a sip of coffee. "Did Lisette encounter the Duke of Bamford in the course of her missions for you?"

"Not to my knowledge." He watched Henriette. "You're wondering how much to trust me."

"I've always trusted you, Raoul."

"Trust is a matter of degrees. And I am the man who made your daughter an agent."

She smiled. "I said I trusted you, not that I'd forgiven you."

"I know all too well the calculus of trust when it comes to loved ones. I won't press you to reveal anything. But I hope you believe I have Lisette's best interests at heart."

"Raoul." Minette, Lisette's younger sister, came into the room with an impetuous rush, dark ringlets bouncing round her shoulders. She bent to give him a hug, then looked at her mother. "Sorry to interrupt. But if Raoul's here now, I can't help but think it's something to do with Lisette."

"Do you know anything about where she is?" Raoul asked.

Minette perched on the arm of the settee where her mother sat. "She got a letter. Late last night." Minette looked down at her mother as Henriette drew in her breath. "I know. I'm sorry. But at first, I thought it was Lisette's business. Only if Raoul's here now, I think it's more serious."

"Do you know whom the letter was from?" Raoul asked.

"No. But she gets letters occasionally. They're delivered by hand. And they have the same seal. Purple wax with an impression of a lion. She always burns them as soon as she reads them." Minette plucked at the blue-striped folds of her skirt. "I thought they were from a lover."

"Why?" Raoul asked. It would have been an obvious assumption with most young women, but Lisette was a former agent. And in all the time he had known her, including the years she'd worked as his agent, she'd been remarkably free from dalliance.

"The look on her face when they arrived," Minette said. "I've never really seen Lisette look like that before. I wanted to ask her more, but I also felt like it was her secret to share and she would when she ready."

Henriette looked at her younger daughter. "Why—"

"I didn't think anything was wrong. Well, not anything Lisette couldn't handle. She's gone off before and not told us anything. You know how capable she is."

Henriette clunked down her coffee cup. "Very well. But this—"

"Why is it worse if she went off with a lover? Lisette isn't foolish. She wouldn't fall in love with a man who couldn't be trusted."

"The most sensible people can be foolish when it comes to love, *chérie.*"

"Was there anything particular about the most recent message she received?" Raoul asked.

"No. Well"—Minette frowned—"with the others she seemed excited. With this one she perhaps looked a bit concerned. But still excited, if that makes any sense. I wouldn't be surprised if her lover is another agent. I mean, don't agents usually fall in love with other agents?"

"Often," Raoul said. "Though not invariably."

"She must have been going to meet him," Minette said. "He probably wrote because he was in trouble and needed her help. Or perhaps he hadn't been able to see her and now suddenly he could. Though I still don't know why she'd have needed to see him in secret."

"Do you have any idea?" Raoul asked Henriette.

Henriette shook her head. "Lisette has never talked about any particular gentleman. I've wondered, of course—a mother does. But even if I'd suspected, I'd never have pushed her to make a confidence she wasn't comfortable making. She'd certainly proved she was her own woman, leading her own life."

Minette looked at Raoul. "You must know something if you're here."

"I was here on another matter. Which may be unconnected to Lisette's disappearance. Though it's difficult not to think there may be a connection. Did you ever hear your sister talk about Désirée Clairineau?"

"Désirée? Not lately. But we both knew her when we were young. She used to bring us the loveliest ribbons and combs for our hair. Do you mean she's missing too?"

"In a manner of speaking. We aren't sure where she is. Meaning in which country. Or even if she's still alive."

Minette frowned. "Désirée could always take care of herself. But it's difficult to connect whatever she might be doing to Lisette's running off with a lover."

"So it is," Raoul said. "And sometimes one can drive oneself mad looking for connections."

LAURA LOOKED up from her notebook as her husband came into the Berkeley Square garden where the children were playing. Clara ran over and flung her arms round her father's knees before darting off to continue her game of chase with Julien and Kitty's daughter Genny.

"Kitty brought the children," Laura told Raoul, as he sat beside her on the bench. "She and Malcolm have gone to see Sofia and Kit Montagu. Though I gather it's really Enrico they want to talk to."

"Apparently Enrico quarreled with Bamford. Malcolm told me before he and Mélanie went to talk to the Bartons." Raoul stretched his arm along the back of the bench, brushing her shoulder. "I hope you're getting a lot of writing done."

"I confess it's hard to focus. But I fear this investigation doesn't play to my strengths."

Raoul's gaze went across the garden where the older children were playing catch. "It's a journey into the past."

Laura watched her husband in the cloudy light filtered by the plane trees. So much of his life had been lived before she met him. So much that went to the complex makeup of who he was. "Your life could have been very different."

Raoul looked sideways at her. "Undoubtedly. How, in particular?"

"If Arabella had left Alistair and run off with you."

"Oh yes. I'd probably have started a newspaper or something. Looked after Malcolm while Bella took on the Elsinore League. Though any version of Bella who would have run off with me would have been a very different person. Given the climate, I'd have probably still ended up arrested. If I hadn't been smart enough to get all of us out of the country. And if I had, we might have gone to Ireland. Where I also could have ended up arrested. And Bella wouldn't have had the leverage with Alistair to get me out. Probably. Who knows. We might have muddled through. Malcolm would have had a happier childhood, I think."

"I'm sure of it."

"Bella would have still been Bella. I can't believe she was beyond saving, but she'd have had to do it herself. I couldn't have done it, however different our circumstances. And I don't think being with me would have given her the resources to do it."

"Alistair seemed to think differently."

Raoul shook his head. "In any chess game there are hundreds of possible scenarios. You have to focus on the one you are in now, given the moves you've made."

"Sweetheart." Laura leant into her husband's arm. "Did you just compare family life to a chess game?"

"No. Maybe."

Laura laughed. "It's all right. I shouldn't have got entangled with Jack. But I can't be sorry I have Emily. I can't be sorry I met you or that we have Clara. There's no sense in replaying any of it."

A ball Colin had thrown overshot Emily, the intended recipient, and thudded to the ground a few feet off. Raoul scooped it up and tossed it back to Colin. "Bella once tried to tell me that if I could have been a full-time father, I'd have been too engrossed in it to properly try to change the world. Of course, assuming she was right, that means I'd have missed what the Revolution turned into, and Ireland, and Spain. Hard, in many ways, to argue there weren't better uses of my time, at least when it comes to preserving my sanity. But I also fundamentally reject the premise."

"Well, no," Laura said. "Look at Mélanie."

Raoul raised a brow.

"She's never let go of her mission. But she's also never let go of being a mother."

"No. I used to worry she'd break herself, but she's never broken any of her commitments. Unlike me."

"Darling—"

"Don't sugarcoat it, Laura." He settled back on the bench, gaze on his children and grandchildren and friends' children. "It was partly the world we were in. I did my best to keep my commitments to Malcolm. But I didn't do nearly well enough." He waved to Emily as she caught another throw from Colin and returned it. "That we all have what we have now is remarkable. I wouldn't trade it for anything. I can't claim we'd be happier if the past had gone differently. But that doesn't excuse my mistakes. That doesn't justify the things I've done. It's folly to dwell on them, as I often say." His gaze shot from Emily to Colin. "But it would also be irresponsible to ignore them."

CHAPTER 43

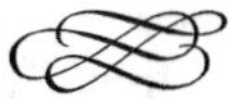

Spring 1817
rue du Faubourg Saint-Honoré, Paris

aura stepped into the salon. Talk and laughter and the clink of glasses spilt through the room. Jessica looked round with wide eyes. Colin clung tightly to her hand, but at almost four he was already well used to grown-up parties. He had been his whole life, from what she could tell.

"Laura." Mélanie Rannoch came forwards with a swish of pomegranate silk and a waft of custom-blended rose, lily, and bergamot and took Jessica from her arms.

Colin let go of Laura's hand and ran to hug his mother's legs, heedless of crushing the silk of her gown. Mélanie touched her son's hair while she cradled Jessica in her other arm.

Malcolm Rannoch joined them and swung his son onto his shoulders. He smiled. So did Mélanie. Her charm dazzled. Malcolm's was quieter. But with both of them, Laura was still struggling to see beneath the surface. Because surely they could not be as warm and caring as they appeared on the surface.

Malcolm handed her a glass of champagne.

"Enjoy yourself, Laura," Mélanie said, detaching her pearls from Jessica's grip.

Laura took a sip of champagne. Dry and yeasty. An excellent vintage. Better than what she'd been accustomed to in her former life, when the champagne had flowed very freely. She took another sip. Dutch courage. An invitation to mingle at a party without watching her charges. A governess's dream. Also an excellent opportunity to pursue her other job. Which was where her dilemma lay.

She moved to the side. Even with employers as indulgent as the Rannochs, there was a limit to how much a governess was supposed to put herself forwards. She found a seat on the edge of the salon and cast a glance round the room. Her dark blue silk faded into the background, but also stood out in the throng of flounced and pintucked Parisian fashions in cerulean blue, blush pink, pomona green, and other fashionable colors.

She should be listening. She should be watching the Rannochs for suspicious behavior. But they were showing their children off to friends. Hardly the setting for espionage. And, of course, if she learnt anything, she'd have to report it. There lay the rub.

"An excellent spot to observe the crowd." A gentleman moved to the seat beside her. Lean, dark-haired. He blended into the surroundings as well. And yet something about him drew the eye. She'd noticed him when she came into the room.

He extended a hand. "The Rannochs do not stand on ceremony. I hope you will forgive me for not doing so either. I'm Raoul O'Roarke. I've known Malcolm Rannoch since he was a boy."

She found herself smiling. Hard not to smile in response to that smile. "I'm Laura Dudley. Governess to the Rannoch children."

"They're fortunate to have you."

"You can't know that."

"I saw you bring the children in."

"I was just doing what I was asked to do. What any governess or nurse would do."

"On the contrary. Not all would look at them as you did. One can read a lot in a look."

"I'm not sure everyone can. But you evidently can."

"I've spent a lot of my life observing. A solitary life gives one the leisure for that."

"You could be describing the life of a governess."

"Are governesses solitary? I would think you have constant demands on your time and attention."

"And we learn to fade into the background. There when we're needed, invisible when not." She glanced across the room. Mélanie was feeding Colin a strawberry with one hand. Jessica reached out a hand from her mother's other arm to tug at Malcolm's cravat.

"It must be an art. Balancing it."

"Oh, it's rather commonplace. No one would think to call it an art. The Rannochs spend a lot of time with their children themselves. That makes it easier."

"You've worked in a number of households?"

It was a natural enough question, but all her warning instincts went up. She'd been talking quite easily, not thinking of what to reveal or conceal. Something about him invited confidences. Which was dangerous. "A few. I've had a number of years to be a governess." Which told the truth without revealing what she'd done in the years before she'd been a governess. Or why she'd become one.

"Difficult to move on, I would think."

"In some cases. In others, it's a bit of a relief. But yes, it's difficult if one becomes attached. And it's difficult not to become attached."

He smiled. "I can understand that. I've lived much of my life alone."

～

SPRIGS OF GREENERY ran down the table. Red ribbon looped round the branches of candles and the wall sconces. A bit too much, perhaps? Hard to tell. It was years since he'd celebrated anything to do with the holidays, except on a mission. But that wasn't what this was. No matter the question in Mélanie's eyes when he'd suggested it. And in Malcolm's.

But they'd agreed. Mélanie on her own would have objected, he thought, but Malcolm had agreed, and she'd drawn a breath, squeezed Malcolm's arm, and agreed as well.

And so he was hosting a holiday party. A family party. Though the very word sounded absurd. Was absurd.

He looked at the greenery again. And the red ribbons, which also wound round the green sprigs. Jessica would like those. She liked to tug at the ribbons on Mélanie's gowns. And the Mivart's staff had provided paper and pastels at his request. Colin and the Davenports' older daughter both liked to draw. Malcolm had. He'd often sat drawing at tables in inns or sitting rooms while Raoul talked to colleagues. How much had Malcolm absorbed of those talks? How much were Colin and Livia Davenport absorbing of their parents' talks now? Would they be agents in the future?

Host was a role he'd played before. Missions called for it, after all. This should not be so very different, but it was. As though he were stepping through a portal into a world he'd never thought to venture into. From which he was likely to be ejected as an interloper at any moment.

The doors opened with a well-oiled creak. He tensed, as he would at rustling in the underbrush in ground set with snipers.

The room filled. Mélanie flashed him an anxious look as he bent over her hand. Malcolm shook his hand with determination. Jessica grinned at him from her mother's arms. Colin ran over to say hello and asked if they could play catch again. Harry and Cordelia Davenport smiled with a friendship unclouded by the tangled layers of the past.

Fanny came over and touched his arm. "It's a long time since we've kept Christmas together."

"I don't believe we ever have."

"I remember you at a Boxing Day party when I was sixteen." She adjusted the chain strap of her reticule. "It never would have occurred to me then that we'd be where we are now. For that matter, it never would have occurred to me a year ago that we would be."

"It wouldn't have occurred to me a month ago. And yes, I know I have no right to be so fortunate."

"I know you're enamored of rights, but in this case, I think you're foolish to talk of them. Everyone in this room looks remarkably happy. Which is just what one wants at this disgustingly sentimental season. Though seeing Chloe's excitement, I was not entirely immune to its charms." She smiled at her eight-year-old daughter, who was playing peep-a-boo with Jessica.

"You're a fraud, Fanny."

"Well, I will confess I quite enjoy spending Boxing Day with you. And it's good to see Malcolm and Mélanie smiling." Fanny paused, gaze on Malcolm and Mélanie. They were standing together, though Mélanie was turned to talk to Harry Davenport, Malcolm to Fanny's eldest daughter Aline and her husband Geoffrey Blackwell, who had been a military doctor in the Peninsula. "I had wondered—"

"What?" he kept his voice easy.

"Oh, just my imagination, perhaps." She waved a hand, though her delicate brows were drawn together. "I'd just thought something had shifted between them. But then while I'm hardly an expert on matrimony, I do realize that happens with couples. Not my affair, of course. But it's difficult not to be concerned. It's difficult for Malcolm to let himself be happy. I was hoping he'd be able to settle into it. I imagine it's challenging for Mélanie. He doesn't share himself easily. And marrying into this world isn't easy."

Raoul looked at Malcolm and Mélanie. They were still turned away from each other, but as he watched, they turned and their eyes met for a moment. If the look didn't have the ease it once had, the closeness was there. Or perhaps he was just determined to see it that way. "They're both capable of a lot, from what I've seen," he said.

"Oh, undoubtedly," Fanny said. "But even the most capable can find challenges difficult to confront. Malcolm and Mélanie have the will to confront them, which may be more important."

The company moved to the table. No one looked particularly horrified by his seating arrangement. Laura Dudley, who had been hanging back, slipped quietly into her chair. If she was surprised to be seated by him, she gave no sign of it. But then he suspected Laura Dudley was expert at concealing a great deal.

"You're kind to do this," she said.

"It's a chance to celebrate with people I care about." That came out a bit awkwardly.

"And it's giving the staff in Berkeley Square a chance to celebrate with their families."

"I did think of that." He studied her for a moment. She was wearing a dark blue silk he'd seen before when she joined the Rannochs at entertainments and a strand of pearls he'd also seen on those other occasions. Her hair was drawn into its usual simple knot. But it was impossible to dim those titian strands. "You didn't want to—"

"Oh no." She reached for her wineglass and took a sip. "I don't have family near. I confess I'm not one for holidays, but I do enjoy seeing Colin and Jessica's delight. It's infectious."

"So I've noticed."

Jessica was sitting in Mélanie's lap, pulling a roll apart. Colin was taking careful bites of the roast potatoes Malcolm had cut up. Laura was watching them as well, a smile in her eyes. Raoul didn't doubt her genuine enjoyment of the children. What else she was doing in the Rannoch household remained an interesting question. There was no particular reason for her to confide in him about her family and circumstances, but he couldn't shake the sense that there was more. Keen instincts? Or a spymaster looking into shadows and mistaking a bush for a bear?

"Their parents want to be with them for the holidays," Laura said. "There's little enough for me to do. They told me I could go away. But I'm with Colin and Jessica enough that I wanted to share this with them. Even though I'm not the sentimental sort."

"One doesn't have to be the sentimental sort to feel sentiment."

"An interesting way of looking at it."

He leant back in his chair and took a drink of wine. "I'm not one for holidays either. But I confess I enjoy spending the day with people I care about." That was true. Truer than he'd realized.

"You've known the family for a long time."

"Since I was at university." That was true too, though an adulterous love affair was probably not what she was thinking of.

"It's nice to see them all so happy to be together." She took another drink of wine. "It's not true at every holiday gathering."

"No."

Colin dropped a piece of potato. Malcolm caught it one-handed. "The holidays are much more agreeable with children," she said. "That's one advantage of being a governess."

"Some would say it's a disadvantage of being a governess."

"I supposed it's a matter of perspective. Much as it is for parents. The Rannochs seem to see the positives in parenting." She reached for her wine again. "Are you settled in London for a while?"

It was a perfectly natural question, and yet he couldn't but wonder if she was probing for information. "For the moment, though I go back and forth to the Continent frequently. My life has been unsettled since Waterloo. Like many of ours." Perhaps not the wisest admission, but Waterloo had unsettled people on all sides of the conflict.

"You were in Spain during the war."

"Working with some of the guerrilleros." That was true, though he'd actually been reporting to the French. "I'm half Spanish."

"And half Irish. And you went to university in Paris."

"You've gathered information as effectively as any agent." He said it lightly.

Her smile was sweet and friendly and looked entirely disingenuous. It was also the perfect smile from an agent to deflect suspicion in such a situation. Assuming she was an agent. Which, he had to remind himself, there was no reason to think she was.

She tilted her head to one side, her blue gaze honest and open and appraising. Clear as a highland stream. Though he'd stumbled on hidden rocks in a seemingly clear highland stream more than once. "People interest me. Teaching is fascinating, but one also has to find the time to put one's mind to other uses. And, as a teacher, I've learnt that one has to fully research a subject to attempt to understand it. Though even then, I try to convey that so much is a matter of perspective."

"Cogently put."

"Governesses might be thought of as singularly powerless. But we are able to share ideas. Even if only a fraction of them are remembered, it can make the work feel worth it."

"Which it should. It sounds a more significant achievement than anything I've managed in many ways."

"You needn't patronize me, Mr. O'Roarke."

"I'm not. I've seen a number of changes I fought hard for come to nothing or go backwards. Actually impacting one person's way of thinking and seeing the world is a lasting achievement."

"There's no guarantee that that person won't change their thinking. Or go backwards."

"No. There's no guarantee of anything. But I think it's far less likely. Lessons learnt in childhood linger."

"You appear to have made a strong impact on Malcolm Rannoch in his childhood from what I've heard."

Raoul kept his fingers steady on his wineglass. What had she heard? And more importantly, from whom? Difficult to imagine Malcolm talking about him in familiar terms. Difficult to imagine Malcolm talking about him at all, after recent revelations, unless he gave way to indiscretion. And Malcolm was far too careful—and far too concerned for Mélanie's safety—to give voice to what must be his true thoughts.

"I was fortunate to be able to spend time with him when he was young," Raoul said. "I think it's often the adults who treasure those memories."

"As a governess, I can say that those often seem to be the memories that linger the most with children. It's amazing how the simplest comment or story or fragment of conversation will stay with them. Sometimes one doesn't realize it until they say some-thing years later. It's heartening. And also rather terrifying. If I let myself think about it, I'd never open my mouth."

"I know the feeling."

She took a sip from her own wine. "The day we spoke in the Berkeley Square garden, you said you don't have children of your own."

"No. As I said, I enjoy my friends' children. And I admire them for putting in the perseverance parenting takes."

"At least for those who do it well."

"Quite."

"It's less work for a governess when they do it well. Of course, the children are more likely to regret being with their governess instead of their parents. But overall, it makes for a far pleasanter household to be part of. The Rannochs' is certainly the pleasantest household I've ever worked in. I can see why you enjoy spending time with them."

He managed not to choke on his wine. It was something of a Herculean feat. He was fortunate to be allowed inside the door of the Berkeley Square house. "One of the reasons I'm glad to be in London, at the moment."

"I imagine Spain is challenging, since the war."

"It's not the Spain I envisioned when we were fighting." That was the unvarnished truth. "But I was always worried about what a restoration of the monarchy would mean." That was the truth as well.

"I admire you. For still fighting for what you believe in. Even when things don't go your way."

"It often feels like banging my head against a wall."

"But you keep on."

"I have a quixotic tendency to still believe something can come from tilting at windmills."

"Perhaps those windmills really are dragons."

He smiled and reached for the bottle to refill her wineglass. "I quite like dragons."

"So does Colin. He draws wonderful ones."

"His father did as well." Memories of drawing paper on scarred tables in inn parlors or gleaming satinwood and marble in salons and hotels flashed into his mind. Malcolm pointing out how the wings would work to catch the air.

Miss Dudley took a sip from her refilled glass. "Children believe in magic. I don't. Or in anything really, beyond the human realm. But it's good sometimes to remember that things we might not think possible can still happen. Not from magic. From sheer perseverance. And perhaps a small amount of luck. Or more than small."

"I admire your fortitude, Miss Dudley."

Her smile lit her eyes but her mouth curved with irony. Something about it broke his heart. "The lives of governesses tend to be singularly free of magic. Except for that we find through our pupils. I gave up expecting magic a long time ago."

"A pity," he said without planning. "I'd like to think it's still possible."

～

March 1818
Pelican Inn, Maidstone

THE PASSAGE, thank god, was empty. He rapped once at the door. Laura opened it and he slipped inside and set the bottle of wine and glasses down on the table inside the door. None tipped over. Which was something of a miracle, given how his hands were shaking.

"All quiet." He managed to pour the wine. Risky to try, perhaps, but it covered the awkwardness and postponed the decision on what else they might do. Which seemed awkwarder now than in those first minutes in the parlor before they'd gone upstairs. When she'd kissed him and said she couldn't bear to be alone tonight.

Laura accepted a glass and clinked it against his own. The wine sloshed but both of them managed not to spill. He took a sip. He probably couldn't feel drunker than he already did. For reasons that had nothing to do with the wine.

She smiled into his eyes with reckless defiance, took another sip, set her glass down, and stepped into his arms.

～

HE TURNED on his side in the tangle of sheets and propped his head on one hand. The light from the candle they'd left lit burnished her hair, spread about her on the pillow.

She turned towards him, as though aware of his regard. Their gazes caught and held for a moment. A moment filled with all the things one couldn't say at such a time.

Her mouth curved in a faint smile that acknowledged the awkwardness. "It's been a long time."

He laughed. "Tell me about it."

Surprise leapt in her eyes.

"It's a risk in my line of work, sharing too much of yourself," he said.

"I would have thought—"

"That it's a tool of gathering information? Sometimes. But not in every role. Not in playing a governess, I would imagine."

"God no. But I'd have thought—"

"At my age, in my position? It hasn't been part of any mission I've undertaken for some time."

Her gaze moved over his face for a moment, as though reassessing long-held assumptions. She reached out and brushed her fingers against his face.

He caught her hand and pressed it to his lips. "Do you want me to stay?"

"Do you mind?"

"On the contrary." He drew her against him and settled back against the pillows. Her head fell into the hollow of his shoulder. After a moment she curled against him, one hand on his chest. He turned his head and pressed his lips against her hair. Every instinct screamed that he'd taken an appalling risk and dragged them both into danger. Yet he hadn't felt so alive in years.

CHAPTER 44

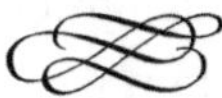

May 1821
London

Enrico Vincenzo faced Malcolm and Kitty across his sister and brother-in-law's sitting room. "Of course, I confronted Bamford," Enrico said. "He was threatening to have Violetta sent home to Italy. Her family are working with the Austrians. That's why she came to England with me. They accused me of abducting her. Which is absurd. As if I could convince Violetta to do anything. You saw her."

"So we did," Malcolm said from the settee across the room from Enrico, where he sat with Kitty. Violetta Barese had arrived in London with Enrico on the night of the Bamford musicale. From everything Malcolm had seen, she was indeed very strong willed and eminently capable.

"Her parents went to Metternich, and he's pressuring Bamford," Enrico said. "We had to hide Violetta."

"Bamford made threats." Kit Montagu moved to stand beside his wife's brother. Kit's voice was more contained than Enrico's, but Kit's expression had a hard determination that hadn't been there when Malcolm had first met him. "We needed to keep Violetta protected. We were afraid Bamford might try to send her back to Italy."

"Did you really think he'd do that, against her will?" Kitty asked. "I didn't know Bamford well, but he struck me as quite fair minded and very kind to his daughters."

"She's a woman," Sofia Montagu said. Her chair was strategically positioned between her husband and brother and Malcolm and Kitty. "And a young woman. We often aren't seen as having a will of our own."

"Fair enough," Malcolm said.

"That's why Bamford came to see us," Kit said. "Metternich had sent word to Bamford through Austrian diplomatic channels. He wanted to know if we knew where Violetta was."

"Did he actually threaten to send her back?" Malcolm asked.

"He said he was concerned for her. That her family were concerned. But we aren't fools. It was clear what he'd try if he knew where she was. So we said we didn't know."

"Which is the truth," Sofia said. "Well, more or less. We know how to find her if we need to."

"Was Bamford angry?" Kitty asked.

"He made a lot of bluster about how we'd see it differently when we were parents." Sofia touched her rounded stomach. "Then I asked him if he'd really not want his daughter to be able to decide her future for herself. I thought he'd bluster more. I was really just trying to score a point. But he went still, and got an odd look on his face. He said he had to admit that the older he got, the more he felt it was important for everyone to decide their own future. And that perhaps that was the one thing he could give his children." She locked her hands over her stomach. "When he left, he looked at Kit and me and said our child would be lucky to have parents who valued its ability to forge its own life. For a moment I quite liked him."

"But you still thought he'd threaten Violetta?" Malcolm asked.

"We weren't taking any chances," Kit said.

"I'd do whatever it takes to save her from an unwanted marriage," Enrico said.

His sister cast a quick look at him.

"I mean, not murder," Enrico said. "You can't think that. I'd never—do you suspect me—"

"We don't know whom to suspect at this point," Malcolm said.

Enrico nodded slowly. "The truth is, I don't know how far I'd go to protect Violetta." He looked from Sofia to Kit to Malcolm to Kitty. "I mean, can you say where you'd draw the line protecting the person you love? There, I've said it. I love Violetta. And I can't say I wouldn't have committed murder. But I didn't." He folded his arms. "You'll have to decide if you believe me."

RAOUL TOSSED a ball to Emily and watched her throw it to Kitty's elder son Leo Ashford. "Capital," he said.

Emily grinned at him over her shoulder, then spun round towards the gate to the Berkeley Square garden.

She had quick instincts. Raoul turned a fraction of a second after his daughter and saw a tall man with dark blond hair and an intent face enter the garden. Raoul put up a hand in reassurance to the children and walked over to the new arrival. "Barton," he said, meeting a pair of intense blue eyes.

"O'Roarke." Gaultier Barton paused just inside the gate. "I've been looking for you."

Raoul gestured towards the nearby bench. Laura had already got to her feet and moved over to Clara and Genny, who were helping Jessica walk Berowne, the Rannoch family cat.

Gaultier Barton moved to the bench with the caution of one on enemy terrain. "I'm sorry to disturb you with your family."

"It's no disturbance," Raoul said. "Especially in the circumstances."

Barton looked across the garden, where the game of catch had resumed. "Your children?"

"My daughters. And my grandson and granddaughter. And the children of my friends. My wife Laura"—Raoul nodded towards Laura, who smiled back—"and our youngest."

Barton inclined his head to Laura. "A lot has changed for you."

"It has indeed." Raoul settled back on the bench. "I understand you have another child as well."

"I suppose you heard that from Bertrand or the Rannochs. They came to see my wife."

"Yes. No sense pretending I don't know. Though I haven't seen them since they got back."

Barton met his gaze. "They're looking for Stroheim."

"If you've spoken to your wife, you know Stroheim's gone missing."

"After the ship he was on, or was supposed to be on, exploded and caught fire, and the man he was supposed to meet was murdered." Barton passed a hand over his face. Even in the gray light of the late afternoon, his skin was ashen. "Régine's fond of Stroheim. She doesn't lightly admit to being fond of anyone, even me. Maybe especially me. But she cares about Stroheim. So she wasn't going to admit anything that might lead to his being endangered."

"Understandable."

Barton leant back on the bench. "I owe Stroheim my life. You know that. He was fond of his cousin Christine, my first wife. Which didn't necessarily mean he'd be fond of me. I don't know that I made her very happy. She thought she was joining the Napoleonic court when she married me. Which she was, in a way. But I was never quite the courtier she wanted. Yet even as our marriage grew more strained, I enjoyed Stroheim's visits. We shared a certain dissatisfaction with developments in both our countries. And we could talk to each other more frankly than we could to most. Still, I wouldn't have thought he'd be the person I could turn to, facing imprisonment. I wouldn't have thought of turning to him at all. Christine was gone. Stroheim and I had fought on opposite sides at Waterloo. When I was arrested, I thought I was as done for as the other poor devils who fought for Bonaparte and were caught up in the White Terror. Didn't seem fair, really, to escape when they couldn't."

Raoul cast a quick glance from Clara, tugging at Berowne's lead below where Jessica held the loop, to Emily, tossing an expert throw to Colin. "I've faced imprisonment. There's nothing unfair about finding a way to live. Especially when you have a family."

"I convinced Régine to marry me to protect Roland. She told the Rannochs as much. No sense in not being frank now. I wanted Régine to protect Roland. I also wanted her to protect herself. If she took Roland out of the country, I figured she'd be so focused on protecting him she'd keep herself out of danger and they'd both be safe." He shook his head with a rueful smile. "Instead, Régine got word to Stroheim. I still don't know how she did it. She has skills I don't. When I got word of the rescue, my first thought was sheer bloody terror for her. She always was tenacious." He shook his head again. "Poor Régine. She never wanted to be married. She married a man who was likely to be imprisoned. But she managed to save me. Then there we were, safe and married. I don't think she ever bargained on the life we have."

"From what I remember five and a half years ago, Régine was quite happy to escape to England."

"Oh, she was happy when we left. And I think she's happy now. Sometimes I wonder if I'm deluding myself into thinking what makes me happy makes her happy. She loves the children too much to choose anything else. And I think she loves me." He stared at the gnarled branches of the plane tree opposite. "Can't help but worry at times that I've trapped her."

"Your wife never struck me as a woman who'd let herself be trapped."

"Only by her own loyalties. Which she scarcely admits to having. But our family challenges aren't what you're interested in now. I'm probably prevaricating." Barton looked up and met Raoul's gaze, his own keen and steady. "Stroheim showed up at our house last night. He apologized for dragging us into this, but said he needed help and wasn't sure whom else he could trust."

Raoul sat very still. "What was he dragging you into? And what did he need help with?"

"He didn't tell us all of it. He said Bamford had been killed, and he thought the killers might be after him too. Or that he might be being set up to take the blame. That the motive seemed to be to cause an incident. But he couldn't be sure. And he wasn't sure whom he could trust in Britain."

"Including the government?"

Barton gave a curt nod. "Especially the government, I'd say. And he wasn't in the country alone."

That was news. "Whom did he have with him?" Raoul asked.

"A woman and child. A little girl. About five or six."

"The woman was his mistress?"

"Possibly, though Régine said she wasn't convinced of it, from the way they interacted."

"What was the woman like?"

"Quiet. Quite lovely. Light brown hair and brown eyes. Or at times they looked green. Warm smile, though there seemed to be shock behind it. As though she'd been dealt a blow she couldn't quite let herself feel yet. A bit older than Stroheim. If they were lovers, I don't think he's the child's father, though he was obviously fond of her. They had food in our kitchen. The little girl slept for a few hours. Stroheim went out and then came back and said he had a safe place for them to go. He apologized for pulling us into it. Said it was safer if we didn't know where they were." Barton looked steadily at Raoul. "I'm trusting you, O'Roarke."

"And wondering if you've made a mistake."

"Trust is always a risk. If you don't trust anyone, you can't move forwards. Régine trusted you and that's why I'm alive today. I'm making the same calculation again." He sat back on the bench. "Of course, you're probably calculating how much you can trust me."

Raoul grinned without rancor. "Always."

CHAPTER 45

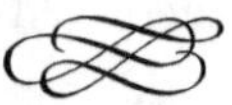

May 1815
Brussels

Julien dropped down across from Raoul on a bench in the beer garden at the end of the Allée Verte. "Haven't seen you for a bit."

Raoul looked up from *Le Moniteur.* "I've been busy."

"I can imagine." Julien swung his legs over the bench. His hair was black, probably from his most recent masquerade. "I saw Mélanie at a regimental ball last night. She was charming everyone. Quite the center of attention. Malcolm was in the library. I think he was passing a code in a book, but I also think he was escaping. But Mélanie got him out later in the evening and they danced together." Julien reached across the table for Raoul's glass of Pilsner and took a sip. "It can't be easy."

"No, I'm sure it isn't. But Mélanie's equal to it. She may be the most talented agent I've ever met."

"I won't argue with you there. But that isn't what I meant."

"My dear Julien. This is no time for cheap sentiment."

"I wouldn't call it cheap. Inconvenient, perhaps. I don't envy people troubled by sentiment. But you won't trick me into thinking it doesn't exist."

"I thought you didn't believe in sentiment."

"I don't think I'm capable of it."

"And you think I am?"

Julien leant across the table, eyes particularly blue. "Don't pretend, O'Roarke. Of course you are. I've seen you."

"I just don't let it get in my way."

"No?"

"You can hardly call my actions sentimental."

"Not sentimental. Driven by sentiment. If you ask me, life is complicated enough without it. But then you waste a lot of time believing in things as well."

Raoul smoothed the pages of the newspaper. "Talking about pretending not to be what you are."

"You don't know who I am, O'Roarke. In any number of ways."

"Don't worry, Julien. I have more vital things to expend my energies on than digging into your past."

"I suppose that should be a relief." Julien pushed the glass back across the table to Raoul. "Where do you see this false fairy tale between the Rannochs ending?"

"We're trying to win a war." And battle between the French under Napoleon Bonaparte, recently escaped from Elba, and the Allies seemed closer every day, for all the holiday atmosphere in Brussels.

"You're too good a strategist not to have thought beyond the end of the war. Tell me you don't always see past checkmate."

Raoul took a drink of Pilsner. It reminded him of Vienna. Without turning his head, he could spot two Dutch-Belgians playing chess, a Prussian major turning the pages of a newspaper, and three British riflemen tossing dice. "I very much hope the end of the war won't be checkmate."

"Do you imagine she'll ever be able to leave?"

"If she wanted to, I'd make sure she could. I suspect she won't ever want to."

Julien frowned.

"You don't agree?"

"No, I find I rather do. I saw them dancing together."

Raoul scanned Julien's face.

"Oh, no," Julien said. "I have a great deal of admiration for Mélanie. Not to mention she saved my life more than once. I'm not going to cause her problems. Mind you, I can't see her being happy as a diplomatic wife. The fact that she can do it for so long proves she's a better agent than I am. I couldn't do it. But once she doesn't have the mission—assuming we get that far—what do you think will keep her going?"

"What keeps any of us going?"

"Isn't that obvious? The game. Or in your case, the cause."

"She may find another way to work for a cause."

"By being a diplomatic wife? Surely you can't bear the thought of the waste."

"Diplomatic wives can wield a lot of power. Look at Countess Lieven. And then there's—" Raoul fixed his gaze on the still waters of the canal beside the beer garden.

"Don't tell me you were going to say love."

"I was going to say being a parent."

Julien's gaze narrowed in the sunlight. But not quite with the quick dismissal Raoul expected. "I don't think that's enough for anyone. Too much of a burden to place on the children. But I'll grant the world would be a better place if more people placed weight on it. She'll need more, though." He reached for the glass and took a drink. "Or she may not drive Malcolm mad, but she'll go mad herself."

~

April 1818

LISETTE VARON REGARDED RAOUL. "You look different."

"Have I aged that quickly?"

"Don't be silly. If anything, you look younger. Not that you ever look old."

"Your tact is admirable, my dear."

Lisette tilted her head to one side, the way she had since she was a child. "You look—happier. As though you have things to think about besides regret."

He smiled. Which he'd been doing more of late. In fact, he'd find himself suddenly staring at a line of trees or at a line of code and realize he had a smile on his face. Because the world seemed full of possibilities. Possibilities he'd given up on years ago. Possibilities that were dangerous and unsuited to the life of a spy. That went against every lesson he should have learnt. And yet. He felt alive. As he hadn't in years. As he'd thought he never would again.

"I've always said regret is a singularly useless emotion." He stopped walking, beneath a swinging sign with an image of a golden ring. "Do you mind if we stop here? I could use your advice."

"On jewelry?" Lisette raised her brows.

"Er—yes."

"For a mission?"

"Not in this case."

Lisette grinned. "She must be very special."

"She's quite remarkable. And deserves far better than me."

They went in to the shop together. "Are you looking for something for the young lady's mother?" the shopkeeper asked, evidently assuming Lisette was Raoul's daughter. Which was far preferable to other assumptions he might have made.

Raoul inclined his head. The shopkeeper pulled out pearls and diamonds, then left them on their own when they said they'd rather browse.

"Is she dark or fair?" Lisette asked, leaning over the counter.

"She has hair right out of a Titian painting." And he could close his eyes and recall running his fingers through it. Pulling out the pins the way he'd wanted to do since he'd met her in a Paris salon a year before.

"Peridot? Aquamarine? Are her eyes green or blue or brown?"

"Blue." And could cut through his defenses with devastating accuracy.

"What about these?" Lisette bent over the counter and pointed to a pair of sparkling blue stones set in silver. "Blue topaz, I think. They'll catch the light beautifully."

The jeweler took out the earrings and encouraged Raoul to hold them up to the lamplight. They did indeed catch the light. He could see them on Laura, glinting in the light of the chandelier in Berkeley Square at the party Mélanie was giving.

"Are they for a special occasion?" Lisette asked when they left the shop, the paper-wrapped parcel tucked in his pocket.

"She's going to a ball. Something of a debut, though she's more than a decade older than you."

"Will you be there?"

"No."

"That's too bad."

"I'm not sure. She has a lot of opportunities available to her. She needs to be able to explore them."

Lisette frowned. "But—"

"Happiness is no less real for being transitory."

"So you don't expect the affair to last?"

I have no right to ask you to feel any sort of obligation. But I feel one.

He'd said it. He'd meant it then. He suspected he'd mean it his entire life. At his age he'd tumbled into feeling like a schoolboy. And acting like one.

Lisette stopped walking and looked up at him, the hood of her blue cloak falling back from her face, strands of honey-blonde hair escaping their pins. "If you really wanted to let her go, you wouldn't be sending the earrings."

Raoul looked down into her blue-gray eyes. "You're very wise. Have I told you that?"

"It's common sense. And you also should know there are different ways of defining what a person has to offer. She's obviously good for you. And I suspect you're good for her, too. Wouldn't you advise someone else not to think too much about the future and enjoy the present?"

"I'm endeavoring to do just that."

"But don't do it so much you give up on the future." Lisette drew a breath of the cold, damp air. "Surely if we've learnt anything these past years, it's that we have to hold on to what's important."

"And?" Raoul scanned her face.

"And what?" She colored lightly in the wintry light. He didn't think it was the cold.

"Far be it from me to pry, but if I were inclined to, I'd wonder if there was someone making you feel this way."

"I don't have time for much, beyond missions."

"Something else to blame me for. Though I'd have said the same."

"But you met her on a mission."

"In a manner of speaking."

"Well, then." Lisette tucked her arm through his own. "There's hope for me. Not that I particularly want anything of the sort right now. Life is complicated enough, don't you think?"

"Sometimes the complications are what makes it worth living."

She laughed. "There you have me."

CHAPTER 46

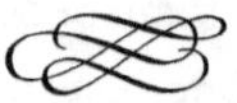

May 1821
London

Kitty stepped through the Berkeley Square garden gate and bent to hug her daughter Genny, who ran over to her. She hugged Clara and Jessica as well, petted Berowne, smiled at Laura, and waved to the older children, then moved to the bench where Raoul was sitting, a thoughtful look on his face. "I passed a man who looked to be leaving the garden on my way into the square. Dark blond hair, intense face."

"Gaultier Barton," Raoul said as she sat beside him. He recounted his talk with Barton.

"I'm glad Stroheim isn't another victim," Kitty said. "You've made more progress than Malcolm and I did at the Montagus'. Though at least we have an explanation for the Levellers' confronting Bamford at White's. Which seems more personal than political." She told Raoul about her and Malcolm's talk with Kit and Sofia Montagu and Enrico Vincenzo. "Enrico fully admits to having had a motive to have got rid of Bamford," she concluded. "But I don't think he did."

"It would surprise me," Raoul agreed. "And in truth I have a hard time imagining Tony's sending a young woman back to her family against her wishes."

"I saw enough of him at the duchess's musicale to agree," Kitty said. "He was also very open-minded about opposing viewpoints. But then so are you." She regarded Raoul for a moment while the children's shouts cut the garden air. "You're very forbearing not throwing my past in my face."

"I could more than say the same. Which part of your past are you thinking of?"

"If your side had won in Spain, we wouldn't be facing the challenges we are now. The challenges that had us appealing to Bamford for help. We might be facing different challenges, but I don't think it would be as bad."

"I tend to agree with you. Though one can never be sure."

Kitty smiled. "You're a model of understanding."

"If it comes to that, you're rather understanding about my divided loyalties during the war."

She regarded him for a moment, a dozen scenes from the past replaying in her mind. So much had shifted when she learnt the truth about Mélanie and Raoul. Odd how new information could change the past. Like rereading a book from a different point of view. "I wouldn't have been at the time," she said honestly. "I don't like losing, and I thought just about anything was justified by achieving my goals."

"Yes," he said. "I know something about that."

She scanned his face in the shadows of the plane tree branches. It was so much more open than it had been in the old days, yet at the same time she often thought he was concealing just as much. But then, perhaps now they were better friends, there were more things to conceal. "I told Mélanie I thought I'd have done what she did. Married a man to spy on him and gain tactical advantage. I think I'd also have done what you did—orchestrate an agent's marriage to gain tactical advantage. Even if that agent was the person I loved. Except that that isn't really all you did, and I'm not sure I'd have done the rest."

"What rest?"

She folded her arms over the appliquéd sarcenet of her spencer. "Orchestrate the marriage of the person I loved because I decided they were better off without me."

"My dear Kitty. There may not have been a marriage involved, but didn't you give up the person you loved precisely because you decided he was better off without you?"

"I suppose so. In a way." Damn, she had walked right into that. She hunched her shoulders. "Also because I wasn't sure it would work."

"Well, then."

"I didn't think I could make it work."

"Precisely."

She fixed him with a level stare. "You're perfectly capable of being happily married."

"So are you."

"Apparently. At least now. Rather to my surprise. In the old days I'd have said I wasn't. But a part of me wanted my freedom. I don't think that was it for you."

"No? I've protected my freedom my entire life."

"Not really, if the stories I've heard are true. And you weren't protecting your freedom eight years ago, if what my husband says is true."

"Julien can be annoyingly sure he has all the answers."

"So he can. But he also has remarkably keen insights." Kitty leant back on the hard metal of the bench. "Ten years ago, I was so convinced I knew the right course for Spain, I'd have been furious with you for seeing it differently. I might not even have been able to acknowledge that you were working for what you thought was best for Spain as well. That there were different ways of seeing it."

"That's remarkably honest."

"You make it easy to be honest. You don't judge. And you've

taught me a lot about not dwelling on mistakes. Though I think you do still dwell on them more than you admit." She looked up at the sound of bootheels on pavement and saw her husband approaching along the side of the square. "I'll let you talk to Julien. I owe the children some time."

❧

Julien scooped up Genny and Clara and swung them in a circle. He petted Berowne, grinned at Kitty, Laura, and Jessica, and waved to the older children, then dropped down on the bench beside Raoul where Kitty had been sitting. "I've been looking for you. Should have tried here first. But it looks like you've just learnt something."

"Yes." Raoul recounted Gaultier Barton's revelation about Stroheim's coming to see him with the woman and child.

Julien listened with his usual attentive silence, gaze narrowed. "So at least we know Stroheim's alive. That's a relief. I like what I've seen of him." He stretched his legs out over the gravel. "This may tie into what I wanted to talk about. Do you remember all those years ago when we were dancing at the Hofburg after the sleighing party?"

"Don't I just. You're an admirable waltzing partner, but one can't but wonder if one's about to get a knife in the side."

"It sounds as though you could say the same about Désirée Clairineau." Julien gave a wave of acknowledgement to his stepson Timothy, as Timothy caught a throw from Colin. "I told you then that I thought Stroheim had only seen Mélanie at Malmaison once, but that he'd been there quite a bit for a time?"

"Yes." Raoul scanned Julien's face. "You said you thought he had another interest there."

"Quite. Specifically, the other interest was Lisette Varon."

Raoul stared at his friend. One was prepared for surprises with Julien. But—"I didn't think you knew Lisette."

327

"With all due respect, O'Roarke, there's a lot you didn't know."

"Granted. But Lisette would only have been—"

"A child? She was older than Mélanie was when she went to work for you."

"Lisette wasn't even an agent yet then."

"I don't think Stroheim's interest in her—or hers in him—had anything to do with intelligence missions."

Raoul shook his head, pieces of the past breaking apart and reforming. "She never—No, I know, there'd have been no reason for her to talk to me about it. And her sister Minette just told me she thought Lisette was hearing from a lover."

"Well, then."

"Why didn't you mention this sooner?"

"In front of Uncle Hubert? We may share some things with him, but there are limits. And if Lisette's acting in secret, I assume she has her reasons."

"A good point." Raoul frowned.

"You're worried about her."

"Of course I'm worried about her. She's little more than a child."

"She was old enough for you to send on missions. Older than most of us were when we started in the game."

"It's different—"

"Now you're a parent?" Julien asked. The shouts from the game of catch carried across the garden. Kitty had joined the older children and tossed the ball to Emily.

"I've been a parent for a long time."

"Sorry. I should have said a parent again. Or perhaps that's not it—I don't think you ever forgot you were a parent."

"No, though I'm not sure I prioritized it enough." Raoul pushed a hand through his hair. "I saw Lisette's mother this afternoon."

"But not Lisette?"

"No. Apparently she went missing last night. Her sister

thought she'd gone to meet a lover. Someone she'd been corresponding with from the Continent. Were Lisette and Stroheim—"

"Not in the most blatant sense, I don't think. Stroheim struck me as the sort with scruples. He too recognized that Lisette was young. She seemed intrigued. It was a long time ago. I have no evidence that they stayed in touch. But given that they're both missing—"

"Quite." Raoul watched Clara catch hold of Laura's slate blue skirt. "Minette mentioned a lion on the seal of the letters Lisette got her from her supposed lover. There's a lion on the Stroheim crest. Not the first time I've been a fool."

"There are lions on a lot of crests. Including the Bamford one. Hard to put it together without knowing their connection. I doubt Lisette is the woman Stroheim brought to the Bartons'. It's hard to imagine anyone's mistaking her for older than Stroheim. And she certainly doesn't have a child. At least, not one she's in regular contact with."

"No. Based on what we know, I suspect Stroheim reached out to Lisette and went to meet her while the woman and child were sheltering with the Bartons. And that Lisette helped them find whatever shelter they have now."

"That fits. It doesn't tell us who the woman and child are. We've certainly known plenty of people to help ex-lovers, so Lisette's involvement doesn't rule out the woman being Stroheim's mistress, but that doesn't really fit Minette's account of the letters between Lisette and Stroheim."

"No. I don't think the woman who went to the Bartons' with Stroheim is his mistress. I wonder—But it's too early for that."

CHAPTER 47

February 1819
London

Tony picked up the bottle and poured two glasses of wine. "The years seem to agree with you."

"Tell that to my back." Raoul settled into his chair and took a drink of Bordeaux. They were in a comfortable pub, not too fashionable but with good wine and dim lamps. "I hear you have another grandchild."

"Yes. My second daughter, Helena, and her husband had a little girl. Of all my children, Helena actually seems happy in her marriage. St. Ives married for love, but the love seems to all be on his side. Hetty wanted him to marry someone else. I wanted him to have his choice. But at times I wonder if he'd have been happier if he'd followed the path his mother wanted. Although I think he'd have had a hard time getting over Sylvie. My daughter-in-law is a clever woman. But then you know that."

"We've crossed paths."

"And swords, as I hear tell. I wouldn't call our family close, but I do manage to stay abreast of news." Tony took a drink from his

330

own glass. "I wouldn't be surprised if I ended up crossing swords with Sylvie myself. I'm never quite sure what she's doing."

"I know something about living in a family of agents."

"Yours seem rather closer. And talking of families, I hear you're about to be a father again."

An unbidden smile sprang to his face. Reckless to be smiling over something that was so complicated. "Yes. It was unexpected—That is, I didn't expect to find anything of the sort at this time in my life."

"I know the feeling."

Raoul stared into the red depths of the Bordeaux. "It's hardly something my life is suited for. But I can't believe my good fortune, for all the complications. Laura is remarkable. And deserves far better than me."

"You plan to marry?"

"As soon as my divorce comes through. I hope before the birth of our child. Margaret has agreed to the divorce, and Hubert Mallinson of all people has offered his help pushing it through Parliament."

Tony raised his brows. "People can surprise you. But I imagine he was grateful that you and the Rannochs got him acquitted when he was accused of murder."

"Yes, that did shift things." Also Raoul suspected the ties he now knew Hubert had had to Arabella Rannoch had played a role.

Tony reached for his glass. "I confess I rather envy you. A chance to start again is appealing."

"I wouldn't say start again. There's too much in my life I wouldn't want to start over."

Tony took a thoughtful sip of wine. "It's odd. You're on better terms with your grown son—the son you couldn't officially acknowledge—than I am with my heir. I enjoy my grandchildren, but I don't see them as much as you see yours. Marriage doesn't necessarily lead to a happy family life."

"Did you expect it to?" Raoul asked.

Tony gave a short laugh. "Not particularly. It was simply one thing I was expected to do. What's more surprising is that now what I didn't have or expect seems appealing."

"That's often true at our time of life."

"And yet you seem more content than I've ever known you."

Raoul sat back in his chair, the stem of his wineglass between his fingers. "I'm not sure I'll be able to marry the woman I love in time to give a legal name to our child. Even if I can, I've dragged both of them and Laura's daughter Emily into scandal. I frequently feel I'm banging my head against a stone wall in my effort to make any sort of difference in the world."

"Content doesn't mean things being easy. I can't imagine you in a life that's easy. You've found things that matter."

"Lately I've let myself get closer to the people I care about. Against my better judgement, in some ways."

"You can't think that's a mistake."

"I don't, so far. But I worry about them."

"Oh well. We always do. I even worry about St. Ives and Sylvie."

Raoul took another drink. It was a vintage that took him back to France. "Have you heard from her?"

Tony stared at a knothole in the table. "Not in over two years. Safer that way. It was clear at the Duchess of Richmond's ball that nothing would ever be the same between us. What we had was born of the situation."

"I'd have sworn it was more than that."

"Careful, O'Roarke. You're talking like a romantic."

"Who says I'm not?"

"You, as I recall. Or perhaps you're saying I was a besotted fool. Which isn't far from the truth." Tony tossed down a drink of wine. "I don't regret what I felt for Désirée. But I see the folly now of making it into more than it was."

"What something is can change. That doesn't lessen its importance."

Tony gave a bleak smile. "You're a good fellow, O'Roarke." He set his glass down. "Our old friend St. Pierre came to see me."

"Good god. I haven't heard from him since Waterloo. I imagine he wants as little reminder as possible of our prior association."

"Quite. He had the audacity to ask for my help getting him preferment with the Bourbon government. Given the service he'd rendered Britain, he said. Which allowed me to pull out my evidence of his having been a double all these years. He blustered a lot, but he was clearly in a panic. I told him I wouldn't reveal any of it so long as he kept his head down. But if he tried to curry favor with the current governments in France or Britain, it would be different." Tony sat back in his chair. "For the first time in months, I was quite pleased with the way something I'd orchestrated had turned out. Our plans all those years ago got St. Pierre precisely where I wanted him."

Raoul laughed. "You were right. Right that he'd continue to be a problem and right that this was a way to control him. Désirée would be pleased." He took a drink of wine. "If you do hear from her, give her my regards."

"I was going to say the same to you." Tony tossed down a drink of wine with an air of finality. "At this point, I'm quite sure she doesn't want anything do with me."

CHAPTER 48

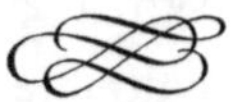

May 1821
London

Hugo Prebble looked up as Roth, Harry, and Cordelia came into his office. "Mr. Roth. And—"

"Lady Cordelia Davenport and Colonel Davenport," Roth said. "They work with the Rannochs on investigations."

Prebble got to his feet. "May I offer you—"

Cordelia gave a dazzling smile and extended an ivory-gloved hand. "There's no need to stand on ceremony."

Prebble's gaze shifted between them. "This means you have news?"

"Not about Lord Rothermere, unfortunately," Roth said. "Have you had news?"

Prebble shook his head. "I saw Hypatia this afternoon. My cousin has always been a contained woman, but she is most distressed."

"You said your cousin's husband entertained friends at the docks at times," Harry said. "Would you happen to have a list of those who attended such parties? It might help with what got the duke on a Prebble & Company ship that night."

Prebble's brows drew together, but after a moment he nodded and turned to pull a ledger off the shelf behind him. "As you may understand, we tracked the names of those who attended and their reactions so we could follow up on wines they might wish to purchase. Of course, my notes are based on what Rothermere told me. He could be a bit disorganized."

"I'll leave it to you to recognize the names," Roth said as he and the Davenports bent over the ledger.

"That's what we really need Cordy for," Harry said.

Cordelia was frowning beneath the silk-lined brim of her bonnet as she turned the pages with a gloved hand. Hard now for Roth to remember he'd dismissed her as a typical lady of fashion when they first met. She was so much more. But her knowledge of the beau monde was indispensable.

"I know most of these people," Cordelia said, "but nothing in particular stands out. Except—" She stared down at a list of guests from two months ago.

Harry whistled.

"What?" Roth asked.

Harry looked up from the ledger and met Roth's gaze. "They're all members of the Elsinore League."

❦

"So this is a League plot after all?" Judith asked, looking round the Berkeley Square library, where the team had gathered.

Mélanie leant forwards to refill the coffee cups. How quickly Judith, who hadn't heard of the Elsinore League until a few months ago, had caught up on the family intrigues.

"It sounds as though it may be," Harry said from the sofa where he sat with Cordelia. "It could all be coincidence, but it's the first link we've found that could explain Rothermere's connection to a plot of this sort."

Malcolm looked at Raoul. "You said Charlotte Leblanc told you the League don't like Bamford."

"So she did." Raoul frowned into his coffee cup. He was perched on the arm of the Queen Anne chair where Laura was sitting. "Though she hardly made it sound a vendetta. Still, there's no doubt Tony made enemies."

"And the League like to tilt international events in their favor," Laura said. "Someone in the League could have had an interest in Austria and Britain's being at odds."

"Quite." Julien clunked down his coffee cup. "All of which, unfortunately, means I need to talk to Sylvie. She used to work for the League and she's Bamford's daughter-in-law."

Kitty turned on the settee to smile at him. "That's one interrogation I can't help you with."

"More's the pity. Perhaps—" He looked round as the door opened and Valentin came into the room.

"This was just delivered for Mr. O'Roarke." Valentin held out a paper. "I thought it might be important, in the circumstances."

"Your tact is always exquisite, Valentin." Raoul smiled and took the paper. It looked to be torn from a notebook, and was sealed with a pin. Mélanie could see black pen strokes through the back of the paper as Raoul read it. It looked like a block code.

Something shot through Raoul's gaze. Relief, Mélanie thought for a moment, though she couldn't be sure. Followed by wariness. He folded the paper and tucked it into his coat. "I need to go out. I'm not sure how long this will take, but I'll report back here when I can." He kissed Laura's hand, shot a quick smile about the room, and was gone, with his knack for an effortless speed that didn't allow for questions.

Roth set down his coffee as the door closed behind Raoul. "There's something else. I'm not sure what to make of it. But just before I went to Prebble & Company with Harry and

Cordelia, two of my patrols reported that a large number of messages were sent back and forth between the Tavistock and the King's Theatre today."

"You monitor who's sending messages from London theatres?" Mélanie asked.

"Not in the general run of things," Roth returned in an even voice. "But we've had suspicious activity centered round the Tavistock. I had to have someone watching. All the more so because I have connections to activity there myself."

"Surely even someone not connected to the theatre could understand there'd be reasons for people at one theatre to talk to another," Mélanie said.

"We would," Roth said. "At least, I would. But any break in the pattern is of interest."

Mélanie reached for her coffee cup. For the first time in a long time she felt like an object of scrutiny with Jeremy. "Did your patrols report anything else?"

Roth pulled out his notebook and glanced through it. "Danielle Darnault called at the Tavistock three times. Not wholly surprising, she has friends there. She had hampers with her the second and third time. Two of the stagehands fetched hampers of food from a nearby by pub in the morning and evening. For a long day of rehearsals, I assume. "

Mélanie thought back to the rehearsal schedule tacked up on the green room wall at the Tavistock. The blanket and pillows that had suddenly disappeared from the green room. The creak she'd heard when talking to Simon. How annoying that the prying patrols had helped.

She looked at her husband. "I think I have an idea of where Stroheim and the lady and little girl might be. I was a fool not to have seen it sooner. But somehow, I never suspected—"

"What?" Malcolm asked.

"Come with me. If I'm right, we'll know soon enough."

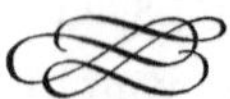

15 June 1815
The Duchess of Richmond's ball, Brussels

Boot heels clattered on marble. Cries cut the air, over the strains of a waltz still playing in the Duchess of Richmond's ballroom. The front door banged open and shut as officers streamed out. Flowers and gloves and even jewels littered the floor.

Raoul slipped through the crowd, crunched over shards of broken champagne glasses, slid between two couples lost in farewell embraces. He cast a glance round. He should leave. He'd danced with Mélanie earlier and said whatever he could say. He'd seen Malcolm across the room. Anything more was dangerous.

"O'Roarke."

It was Malcolm. What he'd hoped for. And dreaded.

"I'm glad I got to see you," Malcolm said. "I'm off to deliver a message. I'm not sure when I'll be back."

Inevitable Malcolm would involve himself. Raoul had known that the moment he'd heard the news tonight that Bonaparte was on the march. He'd known that all these weeks in Brussels.

Malcolm had involved himself in battles in the Peninsula. There was no reason this should feel different. "Have a care. You aren't a soldier."

"Oh no. Just fetching and carrying. But I've been involved in this for a long time. I know so many people fighting."

"And you feel you need to see it through."

Malcolm shifted his weight from one foot to the other. "I suppose so. Yes."

"You wouldn't be the man you are if you didn't." Raoul clapped him on the shoulder. Because he was no longer a boy he could embrace. "But you have a family to come back to."

"Believe me, I know. Fortunately, I'm at much less risk than most of the poor devils rushing off to report."

"Your wife and son are staying in Brussels?"

"For now. Suzanne's quite capable of getting to Antwerp, if needed." Malcolm gave a quick smile. "I used to worry about you. Whenever we said goodbye. I knew you were risking dangers more often than not. I'm glad I don't have to worry today." He gripped Raoul's hand for a moment. "We always seem to be seeing each other when there isn't time to talk properly. When this is over, I hope we can catch up. It's been too long."

Raoul put his hand over Malcolm's own. "Yes. It has been."

"Something to look forward to, then. We all need that just now." Malcolm hesitated a moment. "O'Roarke? I'm only carrying messages. But if, by any chance, Suzette does have to take Colin to Britain without me—the next time you're in London, perhaps you could look her up. There'll be plenty to provide for both of them. But it's not an easy world to move into. I think you understand that. She'd need friends."

Raoul's throat tightened with conflicting emotions. Self-disgust high among them. "Of course."

"Thank you. I knew I could count on you." Malcolm gripped Raoul's arm. "Colin likes you. You'd be a good friend to him too. You were always a good friend to me."

"I'll always do my best to be a good friend to your family." Which was highly debatable, if one knew his actions. Lying was second nature to him. But some lies cut to the bone.

"I know that, but it's good to hear it." Malcolm tightened his fingers on Raoul's arm for a moment. "I'm sure I'll see you soon. Take care. I must find my wife."

～

"I MIGHT HAVE KNOWN I'd see you here." Julien St. Juste stopped beside Raoul.

Raoul scanned the green rifleman's uniform.

"Oh, don't worry," Julien said. "I'll get out of this before the fighting. I don't suppose you're going to be so careful."

"I don't think it's a time to be careful. One way and another, a lot is going to be determined in the next few days."

"I can't argue with you there."

Raoul watched the younger man, a host of memories shooting through his mind. Julien sticking a stiletto in a man's ribs in the boulevards without breaking stride. Julien jumping in front of a bullet meant for Raoul. Julien with cheeks suspiciously damp when Josephine lay on her deathbed. "Take care of yourself, Julien."

"Always do. I can't say the same for you."

A young woman in a pink dress went rushing past them and flung herself into the arms of a man in a lieutenant's uniform. "In the event I don't return—" Raoul couldn't quite say it.

"She can take care of herself, O'Roarke. But if you don't survive, and Rannoch doesn't, I'll do my best to see she and the boy get somewhere safe." Julien drew a breath. "Sorry, I shouldn't have mentioned Rannoch not surviving."

"No. We all have to consider it." The girl in pink had her head pressed to the lieutenant's shoulder. The lieutenant put his lips to her hair, but the light of adventure was in his eyes. Raoul wrenched his gaze back to Julien. "I just saw Malcolm. He asked me to be a friend to Mélanie and Colin in the event he doesn't return and they have to go to Britain."

"Well, at least that's something you can promise to do. Though I imagine you weren't in a state to appreciate the irony."

"It was not lost on me. Though I might use words other than irony. Self-disgust comes to mind." Raoul glanced away again. But there was no one else to say it to. "I'm concerned about Malcolm, but he's more likely to come through this than I am. If I don't—"

"Mélanie knows."

"Yes. I think so. But if I don't return, I'd appreciate it if someday you'd find a way to tell Malcolm I was thinking of him."

Julien's gaze went still for a moment. "I'll manage. Don't worry. But I think you still have some of your nine lives left. Do me a favor and stay about, O'Roarke. You make life far more entertaining."

"Raoul." Désirée Clairineau was at his side in a stir of satin and a waft of jasmine scent. It was the first time he'd seen her that night, but somehow he wasn't surprised to see her in any setting. Her eyes glittered with the tensions of the moment, but her skin was glowing. She looked like the girl he'd met sixteen and a half years ago. "Everyone seems to be here." She squeezed his arm, a friend finding a friend in the midst of chaos. "It's like Vienna. Only more intense. That was the first act. This seems to be the climax. One way and another, nothing will be the same. One should be able to appreciate the suspense, though I confess I could do without it."

"Indeed. Difficult to plan when both sides of the whole board are moving at once. Do you—"

"Have an exit strategy?" She smiled, the smile that had faced down danger as long as he'd known her. "Of course. I could say the same to you. Though I don't suppose you're running right now. At least, not away from battle."

"I need to go where I can be the most help."

Her fingers tightened on his arm for a moment. "I'm decent with a knife, but I wouldn't be much good on a battlefield." She hesitated an almost imperceptible fraction. "Have you seen Tony?"

"I haven't spoken with him tonight. Have you—"

"Not yet." Her eyes still glittered, but a shutter had closed over her gaze. "There are things I need to say to him." Two girls in white rushed past them. Désirée smiled without irony. "The impetuosity of youth. Though I admit it's a situation that tends to make one impetuous. I hope it doesn't make Tony too impetuous."

"He doesn't need to be involved. But he's likely to think he has to be." Much like Malcolm.

"My fear precisely. If more men understood that just because the world chooses the idiocy of warfare to decide things it doesn't mean they need to be involved."

"I agree with you on the idiocy. Yet I confess to feeling I need to be involved."

"I wouldn't have expected you to be immune." She pressed his hand and reached up to kiss his cheek. "Take care of yourself, Raoul. Whatever happens, you'll be needed after." She drew back. "You said you hadn't spoken with Tony. I don't suppose you've seen—"

"He went into the duke's study with Wellington and some others. But that was a bit ago."

She squeezed his fingers. "Thank you. Look after yourself. I need to find Tony."

~

"O'Roarke." Tony came down the stairs pulling on his gloves. "I should have known you'd be here. I'm glad to see you."

Raoul moved closer to the stairs. "I'd have paid my respects earlier, but it seemed a good time to keep my distance."

Tony tugged at his second glove. "I'm off with Wellington to offer reports. He'll have need of all the help he can get."

"So I'd have expected. I'm—"

"No"—Tony put up a hand—"don't tell me where you're headed. You can't tell me the real story. I can hazard a guess. And I hope you survive."

"I could say the same." Raoul put a hand on Tony's arm. "Malcolm's headed to the field as well. I suspect he'll feel compelled to do more than is required of a diplomat. Perhaps if I ask you to keep an eye on him, it will help keep you both out of danger?"

Tony gripped his hand. "I'll do my best. I suspect we're in for something none of us has ever quite seen before." He cast a glance round the hall. A young man in a captain's uniform had swept a dark-haired young woman into his arms and was kissing her with an intensity normally not seen in public. A hail of her crystal pins tumbled to the floor. "If it goes against us—or however it goes, if I don't come back. She's in Brussels."

"I know. I saw her tonight."

"So did I." Tony's throat tightened. "She assured me she'll be perfectly all right. I know she can take care of herself, and she'd clout me for suggesting otherwise. But I can't help but worry. Especially now. She—well, never mind about that now. But can you—"

"She's a friend," Raoul said. "I'll do my best. No matter what."

Tony's gaze locked on Raoul's own. "Thank you."

They regarded each other for a long moment. So much hung in the balance. The game was shifting. The board itself was shifting. It was never going to be the same, whichever side won on the field in the next few days.

"It's been a privilege, Tony," Raoul said.

"Likewise." Tony gripped his hand. "And O'Roarke?"

"Yes?"

"Have a care."

CHAPTER 50

May 1821
London

Raoul slipped through the trees to the bench by the Serpentine where they had talked so many times. Where he'd also met with Archie. The most innocuous public setting could be the best for meeting a contact.

He hesitated, still in the shadow of the trees. The hope of the moment in the Berkeley Square library when Valentin had handed him the coded message still thrummed through him. Yet though the code should only be known to the two of them, codes could be stolen. The handwriting had been familiar, but it was difficult to be certain with block capitals.

The water of the Serpentine was still. So were the trees and the surrounding landscape. He stepped forwards, senses keyed, and slid onto the bench. Nothing to do now but wait. And stay alert.

The trees stirred. Instinct slammed into place. He ducked before he even heard the report. The bullet whistled over his head and pinged off the water. He dropped to the ground. Another bullet shot overhead as he rolled into the water. He stayed underwater until he got deep enough that he could swim, and then struck out as long as his breath held.

When he couldn't hold out any longer, he ventured above the water to see a single figure hurrying towards the bank. Relief shot through him.

"I'm sorry." The new arrival extended a hand as Raoul made his way to the bank. "This wasn't my intention."

"Tony." Raoul accepted the outstretched hand. "Timely, as always. I can't tell you how glad I am to see you."

CHAPTER 51

15 June 1815
The Duchess of Richmond's ball, Brussels

Tony moved to the French windows on the side of the ballroom that had been left open to let in the warm night air. He'd seen a flash of silver net. And they had a history of meeting in gardens and on terraces.

As he stepped through the window, she disengaged herself from the shadows.

"Silver over white satin may not have been the best choice," he said. His voice was thick to his own ears.

"I wasn't planning on secret meetings. Failure of imagination, perhaps." She moved to his side, less than an arm's length away, the bones of her face caught by the light from the windows.

Those days in Vienna had been glorious, but tinged with the knowledge that nothing was going to last. "I know you don't like to think of losing," he said. "But you may need to leave Brussels."

"And I may find France unsafe? You're right, I hate to lose, and I shall be thoroughly cross with you if we do. But I've always been one to plan for contingencies."

He smiled despite himself.

"I suppose you're going to be foolish and not stay sensibly out of the fray," she said.

"Just going along to make reports. Other diplomats will be there."

"Other diplomats don't run the risks you do." She moved to his side and put her hands on his chest. "You've always been a romantic, Tony. But throwing your life away isn't romantic. It's foolish."

It was more than seventeen years since they'd first met. And they'd been enemies the whole time, barring the uncertainties of the Peace of Amiens and the months Bonaparte had been on Elba. Their world was going to change in the next few days. Though god knew into what. "I won't argue with being a fool, and perhaps not with being a romantic. But I have no intention of throwing anything away."

Désirée tilted her head back. Her side curls fell about her face in a riot of tarnished gold, reminding him of all the moments he'd run his fingers through her hair. "You're not just gambling with your own life. You have people who need you. You have children."

He gave a short laugh. "My children are grown. Well, Rosalind's a teenager, but I don't think she'd admit to needing anyone. They're all past needing me. If they ever did."

"I'm not sure one's ever past needing a parent. But your children aren't all grown." Désirée took his hand and put it against her stomach.

Warmth. Flesh that was more rounded than it had been in their most intimate moments in Vienna. Nothing more tangible yet. But the truth was there in her eyes. For all the lies between them, he didn't doubt this. His world had shifted.

She closed the distance between them and put her mouth to his own. "I love you to distraction, you provoking man. If you don't realize that, you aren't half the agent I thought you were. We have a lot to talk about. Come back, so we have a chance to do so."

CHAPTER 52

May 1821
London

Simon got to his feet as Mélanie, Malcolm, Julien, and Kitty came into his office at the Tavistock.

"It's all right," Mélanie said. "If you'd rather ignore this, we'll explore on our own. I have a very good set of picklocks."

Simon's gaze shot from her to Malcolm to Julien to Kitty. "I know. Secrets hamper your investigation."

"No," Malcolm said, "I understand."

"I'm glad you do. I'm not the hell sure I do. Save that Jennifer and Manon wanted to keep it secret. And it didn't seem to be my choice to go against them."

He moved across the room and opened the door to the storage room behind it, which was normally used to keep extra costumes and props. "We have visitors," he said. "And I think it's time we spoke to them."

The room beyond was more crowded than Mélanie had ever seen it. The gateleg table in the center held an open hamper, a plate of bread and cheese, a bottle of wine and an array of glasses. Manon and Jennifer were at the table, serving food. Tristram Gresham and Danielle Darnault sat on straight-backed chairs. A tawny-haired man, unmistakably Franz Stroheim, perched on a trunk beside Lisette Varon. A woman Mélanie had never seen before, with golden brown hair and a distinctive, high-cheekboned face, sat on a sofa draped with the blanket that had disappeared from the green room, beside a little girl of about five, who was plaiting a doll's hair. The pillows from the green room were on either side of them.

"They worked it out," Simon said. "We're at the point where more secrets are dangerous. And we were about to tell them anyway."

"Mrs. Rannoch. Rannoch." Stroheim pushed himself to his feet. "You mustn't blame—"

"We don't blame anyone." Mélanie cast a quick smile at Lisette, who was looking particularly anxious. "We're sorry for what you've been going through, and glad you found a refuge." Her gaze moved to the sofa. "I believe you are Désirée Clairineau. And you"—she smiled at the little girl—"I think are Sophie?"

The little girl's eyes widened, then she cast a quick glance at her mother. Well-trained. Colin, Jessica, and Emily wouldn't admit their names either.

"It's all right, *petite*." Désirée Clairineau touched her daughter's hair and then smiled at Mélanie. "I've heard about you, Mrs. Rannoch. And about you, Mr. Rannoch. Your father is very proud of you." Her gaze moved on to Julien. "You're Julien St. Juste. At least, you were."

"I think I'll always be Julien St. Juste, whatever else I'm called. I believe we've met once or twice, though we were both in disguise."

"So we have." She smiled. A warm, disarming smile that seemed wholly genuine and was probably all the more effective an asset for a spy because of it. "Like you, I've used many names, but I think I'll always be Désirée Clairineau." She turned to Kitty. "We haven't met, Lady Carfax, but I've heard a great deal about you as well." She cast a quick glance round the room. "Please sit down. Explanations will take some time. I think there's another bottle of wine in Danielle's hamper?"

Manon and Jennifer opened the second bottle and poured both bottles into a variety of drinking vessels—chipped teacups, goblets that looked to be stage props. Mélanie and Malcolm sat together in a frayed velvet armchair. Julien and Kitty pulled a cushioned metal garden settee from the jumble of furniture against the wall.

Désirée took a sip of wine. "As I'm sure you've realized, Sophie and I came to London with Franz."

"In fact, I think perhaps that was the real reason for your secret trip?" Malcolm looked at Stroheim.

Stroheim nodded. "France has been getting increasingly dangerous for Désirée. In truth, it always was."

Désirée shrugged. "I was stubborn about leaving. But I had to admit it was no longer safe for me and Sophie." She tightened her arms round her daughter. "I know you know Franz and Tony were acquainted. One thing I suspect you haven't learnt is that Franz is my nephew."

"Despite not being so very much your junior," Stroheim said with a quick smile. "My grandfather had a liaison with a French actress on diplomatic mission to Paris before the Revolution. He remained in touch with his daughter."

"And my half-brother—Franz's father—was always generous, despite our political differences," Désirée said. "He and Franz have been concerned about us since Waterloo. As was Tony." She drew in a quick breath. "We quarreled about it, but then—"

Three quick knocks at the door interrupted her. Simon opened the door. Raoul stepped into the room, soaking wet, shivering, coat stained with mud. Another man was behind him in the shadows. "I think we can shed some light on this." He stepped aside to reveal the Duke of Bamford.

Mélanie stared at the man whose supposed murder they had been investigating. Beside her, Malcolm had gone still, though she heard his quick indrawn breath. Kitty gasped, then smiled. Julien's gaze narrowed in appreciation.

Désirée regarded her lover with relief, but not surprise. "I'm glad you found him, Tony. But it appears not without some misadventures."

"No." A look shot between Bamford, Raoul, and Désirée, weighted with memories.

Manon moved quickly to one of the racks of costumes and produced dry clothes. Raoul went into the adjoining room and emerged in a flowing shirt with a rather piratical look, dry breeches, and bare feet. He perched on another chest and accepted a glass of wine. Bamford had already settled on the settee with Désirée and Sophie, who snuggled against him. She had his eyes, Mélanie noted. And the easy trust of a child who has spent a lot of time with a parent.

Raoul (who had stopped shivering, Mélanie was pleased to note) looked at Bamford. "I always knew you were a good actor. But I don't think I properly appreciated your talents. Your portrayal of the broken-hearted ex-lover for the past few years quite took me in."

Bamford settled back on the sofa, fingers brushing Désirée's shoulder, Sophie cuddled between them. "That I managed to deceive you is about the highest praise I can imagine."

"After Waterloo, everything was different," Désirée said. "We all knew it would be. I said as much to you at the Duchess of Richmond's ball, Raoul. I told Tony that night that we were going to have a child. I think that night brought out all sorts of unexpected feelings for a number of us. It seemed intensely important to me that Tony know before the battle. I had hopes it might keep him from particularly reckless acts of daring."

"Which I was too old for, anyway," Bamford said. "But it did help."

Désirée glanced down at their daughter, who had returned to plaiting her doll's hair, though she appeared to be listening intently. "Nothing could be the same for Tony and me after Waterloo. But that didn't mean staying apart. In fact, there was less reason to stay apart than before. And at the same time, more risk. We all know how useful a creative fiction can be. In our case, the most useful fiction was that we'd fallen out. Tony was worried about me, and even I confess that with a child in question, one begins to think differently. There was a cottage in Normandy we'd stayed at sometimes. For a number of reasons, it seemed a reasonable time to retreat. Tony visited as much as he could. He was able to be there when Sophie was born. I didn't precisely mean to retire from the field. But the game had changed. I found having a small human to tend to remarkably entertaining. I wrote some rather blistering articles. The most recent of which Danielle's husband and his friend Mr. Blayney have published. Tony continued to visit when he could. In some ways, perhaps we were living in a world out of time as much as we had been in Vienna."

"In my case, perhaps a more real world than I'd ever lived in before," Bamford said. "But people were looking for Désirée. It was increasingly dangerous."

"I could no longer claim Sophie was safer in France," Désirée said. "So I agreed to bring her to London. It seemed mad, but perhaps no madder than other choices we'd made. We think of ourselves as farseeing strategists, but in truth life as an agent often means reacting to the moment." She looked down at her daughter, who smiled up at her. "Which I now know is not so different from raising a child."

"With people looking for Désirée, travel was dangerous," Bamford said. "Stroheim and I had been in touch since the war—"

"They know," Stroheim said. "That Désirée and I are family."

"Good." Bamford nodded. "That makes things easier. Stroheim

and I concocted our secret meeting as cover for Stroheim to bring Désirée and Sophie to London."

"Because, in fact, neither of us has any desire to see Britain supporting Austria's intervention in Naples. Or anywhere else," Stroheim said in a hard voice.

"I got word as I was dressing for the Marchmain dinner that they'd arrived," Bamford said. "I went to the ship. I was supposed to meet Stroheim there and he'd take me to Désirée and Sophie. Instead I found a bullet hole in the window. And other signs of disruption, though someone had attempted to restore order. I searched and found a body had been stashed in a cupboard. I can't be sure, for we weren't well acquainted, but I think it was Lord Rothermere."

"That makes sense," Raoul said. "He's been missing since that night."

Bamford nodded. "I dragged him over to the window to see what I could do for him, but he was plainly beyond help. Then the explosion went off. The force knocked the oil lamp over and the oil spilt on Rothermere. I knew I had to run. And then I looked down at Rothermere and realized he wouldn't be recognizable when found. That's when I suddenly had the mad thought that I could be free. As the Duke of Bamford, I was going to be the center of the investigation and my every move would be watched. I needed to be free to find what had happened to Désirée and Sophie. That was all that mattered in that moment. I pulled off my signet ring and put it on Rothermere's hand. Then I went over the side of the ship." He looked at Raoul. "Did you guess?"

"I wondered." Raoul curled his hands round his glass of wine. "From the moment I saw the signet ring, I think, though I didn't quite let myself admit it. More as the day progressed. I started to wonder if you and Désirée were as estranged as I had thought when I realized your relationship with Maria Parker was cover."

"Ah, the lovely Maria," Bamford said. "She's been a good friend to me."

"I was quite sure the woman Gaultier Barton reported seeing with Stroheim was Désirée. And that the little girl was yours." Raoul smiled at Désirée. "I remembered how your skin glowed at the Duchess of Richmond's ball. I should have guessed then. But none of that necessarily meant Tony was alive. I couldn't be sure how much was my own hoping. And I assumed you had your reasons for disappearing, Tony. Where did you go last night?"

"To Gresham." Bamford looked at Gresham, who had been sitting by in remarkable—for him—silence. "We've been allies for some time."

"Stroheim brought us together," Gresham said, with a nod at Stroheim. "I met Stroheim several years ago on one of my visits to Italy. I don't want to betray his secrets, but he's been very sympathetic to the Italian rebels. I was working with Bamford to arrange things for Stroheim and Désirée and Sophie."

"Which is the real reason you premiered music from your new opera at Bamford House," Mélanie said.

"Don't tell Hetty," Bamford said. "She was so proud of having secured the premiere."

"I never thought to find myself working with a Tory," Gresham said, "but it was a remarkably smooth alliance. Well, except for a bit about Lady Rosalind—" He coughed and glanced at Sophie.

"Rosy can take care of herself," Bamford said.

"Not my finest moment. In a number of ways." Gresham took a drink of wine. "Bamford and I were making arrangements for Désirée and Sophie and Stroheim's arrival when we had our 'quarrel.' We heard footsteps outside the door and started yelling to divert suspicion."

"When I asked you about the quarrel, you told me Bamford was trying to find Désirée," Kitty said. "Why bring her into it?"

"I was thinking off the top of my head," Gresham admitted. "But if you were looking into Bamford, I figured you'd hear about Désirée, and she was safe in London at that point."

"I went to Gresham's lodgings after I escaped the docks,"

Bamford said. "I was as dripping wet as Raoul was tonight. Gresham got me dry clothes and took me to the theatre—the King's Theatre, not the Tavistock." He looked at Kitty. "I was hidden there when you spoke with Gresham, Lady Carfax."

"Understandably," Kitty said.

"Meanwhile, I'd been on the quay when the ship exploded. I was delayed by traffic getting to the docks or the explosion would have caught Bamford and me as intended." Stroheim took up his part of the story. "All I could think was that I had to get Désirée and Sophie to safety. I wasn't sure whom I could trust. We went to the Bartons, and while Désirée and Sophie stayed there, I reached out to Lisette." He hesitated a moment. "We've been friends since long ago at Malmaison."

"So we learnt," Raoul said.

"We couldn't involve you," Lisette said. "It wouldn't have been fair. At that point, we'd heard the reports that the duke had been killed."

"It's difficult to know whom to trust," Raoul said. "You needn't apologize for it."

"It's not that." Lisette colored, then leant forwards, gaze intent. "You know I trust you. But this was our problem to solve. We weren't sure whom we were working against. And I didn't know how much danger you were in yourself. But Désirée knew Manon and Jennifer from Paris."

"Rather better than either of us let on," Manon said. "I got to know Désirée quite well just before and after Waterloo. The girls and I visited her when Sophie was a baby. I went to Jennifer when Lisette told me Désirée and Sophie needed help."

"And they went to me," Simon said, "though they may try to keep me out of it."

"They gave me costumes that Franz and Désirée and Sophie could wear to slip into the Tavistock," Lisette said.

"We'd just got them hidden when Raoul called at the Tavistock," Jennifer said. "I must say Manon was a cool customer in the green room."

"Best to confront danger head on," Manon said. She looked at Raoul, her former spymaster. "Sorry."

"On the contrary. My compliments."

Manon gave a faint smile. "After you left, we debated if we should tell you the truth. But we knew you were talking to Hubert Mallinson."

"Talking to him doesn't mean we'd share things," Julien said.

"No, but it increases the risk," Manon said. "And we needed to let Tristram know Désirée and Sophie and Stroheim were safe."

"To our intense relief," Gresham said. "We were able to let them know Bamford was alive."

Danielle picked up the bottle of wine to refill glasses. "It seemed safer for me to take messages to the Tavistock than for Tristram to do so. Everyone knows I'm friends with Manon and Jennifer. Oh, by this time Tristram and Tony had updated me. I was sadly uninformed the night of the musicale. In fact, I now know my husband knew more about the plan than I did. But I did learn a fair amount from Tristram and Tony afterwards "

"I knew Danielle in Paris," Bamford said.

"You mean you worked with her for British intelligence," Julien said.

Bamford met his gaze. "Possibly. With Danielle's help I was able to join Désirée and Sophie."

"Suitably disguised," Danielle said. "You made a far more fetching lady than most Falstaffs."

Désirée reached up to grip Bamford's hand where it rested on her shoulder. "Once we could put our stories together, we agreed we needed to reach out to all of you. Especially to Raoul. Tony wanted to talk to him away from the Tavistock. So he sent a coded message."

Bamford turned to Raoul. "I wish I'd gone to you sooner, though. Because while I thought the plot was directed at Stroheim and me, I'm beginning to think whoever attacked me was also behind the attack on you today."

"It's possible," Raoul admitted.

"What exactly happened to you?" Malcolm turned to his father with an easy tone that held an edge.

"Someone shot at me," Raoul said. "While I was waiting for Tony by the Serpentine."

"Someone wanted both of you dead," Désirée said. "And possibly Franz as well."

Raoul looked between Bamford and Stroheim. "Who knew about your meeting?"

"Metternich," Stroheim said. "We needed that to make it seem official. My father. The Countess Lieven, because Metternich told her. Other than that, we kept as quiet as we could."

"I didn't tell Castlereagh or Hubert Mallinson or anyone else," Bamford said. "I may have implied to Metternich that official channels were more involved."

"Someone has to have set up the meeting on the Prebble & Company ship," Malcolm said.

Bamford frowned. "That came through Metternich in a round-about sort of way. Billy Fitzsimmons married a Russian girl he met at the Congress of Vienna. Her brother is an attaché at the Russian embassy now. He's close to Countess Lieven. I don't think she told him the whole story, but she shared enough that he told her Fitzsimmons could get the use of the ship. She suggested that to Metternich. Safer than meeting in someone's house or at an hotel. We needed to follow their plan so as not to rouse suspicions."

"Sylvie followed you to the docks," Julien said.

Bamford grimaced. "I'm not surprised. But I don't think she knew a great deal in advance."

Malcolm leant forwards, hands on his knees. "What do you know about the Elsinore League?"

Bamford went still, his fingers suddenly taut against Désirée's shoulder. "Rumors. I made it my business not to tangle with them. To own the truth, they struck me as a set of pretentious poseurs."

"They are," Julien said. "And also deadly. Rothermere recently entertained a number of their members at the docks, offering samples of his wines."

"Including Billy Fitzsimmons," Malcolm said.

"Suggestive," Bamford said. "But correlation doesn't prove causation."

Malcolm's gaze moved from Raoul to Bamford. "The question would seem to be why someone would want to get rid of the two of you. What secrets did you share? You needn't reveal the secrets, but you damn well better reveal who might be after you."

Raoul and Bamford exchanged glances. Bamford glanced at Désirée. "Don't look at me," she said. "I don't know half the things the two of you were up to."

"It's hard to see how rescuing people from the White Terror would lead to attacks on us," Bamford said.

"Unless someone had a particular interest in seeing those you rescued face imprisonment or death," Julien said.

"We don't know the attack on me is connected to the explosion," Raoul said. "The explosion could be aimed at creating a breach between Britain and Austria."

"It strains credulity that they aren't connected," Malcolm said.

"Credulity has been strained before."

"I'll talk to Sylvie," Julien said. "She's one of our best sources on the Elsinore League. And sometimes I can get her to talk."

Mélanie looked at Malcolm. "Beverston might be able to help."

"I'll talk to Charlotte again," Raoul said. "I'm not sure what she'll let slip, but even her silences may reveal something." He looked at Bamford and Désirée. "Do us all a favor and stay here. Your help is invaluable, but we've already been through losing you once."

"Don't worry." Désirée gripped Bamford's hand. "Having

decided I want to hold on to him, I'm quite tenacious about not letting go."

Raoul grinned and moved to retrieve his half-dry shoes and coat.

"Father," Malcolm said.

Raoul looked back at him.

"Have a care," Malcolm said.

Raoul grinned. "Always do."

CHAPTER 53

"Are you telling me the League were behind Bamford's murder?" Sylvie asked.

"I'm asking you if you think they might be." Julien leant against a marquetry table in the Bamford House salon. He hadn't revealed that the duke was alive. That was for Bamford to do when he was ready. Which partly had to do with when it was safe.

Sylvie folded her arms across the vandyked bodice of her gown. "I don't work for the League anymore."

"You knew them. Who might want to drive a wedge between Britain and Austria? Or want to get rid of both Bamford and Raoul?"

"Surely you'd know more about who might want to get rid of Raoul than I would."

"Back when they wanted to hire me. They claimed they wanted me to get rid of Raoul for them."

"That was partly an attempt to get your attention. But—" Sylvie chewed on one of her nails. "I don't know why I'm telling you this. I don't believe in debts, but I suppose I owe you one of sorts. You saved my life, which is more than I might have done for you." She adjusted the beaded gauze sleeve of her gown. "There was someone in the League who wanted Raoul gone then."

"Alistair."

"No. That is, I don't think Alistair would have minded if Raoul were gone. But he wasn't the driving force behind it."

"So who was?"

Sylvie met his gaze, eyes clear and blue and open. And just possibly truthful. "I don't know."

Humphrey Smythe, Viscount Beverston, regarded Mélanie and Malcolm across his study. "Odd how the world changes. I'd genuinely like to help. But I've had nothing to do with the League for months. I can confirm Rothermere was a member. Certainly not in the inner circle. I never dealt much with him."

"Alistair mentioned him once," Nerezza, Beverston's daughter-in-law, spoke from the sofa where she sat with her husband Ben. "He said connections to trade might be regrettable, but they had their uses."

"And Billy Fitzsimmons?" Malcolm asked. "Or any of the others on this list?" He held out the list Cordy and Harry and Roth had found of the Prebble & Company party at the docks.

"All League members, as you know," Beverston said.

"Would any of them have had reason to dislike Bamford? Or to want to cause disruption between Austria and Britain?"

Beverston frowned at the list, brows drawn. "Lionel Buckfield might. He's married to Thirleton's sister. And from what I hear—not from the League, but from gossip in Westminster and at White's—Thirleton's angling to be made foreign secretary. An international incident could shake Castlereagh's position."

"Castlereagh didn't know about Bamford and Stroheim's meeting," Mélanie said.

"Precisely. But if he says so, he'll either appear to be lying or look like a man who wasn't in control of foreign policy. Either could be ruinous. And if Castlereagh fell from power, Bamford is widely seen as his likeliest successor. So this could have been an attempt to get rid of both of them."

"What about O'Roarke?" Malcolm asked. "It's hard to see how getting rid of him could cause trouble for Castlereagh."

"Alistair hated him," Nerezza said. She cast a quick look at Ben, who looked back at her with a reassuring smile. If it weren't for Nerezza's entanglement with the League and Alistair Rannoch, he often said, they might never have met. "But he once said it was ironic that others hated him even more."

"Who?" Malcolm asked.

"He didn't say." Nerezza looked at Beverston.

Beverston shook his head. "Alistair hardly shared things with me. And he was never inclined to talk about O'Roarke. But—"

"What?" Malcolm's voice was tight.

"Alistair once said that the most dangerous thing O'Roarke had done wasn't a betrayal. It was a collaboration."

"HE'S ALL RIGHT." Kitty squeezed Laura's hands. "Soaking wet, but he'd mostly dried out by the time he left again. None of the bullets came close. If anything, he looked energized by it all."

"Of course he was." Laura choked on a laugh, though fear lurked in her eyes. "He thrives on danger. But they're likely to try again."

"He's on his guard now." Kitty glanced at the far end of the Berkeley Square library, where the children were playing Lottery Tickets. She'd been used to seeing Julien go off into danger when she first knew him. But for all the risks they both still ran, their lives were safer now. Much as they might sometimes chafe at the restrictions, they couldn't either of them fully go back to their old life in the field. She'd told Julien as much when they'd talked about

Spain the night before. "He should be back soon," she added. "You'll feel better when you see him."

Laura gave a tight smile. "I'm used to it. I knew what I was getting into when I married him. Before." She too glanced at the Lottery Tickets game. Clara, in Emily's lap, had grabbed a mother-of-pearl fish. "Sandy and Bet went out to dine with Ben and Nerezza. They wanted to stay here, but I told them it would be good for them to get out. Besides, if this is connected to the League, Nerezza may have information."

"Malcolm and Mélanie went to talk to Beverston," Kitty said. "If—"

She looked over her shoulder at the opening of the door, hoping it was Raoul. Instead, Valentin stepped into the room to usher in Antonio Diaz.

It was less than twenty-four hours since Kitty had seen Antonio at the docks, but it felt like another world, before the explosion and all that had come after.

"I went to Carfax House," he said. "They told me I could find you here." He hesitated, looking round the room.

"My children." Kitty nodded to the far end of the room. "And those of my friends. And this is Laura O'Roarke, Raoul's wife. But I thought you were off to the Argentine and didn't have time to see us?"

"I turned back on the road to Falmouth after the news I heard." Antonio inclined his head to Laura and took a step into the room. "Is it true the Duke of Bamford was killed?"

"I'm afraid so." Kitty wasn't prepared to reveal that Bamford was alive. "Had you heard talk about him?"

"Not his name. But I'd heard rumors from foreign agents about an English duke people wanted removed from the field of play."

"Because of Austria and Naples?" Kitty asked. "Or Spain?"

"Neither. Because of the past. Someone with powerful friends wouldn't be safe while this duke was alive."

CHARLOTTE LEBLANC REGARDED Raoul across her favorite table at the coffeehouse in Piccadilly. "Are you saying you'd trust information from me about the Elsinore League?"

"Not necessarily." Raoul relaxed back into his chair. "But I would be interested in what you have to say. To begin with, is Lord Rothermere a member?"

Charlotte curled her fingers round her cup, weighing her answer. "On the fringes. But yes."

"The sort who might arrange to get important people to a particular location—say, a ship he owned—at the behest of more powerful members?"

"Possibly."

Raoul stretched out a hand for his own coffee. "And are there members who would like to see Britain and Austria at odds?"

"With all the interests in the League? Can you doubt it?"

"Who?"

"No comment."

Raoul took a swallow of coffee and pushed back his chair. "That's more than I expected. Thank you."

"Raoul." Charlotte's voice stopped him as he got to his feet.

He looked down at her with a raised brow.

"God knows why I'm doing this," she said. "But you always brought out more sentimentality in me than most people do. Which isn't saying a lot from me. But still." She met his gaze, her own dark and steady. "It's more than Austria and Britain, though that's part of it. But I've also heard rumors. They're serious about getting rid of Bamford. And you. Far more serious than they were when they attacked you a few years ago."

"Do you know why?"

"Only that your knowledge makes you dangerous."

Raoul nodded. "That's a lot, Charlotte. Thank you."

"You have no way of knowing any of it is true."

"No. Still."

"Be careful, Raoul." Her hand shot out across the table. "The world would be a less interesting place without you in it."

"I wouldn't have survived this long if I weren't careful." Raoul smiled at Charlotte and made his way out of the crowded coffee-house into the early evening bustle of Piccadilly. People could surprise you. Of course, knowing Charlotte, her admission of sentiment might be a carefully calculated ploy. The fact that he couldn't immediately see what she had to gain by putting him unnecessarily on his guard didn't mean that she didn't have her reasons.

Not that he hadn't already been on his guard after this afternoon. But he'd long since learnt that one couldn't hide. Or he'd have spent his whole life hidden away.

He turned down Berkeley Street, past the palatial bulk of Devonshire House, where Bella had taken him for parties, still damp coat pulled close against the rising wind. It whistled down the street, always a challenge when one was alert for the sounds of anyone following. He'd thought he'd heard or glimpsed someone once or twice the past day, even before the attack by the Serpentine. It wasn't the first time and wouldn't be the last.

He ducked into a doorway, waited two carefully counted minutes. Nothing stirred in the gathering shadows. No sound beyond the wind and the rattle of carriages from Piccadilly. He started back towards Berkeley Square.

He heard the vibration before he caught the rush of movement from the right. He spun round and dealt a blow to his attacker's jaw. But as he did so, he felt the slice of cold steel in his side. His feet slid from under him.

He hit the pavement, seconds before the world faded to black.

CHAPTER 54

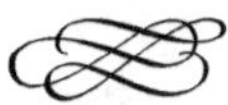

"I keep thinking we should have stayed." Sandy cast a glance back at the Rannoch house as he and Bet descended the stairs.

"Laura assured me it was fine." Bet tightened her fingers round her husband's arm. "The others will be back soon. Besides, Nerezza and Ben may be able to shed some light on what's going on." They were on their way to dine with their friends Nerezza and Benedict Smythe. Ben's father, Lord Beverston, had been connected to the Elsinore League as had Nerezza. Bet shared her husband's qualms about going out in the midst of a crisis, but the children were happy and there was little else they could do to help in Berkeley Square. And it was important to her that Sandy not miss a chance to see friends. He'd given up so much because of their marriage. Because of her, really.

They made their way through golden pools of lamplight along Berkeley Square. A carriage was drawn up to let off a couple going into a house blazing with candlelight. Another was picking up a family from the house at the corner. Bet kept her gaze carefully averted. She was likely to receive the cut direct and that only upset Sandy.

They crossed at the end of the square and started down Berkeley Street. Quieter here. But a dark shape caught her eye beside a doorway. Not a box or a crate. Too large to be a dog. What—

Sandy was already running. He bent over the body and called to her in a voice hoarse with shock. "It's O'Roarke."

~

Geoffrey Blackwell straightened up from the bed where they'd placed Raoul when Sandy and Valentin (summoned by Bet) had carried him back to Berkeley Square. Ten minutes before Malcolm and Mélanie had returned to the house to find the world upended.

Malcolm had known Geoffrey, a distant cousin, since childhood, long before Geoff became a military doctor in the Peninsula and later married Fanny's daughter Aline. Geoff's piercing dark gaze was steady now, as Malcolm had always known it, but weighted with regret. "He's lost too much blood."

Malcolm stared at his father's white face against the white of the sheet. Raoul's eyes were closed, the bones of his face sharp against his skin. Countless scenes from childhood through today shot through Malcolm's mind. He'd loved Raoul from babyhood. He'd briefly hated him. He'd found him a mystery. But he couldn't imagine the world without him.

Beside Malcolm, Mélanie was utterly still. Laura stood at the head of the bed, holding Raoul's hand, gaze shrouded. Julien and Kitty were standing a little way off. But Malcolm could feel the horror that gripped all of them. For a moment, he wanted to smash his fist through the window.

"I've heard stories of the Incas transferring blood from one person to another as early as the sixteenth century," Kitty said in a quiet voice.

Geoffrey's gaze shot to her.

Malcolm reached out and gripped Geoff's arm. "Can it be done?"

Geoffrey glanced at Raoul for a moment, met Kitty's gaze and then Laura's, then looked back at Malcolm. "I've heard the stories of the Incas as well. Over 150 years ago, Richard Lower successfully transferred blood from one dog to another. There've been attempts to treat humans by transferring blood from nonhuman animals. Most have failed. Leacock did some persuasive work on the risks of transferring blood from one species to another. But James Blundell recently saved a woman who was hemorrhaging after childbirth by transferring blood from her husband's arm."

"Can you do it for Raoul?" Malcolm's voice scraped against his throat.

"It's dangerous, Malcolm. Blundell's brilliant and he's tried it again, but it hasn't always worked."

"But without it, Raoul's going to die?"

Conflict shot through Geoffrey's eyes. "One can never be certain. But from all my experience as a physician—yes."

Malcolm held Geoffrey's gaze. Everything else had shrunk down to the needs of the immediate moment. "If Allie were in O'Roarke's condition, what would you do?"

Geoffrey drew in and released his breath. "Anything I could to save her."

"So you'd try this?"

Geoffrey gave a contained nod. "With my own blood, if I could get someone else to operate. It would be hard to ask someone else to be the donor."

"Is there a risk?" Mélanie asked. "To the donor?"

"Not as much as to O'Roarke. But there's always risk of infection. Or bleeding too much. I'm precise, but we're talking about opening a vein."

"Malcolm—" Mélanie said.

Malcolm swung round towards his wife. "You know damn well he'd give every drop of his blood for either of us."

"I'll do it," Laura said.

"No." Malcolm shook his head. "Raoul couldn't live with anything happening to you."

"I'm his wife," Laura said. "He'll accept that it was my risk to take. He'd never forgive himself if he was the cause of something happening to you."

"Stop it, both of you." Mélanie moved between them. "I'll do it. That way, there's one person healthy in each set of parents if anything goes wrong. And I owe him my life more times than I can count."

"No." Malcolm gripped her arm. Her skin was ice cold.

"No one can doubt the heroism of any of you." Julien pushed himself away from the wall. "But there's an obvious solution. I'll do it." He shrugged off his coat.

Malcolm swung towards him. "You don't need to—"

"I may not be his son, but you aren't the only one indebted to him." Julien reached for the buttons on his shirt cuff. "Don't tell O'Roarke that if we both survive this, by the way."

"There's no need for you to—"

"I'm the obvious choice." Julien undid another button.

"Why—"

Julien pushed up his sleeve. "Because I've shed more blood than anyone in this room. Than most people on this planet, if it comes to that. Call this a debt."

"This isn't the way you talk, Julien."

"I'm quite happy living the life I live. I don't believe in debts, in the general run of things. I'd happily go on with my life without atoning for my sins. But if someone has to do this, it seems quite clear it should be me." He glanced at his wife. "Kitty and I've always known we lived in a dangerous world, and that there were limits on what we might have."

Kitty nodded.

"No," Malcolm said.

"Darling—" Mélanie said.

"I can't let any of you—" Laura began.

"I'm afraid practically you may not all be equal," Geoffrey said. "I suspect not all blood is the same, and that's why sometimes these attempts work better than others."

"Do you know what makes it different?" Mélanie asked.

"No. And I can't even claim to have a theory. But I suspect as O'Roarke's son, Malcolm is likely to be the best donor."

"Then let's not waste time," Malcolm said. "What do we need to do?"

Mélanie's face was white, but she didn't protest. Nor did any of the others.

Geoffrey nodded. "We'll need boiling water. Mélanie, I normally wouldn't ask a patient's wife to assist, but I know you'll have steady hands. If we're going to do this, there's no time to waste."

CHAPTER 55

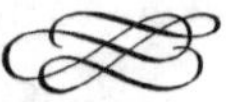

"He'd never have forgiven himself if he hadn't tried this," Julien said.

"I know." Mélanie stopped pacing on the library hearthrug. Malcolm, now almost as shockingly pale as Raoul, was upstairs resting while they waited to see if the blood Geoffrey had syringed into Raoul was enough to save him. And to make sure Malcolm didn't develop an infection. "In a sea of bad options, there was nothing else to try. Raoul would appreciate that."

"He *will* appreciate it," Kitty said. "When you can tell him the story."

Mélanie managed a smile, then dug her fingers into her hair.

Laura was sitting still in one of the Queen Anne chairs, knuckles white in her clenched fingers.

Julien moved to her side and crouched down beside her chair. "He'd also appreciate helplessness. That's what a spymaster faces, sending agents into danger. Some don't feel it at all. I'd have said Hubert was in that category until recently. Others like O'Roarke learn not to show the feeling."

Laura managed a smile. "Has anyone told you you're very kind, Julien?"

He squeezed her shoulder. "Don't talk rubbish."

The door swung open and Hubert walked into the library. "Is it true?"

Julien straightened up. "That depends on what you've heard. O'Roarke was seriously wounded."

"Is he alive?"

"Yes. Blackwell's trying to give him some of Malcolm's blood."

"What the devil —"

"There were no other options," Mélanie said. "And according to Geoffrey, Malcolm was the best candidate."

Hubert moved to her side and touched her arm. "I'm sorry. I can't quite imagine the world without him."

"Nor can any of us," Julien said. "We all owe him, one way and another."

Hubert looked at his nephew. "We have a minimal amount in common, Julien. But I'd agree with you there."

Julien stared at Hubert.

"Don't look so shocked, Julien. Just because I don't always act on my feelings—"

"*Always?*"

"—often—doesn't mean I don't have them. How much risk is Malcolm at?"

"We aren't sure," Mélanie said. "We aren't sure of anything."

Julien moved to her side and put an arm round her.

"Did the same person who attacked O'Roarke kill Bamford?" Hubert asked.

Mélanie looked at Hubert from the circle of Julien's arm. "The same person tried to kill both of them. Sit down, Hubert. We have a lot to tell you. And it may help us get through the waiting."

They were halfway through the story when the door opened again to admit Harry and Cordy and Frances and Archie and Judith and Jeremy. Cordy went right to Mélanie and hugged her. Over Cordy's shoulder, Mélanie saw Harry, face set with fear, Frances, hands gripped together, Archie, arm round Frances, face drawn. Judith and Jeremy hovered a little behind, but Jeremy met Mélanie's gaze and gave a quick smile.

"We didn't want to make things worse by descending on you," Frances said.

"Nonsense." Mélanie moved from Cordelia to hug Frances. "It helps so much that you're all here."

"Sit down and listen to the story we've been telling Hubert," Julien said. "It's a good distraction."

A little of the pallor left Fanny's face when they got to the news that Bamford was alive. "I always liked Tony Bamford. And the League were behind the attacks?"

"According to Beverston, Lord Thirleton wants to push Castlereagh—and Bamford—out and become foreign secretary."

"That fits what I've seen and heard in Westminster," Hubert said. "But it doesn't explain targeting O'Roarke."

"Someone in the League has something personal against him," Julien said. "At least according to Sylvie. Someone other than Alistair. And whatever it is, apparently it connects to Bamford as well."

"And to the past," Kitty said. "My source told me that. Someone with powerful friends wouldn't be safe while Bamford was alive."

"And Beverston said Alistair told him the most dangerous thing Raoul had done wasn't a betrayal," Mélanie said. "It was a collaboration. Presumably with Bamford."

"Damn it—" Hubert said.

"That doesn't mean either was a double agent," Harry said. "Agents find reasons to collaborate with other agents."

"Was the person who shot Lord Rothermere trying to kill him or Bamford?" Judith asked.

"Difficult to know," Julien said. "It's possible the League thought Rothermere knew too much and decided to get rid of him. But Rothermere was fair-haired and of the same height and much the same age as Bamford. The idea could have been to make

sure Bamford was dead before the explosion went off. If Rothermere went on the ship—he may not have known about the explosion, perhaps he went to leave a bottle of wine for the guests—the
assassin could have mistaken him for Bamford."

"That was my thought," Jeremy said. "They couldn't have
counted on the explosion killing anyone for a certainty. And we
did find a decanter and glass."

"And then the killer hid Rothermere in a cupboard?" Cordelia
asked.

"If the killer realized they'd got the wrong person they may
have been scrambling to cover things up at that point," Kitty said.

"Or if they were hired for the job, they might not have known
they had the wrong person," Julien said. "They could have always
planned to hide the body so Stroheim wouldn't run the moment
he stepped onto the ship. They needed Stroheim to create an
international incident, but killing him doesn't seem to have
mattered as much."

"So we're looking for someone with a grudge against both
Raoul and Tony Bamford," Fanny said.

Mélanie looked at Malcolm's aunt. "You've known them for
years."

"Yes, but I didn't know of their association. I could scarcely tell
you acquaintances they had in common, much less enemies."

Archie stretched out his bad leg. "The only person I can think
of is Reynald St. Pierre."

"What on earth does he have to do with Raoul or Tony?" Fanny
asked her husband. "He went back to France decades ago. And
never made much of himself, from anything I heard."

"He was selling information to the British," Archie said. "I
suspect Hubert knows."

Hubert grunted. "He wasn't much of a help."

"In fact, he was such a problem that Bamford convinced Raoul
to turn him into a double agent," Archie said.

Hubert's brows snapped together.

"Even you don't know everything, Uncle Hubert," Julien said.

"I know that. But what the hell did Bamford think—"

"That he could watch what St. Pierre did and that he'd have a hold over St. Pierre if ever he tried to curry favor," Archie said. "He never forgave St. Pierre for his role in the rue Saint-Nicaise affair."

"That was bungled," Hubert said.

"That was an attempt to take out a foreign leader that killed a shocking number of civilians," Julien said in precise tones.

"So St. Pierre was reporting to O'Roarke all these years?" Hubert demanded, gaze on Archie.

"Apparently St. Pierre would try to play O'Roarke and Bamford off against each other, and instead they controlled him. A couple of years ago, St. Pierre asked for Bamford's help getting preferment with the Bourbon government in light of his supposed service to Britain. Bamford pulled out evidence of St. Pierre's duplicity and threatened to expose St. Pierre if he dared raise his head."

"I have to admit that was cleverly done." Hubert pushed his spectacles up. "Bamford told you all this?"

Archie met his gaze. "How else would I know it? I'm more concerned with getting at the truth than with other niceties."

Mélanie tensed. Because unlike her and Raoul, Archie didn't have a pardon, and at least in theory, Hubert didn't know Archie had been working with Raoul. She saw a wary flash in Harry's eyes at the risk to his uncle.

Hubert grunted. "As you say."

Fanny was frowning. At first Mélanie thought it was over the risk to Archie, but then she said, "It's odd, because she and Hetty Bamford were such good friends."

"Who and Hetty Bamford?" Mélanie asked. Frances's mind could make quick leaps, but normally Mélanie could follow them.

"Helen Tarleton. She and Reynald St. Pierre were madly in

love, only he was an emigré without a portion and her father forbade the match. Reynald ended up going back to France. And Helen married Lord Marchmain."

A dozen fragments of information shifted in Mélanie's head. Into a chilling pattern.

CHAPTER 56

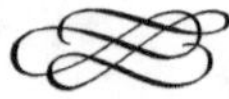

Before Mélanie could put her thoughts into words, the door swung open. She looked round, expecting Geoffrey, every nerve stretched taut. Instead, Valentin stepped into the room. "Lord Marchmain has called." He cast a concerned glance at Mélanie. "I would have told him you weren't at home. But—"

"Quite." Mélanie got to her feet. "Please show him in."

She took a step forwards, aware of the others ranged behind her. Even Hubert.

Lord Marchmain came quickly into the room, then hesitated on the threshold at the sight of the company.

"Come in," Mélanie said. "I'm afraid you find our household somewhat disrupted. Sandy is upstairs with the children."

"I'd like to see him. But I've come to see you. How is O'Roarke?"

"You know?" Mélanie folded her arms over her chest. Both Julien and Harry took a step closer to her.

"Yes. That's why I've come."

"Do you want to talk to me alone?" Mélanie asked.

Marchmain's gaze swept the room again. "No. If I'm right, this will impact all of you."

Mélanie nodded. "Then please sit down."

Marchmain moved to a chair by the fire as they all returned to their seats. "I suspect you've already guessed that the same person was behind the explosion on the ship and the Duke of Bamford's murder and the attack on O'Roarke tonight."

Mélanie jabbed her hair behind her ears. She'd completely pulled out the pins that usually held it back at the sides. She had her voice under control, but her fingers were shaking. "We have," she said. Without adding the new theory they had just developed that cut close to Marchmain.

Marchmain nodded. "As perhaps you know, Bamford and O'Roarke had been acquainted for some years. And had worked together."

Mélanie tensed. Marchmain wasn't a powerful politician, but he sat in the House of Lords with the Tories. If he knew about Tony Bamford and Raoul—

"We know," Hubert said. "The question is how do you?"

Marchmain returned Hubert's gaze. Few people could stand up to Hubert Mallinson so directly. Mélanie revised her opinion of Sandy's father. "They both had a man named Reynald St. Pierre reporting to them."

"We know that as well," Hubert said. "St. Pierre was a traitor to England and France."

"He had also once wanted to marry Helen. Who is now Lady Marchmain. And Helen wanted to marry him. Very much." Marchmain's fingers stilled on the arms of his chair. "I always knew she never got over him. Though it was a long time before I realized how much he meant to her." Marchmain passed a hand over his face. "I never wanted anything to do with the Elsinore League. But after Helen's affair with Alistair Rannoch, I realized she was entangled in something very dangerous. I made it my business to know more." He flushed, though his gaze remained steady. "Reading one's wife's letters sounds like the act of a jealous husband. And perhaps I was cloaking my jealousy in concern over international intrigue. Suffice it to say, for many years I had made it a habit to examine my wife's papers. I'd seen enough that I had horrible suspicions when Bamford was killed."

"Are you saying you knew—" Fanny, usually so direct, couldn't put it into words.

"No. Not last night. Not for a certainty. But when Lord Thirleton called today, I contrived to overhear him and Helen. Just after Thirleton left, our footman returned from an errand with the news about O'Roarke. I'd overhead enough from Thirleton and Helen to guess what must have happened." He looked at Mélanie and then at Laura. "If I'd had any suspicion before, I'd have done everything I could to stop it."

Laura nodded, gaze dark and steady, hands clasped tight in her lap. Kitty, who was sitting beside her, put an arm round her.

Marchmain shifted in his chair. "I confronted Helen this evening. Perhaps the most honest conversation we've had in the thirty-some years of our marriage. I didn't think she'd admit as much as she did." His face twisted for a moment. Mélanie suspected he hadn't fully accepted it himself until his wife's admission. "In truth, I think she couldn't bring herself to deny her feeling for Vincent St. Pierre."

"She arranged the explosion on the ship, the man who shot the Duke of Bamford, and the attack on Raoul," Mélanie said.

Marchmain gave a quick nod. "In concert with Thirleton, who had his own reasons for wishing to get rid of Bamford and cause chaos in foreign policy." He passed a hand over his face again. "I would scarcely have believed such things were possible until now."

"One doesn't," Julien said. "Until they occur. Well, not unless one lives the life most of us do."

Marchmain spared him a brief look.

"Where is Lady Marchmain now?" Hubert asked.

Marchmain turned his gaze back to Hubert. Mélanie could see the palpable weight of the consequences in his gaze. "On the way to the coast. To go to France and join St. Pierre. I realize you could still catch her. In truth, I'm telling you so that you have the chance to. But I ask you not to. Do what you will with Thirleton and the others. But let Helen go off in obscurity. For the sake of what is left of my family. And because I don't think any of us wants the situation that would result from Helen's crimes being exposed."

"You're right," Hubert said. "We don't. But Lady Marchmain was very determined to get rid of Bamford and O'Roarke. What makes you think she'll stop now? Especially if she's gone to join St. Pierre."

"Because I got her to write out a confession," Marchmain said. "It was the price of my helping her to flee. I promised to keep it hidden. But I told her it would be made public if anything further happened to O'Roarke. Or to me."

"Ingenious," Hubert acknowledged.

"I was improvising the best I could."

Hubert shot a look at Mélanie. Mélanie started, realizing Hubert, of all people, was asking her permission. She inclined her head.

Hubert pushed his spectacles up on his nose. And then turned to Jeremy Roth.

"Why are you looking at me?" Jeremy asked.

"Because you're the representative of British justice in the room," Hubert said.

Jeremy choked. He cast a quick look at Judith, who gripped his hand, then said, "As you say, detaining Lady Marchmain would lead to a number of complications. I can't imagine anyone in this room would wish that. Or anyone in the British government. Not that I would necessarily put the government's wishes first. But in this case, I think we are in rare alignment."

"Provided O'Roarke recovers," Julien said, a dagger's edge to his voice.

"Provided that," Jeremy agreed.

"And you?" Marchmain looked at Hubert.

Hubert folded his arms across his chest. "You've heard them. I'm merely a private citizen who dabbles in intelligence, after all."

The door opened on the silence that followed his words. Mélanie looked round, fear thrumming through her again, and met Geoffrey's steady gaze. "O'Roarke is awake. It's too early to be certain, but it's a good sign. He's asking for Laura."

CHAPTER 57

Raoul turned his head on the pillow. His mouth tasted like cotton wool. His head throbbed as though he'd been dealt a blow with the flat of a sword. Even shifting his head a fraction of an inch felt a huge effort. Yet he was alive. Breathing, even if his chest hurt.

His wife moved into focus. Strands of coppery hair escaped round her face. Blue-black smudges showed beneath her eyes. She had never looked more beautiful.

He managed to slide a hand out from beneath the covers. Laura's fingers closed round his own, tangible and reassuring. "I thought I was done for." His voice came out hoarse and cracked to his own ears.

For a moment, Laura didn't seem able to speak. "You lost a lot of blood. Fortunately Malcolm was able to give you some of his."

Raoul blinked. His brain still felt fuzzy, so it wasn't surprising Laura's words didn't make sense.

"Geoffrey was brilliant," Laura added.

Geoffrey Blackwell was standing at the foot of the bed, face contained as ever, gaze alight and focused. "I would thank you for letting me try a new technique, but I was too damned afraid I'd botch it. Your family and friends were eager to help. And in the end, your son saved you."

Raoul turned his head to the other side. Malcolm was sitting up on the sofa, a bandage wound round his arm. He'd spoken when Raoul first woke up, but Raoul hadn't quite made sense of what his son was doing there or properly taken in the bandage. Mélanie, who had come into the room with Laura, was beside him.

Malcolm gave a faint smile. "I've always been afraid every goodbye we say will be the last. And felt powerless to stop it. Today, there was something I could do."

SANDY TRENOR LOOKED at his father—or his legal father, which was part of the problem—across the small salon. He'd come to talk to Marchmain while Bet stayed with the children. He hadn't wanted to inflict his father on Bet. And now, given what Marchmain had just told Sandy about his mother, Sandy could only be relieved Bet wasn't here. To the extent he could think at all.

"You just let her go?" Sandy demanded.

"There were few other options. That is, there were a number, but they all seemed worse." Marchmain hesitated. "I'm sure she'll write to you."

"Why would she?" Sandy's voice cut with a force he hadn't intended. Not that he could really intend anything at all. That would require rational thought and rational thought seemed to have quite deserted him. "She hasn't spoken to me in months. Why should it be any different now she's fled as a murderer?"

"Alexander—" Marchmain put out a hand, hesitated, touched Sandy's shoulder. "She's your mother."

"She gave birth to me. She never—She wasn't the sort of parent the Rannochs are. The sort I hope to be. The sort I know Bet will be." He almost added "the sort you were," but he wasn't sure he had the right to say that.

"How is Miss Simcox?" Marchmain asked. "That is, Mrs. Trenor. Elizabeth."

"She's well, thank you." Sandy passed a hand over his face. "It's been—she's been concerned. About what lies ahead. But we're settling in. The Rannochs have been very kind to us."

"I trust you're both happy."

"We're together. That's what we want." Sandy swallowed. "I suppose it's what Mama wanted with Reynald St. Pierre. Or, no. She wanted him back in power. Even if it meant killing the people in his way. If she'd just run off with him in the first place, she could have saved a lot of grief."

"I don't pretend to understand her," Marchmain said.

"God knows I don't. She was so determined to keep me away from Bet. But if she loved Reynald St. Pierre so much, surely she'd have understood what it means not to marry the person of one's choice."

"St. Pierre was—"

"An aristocrat? That's it, isn't it? Bet didn't count because she's from St. Giles."

Marchmain shifted, the lamplight falling over his shoulder but leaving his face in shadow. "When you told me of your betrothal last autumn—I spoke out of shock. Normally I pride myself on thinking things through better."

"I doubt thinking this through would have helped."

"I'm not sure about that." Marchmain's fingers flexed, as though with a gesture he couldn't quite permit himself to make. "Your mother and I have known each other since we were children. The family properties adjoin. You know that. I wouldn't quite say the marriage was arranged, but it was certainly pointed out to us both that it would be an advantageous match. I was at an age where all my friends were beginning to marry. I never expected anything different.

" He looked at Sandy, as though reading his discomfort. "I know, not the sort of things one wants to hear about one's parents. But it's past time for some plain speaking in our family. I liked your mother. She was a pretty girl. I was proud of having won her. She seemed happy at the prospect of being my wife. Or perhaps of being the future Lady Marchmain. But even then I knew she wasn't over St. Pierre. It would be absurd to claim we were deeply in love. I'm not sure either of us would have said so, even in the haze of our wedding journey. Certainly we'd have never risked giving anything up for each other. On the contrary, securing the estates was part of the allure."

"Isn't securing estates what marriage is supposed to be about? That's what you're both always telling me. That that's the basis of a stable union."

"That's what I'm trying to say, Sandy." Marchmain put out his hand and let it fall. "Perhaps if we'd married for other reasons, the marriage would have turned out differently."

"And you wouldn't be stuck with a son who isn't really yours?"

Marchmain flinched as though Sandy had struck him. Even now, they rarely put it into words. "You've been my son since you were born, Sandy. Alistair Rannoch can't change that. And having you is one reason I don't regret the past. But if your mother and I had started out caring more, we might have stayed together longer. That is, our marriage might have held together better. Which might have made things different for our children." His mouth twisted and his voice scraped raw.

Now it was Sandy who took a step forwards and touched his father's arm. "You aren't responsible for Matt's crimes."

"No. But we raised him. I can't help but wonder what might have been different. You'll understand when you have children, though I hope to god you never face anything like this. And I very much doubt you will." He studied Sandy's face. "You've been willing to risk a lot for Elizabeth."

"I love her. I'll do what it takes for us to be together."

"And she obviously doesn't care about your fortune. I liked her when I met her. A very sensible and kind seeming young woman. I'd like to see her again."

"Father." Sandy's voice came out tight with strain. "I'm glad we can speak. But you must know that I'm not going to ask Bet to see you when you won't acknowledge her publicly."

"Of course not. That would be most ungentlemanly of us both. I meant I would like to see you both together. In the hope that I can present my daughter-in-law to society."

Sandy stared at his father. "You can't—"

"I want to know your wife, Sandy. I want to be part of your life, if you'll let me. I don't want to waste any more time. I want to meet my grandchildren."

Sandy drew a hard breath. Hope could hurt. "Mama—"

"Your mother's taken herself out of our lives. Our family may be shattered, but it's up to you and me to attempt to rebuild it. Of course your allowance will be restored."

"It's not about that. But I don't—I don't want Bet hurt. It's difficult enough for her in this world. I don't want you to meet her and be part of our lives and then walk away."

"Christ, Sandy—No, you have a right to fear that, based on the past. But I won't. I'm making you that pledge. I've stood up for few enough things in my life, but I'm not a complete coward. I won't let you down. Not that there's any reason you should believe me."

"That's the odd thing." Sandy smiled and took a step towards his father. "I'm quite sure I do. Let me present my wife to you."

CHAPTER 58

Tony considered his wife. The high forehead and delicate chin and wide eyes were those of the girl he'd proposed to. The girl who had dazzled any ballroom she stepped into. Who had dazzled him, but not so much he'd forgot he was a duke proposing to a future duchess. The girl who had known just what to say, just how far to go to be witty and clever without descending into scandal. How to charm without going over the line. How to control a room without ever letting anyone see she was doing it.

"I'm sorry, Hetty," he said.

She raised her brows. They'd always had a perfect arc, though the angle was sharper now. "You needn't be. I'll own we were all distressed, but knowing the circumstances I can understand why you didn't tell us. Though it certainly never occurred to me that Helen was the cause of the attack." She shivered and drew her shawl about her shoulders.

"There's no way you could have known," Tony said.

"No. But I can't help but think I should have done. I'd known her almost my whole life. She'd always been tenacious about getting her way. And ruthless when crossed. I knew she never got over St. Pierre. But it never occurred to me—When I think of how she tried to comfort me when the Rannochs broke the news of your death. I couldn't wait to get away from her. But because I couldn't bear her fussing. Not because I had the least suspicion—" Hetty shook her head. "Now you're back, I confess that part of me did wonder if you were still alive."

"I'm impressed."

"I may not be able to claim to know the inner workings of your mind and heart, but we have been married for over three decades. I've absorbed a certain amount of your work."

"My work would have been next to impossible without you. I don't think most properly appreciate the role of diplomatic wives."

"I meant your other work."

"That too. I couldn't have begun to do it without you here to take up so many responsibilities at home. But I meant I'm sorry for all of those thirty-some years."

She folded her hands. "You mean for our marriage?"

"For a marriage that wasn't what I think a marriage ought to be."

"Tony." Her tone was at once affectionate and mocking. "I became a viscountess and then a duchess. I manage one of the finest town houses in London and one of England's most beautiful country estates, along with five other properties. Our children have had every advantage. You're kind and considerate. I have everything I expected when I married you. And far more than many of my friends. No, I don't mean Helen, who is in a class by herself. But other girls from our season, who perhaps married with more stars in their eyes than I had. Not that I didn't permit myself a few starry-eyed imaginings about you."

"As did I in those early years. But I don't think I thought marriage could be more than what we had. Or, for years. I had no model of it. Odd that it takes the younger generation to make that possible."

"The Rannochs?"

"Among others."

She regarded him for a moment with a faint smile, part affectionate, part wistful. "You're leaving, aren't you?"

"How did you know?"

"Partly a shot drawn at a venture. But how else to explain all of this? You want to be with the woman you love. And your child, who is still quite young. It makes sense."

"It wouldn't have made sense to me three decades ago." He watched her. "I recognize that I'm breaking up—"

"The charming illusion of our lives? I don't need a Duke of Bamford to be Duchess of Bamford. Unless you're planning to fake your death again. But I don't advise it. St. Ives isn't ready for it. Sylvie may be, but I'm not sure we want to see the use to which she'd put the added power."

"No. A good point. And no, pretending to be dead was born of impulse and situation. I won't try it again. I'm not quite so lost to a sense of my responsibilities."

"I don't think you're lost to them at all, my dear."

"You're very kind, Hetty." He drew a breath, reached for the glass of port he'd poured at the start of the conversation, took a sip. "I'd like to live at Sawden Park with Désirée and Sophie. Wilcox can manage Chevenings and the other estates very admirably. He's done so for months on end when I've been out of contact. From the moment I came into the title, really. I'll still visit the other properties once or twice a year. St. Ives can take on more too. It will be good for him. He can visit us at Sawden as well. All the children can." He bit back what he'd been about to say, took another drink of port, said it anyway. "You can as well. Though I wouldn't—"

"On the contrary. I find Sawden very agreeable. And I'd quite like to get to know Mademoiselle Clairineau and Sophie." Hetty picked up her own glass, took a sip, and regarded him over the rim. "Tony. You're very busy. And you've been home less and less in recent years. I don't suppose you've noticed that Wilcox and I have always got on quite well."

"Of course. Wilcox is an admirable steward. And you've always —good god." He broke off before he could even voice to himself what he'd been about to say next.

Hetty raised a brow. "Is it so hard to believe?"

"My dear. I've always assumed—"

"That I had lovers?"

"Well—yes. After—"

"The first children?"

"After the first years. After—the bloom was off, I suppose. We were never—but we did believe in the romance at first. At least I did."

"I did as well. No need to doubt that. But I think we were both aware when it shifted. And my sense is that neither of us blamed the other."

"Certainly not on my side."

"So it can't be a surprise."

"No. But I saw you—"

"You thought I was too much of a snob to have an affair with a steward?"

"No." He took another drink of port. "Of course not."

"Liar."

"Hetty—It's just never how I pictured you."

"Having affairs or having affairs with a steward? Or are you simply unable to imagine that John and I kept it secret from you, a seasoned agent?"

"No. That is—"

"I can see how it would be frustrating. But you weren't particularly focused on either of us. There was no reason for you to be. We were both fulfilling our roles rather well, I think." She frowned. "Unless you're jealous?"

"That would be singularly unfair of me."

"There's no fairness about it. One can feel twinges of jealousy at the most unexpected times. I'll confess to having felt them myself, on occasion."

"My dear." He crossed to her side and took her hands. "If you and Wilcox are happy together, I'm delighted. I hope it means this new arrangement will make matters easier for you."

"We've been getting on quite well. But, yes. John in particular will be relieved that you know. Though I don't quite know how I'm going to break it to him. He's rather particular about such distinctions, as I think you know. Best leave it to me. I'll be able to put it more tactfully."

He touched her cheek. "You're a wonder, Hetty."

She caught his hand and twined her fingers round his own. "Life is complicated, Tony. Our lives will continue to be complicated. Yours, in particular. But there's no reason this has to be complicated."

"You'll manage the Bamford estates far better than I could."

"I wouldn't say that. But I'll certainly know when we need to reach out to you." She considered him for a moment. "Beyond everything else, we've always been friends, haven't we?"

"I hope so. I'll confess, at the beginning I don't think I was quite capable of thinking in those terms. But that's certainly what we've been through the years. And the children—"

"They'll be all right. St. Ives has a lot of growing up to do and things with Sylvie will never be easy, but this won't make it worse. Frederica's marriage is a disaster, but at least she seems to see Percy clearly. We may set a good example for her by separating. Helena's managed to be surprisingly happy despite us. This won't affect her. I'm not quite sure what Rosy's got herself into, but it's not to do with us."

"I'm not entirely sure of that. Rosy's very much involved in politics. And that's something I won't be able to ignore."

"But your going to Sawden won't impact it. Not so long as you keep an eye on things. I don't think any of them has illusions about our marriage. So now we can put our minds to setting a better example."

"I won't embarrass you, Hetty."

"I never thought you would, my dear." She drew the folds of her shawl about her shoulders. "I'm not necessarily opposed to a divorce, you know."

Tony started. As much as Hetty had surprised him in the past half hour, this was a new level of shock. "I wouldn't ask—"

"I know you wouldn't. That's why I brought it up. The children are settled. We needn't worry about scandal for them. But it would make things easier for little Sophie. And other children you may have. Unless you think Mademoiselle Clairineau wouldn't have you?"

For a moment Tony tried to imagine asking Désirée to become Duchess of Bamford. It had been difficult enough to convince her to live with him in England. "I'm not sure."

"Talk to her about it. No need to rush any of this."

"Do you want to marry Wilcox?"

"Possibly. If I could convince him not to worry about the scandal. I'll confess I'm conventional enough to find the thought of marriage rather agreeable, A different sort of marriage, as you said." Hetty reached up and kissed his cheek. "I fully believe saying too much is one of the ills of modern society, but it's good to have talked this out. Past time." She stepped back. "I'm happy for you."

"That's generous of you."

She smiled, the smile of the girl he'd married. "Why wouldn't I be happy for one of my oldest friends?"

~

"I ALWAYS THOUGHT your wife sounded sensible," Désirée said. "But I didn't realize quite how much I'd like her."

"I'm fortunate to be surrounded by remarkable women." Tony

slid his arm round Désirée. He hadn't mentioned Hetty's offer of a divorce yet. One thing at a time.

They stood together looking out at the Bartons' garden where Sophie was playing with Roland and Mylène. "There were a few hours where I thought you were dead," Désirée said. Her gaze was fixed on the garden, but her voice was husky. "I won't say I thought my life was over, because it couldn't be. I have a child. But they were the worst hours of my life."

"I'm sorry. If I could have—"

"You did everything you could." She gripped his hand, still not meeting his gaze. "But there's nothing like that for making one appreciate what one has."

In the garden, Sophie and Roland were making a great show of pretending not to find Mylène, who was hiding behind a tree. She jumped out at them and all three dissolved into giggles.

"Past time we realized what's important," Tony said. "I'm damned if I'm going to spend more time living the life someone else set out for me. Those children understood that. Kit and Sofia Montagu and her reckless brother. He had the courage to stand up for the woman he loved. And her right to make her own choices."

He held Désirée for a moment, face pressed into her hair. Then he drew back and laughed. "I don't think I've ever felt so free. You rescued me."

She ran her fingers through his hair. "As I recall, we've both rescued the other more than once."

"You let me have a life. You showed me what was possible."

She gave a choked laugh. "Betrayal?"

"Partnership."

CHAPTER 59

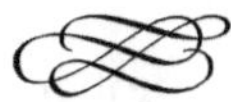

"It's amazing," Tony said. "How one can live with a person for over three decades and still be surprised."

Raoul turned his head from the chair by the window. To which he'd progressed from the bed. He might even venture downstairs for dinner tonight. "Not for the worse, I presume."

"On the contrary. Hetty's remarkable."

"Have you asked Désirée?"

"If she'd be willing to marry me? I can't quite put it into words. Even living outside society, I'm not sure she could bring herself to be a duchess."

"I think there's a lot she'd do for Sophie. Not to mention for you."

Tony gave a twisted smile. "Possibly. We're a bit old for fairy tales, but I'll own a part of me wants to grasp hold of whatever I can."

"I don't think one's ever too old for fairy tales."

Tony leant forwards on the chair he'd drawn up close to Raoul's armchair. "You're sounding quite unlike yourself."

"Nothing like being confined to a sickbed to give one time to think."

Tony's face went serious. "I'm sorrier than I can say—"

"You're hardly to blame for St. Pierre's crimes. Or Lady Marchmain's. Let's focus on the positive. We're both alive. And perhaps now we have the ability to be friends."

"Haven't we always been friends?"

"Oh, yes. Long before I used the word about anyone. But now we don't have to hide it."

Tony grinned. "I'm all for not hiding things. Of course, in a world where Désirée can admit she loves me, anything seems possible."

"Believe me, I think the same about Laura every day."

Malcolm rapped once and stepped into Raoul's room. A relief to see his father sitting by the window, more color in his face. His visit with Bamford seemed to have done him good.

"Are you still thinking of coming down for dinner?" Malcolm asked.

"Most definitely. I may need help shaving."

"No one will care."

"I'll care."

Malcolm dropped into the chair nearest Raoul. "Bamford stopped to thank us on his way out. I must say in all the years I've known him I don't think I've ever seen him look quite so happy."

"He's free of it. For the first time since I've known him."

"What?"

"Being Duke of Bamford. Or rather, being the sort of duke he thought he needed to be. Tony may not be a Radical, but I think he was always at odds with his position."

"Malcolm regarded his father for a moment. "Is it too soon to offer you a glass of whisky?"

"Raoul grinned. "I was wondering when you'd ask."

Malcolm returned the grin and poured two glasses from the

decanter on the chest of drawers. There was so much to say. Difficult to know where to start. He studied his father over the
decanter. "You must have been horrified by the life I chose."

"When you became an agent? God, yes. I could have cheerfully
murdered Hubert. I think Henriette felt the same about me when
I recruited Lisette."

"I was thinking of when I became a diplomat. I was working
against everything you taught me about."

"You were working for your country."

"The country you were working against."

"I was working against what Britain stood for in Ireland and
Spain."

Malcolm returned to his chair. "I should have known."

"What?"

"That you'd be working with the French. Stroheim did."

"Stroheim had worked with me. Supporting the guerrilleros
would have been a valid way to work for change in Spain. Not the
path I chose. But I can imagine it."

"You still believed in the Revolution."

"I did. And I believed the Bonaparte regime was the best
chance we had of preserving some of it. I'd make that call again.
But I can certainly understand someone's feeling differently."

Malcolm cradled his whisky glass in his hand. "I didn't feel
anything at all when I took on my work."

Raoul's gaze settled on Malcolm's own. "I know. And that's the
part of it I hate. How you felt at the time you became a diplomat
and agent. At the same time, I'll never stop being grateful to
Hubert for giving you something to hold on to."

"He gave me a disaster to hold on to that had me hating myself.
But yes, I admit there were worse options. But you can't deny it
put us on opposite sides."

"We were always going to be on opposite sides."

"Were we? I believed in the same things you did."

"We came from different worlds."

"You're a bloody aristocrat, O'Roarke. As much as I am."

"I wasn't going to turn you against Britain."

"You think Britain matters to me that much?"

"Perhaps not. But the turning against it would have done."
Raoul watched him for a moment. "That you listened at all to any
of the things I said to you meant an incalculable amount."

"Yes, well, that's comforting to hear. But I'd have spared myself
a lot of self-hatred if I'd never gone to work for Hubert. Or
Castlereagh. Or Wellington." Malcolm took a drink of whisky. "Do
you think Stroheim will want to stay in England?"

"Possibly." Raoul curled his fingers round his own glass. "I
certainly think he finds things to love here. But it would mean
turning his back on his country. And his heritage."

"It rather depends on how he defines his heritage. We don't
know what other influences there were on him." Malcolm
watched his father. "Did you ever think about telling me? All of it?
Who you were? What you stood for?"

"Would you tell Colin, in the same circumstances?"

"I'm not sure. It's difficult to imagine having a relationship
with Colin without being able to share my thoughts for him with
Mel."

"Quite."

Malcolm looked at the man who had raised him, distant
memories from the shores of Lake Como dancing in his mind. "It
must have been hell."

"Arabella was challenging." Raoul's gaze was steady and opaque
as dark glass. "What the secrets put you through was
unforgivable."

"I managed."

"Oh yes. But it shouldn't have been so hard."

"I wish I'd known sooner. I wish I'd been clever enough to
guess."

"If it's any comfort, I wouldn't have cared much for what that
said about my skills as an agent."

"Did you think about it? Trying to keep the secret from me?"

"My dear Malcolm. Unfortunately, there were few times, once you were able to talk, when I was with you and didn't think about keeping secrets from you."

"Point taken."

"Don't you think about trying to keep secrets from Colin and Jessica?"

"Well, yes, if you put it that way. But not the secrets of who we are."

"Isn't being an agent part of who you are?"

"Not perhaps a part I'm eager to acknowledge. But at the risk of making Hubert happy—yes. Not that we precisely hide it from the children. Though I suppose Mel still—I wish she didn't have to hold things back."

"There are always going to be secrets one keeps to protect others."

Are you still keeping any? Malcolm bit back the words. Because they would only push Raoul to lie. And he didn't want any more lies between them. "There are secrets and secrets. I think Colin and Jessica know who Mel is at the core. And I think I always knew who you were."

Raoul nodded. For a moment it didn't seem he trusted himself to speak.

"Which makes it all the more frustrating that I didn't see where your loyalties would have taken you."

"You were coming at it from a different perspective."

"But you shared thoughts with me. And ideas."

"So you could form your own opinions. Not so you could be a copy of me. You don't see your children being a copy of you, do you?"

"God no. Not even of Mélanie. And she doesn't."

"Well, then."

"I still think you must have been horrified."

"Why?"

"I suppose because when I look back at the choices I made at that time in my life, I'm horrified."

Raoul reached forwards and touched his arm. "If anything horrifies me, that does."

"I gave up. You never did. With far greater reason to despair than I had, if it comes to it."

"I'm not sure about that."

"Your own revolution imprisoned you."

"It wasn't my revolution. But it was a hard lesson."

"But you didn't give up. And Ireland. And Spain. And Waterloo."

"It might be the definition of madness."

"Or tenacity. As you might say, it rather depends on the outcome."

"I was close to giving up. When Arabella got me out of Ireland and over to France, anything I could do felt rather academic. That's the man I was when I first met Désirée Clairineau and first worked with Tony."

"But it didn't last."

"No, I clawed my way back to a sense of purpose. I'd had practice."

"What about Bamford?"

"What about him?"

"Did he believe in what he was doing?"

"I never asked him in those terms. He was always able to see the human element. He disagreed with his superiors. It was one thing we had in common. Striking out on our own. And a frustration with incompetence. But he wasn't a secret Radical."

"So he wasn't working against everything he believed, in the way I was."

"Malcolm."

"Sorry, that was overdramatic. Though not untrue."

Raoul's gaze narrowed on a scuttering cloud outside the

window. "Tony was searching for something. He was good at being a duke, but it wasn't the life he really wanted."

"And he has it now?"

"I hope so. They'll neither of them be content with simple country domesticity for too long. But I imagine they'll find ways to keep busy. One never really knows where life will lead one beyond the moment."

Malcolm regarded Raoul over his glass. "You've never blamed me for it."

Raoul's brows rose in rare surprise. "My dear boy. What in God's name would I blame you for?"

"The mess in Spain. If my side—or the side for which I was working—hadn't won, you wouldn't be facing what you're facing now."

Raoul took a sip of whisky and set down his glass with care. "Though I would never discount anyone's work—particularly yours—such things rarely come down to one person."

"No. But to the extent I had an influence at all, it was for the wrong side."

"Wrong and right and sides are difficult to define. Kitty was working for the same side as you. Now she's trying to create change as much as I am."

"I love Kitty and have a great deal of respect for her. That doesn't mean we weren't both wrong during the war."

"As I've said, we all make choices. We can't always tell where they may lead."

"You could tell where what the British were doing would lead for Spain. Better than Kit and I could."

"I had my experience of France and Ireland to draw on. And somewhat different loyalties when it comes to France."

Malcolm took a drink of whisky. It burnt his throat, at once rough and familiar. "I can see doing a lot to avoid something like that coming to pass. It—throws things in perspective."

Raoul's gaze lingered on his own. "Loyalty, as I've said, is a matter of choices."

Malcolm tossed down another drink of whisky. "Well, I didn't choose very well."

"I think Tony's come to the conclusion that his first loyalty is to his family." Raoul took another sip of whisky, then set the glass down again, as though afraid to jostle it. "I owe you a great deal."

"Any of us would have done it. I was the best candidate. You'd have done it for any of us."

"Yes. That doesn't change the debt. I was conscious long enough after I was wounded to be sure my life was over. It's rather stunning to see you all again."

Malcolm nodded. It was difficult to speak. Difficult even now to know if he should speak. "For as long as I can remember," he said, choosing his words with care, "every time I've said goodbye to you I've wondered if I'd ever see you again. It was so very present I didn't really dwell on it. But it was there at the back of my mind."

"I'm sorry. That's a horrible burden for a child to grow up with."

"You don't need to be sorry. I was proud of you. I am proud of you. But if it goes on like this, you're going to get yourself killed. Perhaps not today, perhaps not tomorrow. But at some point." Now he'd started to speak, the words spilt out. "Emily and Clara and Colin and Jessica will grow up without you. Laura will find a way to go on, but she'll never love again, not like this. Julien will be more devastated than I'd once have thought he could be by anything. We both know what it would do to Mélanie—she'll never quite be the same. Kitty and Harry and Cordy and Archie and Frances will all be devastated. Tony will be certainly be. Désirée too, I think. Even Hubert, more than he'd admit." Malcolm drew a breath. "And I won't be very happy either."

Raoul's gaze caught and held his own. The past stretched

between them. So many memories, so many things still unspoken. "Once, I'd have never thought to hear you say that."

Malcolm stared into the glass in his hand. "Once, there were a lot of things neither of us would have said. Once, I'd have thought I didn't have the right to ask anything of you." He dragged his gaze to Raoul's face. "But I've come to believe I do. And this may be unfair. But for god's sake, stop. Start a Radical newspaper, stand for Parliament. Find some way to make your voice heard—because god knows it needs to be heard—that doesn't involve risking your life."

Malcolm stared at his father, not quite able to believe he'd actually said it.

Raoul looked up at him, gaze steady. For a moment, the balance of their lives tilted between them. "All right."

"What?" Malcolm could scarcely frame the word over his shock.

"You're right. You do have the right, and more, to ask something of me. This seems the least I owe you. And just possibly what I owe myself."

❧

"It's all right." Raoul touched Laura's cheek. "I'm still a bit fragile, but I'm not going to break. I think I'll be up to a game of tag soon."

"One step away from a mission," she said lightly.

They were in their bedchamber after dinner, the first dinner Raoul had eaten with the family since he had been attacked. He was leaning on a walking stick, but his color was almost back to normal and his eyes had their old fire. It would be some time before he could contemplate a mission. But probably sooner than anyone expected. Especially her.

She went to tuck the covers round Clara in her cradle, because tears suddenly prickled her eyes.

Raoul followed her across the room. She turned to him—because hiding things from him never worked. He smiled and touched her cheek again. "Do you think you could bear it if I was about more?"

Something leapt inside her. She tamped it down. "Well, I was rather hoping you'd wait for a bit before going back to Spain."

"I'm thinking of turning my networks over to Raimundo. He's in Spain, he can handle them well. I can advise him if he needs it."

"And?" It wasn't wholly surprising he'd trust his networks to his nephew. But only if he was needed elsewhere.

"And what?"

"Are you going back to Ireland? Or"—she hesitated—"South America—"

"Good god. You can't think I'd go to South America, sweetheart."

"I don't want you to be constrained. I told you that at the start."

"Yes, and it's a bit unfair when there are certain choices you'd never make yourself." Raoul moved closer to the cradle and adjusted a fold of Clara's quilt. "I think I'll stay here. Find something to keep me busy that's somewhat less likely to get me killed. My parents wanted to make sure I could stand for Parliament. Though Julien might claim I'd end up bored to death."

Laura stared at him. "You're serious."

"Yes, actually." He looked up from the cradle. "Never more so."

She drew an uneven breath. "I'd never ask you to do this."

"I know."

"But if you're doing it for me—"

"I'm doing it for Malcolm, partly. Because he asked me."

"He asked you?"

"He made a quite convincing case. And I'm doing it for Emily and Clara and Colin and Jessica. Because I want to watch them grow up and help them how I can. But mostly I'm doing it for myself. There's too much I don't want to miss."

Laura locked her hands behind her. "You'll miss what you're giving up."

"Oh, I don't doubt it. But then life is about choices, as I always say. And there are tradeoffs. I'd miss a great deal more if I went on as I was." He leant in and kissed her. "Are you sorry?"

"Oh, my darling." Laura wound her arms round him. "I couldn't be happier."

~

"Darling?" Mélanie looked up at her husband. He'd been quiet at dinner and he'd had a bemused look on his face ever since they'd said goodnight to the children and gone into their bedchamber. "Is something wrong?"

"I'm not sure." Malcolm frowned at his hands for a moment, then sat beside her on her dressing table bench. "I'm still not quite sure I actually did it."

"Did what?" Mélanie looked up from petting Berowne, who was winding against her rose gauze skirt.

"Asked Raoul to give up being a spymaster."

Mélanie's fingers froze on Berowne's fur. "You—"

"He's going to get himself killed." Malcolm's voice turned rough, like rope worn to where it's about to snap. "I've been afraid of that for as long as I can remember. I didn't want to force him to change, but damn it, I wanted him to realize what he's risking and know he'd be missed."

Mélanie's gaze flickered across her husband's face. "What did he say?"

"He said yes. I still can't quite believe it." Malcolm held her gaze in the shifting light of the tapers on her dressing table. "Do you hate me?"

"I can't tell you how relieved I am." Mélanie leant forwards and slid her arms round him. "You're the only one who could have asked him. I think Raoul's always understood what it means to be a parent, better than either of us realized for a long time. But it took you to remind him of where he's needed most."

HISTORICAL NOTES

Raoul O'Roarke, Tony Bamford, and Désirée Clairineau are fictional, but their adventures are set against real historical events. Writing about Raoul's past and his friendship with Tony and Désirée let me return to some key historical events we have already seen in the series, such as the Congress of Vienna (I couldn't fit the sleighing party into *Vienna Waltz*) and the Duchess of Richmond's ball, and also explore new one such as the rue Saint-Nicaise plot.

Geoffrey Blackwell could have known about James Blundell's successful transfusion in 1818 to save a woman suffering a hemorrhage after childbirth. Blood groups were not identified until almost a hundred years later. Fortunately, Malcolm and Raoul do indeed share a blood type.

For further information about the historical events in *The O'Roarke Affair* see:

Alsop, Susan Mary. *The Congress Dances*. New York, Simon & Schuster, 1985.

Boigne, Adèle d'Osmond, Comtesse de. *Memoirs of the Comtesse de Boigne,* vol. 1. New York: Helen Marx Books, 2003.

Clayton, Tim. *The Secret War Against Napoleon: Britain's Assassination Plot on the French Emperor.* New York: Pegasus Books, 2005.

Cooper, Duff. *Talleyrand.* New York: Grove Press, 2001.

Creevey, Thomas. *The Creevey Papers: A Selection from the Correspondence & Diaries of Thomas Creevey, M.P.* Edited by Sir Herbert Maxwell. London: Murray, 1904.

Frazer, Augustus. *The Letters of Colonel Sir Augustus Simon Frazer, K.C.B.* London: Longman, Brown, Green, Longmane, & Roberts, 1859.

Granville, Harriet. *Letters of Harriet Countess Granville 1810–1845,* vol. 1. London: Longmans, Green and Co., 1894.

Gronow, Rees Howell. *Reminiscenes and Recollections of Captain Gronow,* vol. 1. London: John C. Nimmo.

Jones, Proctor Patterson (editor). *Napoleon: An Intimate Account of the Years of Supremacy.* San Francisco: Proctor Jones Publishing Company, 1972.

Kincaid, John. *Adventures in the Rifle Brigade.* London: T. and W. Boone, Strand, 1830.

King, David. *Vienna, 1814.* New York: Harmony Books, 2008.

Longford, Elizabeth. *Wellington: Pillar of State.* New York: Harper & Row Publishers, 1972.

McGuigan, Dorothy Gies. *Metternich and the Duchess.* New York: Doubleday & Company, 1946.

Mercer, Cavalié. *Journal of the Waterloo Campaign.* London: Greenhill Books, 1989.

Stuart, Andrea. *Josephine: A Life of Napoleon's Josephine.* New York: Grove Press, 2004.

Zamoyski, Adam. Rites of Peace. New York: Harper Perennial, 2008.

A READING GROUP GUIDE

1. How does being a parent impact Raoul's actions and those of other characters—Tony, Désiréc, Régine, Mélanie, Malcolm, Kitty, and Julien?

2. What do you think lies ahead for Tony and Désirée?

3. How might Raoul's life have been different if Arabella had been willing to run off with him? Do you agree with Arabella that he wouldn't have achieved as much?

4. What do you think of Malcolm's request of Raoul at the end of the book?

5. How are the choices and compromises that Raoul and Tony face in their work in intelligence similar? How are they different?

6. How does what we see of Raoul's relationships with Malcolm, Mélanie, Laura, and Julien during the book

drive the scene where they are all trying to save his life?
Whose actions in that scene are most surprising?

7. Tony, Julien, and Bertrand all pretend to be dead for varying lengths of time. How does this change the course of each of their lives?

8. Which scene from Raoul's past do you think is the greatest turning point for him? Why?

9. What do you think lies ahead for Lisette Varon and Franz Stroheim?

10. How does the book, particularly the scene where the meeting between Tony and Stroheim is revealed and the scene with Marchmain at the end, show how Mélanie's relationship with Hubert has shifted? What does this imply for the future?

11. What do you think Raoul will do next?

12. How do you think the ending of the book will shift the dynamic among the central group of investigators?

THE DUKE'S GAMBIT

SECRETS OF A LADY

THE MASK OF NIGHT

THE DARLINGTON LETTERS

THE GLENISTER PAPERS

A MIDWINTER'S MASQUERADE

THE TAVISTOCK PLOT

THE CARFAX INTRIGUE

THE WESTMINSTER INTRIGUE

THE APSLEY HOUSE INCIDENT

THE WHITEHALL CONSPIRACY

THE SEVEN DIALS AFFAIR

THE ACKERLEY INHERITANCE

THE O'ROARKE AFFAIR

ACKNOWLEDGMENTS

Every book is special, and I can't imagine having a favorite book any more than having a favorite cat (I'd say a favorite child, save that I only have one child). But this was a challenging and emotional book to write. It's a core book in the series, while at the same time in many ways unique. I've been planning it for a long time and the story let me explore a number of key moments in the series from a different perspective.

It takes the help and support of an amazing number of people to bring a book into the world. My amazing agent, Nancy Yost, has been a wonderful support to the Rannoch Fraser Mysteries from the start. As always, huge thanks for her insights and brilliant eye for framing the story and editing cover copy. Thanks to Natanya Wheeler, a fabulous Director of Digital Rights, for shepherding the book expertly through each stage of the publication process. Natanya also designs the covers for the series. For this book, she brought to life a favorite scene of mine at the sleighing party at the Congress of Vienna (which I've wanted to dramatize for years) with wonderful care and attention to detail, including a great rendition of Mélanie Rannoch. To Sarah Younger for helping the book along through production and publication, and to Sarah and Christina Miller for superlative social media support. To Zoe Bryant for another great set of character and quote cards. And to the entire team at Nancy Yost Literary Agency for their fabulous work. Their creativity and dedication make all of them a dream to work with. Raoul, Malcolm, Mélanie, and I are all very fortunate to have their support.

Thank you to Eve Lynch for the meticulous and thoughtful copyediting. I love sharing the Rannochs with you and so appreciate your care for getting their story right when it comes to everything from historical usage to series continuity.

Thank you to Kristen Loken for a magical author photo. This one is particularly special because we were back in San Francisco's War Memorial Opera House for the Merola Grand Finale. Your brilliance never fails to amaze me, Kristen!

I am very fortunate to have a wonderful group of writer friends near and far who make being a writer less solitary. Thanks in particular to Lauren Willig for sharing the joys of historical research and the challenges of juggling life as a writer and a mom. To Penelope Williamson, for sharing adventures (including wonderful writer escapes to the Oregon Shakespeare Festival), analyzing plots from Shakespeare to *Scandal* to *Miss Scarlet & the Duke*, and being a wonderful honorary aunt to my daughter. Thank you to the #momswritersclub for bimonthly chats that are energizing and inspiring, and especially to Shay Galloway, with whom I now co-host the chats, and to Jessica Payne for starting the group and to Jessica and Sara Read for their wonderful #MomsWritersClub YouTube channel on which Mélanie and I had the fun of doing a guest interview.

Thank you to the readers who support Malcolm and Mélanie and their friends and provide wonderful insights on my website and social media, and especially on the Goodreads Discussion Group for the series.

Thanks to Gregory Paris and jim saliba for creating and updating a fabulous website that chronicles Malcolm and Mélanie's adventures.

And thank you to my daughter Mélanie, for brainstorming *The O'Roarke Affair* (including ideas for a couple of key action scenes and plot points), proofreading, and supporting me all the way through the process. I am so proud that my website now includes "Mélanie's Corner" for her stories, starting with her wonderful series *Talea's Mysteries*. From the time she could touch the keys, Mélanie has contributed something to each of my books. This is Mélanie's contribution to this story – "another epic book in an amazing series by the best mom in the universe, (or any universe). I really love the whole series but this book is really good and might be one of my faves. My mama is amazing, and I love her more than anything else in any universe."

ABOUT THE AUTHOR

Photo by Kristen Loken

Tracy Grant studied British history at Stanford University and received the Firestone Award for Excellence in Research for her honors thesis on shifting conceptions of honor in late-fifteenth-century England. She lives in the San Francisco Bay Area with her young daughter and four cats. In addition to writing, Tracy works for the Merola Opera Program, a professional training program for opera singers, pianists, and stage directors. Her real-life heroine is her daughter Mélanie, who is very cooperative about Mummy's writing time and is starting to write herself. She is currently at work on her next book chronicling the adventures of Malcolm and Mélanie Suzanne Rannoch. Visit her on the web at www.tracygrant.org.